R. S. ST

Albie's Struggle

A NOVEL

ISBN 978-1-7360286-0-5

Albie's Struggle is a work of fiction. Names, characters, businesses, events, locales and incidents are either products of the author's imagination or, as in the case of real locations such as New York City and New Hampshire and aspects of the real world such as Grand Central Station and articles published in *The New York Times*, used in a fictitious manner. Any resemblance to actual persons, living or dead, is coincidental.

TABLE OF CONTENTS

For my father.

MY CAMP

. . . each one had six wings: with twain he covered his face,
and with twain he covered his feet, and with twain he did fly. . . .
Then I said: 'Here am I; send me.'
–ISAIAH VI

"I had run my uniform camp shorts and tee shirt sweaty by the time I stumbled to my refuge beside the lake. On my grassy mattress that sloped down to dark water, beside trees an arm's length out of reach, I rested my head on the pillow of my fingers interlaced. Leaves above me divided the air into shade and sun. Motes and insects twinkled, appeared and disappeared, as they sifted through those quiet bands of light and darkness: so much motion amidst the stillness!

"My breath eased. Two dragonflies hovered, one behind the other. Their many wings glinted as they subsided from shade into light; their silhouetted bodies flashed purple pink, like the filament in an electronic tube that has just come on.

"With the flash, the crack of a bat echoed across the lake from far to my left. Shouts of boys, deeper cries of men who drove them: baseball. A sharp sound nearby, a broken stick. I caught my breath and set aside the dragonflies' pursuit and coupling to listen.

"Silence. Leaves moved. Another stick broke, more leaves, a step. More steps came my way through the forest, along the lakeshore, from beyond the next cove, from where the Indian Circle was, and the baseball field. A slow cadence: adults. Shoes off and in my hand, I was up and in the water to wade over slimy stones my feet knew well, through cattails and lily pads, to the cleft in the trees. I crouched like a stone and rested my shoes on a root above the surface of the water. Behind me the great trunks and a tangle of thorns protected me from the counselors on the path around the lake. Deep in shade I was open only to a boat or to someone with binoculars on the wooded shore half a mile opposite.

"I hunched down, damp but not cold. My heart ran raprapraprap, so every forceful beat ended in a tap instead of a whoosh as my path through the lily pads trembled and disappeared. The counselors were baseball players: even if they saw the disturbance they would not understand.

"Just in time: slow adult steps stopped in the clearing.

"'Little fucker ain't here.'

"'. . . where he came last time.' That was Uncle Jesse, my cabin counselor.

"'I thought you gave him a noogie.' That older, darker voice was the Head Counselor, Uncle Charlie. So it had been a serious pursuit. I considered my next move. In the days I had hidden from baseball I had explored through a swamp halfway around the lake, but I had not reached the end of the camp property.

"'Yeah, sure. . .' Uncle Jesse sounded uncertain. They meted out discipline in noogies, blows of an adult fist on a boy's shoulder. Brief pain, humiliation, sometimes a black and blue.

"'. . . seriously wrong with him,' Uncle Charlie said. 'You gotta straighten him out before visiting day.'

"'. . . if we can't find him,' Uncle Jesse said. 'But I think he was here.'

One of them threw a rock out among the lily pads. I had read the story of Cadmus; I imagined that the green and white leaves became the ringlets of strange warriors who arose from the slimy shallows to smite them. Afterwards the two counselors would lie one on top of the other, their red wounds faded, white bones exposed, their torn, sodden remains strewn with dirt and leaves and twigs. A passerby who found them would not be sure whether they were two corpses or one.

"They stood a few feet away. '. . . when he comes back from dinner,' Uncle Charlie said, 'and I'll straighten him out.'

"Heavy footsteps dwindled away. Dragonflies with two pairs of wings hung in the dark and light over the lily pads, two, three, four of them, now alone and now in pairs. I marveled at how fast they moved their pairs of wings with no sound I could hear. When I was sure I was safe I waded back to my landing to lie in the sun, where my shorts and the bottom of my shirt would dry."

ONE

In the beginning she read to the boy on her lap. On that dark velvet sofa he closed his eyes to dream the pictures she pointed at alive, until the day he guessed that the story hid in the black marks on the page. He seized her tanned finger and forced her red nail toward the words. "Read to you," he demanded.

"This is Ferdinand," his mother said, "over here."

"No. Read to you."

Her finger dragged the tiny fist across the page as she sounded out the words, and the boy she carried under one arm began to read. "He's very strong," she told his father that evening.

"In this world he'd better be," he said.

His name distinguished him from everyone else. Every thing has a name. Bed is 'bed,' Mother 'Mommy,' the canary 'Junior.' Some things need two names. 'Bed' names all the beds in the apartment; his bed is 'my bed.' His parents call him Albie, when they don't change it into something else, like *Babble-boy*.

Albie was sick for the first day of kindergarten. On the third day of classes, Mother, once a teacher herself, took him to school by taxi to command special attention for her four-and-a-half-year-old son. She led him over dark green linoleum squares, past finger paintings on bulletin boards and up an elevator. At the principal's office, they waited on an oak bench between a counter higher than his head and an oak railing with a gate. He perspired in a yellow slicker over his long-sleeved striped tee shirt and corduroy overalls, and shiny black rubbers over brown oxford shoes his mother had tied for him.

His mother's skirt was navy blue. Incandescent lights in the ceiling sat in metal housings like the fan in his grandmother's kitchen. Adults spoke. A woman opened the gate and led them over brown linoleum past other women at desks to a door in the opposite wall. Beyond a carpet, behind another desk, stood a woman taller than his mother with gray hair like his grandmother's.

The woman's light eyes gazed above his head. She talked and his mother talked. After some time the woman bent down. "Will you tell me your name?" she said.

"Want to see how high I can jump?" Heavy with rain gear, he jumped two inches into the air and returned to the thin carpet with a rubbery slap.

The woman with gray hair said, "What is your name?"

His mother's dark eyes reassured. "Albie," he said.

"Albie Greenberg," his mother said. Albie knew that.

The tall woman said, "I am Mrs. Drumm," and reached down to take his hand.

Mother told him to say good-bye to Mrs. Drumm. A different woman held the oak gate open and escorted them down a cooler corridor to a double metal door. The wired glass in each half of the door was too high to see through. His mother bent down. "Here we are, sweetheart. This is your class."

The woman and his mother each opened half the door. Beyond an alcove, in the largest room Albie had ever seen, groups of children played and ran on a floor so vast that the lines of square linoleum tiles disappeared together in the distance. Above the height of adults on the far walls, metal strips divided tall windows into many small glass panes.

Albie's hand found his mother's and squeezed hard. His slicker and rubbers oppressed him, but he did not want to take them off. A woman slighter than his mother approached them in shiny dark blue shoes and spoke to his mother.

The woman squatted. "Albert? I'm Miss Marcus. Would you like to see where we hang our coats?"

Behind the coat room in a giant bathroom, three toilets stood in separate stalls and three sinks stood side by side. The floor was hexagonal white tiles like at home.

"Would you like to play now, Albert?" Miss Marcus said.

Albie held his mother's hand. "Albie," he said.

"Albert." Miss Marcus waved at another woman across the classroom and pointed. The other woman touched a tall boy in dark brown pants and led him all the way across the huge classroom to Albie and his mother.

"Albert, this is Albie White," Miss Marcus said. "Albie, this new pupil in our class is Albert Greenberg."

Albie White was much taller, with big, fleshy earlobes. He said "Hi," and picked his nose. Albert Greenberg squeezed his mother's forefinger tighter and put his right hand in his pocket. He wanted his rubbers back.

"You see,"—Miss Marcus shook her dark hair—"we can't have two Albies in one class."

They had three sinks there, and Albie had more than two beds in his apartment. For his kindergarten class to call him Albert set him apart. If he were normal he would be Albie.

As long as Albie could remember, the big dark wood radio, polished to a furniture luster, sat in the living room on a brass-edged mahogany table. The baritone snap! of the switch spoke the importance of the news to come. As the radio warmed up, an amber light glowed behind the long rectangular dial and a green eye flashed and focused at you.

Albie's father loomed above him, smoking his pipe. "Don't touch the radio," he said.

"Why?"

"It's the news."

Albie and his mother watched from the sofa as a strange man's voice recited secrets of men to Albie's father, who leaned close to adjust the dial until she shuffled off to the kitchen.

When he was five Albie discovered the radio page in the newspaper. He studied the schedule until he was sure. Amazing! Dick Tracy and the characters he knew from comics were in the radio, too! He tiptoed into the kitchen. "Mommy?"

She stirred water and ice cubes in the glass measuring pitcher with red lines. "Yes, my sweetie?"

"What time is it?"

"A quarter to five." She pointed to the clock on the kitchen wall. "The big hand is before the nine, and the little hand is before the five."

"When is five o'clock?"

"Soon. Are you getting hungry in your tummy?"

He held up the newspaper. "Can I listen to Dick Tracy?"

She hesitated. "We'll turn on the radio together," she said, and smirked the way naughty girls at school did. In the living room she held her glass and told him what to do. "Turn that, a little more. Now turn that past the seven."

A roaring man's voice filled the room, and static. He jumped back.

His mother laughed. "You turn this until the eye is almost all green." She adjusted the knobs. "This one is the volume."

Books said Volume I and Volume II on the spine; he was ready for a story. Once the man announced Dick Tracy, Albie was gone with Dick and Pat to investigate a shooting in a tarpaper shack on the ice of a frozen lake far to the north.

When the music welled up he came back to find his mother staring at him with sad eyes. "Did you like that?" she said.

He held up the newspaper. "Terry and the Pirates is next."

"Aren't you hungry?"

He shook his head. He could imagine better when he stared right at the radio's green eye. He hardly moved during Terry and the Pirates and Tennessee Jed and Sky King, but while Sky King was still in the air over his ranch looking for the rustlers, his mother reached past him to turn the radio off.

"Wait!"

She pulled him by the arm to the kitchen.

"It's not over yet!"

"Your father's coming home."

"Please!"

"You better eat," she said, and drank.

Albie slid soft green beans from side to side with his fork. The front door opened. Voices, a hand slapped flesh, a giggle, the snap of the radio switch. Sound filled the living room. His father's voice came even louder: "Who changed the station?"

His mother's first words were too soft to make out. She said, "I made him turn it off."

His father shook the hall, filled the kitchen door. "I told you never to touch the radio!"

Albie leaned close to his plate and poked at the mashed potatoes.

"Answer me!"

He pushed back his chair and darted between his father's thigh and the door jamb to his room, where he put his head under the pillow.

After the first day of first grade his mother took him to a restaurant where old women sat at tables wearing hats. "Do you want a milkshake or ice cream?" she asked.

"A chocolate milkshake and strawberry ice cream," he told the waitress.

"We don't give ice cream *and* milkshakes to little boys," the waitress said. "That's the rule."

He had seen the high sign his mother gave the waitress, so the rule was a fake. Still, he lived in terror that he might violate some real rule for which they would doom him to wander the dangerous world forever, unable to return to the comfort of his room. He also chafed at the confinement of his room, and dreamed of escape.

If only Albie could have a pair of binoculars like his father's! With binoculars he might see what happened to him, where he had come from, and where he was going. Albie had only six years to remember, yet weeks, months, even years remained as blank as the uncolored places marked *terra incognita* in the historical atlas his father kept on the living room shelf.

Real binoculars would come from an old shop in a city, a dark place below street level, as local and as fixed as the double store front at the end of his block, before the Avenue, ten steps down from the sidewalk. One half was a liquor store, whose window display changed every few weeks.

At Thanksgiving a cardboard turkey driven by a hidden motor pecked incessantly at a cardboard liquor bottle. A month later a cardboard Santa Claus dipped a ladle into a cardboard punchbowl again and again. For the New Year a cardboard reveler in black tie brought a cardboard horn to his lips and took it away, as his cardboard consort in her long cardboard dress admired him. Albie figured out all by himself that the displays, which had seemed quite wonderful and various at first, must all be driven by the same motor capable of only a single reciprocating motion. The display had possessed the power to astound Albie until Albie understood it to be a fake, when his astonishment melted away and the power became his.

"Hello, Mike," Albie's mother said.

"Good Afternoon, Mrs. G." The clerk winked at Albie. "The same again, is it?" He climbed a ladder to get her a frosted white bottle and a dark green bottle with a yellow label. Mother gave him money and he gave Mother money.

That was easy to understand and therefore safe. All the bottles from which the man must choose stood exposed in plain sight under bright bulbs, even if he might have to climb the ladder to read a label.

"Thank you, Mike." Mother led Albie out through the sunlight that sparkled off the bottles in the window. In the Chinese laundry next door, brown-wrapped parcels of ironed shirts piled to the ceiling stopped what little light penetrated the dust and the words HAND LAUNDRY painted in red on the glass.

Behind this bulwark, an old man with thick glasses ironed on a wooden board behind a tiny counter. Mother opened her red snakeskin purse—the scales felt scratchy when Albie ran his hand over it—and extracted a yellow paper with letters and numbers, and Chinese writing as well.

Dark, dark: in winter, when the late afternoon light that sneaked between the parcels was too dim to iron by, Mr. Hong turned on a small bulb over the counter. No talk at all, only the hot, not-quite-soap ironing smell, until Mr. Hong had located the parcel, compared the paper Mother had given him with the one bound to it by white string, muttered as he clicked his abacus and announced the price. Mother gave Mr. Hong money and Mr. Hong took his hand off the parcel and gave Mother money.

Mother let Albie carry the parcel up the steps. "Hold it under your arm," she said, "not by the string."

"Why?"

"If the string breaks you might drop it."

Albie put the parcel under his arm.

"Don't squeeze so hard," Mother said as they crossed the street.

"Why?"

"You might wrinkle Daddy's shirts."

Elbows at his sides, Albie bent his forearms to make a shelf on which he bore the parcel up the block. It would be more fun to carry the bright bottles, but Mother never asked him to.

As they walked, Albie strained to see beyond home to the park. He coveted his father's binoculars in their old brown leather case, scarred and scratched by a generation of use. The foot-long brown strap had been extended by another strap attached with buckles so it could go over your shoulder or around your neck. The binoculars sat inside a red velvet lining worn thin and gray in places: solid, heavy, cold metal and glass, black. The lenses iridesced like the slicks that floated in the puddles beneath parked cars. Around one eyepiece were engraved white lines and numbers, pluses and minuses, letters that referred to mysteries. The smooth, heavy motion of the knurled knob between the two barrels suggested importance and authority, and yet when you let go, the turning stopped at once. The leather strap on swivels on the binoculars themselves had become so old and cracked the rough brown leather showed on both sides.

As small as Albie was, if he promised to be careful, his father let him hold the binoculars and look out the window. Albie caught his breath, so close the human faces of people on the street came to him. With binoculars he might learn what he did not know about how other people lived, hence how to live himself.

That was it. The secrets of how to live lay hidden from him in dark parcels marked with incomprehensible labels, like the packages in the Chinese laundry, while he dreamed of moving out, or up, to a world in which the possibilities were explicit and bright, where he could understand how things worked, a world like the liquor store.

The four grandparents talked and quarreled at the dinner table every week until after Albie's mother put him to bed, but he awakened in a quiet house where morning sunlight through the Venetian blinds drew lines and shadows on his bedroom ceiling.

In the middle of the ceiling a frosted glass dish decorated with clear sparkles diffused the light of incandescent bulbs. Once a dark spot appeared in the dish and stayed there for days. He could see it better at bedtime when the light was on.

His mother wore red cloth shoes with white rope soles on her slender legs. "Mommy," he said, "why is there dirt in the light?"

She glanced up. "It's a fly."

"Why did it fly in there?"

"It got lost. It meant to fly out the window to escape."

Albie squinted so he could bear the painful brightness. He could still see the fly. "Why doesn't it fly out?"

"It's dead."

"What's dead?"

Silence, the length of a heartbeat, and his beautiful mother said, "It means he can't fly anymore." Her perfume smelled like flowers. Even after she switched off the bulbs, a little daylight from the window reflected in her dark, dark eyes. "Good nighty night," she said.

"Mm nighty night," he murmured into his pillow, and faded into another world even as she closed the door.

Another night as he watched from his window, the lamp on the bed behind him lit his pajamas and projected his disembodied image onto the glass so it hung above the street. If he could see himself, the large figures on the brownstone stoop opposite could see him too. Uneasy, he turned out the light and returned to the sill.

Now that he was invisible, those much older boys, men really, could not hurt him. Perhaps in time he could learn to pass among them and be taken for one of them—but doubtful. They argued, laughed, pushed each other, smoked cigarettes and drank beer on the dark summer street. That night they were louder than usual when a tall, thin man in a suit strode down the block from the Avenue.

He wore a hat with a small brim tilted down like a lamp shade so Albie could not see his face. A voice shouted. Even as Albie watched, the tall man drew his arm back and thrust it forward. They all fell silent. The tall man ran back toward the Avenue with long, loping strides, his arms out before him, as if he were swimming. The back of his jacket flapped as he disappeared into shadows. A woman's voice shrilled, "You're bleeding, you're bleeding!" Another voice, "Get a doctor!" And hubbub.

Albie felt afraid in his window, but a moment later he didn't feel anything at all. If he dreamed that night he did not remember it the next morning.

Saturday morning his father emptied a canvas bag that had lain on the floor of the hall closet for years. A pair of socks, a cardboard box of fish hooks, a small pocket knife. "That was mine when I was in third grade," Albie's father said. "Do you want to hold it?"

Albie did. Cold, heavy, a real knife, not a toy. The stag handle felt smooth despite the shadows in its surface.

"You can have it," his father said.

Albie, unbelieving, met his father's eyes.

"Ask me to help you open it," his father said. "And don't take it out of the house. It's against the law to carry a knife."

"Thank you." Albie didn't admire it as much as he had before, but he enjoyed its weight in his pocket as he left the room.

The next day he studied the knife when he was alone. The bigger blade faced backward and was easy to open, but he imagined that the smaller one, which faced forward and was harder to grasp, might be the sharper. It would be there, in time of emergency—but his father had forbidden him to open the dark gray blades alone.

Uncle El who limped came to take Albie to the zoo during the April vacation.

"Can you walk that far?" The soft concern in his mother's voice was the kindness Albie expected when she woke him for school in the morning.

"Yes, Chana, yes, I can walk with a small boy to the zoo." But when Uncle El shifted his weight Albie saw that his leg was short.

"A taxi." His mother picked up her dark blue pocketbook from the hall table.

"An angel." His uncle bowed. He lifted his mother's beautiful fingers toward his lips, but didn't quite kiss them.

"Oh!" His mother turned away. "By five o'clock," she said in the toneless voice she had at the end of the day, when she drank water from a glass with ice cubes.

On their way through the park Albie held his uncle's hand. When the older man did not speak, Albie pulled away to run into a stand of bushes behind the park benches, or up the hill and down. One time Uncle El called, "Wait! Be careful!" His panicky voice stopped Albie, who was already ten yards up the hill again.

"What's wrong?"

His uncle coughed the way he always did. His stubbly gray whiskers didn't hide purple ropy scars on the side of his neck. "Wait, it's not safe." he said, and peered up toward the brow of the hill.

Albie followed his glance. The steep part of the hill was empty of big boys who might threaten him. Beyond the steep part were trees, and behind them a police car sat on the flat place where in winter the children waited with their sleds for a turn to slide down the hill. Two policemen smoked cigarettes beside the car. One gestured with both hands with the cigarette in his mouth.

"It's okay," Albie said. "They're policemen."

"Policemen!" His uncle clutched Albie's hand and dragged him at a clumsy run, step-STEP, step-STEP, to the arbor that led to the road crossing. Uncle El looked back over his shoulder. The policemen were still smoking outside the car.

"What's wrong?"

"Okay, okay." The voice shook.

"What is it? My mother says if anything happens, I should ask a policeman . . ."

"I will tell you," his uncle said, but he towed Albie past the boccie field in silence, down the path between two meadows to the broad cement expanse where Albie had learned to ride his bike. Before a statue Uncle El's mouth moved while his eyes twisted in anger. He stopped walking and set his jaw. "Yes! Here you must ask a policeman!" He nodded. They walked on. "It was different in Europe," he murmured. Albie might not have heard, had he not been watching his uncle's face.

Near the zoo his uncle's limp worsened. The older man relaxed his moist grip; Albie pulled free to run as fast as he could to the wooden rail fence that separated the bicycle path from the autos; when he ran back he took his uncle's hand again.

On their way down the steep hill into the zoo, Uncle El rested a hand on Albie's shoulder. "We stop here," he said. Two polar bears lived behind an iron fence painted black. One of the animals jumped into murky water and swam around. The other bear stood on four legs and swayed its head from side to side as it watched his uncle.

"Uncle El?"

"Yes?"

"What happened to your leg?"

The man's face reddened. "My foot . . ." Man and boy stared at each other. Albie thought that his uncle was angry. After a silence he said, "In Europe . . ." Albie waited with open eyes. "A bear, it was a bear that gave me a bite, yes, a bear." The uncle's tone was colder than when he joked with Albie's mother. Albie touched the stag knife handle in his pocket.

When they had rested they continued under the brick arch into the stench of wild urine in the lion house. Albie couldn't imagine how the bear had bitten his uncle's foot. "Uncle El?" he said, as they walked back out into the light of day. "Why wasn't the bear in a cage?"

A glare came into his uncle's eyes as he spoke to the air in front of him. "Ha! Not a Russian bear, no, this bear bites . . . ." His speech became incomprehensible, and he gestured with the hand that wasn't holding Albie's. Albie was afraid to ask again. He wanted to grow up so he could open the pocket knife to protect his uncle from the bear.

"Today we will make Easter baskets," Miss Ginty told the second grade in a scratchy voice. Her little glasses sat on her nose and their sparkly chain hung around her neck. The children filed to tables where she had laid out colored construction paper, scissors, paste and crayons.

"First you fold the basket, then you fold the handle," Miss Ginty said. "Raise your hand when you're ready to paste."

Her black shoes had thicker heels than his mother's, and laces. Albie wanted to draw rocket planes. He chose pale green construction paper and a crimson crayon. As the rocket plane took shape, he gave it golden exhaust.

"What's this?" Miss Ginty said behind him.

"It's a future plane." He spoke with his eyes on his orange moon, unbound by the gravity of the classroom.

"Stand up."

Albie stood up. Miss Ginty held up his drawing. The other children folded and pasted; Suzy, across the room with her little red pocketbook over her shoulder, drew eggs on the outside of her finished basket.

"This boy," Miss Ginty said, "is wasting valuable construction paper." The other children glanced over and returned to their work. "Sit down," Miss Ginty said. "If you fold properly, this"—she put the drawing on the table and tapped it with her finger while her other hand held him up by his shirt—"will be inside, so no one will see it."

Chastened, hot, Albie folded properly, and pasted. He chose black paper for the handle. He covered the one tear that fell with paste.

At the end of the hour he wiped his hands on his shirt. The class lined up in twos to return to their classroom; they carried the Easter baskets in their outboard hands. As the line passed the trash bin near the stairway Albie dropped his basket in.

Suzy broke out of line. "Miss Ginty!" She ran back to the art room. "Albie threw his basket away."

The line waited at the stairs. Miss Ginty hurried after them in her heavy shoes to seize Albie by the shirt again. "Get it out," she said.

He reached through the swinging top.

"Don't you want your Easter basket?"

He thought she wanted the truth.

"You come with me." Miss Ginty haled him to the principal's office, where he clutched his no longer square green and black basket on the oak bench until Mrs. Drumm told him he could go back to class.

Uncle El rented a movie projector and screen and reels of cartoons for Albie's seventh birthday party. The intensity, the joy of moving pictures, in color, right in his own apartment! Excitement dizzied him; he sat mindless of friends, of ice cream and cake, even of the shiny projector. A gargoyle broke free from a building to become a winged white horse, who galloped into the blue sky to befriend the flying mouse. At the end they disappeared together into the center of the screen, where the final logo covered them and music played before the film detached to tick-tick-tick as the unconstrained wheel spun until Uncle El could stop it. The bright-as-dreams cartoon world yielded to the drab colors and dim light of the winter apartment.

Albie mourned the loss. After the other children departed clutching their favors and paper hats, he begged to watch the film again and again, until bleary-eyed, he let his father carry him to bed. He muttered to the winged horse as he fell asleep.

His mother taught him to cross the street and permitted him to do so. "But don't cross the avenue," his father said.

"Why not?"

"Because the traffic is coming from both directions."

"I look both ways."

"And don't go into the park alone."

"I do look both ways," Albie said.

"You might meet bullies in the park." His father lit his pipe, shook the match out. "Big boys, with knives. Go with Uncle El."

"Stevie can cross the avenue."

"He's older."

"Clinton in my class can cross the avenue."

"Do you hear me? I know what might happen. I'll tell you when you can cross the avenue!"

He went with his cousin Stevie, one year older but much taller, to buy illegal fireworks in mysterious Chinatown: Mott, Pell, Doyer streets, right off the Bowery, darkness under the elevated railway, narrow sidewalks, strange smells. A man with yellow skin and a cigarette in his mouth unloaded pails of something from a small truck.

Albie saw few Caucasians, no policemen. He tugged Stevie's sleeve. "Are we lost?"

Stevie examined a piece of paper from his pocket. "No," he said, but he peered at one street sign after another.

"Boy lost?" said a thin, bent-over Chinese man with sparse gray hair.

"Don't say anything," Stevie said under his breath.

"No," Albie said, "we're not lost."

"Boy hungry?"

Albie reached into his pocket. "My mother gave us money for lunch."

The man waved air toward himself. "Boy come." He led them into an alley.

Stevie gripped Albie's arm. "Ask him about fireworks."

The man hurried ahead through the alley to another street, where steps descended to a basement entrance. The doorway was painted red; the sign over the door was in hand-painted yellow Chinese characters. The man opened the door. "Boy come," he said.

Stevie hesitated on the sidewalk, but the man with gray hair beckoned to Albie with his dark, narrow eyes wide open and his mouth in an O. Albie trusted his eyes, and went in. The restaurant floor was tiled like a bathroom. Chinese men crowded at small wooden tables without cloths. A musical buzz of talk Albie could not understand filled the steamy air. A high glass counter separated the diners from cooks at the back.

Stevie tugged Albie's sleeve. "We better get out of here," he whispered.

The man who had led them to the restaurant pointed at two empty chairs on one side of a small table at which a fat Chinese man was eating something with chopsticks. "Boy hungry." Albie slid over. The menu on the wall was all ideograms he could not read. Stevie and Albie were the only Caucasians in the restaurant.

The man who had brought them shouted at the cooks behind the counter. Someone set a huge bowl in front of them, small bowls, flat porcelain spoons, chopsticks, glasses of tea. The man ladled soup into their small bowls, opened his eyes wide again, and gestured.

Albie dipped his spoon into the soup, blew, and tasted. "It's good."

Stevie frowned at the man and at the soup. He tasted his glass of tea. "Uncle El drinks tea in a glass," he said, and added sugar.

"Try the soup," Albie said.

Stevie tasted. "It's chicken soup, but it's salty." He poked in his bowl. "It's got kreplach."

Albie smiled up at the man who had led them to the restaurant. "Thank you." He slurped. "Try the meat with the red edge," he said, still chewing.

Stevie emptied his bowl, and ladled out more soup for both of them. "This is better than the chicken soup my mother makes," he said. "What about you?"

"I've never had chicken soup."

An expressionless man at the next table watched them eat. The man who had led them to the restaurant was gone. Now Albie felt alien and unwelcome because of his pale skin, his open eyes, his curly hair, because he could not read the ideograms on the menu on the wall. It was what he felt all the time, only more obvious and more intense.

He hurried to finish. They paid and left. Albie had lost something, and missed it; someone had lost Albie, but had not come to find him.

In his own room Albie could read by an incandescent lamp warmer than the gray cold world outside. Here were comfort, peace, security. Yet even in this bed, even with the covers drawn up over his head so he lay alone in the dark with his own smell and his hands warm between his thighs, his eyes shut tight so he could see the sea of colored stars that still carried him off to dreamland—even in this sanctuary—Albie felt a cold, uneasy certainty that he did not belong.

His room was his shell. Albie hurled his door shut against his family with an angry slam. Thin winter light from the window penetrated, gray and cold, hardly light to dream by. But he had his books. The incandescent light that lit them was under his control. As he lay in his bed, his feet toward the window, the dreary world outside cast a shadow on the pages of his book. The book: a small shield against the world he yearned to make his own.

Albie's pull on the beaded chain clicked life into the brown Bakelite reading lamp clamped to the head of his bed. Warm, golden light sprang out to animate the words on the page. Far beyond the words, the window, now darker, no longer transmitted the cold unfriendliness of outside, but rather reflected the world Albie created for himself in the artificially illuminated reality of his own room.

Once or twice a month Stevie's mother, Albie's aunt, took the boys to play in the park. "Mind that you don't go too far," she said, and settled onto a bench in a long brown dress and brown hat to read a book with a yellow paper cover. Albie and Stevie picked up pebbles and threw them, waited until she had closed her book a second time. "Not too far," she said.

"Yes, mother," Stevie said, but once she was absorbed again they climbed the rocks, dug in the woods, even crossed the bridle path to scale the wall and cling to the top with their fingertips.

At the end of the afternoon they were filthy. Stevie's mother scrutinized

Albie over her glasses, then through them. "Hannah should make you mind better." She stalked ahead. Albie followed her and Stevie up the path, out of the park, and home. They buzzed and ascended in the elevator. Hearty women's laughter sounded through the apartment door before Albie's mother opened it.

"It's not my fault," Stevie's mother said. "You should teach him to be clean."

Albie's mother held him to her with one hand and smoked with the other. "How the hell are you? Come in and have a drink."

"Certainly not." Stevie's mother tugged Stevie back toward the elevator.

When the elevator door had closed, Albie's mother walked him into the living room with her arm around him. "This is my little boy." A woman in a red and white dress with a bow sat on the couch. Her high-heeled white shoes lay on their sides in the middle of the carpet. "Say hello to Della," said his mother.

"Hello." He didn't want to look at the woman, but he smelled her perfume, and saw cigarette butts stained with two colors of lipstick.

"Take a bath," his mother said.

He was eight years old. He shook Ivory Flakes under the spigot, ran the water himself, undressed, and soaked. Some day he would grow as tall as Stevie.

The bathroom door opened. "He's a cute one," Della said.

"Have you washed yet?" his mother said.

"Sort of." He stirred the suds with one hand.

"Stand up," his mother said. "Let me see you."

He glanced at Della.

"Oh go on. Della's like family."

He stood up, grateful for the suds that clung to him.

"He's growing so big," said his mother, "isn't he, though?"

Della sipped her drink, puffed her cigarette. Something she said under her breath made his mother laugh. When Albie realized what Della and his mother were looking at, he bent forward and covered himself with his hands.

"We'll leave you be for now," Della said. Both women laughed as they left the bathroom.

Albie sat back down in the tub and splashed his face with bath water less hot than his eyes. A little later Della's voice said, "Take care of your little Jewish boy," before the front door closed.

The flat slam of Albie's door contained the baritone authority of men's violence, of action taken regardless of consequences. Where had he heard that sound before? Had Tennessee Jed's pistol sounded like that, or Dick Tracy's? No, when those valiant defenders of good order fired at evil, their sound was shorter, cleaner, more surgical, without some dark implication which resided in the slam of the door. When the hero fired, the end was in sight: good was about to triumph, the widow would receive her moiety soon, and the wicked his just deserts.

Despite his anger, despite his retreat, the slam of Albie's door was not the end. In his imagination the dark core of that sound whirled into a vortex of constant rapid motion, like water in the bathtub or the toilet, going down to darkness. It grew louder and harder to bear, it threw him to one side and the other, he could not hold on.

It was the subway Stevie and Albie had taken to Chinatown! He stood in the front car next to the driver's closed booth and leaned against the glass door to peer through its crisscrossed lozenges of steel grillwork at the dark tunnel. The point of light which was the next station glared off the bright rails which joined and faded in the darkness ahead.

This subway train would not slow for the station. The dark roar, the clack of wheels, the high-pitched scream of steel on heavy steel grew louder as the train accelerated. The chain harness outside swung left and right as the train threw him sideways, and sideways again. The station rushed toward them, embraced the train and swallowed it, then with a noisy rattle it was gone! The motion threw Albie against the door of the driver's compartment, and from there against a strange big boy he had not noticed before.

The danger, the danger! The big boy's cruel smile! The slam of the door echoed and whirled about Albie, rang in his ears, as the train tried to fling him to its dirty red composition floor. To get his balance he spread the flat of his hands against the cool glass of the door, which rattled in its frame. Far ahead up the track the lights which might have slowed the car were green, all green, to suck the train further and faster into dangerous darkness on the way to neighborhoods, people, experiences Albie could not imagine or control.

He choked back a sob, cowered away from the bigger boy, closed his eyes; to brace himself better he let his forehead touch the cool glass of the door, and he was soothed.

Now Albie stood in his room at the mirror on his closet door. He leaned forward, palms and forehead against the glass as turbulence inside him shook louder and more insistent than the metal violence of the subway. His room, his place, had become unstable. He must cry out a warning, but whom will he warn? The world will collapse in gore and ear-splitting noise, explode in a violent intrusion. Strange hands will rip him from the only comfort that has ever been. Help me, he would cry, if someone would answer him.

Beyond the walls of his room his mother shuffled past his doorway. Albie's pulse cried Hish! Hish! Hish! in his ear. As he took a deep breath in, the pulse paused. I have died! he thought with a gasp, but as he released the deep breath his pulse came back like an express train train in full pursuit of the end of the tunnel, Hish! Hish! Hishhishhish!

He could not go back through the door he had slammed to the family intensity, the craziness, the billowing clouds of unmanageable feeling that darkened, suffocated, threatened. Of course not: he was in full retreat. He touched his window. Shut in his room with a plate of food he had refused to eat he would sneak to the window, open it, and scrape the scrambled eggs or the overcooked green beans off the plate into the air where they would fall to a silent stop on the pavement below. Thus would he rid himself of the reproach of uneaten food, and earn his mother's grudging approval of his acceptance of her terrible cooking.

But what he did was a waste. The mess it made on the street would not be there forever because stray dogs, God's rain, nameless agencies would reduce the splatter of egg to ordinary city grime before the next time Albie walked there. So if he were to jump, die, and lie broken on the gritty sidewalk, he might dull for an hour the tiny flakes of mica that reflected the sun, a temporary inconvenience.

And the waste: if he did not eat his food (as he often did not, yet he did not starve) his parents would invoke the Poor Children In Europe, nameless persons unknown to Albie, whose gratitude his parents daily compared with his own. But Albie felt poorer than they, and desperate.

Escape! He will raise the sash one awkward inch at a time to prevent the shriek of wood on tin when a stuck window yields. He will climb up onto the radiator cover and window sill. On elbows and knees he will maintain a handhold while he extends one cautious foot backwards over the rough granite of the sill outside, into empty space five stories above the street. The sill will push his pants up his leg; the gray stone will scrape his shin. He will endure the little start of fear and pain as blood wells up.

He will concentrate on the fearful knowledge of his right foot unsupported, until his skill, his control, brings the toe of his shoe to the half inch ledge of the decorative groove in the brickwork.

Inch by terrible inch he will edge backward. His hands will cling to warm, familiar things in his room until the very last minute, as his thighs and his smooth belly scrape across the sill, and his toes lodge below the window. He will hold on as the wind whirls green park air and truck exhaust through the canyon of the street. He will hear the bell, the cry of the knife grinder—"I cash old clothes!"—and the groans of a bus changing gears on the Avenue. He will tremble with the excitement of freedom: the choice is his!

He will edge his soft cheek sideways against the rough mortar of the facade, to peek into his parents' bedroom window. He will slide past the living room with its green wool rug and polished mahogany furniture, past the Manleys' next door apartment he has never entered, to gain the corner of the building. Or he will climb ridge by ridge to the apartment above where the girl with dark eyes lives, or the one above that, or higher, higher, fingers and toes, until he reaches the parapet, pulls with both hands, and rolls over to land on his back on the tarry gravel roof, halfway to the stars, and safe.

Albie and Stevie ran past a workman pushing a hand mower over a patch of grass in the park. At the end of each row the rusty iron wheels clattered on pavement as the man backed and turned, but when he bent forward to push straight ahead the creak faded and the sick—sick—sicksicksick of the whirling blades threw a green cloud into the air behind the mower.

The smell of the cut grass reminded Albie of something about bodies he couldn't quite remember. His father had taken the family by car to see the golf club he had joined. In the formal dining room, heavy curtains framed tall windows and silence imposed: if Albie were to speak someone would hush him. "The food is very good," his father said, and led them through a darker room which smelled of liquor where a man in his shirt-sleeves polished a glass as he listened to a staticky radio.

"Would you like something?" Albie's father said.

"Sure," his mother said with her naughty face on. His father started toward the bar. "I'll come to you, sir," the bartender said as he picked up a red jacket with brass buttons.

The family sat at a glass table overlooking a lawn and a bright blue swimming pool. Albie asked for a Coke. From the terrace edge he watched a man guide a power mower with only his fingertips. "Look!" he said. "He doesn't have to push it!"

His father shook his head. "Those are dangerous," he said. "They can take off a foot. I had a case where a pebble flew up and put out an eye."

The sweet odor of new-cut grass thickened the air as the man and the mower traversed a gentle slope. The bartender brought two Cokes on a tray for Albie and his father. He gave Albie's mother a glass with a skinny straw and fruit in it.

"You have to be careful," his father said.

His mother clanked her glass down. "The push ones are just as dangerous," she said. "I gave your uncle a ride on one, down on the shore." She drank again. "He was five years old."

"And?" Albie's father voice was cross.

His mother giggled. "He had to go to the doctor, with blood all over."

His father pointed beyond the swimming pool to men swinging golf clubs. "That's the first tee," he said, "it's a par four." He rubbed Albie's shoulder. "Nine is old enough to start caddying."

Albie's mother pushed her chair back and stood up. "I'm going to the bathroom." She emptied her glass. "So he had blood all over his deedle," she said to his father. "So what? It was an accident." She took a big step toward the clubhouse and came back. "You talk like I meant to cut it off," she said, and went away again.

"I won't do anything dangerous," Albie promised his father.

Albie supported himself on the warm radiator cover and leaned his forehead against the windowpane to regard the cold winter air below before he made his way to the full length mirror on his closet door.

The image of the two windows behind him bounced back from the mirror, brighter than the silent reflection of a slender boy, small for ten, pale skin in shadow under curly hair, who held himself still and watched for danger. Albie approached: one step, two. His image grew larger than the windows behind him. He touched the glass, as cold as the window; the unfamiliar figure reached out, too, to touch his hand.

The traffic rattle outside and the murmurs of the family fell to silence as Albie examined the face before him, and drew near. Too close! Albie lowered his eyes and dropped his chin, and the shadowed mirror boy tilted his head down as well to regard Albie out of the well of darkness that was himself.

Hands against the mirror, Albie closed his eyes and touched his forehead to the glass, which warmed at his touch. The figure in the mirror did the same. Albie controlled the mirror boy better than he could control the thoughts that led him from books to the land of dreams, or the roundabout routes that did not return him home until morning.

Lean closer, closer, the mirror boy seemed to say. If Albie could only give the other what he wanted, he would receive it too, and be free. Tingles sparkled up the side of his neck and his scalp tightened. If he dared to press forward, the mirror might soften and slide around him in a line he would feel with the skin of his forehead, slip down to a ring around his face. No! He drew back as wave after wave of fear filled his body; he squeezed his eyes shut to block the other's voice inside his head.

It would be like when he let his bottom down to the hard tub in a too-hot bath. He bent his knees and hips, arms on the sides; feet flat slid forward, and a ring of water climbed his leg to surround a dry oval of kneecap skin. That ring stood up the thickness of a raindrop as the dry place shrank, until surface tension no longer held and water rushed to water across his knee with a tiny sound. Gone! Albie gave himself up to the heat of the bath. That moment on the edge, the moment between things, was over.

Eyes still closed, he pushed the mirror away until the closet door latched. He felt his way to his bed and exhaled a breath held much too long to recline in silence. He let a long moment pass before he turned on the light and reached under the bed for the book he had been reading the night before.

Albie awoke cranky and sweaty, with trouble in his body, but he could not say where. His room was darker than closed eyes. He had fallen away, twirled by the sun's gravity on a cometary course more extreme than any wandering planet. He would be gone for years, for ages, and when he returned, time would have crushed those who scorned him, and swept them away. The bright, sweet smell of a spring day would float up to welcome him over city sidewalks, past rusted trucks racing their engines, through a window he would be strong enough to open. When he returned they would welcome him, because he would have become normal.

Albie's mother darkened his room. Even modest daylight from the airshaft hurt his eyes; he had not recovered from measles the way the doctor had told her he would. On the fifth day the large doctor came to touch and press him again. He pried up an eyelid to shine a light into Albie's eye.

Albie turned to the wall with a sob.

"Oh," gasped his mother, "cooperate with —"

The doctor raised a hand to hush her. They left the room. When his mother returned to sit on his bed, the glare around the margins of the shade had faded and incandescent lights glowed elsewhere in the apartment. Albie's canary Junior was quiet in his cage.

Mother offered him Jell-o. It hurt to shake his head. "Please, honey, drink some ginger ale."

Her touch was a molestation. He curled up to rest his forehead on the cool plaster wall.

"If you can't drink, Doctor Campbell is going to give you fluids in your vein."

He didn't respond.

"I went through hell in the hospital," she said, "but when it was over I felt like tearing down buildings."

He was ready to tear down this building right now, to pull the whole world down, because it was wrong. That was why he never felt right in it. Perhaps God awakened like this, cranky and sweaty, with trouble in his body, with pain in his head, and flooded the earth to rid himself of annoyance.

God's trouble was the world, but Albie's lay inside him. You catch disease from a sneeze, or if you share a glass, but most people stay well, so Albie must have a flaw — despite his father's corrections. He had to try harder. If this uncomfortable feeling was transmissible, couldn't he also acquire normalcy from the outside? He would associate with people who acted according to the gospel of grade school readers and the covers of the Saturday Evening Post so that when, in time, he came to resemble them, he would feel inside the way he imagined they felt all the time — normal.

That was the goal, but now he was a small boy in bed in a dark room late in the afternoon, whose life had become intrusion by others, even others like his mother from whom he was not distinct. The only place he could be himself was at his own core, where something grand lay, where he would find escape and salvation as deep inside himself as the cranky, sweaty feeling was.

At the same time he wanted to escape his stifling family to find clarity unmuddied by his own particularity and bad feelings. Albie never doubted that the two extremes were the same. His world was a snake with its tail in its mouth that at every moment inflicted on itself a mortal wound. Albie tasted in his imagination a snake's scaly tail that would rattle if only his dry tongue did not prevent it.

The cure for the poison is to suck it out. You open your mouth on a snakebite to suck the poison into a space inside you which is actually outside you. Listen, boy, you can not escape. All this biting, this poisoning, the risk of sucking out, is part of eating, of nutrition. Here boy, eat, eat more, you're so skinny. Take food, eat! If he doesn't eat he will die.

Albie's mind labored in a thick state between sleep and wake. His mouth was so dry his tongue felt hot when he tried to move it. Chatter in the kitchen slipped by, but the doorbell roused him. His mother's voice, a heavy tread in the corridor, conversation outside his door.

"Sweetie." His mother stood behind Dr. Campbell's large presence. The doctor's coat smelled cold as he put down black leather cases in the dark room.

"The light . . ."

"His poor eyes," his mother said.

"I have to see."

A snap. Albie opened his eyes to blinding light and headache. The huge man unpacked a glass bottle, tubes, gauze pads. The bright orange dream color he poured on a pad looked green for a moment.

"Your hand," Dr. Campbell said.

Albie's tongue stuck to the roof of his mouth. By the time he succeeded in moving it to his upper teeth, Dr. Campbell had tied a rubber knot that pinched his skin. The orange chemical he painted Albie's little forearm with smelled metallic and turned his skin red. "Wait," Albie wanted to say, but Dr. Campbell crushed his fingers together and pierced his hand with a metal needle. Albie struggled. Dark red blood dripped out of the needle onto his knuckles.

"Don't move," Dr. Campbell said.

The needle hurt. Cold coursed up Albie's forearm. His mother made a little hushing sound as she reached over the headboard to touch his forehead. Albie closed his eyes and whimpered. His upper lip stuck to his lower.

"Hold this up," Dr. Campbell said.

Clothes rustled, the chair moved, a ripping sound, another new smell. Albie opened his eyes. Dr. Campbell was strapping his hand to a board wrapped in muslin. A tube led from his hand to a glass bottle his mother held above her head. "The stand?" Dr. Campbell took the bottle from his mother, who moved around him in the small room. Junior fluttered; the cage crashed and jangled as she set it on the floor. The doctor hung the glass bottle upside down from the hook inside the metal ring.

Albie could still feel the needle. "Mommy?"

"Shh." She touched his forehead.

". . . come back later," Dr. Campbell said. "We still may have to go to the hospital, Mrs. Greenberg."

"I don't want to lose him."

The light went out. Albie curled himself up under the warm covers. He left the hand with the needle out in the room.

When he awoke in darkness his mouth was still stuck but he felt better. He sat up on the side of the bed. Faint light entered around the sides of the shade from lights in other apartments on the air shaft. The cage rattled as Junior jumped from a perch to the swing.

Albie sat up. His head hurt less. He wiggled his fingers to feel where the needle went into his hand. He crossed to the window to lift the shade so he could make out the upward course of the plastic tube from the tape over the needle. The metal ring on the upside-down bottle was the same size as the wire on top of Junior's cage.

Albie jiggled the cold metal stand to swing the bottle the way he rocked Junior. The swinging bottle moved the tube, which tugged his hand. It didn't hurt. Albie pushed harder, pulled, pushed; the bottle swung.

The doorbell startled him. Guilty, he hurried under the covers. The stand fell away and landed with a crash; the tape tore and his hand hurt and he closed his eyes to appear asleep.

Dr. Campbell pushed open the door of his room. The light went on. His mother screamed and Dr. Campbell crushed his hand. "My bag," he said. "A towel—"

The wet on Albie's hand was red. The sheet was red. The tube hung down to the floor. From outside the small room, his father shouted, ". . . explanation!" Albie was too sick to care who his father was angry at. Junior sang and jumped from one perch to another in his cage next to the broken bottle on the floor.

Three adults crowded over Albie to examine the new bandage on his hand. Dr. Campbell touched Albie's neck and laid his palm on Albie's chest. Albie's mother touched his forehead. "He's cooler." She spread a towel over the dark blood on the sheet. His father picked up Junior's cage, but he waited for Dr. Campbell to take the bottle off the hook before he carried the cage and the stand back to the corner of the room. Junior sang through the flowery cover fastened around the cage.

"Can I have ginger ale?" Albie said.

His mother waited for Dr. Campbell to nod. His father slumped against the radiator with a hand over his closed eyes until Dr. Campbell had packed his bag. The trouble was leaving Albie's body, and Albie would miss it.

Miss Steidel set a machine with knobs and dials and a spool of shiny silver wire on top in front of the second grade. She played the two piano chords that demanded silence and attention. Albie was smaller than all the other boys and most of the girls, so he sat in the first row.

"Children," Miss Steidel said.

Clinton whispered in back. Miss Steidel played the chords again and stared at him. "This is a wire recorder," she said. "We can sing into it, and hear ourselves. The machine is very delicate, so we will sing beyoo-tifully."

Miss Steidel paraded from the piano to the machine to turn a switch. A light came on, and the cylinder of wire moved up and down. "Do, Re, Mi, Fa, Sol, La, Ti, Dooo," Miss Steidel sang into a silver microphone. She snapped switches once, again. A tinny Miss Steidel sang, "Do, Re, Mi, Fa, Sol, La, Ti, Dooo!" and ended with a shriek while the flesh teacher pressed her lips shut.

All the children talked at once. "Can we try it?" "Please, can I?" "Oooh," flat hands high in the air.

"Stand up, class," Miss Steidel said. "*The Wassail Song.*"

Chords again. Everyone sang. The tune was merry, so Albie sang out. "Love and joy come to you, and to you your wassail true . . ." Remembering words was easy for him.

Miss Steidel pulled on her earring to listen at the end of the first row. She left Barbara Gianni to crouch in front of Judy. She moved a hand up and down and touched Judy's hair. She came to Albie.

"God bless the master of this house," Albie sang. Miss Steidel frowned.

Albie sang hard, and peeked over Miss Steidel's shoulder at the wire recorder. Miss Steidel's frown deepened.

Albie belted it out. "And all the little children . . ." Miss Steidel pointed with her finger. "Albie, why don't you stand in the back and hum?"

He stood in the back but he didn't hum. When he got home, his mother was talking on the telephone with no lights on in the apartment. He waited a long time until she finished and got him a glass of apple juice. They sat together on the sofa. "What happened in school today?" she said.

"We sang Christmas carols, into a wire recorder."

"A wire recorder, that's wonderful."

Miss Steidel had sent him to the back to protect the wire recorder from his singing. They sat in silence while the last afternoon light faded from the sky. Albie sipped his apple juice; his mother sipped from a glass too.

"Did you sing in school?" he said.

"I know a song," his mother said after a pause, "but it's naughty."

Albie waited.

"I'll sing it, but I have to make dinner." She straightened herself on the sofa and piped in a little voice:

"'Twas a year ago our baby died,
"He died committing suicide.
"We know he died to spite us
"Of spinal meningitis.
"'Twas a nasty baby anyhow.
"We ate him."

Albie sat in the dark living room a foot away from his mother. When she walked to the kitchen, she bumped her leg on the edge of the coffee table. He heard her pull the beaded chain on the kitchen light. He sat still in the dark with his glass of apple juice tilted so it pooled at his lip for another long time before he went to his room to read.

Albie watched pale gray morning lines slide off the Venetian blinds onto his ceiling until a yellow glow reflected from passing headlights told him that people were moving. A new day had arrived. He donned the shabby slippers beside his bed, pulled his plaid flannel robe over his pajamas, and hurried to his parents' bedroom door.

From the dark of the hall he pushed it open a little to see similar lines cast by their Venetian blinds on their ceiling. Their bedroom was a deeper, more private retreat than his; their many bureau drawers were closed to him. The rich night animal smell in their room invited him and forbade him.

Even if they were still asleep they would soon awaken. He tiptoed toward their dark stillness, and held his breath as he suspected they were holding theirs. He fingered the covers over his mother's shoulder. "Mommy?"

After the pause that seemed too long she raised the covers to invite him to lie beside her. His thin ankles and feet, cold even in slippers, warmed in the dark place of legs as he snuggled in. Beyond her his father mumbled, reached over her to rub Albie's head, and made his way around the foot of the bed to their bathroom. He closed the door.

What was Albie missing in the secret world of two people in one bed? What he sought was not in the movies. At the end of a Saturday afternoon adventure, the joining of hero and heroine as their lips approached but never touched was false, and silly. "Oh, no!" Larry said, throwing a hand over his eyes, as the embrace faded and the credits began. The catcalls of the other boys expressed the power of the dark mystery that drew Albie on.

Outside the movie he blinked in daylight as Larry's mother invited him home with them for cake and milk. After the snack Larry's brother, who was thirteen, showed them magazines filled with pictures of women in strange clothes that didn't cover them. Albie wondered at their breasts because his mother was slender. The darkness beneath the gowns where the women's legs came together made Larry's brother blush.

Larry's brother said, "I got something else!" His hazel eyes gleamed. An olive shadow on his upper lip was the beginning of a mustache. He closed the door of the room against his mother rattling pots in the kitchen and climbed on a chair to take a cigar box from the back of the top shelf of his closet. With the box under his arm he pulled the shades and switched on a lamp.

"You better not tell," Larry said.

The cigar box contained a single black and white photograph: a woman with short hair lay back on an oldfashioned sofa, like his grandmother's. She wore stockings, high-heeled shoes, and a long pearl necklace. As she lay back on the sofa, she licked her lips at the camera past uncovered breasts which sagged to the sides. One of her hands was behind her head. The other lay on her thigh, her extended index finger in the top of the cleft between her legs.

It was too much for Albie to take in. "Who is — " he said, but Larry's mother was coming, the picture back in the box, the shades up, the closet door slammed, all in a moment.

From his window Albie watched couples hold hands or walk with arms about waists. One summer afternoon a woman in a white bra smoked a cigarette in a third floor window across the street. Her dark curls fell over her shoulders; she watched cars pass and children play stoop ball below her. A man in a ribbed undershirt like Albie's father's came up behind the woman. Dark hair slicked down, a mustache, he cupped her breast. She smoked a long minute before she flicked the cigarette away so it bounced off the brown stone of the stoop. Her eyes swept over Albie's window before she embraced the man and white curtains floated together in the warm air.

Albie imagined he climbed out his window at night. At the edge of the cool, rough granite ledge he hesitated, let go, pushed off sideways. With his eyes on his dark window he tumbled downward until the cool air accepted his weight. When it caught him, he filled his lungs. On this night the air lifted him up, and he could fly!

To fly! He lay prone on the currents like Superman above brownstone stoops and parked cars. He rode a crest of black air toward the Avenue he had visited with his mother late that afternoon.

As he flew he could see the blue center dot in the red tail lights of a car driving past and the woman on her stoop in a flowered house dress, hair as black as his mother's. Her perfume was plum and fire, thicker than his mother's, her sallow face impassive. The street light shone on the corner of her eye, the small hairs and drop of sweat on her upper lip. She could not see him.

Arms spread, he glided toward where the pale blue sign of the bar on the corner flashed and flickered. Four bums leaned against the brick and drank from a bottle; Albie anticipated the liquor smell and arched over the Avenue in a smooth parabola at a height of five stories. His fingers stirred the night air to turbulence above the colored blaze of still-open stores and passing traffic. Up there the wind reduced a bus, a taxi, the men on the corner to irrelevance, and he flew over them.

In the next dark street he brought his arms to his sides to let himself coast down to the tops of the cars, and lower, to the level of their tires. He drifted a foot, a hand's breadth above the pavement with the clarity and coolness of the night air in his nostrils. He could fly as long as he only looked. A leaking hydrant had moistened the asphalt black, or perhaps one of the huge gray trucks had passed with its skirt of water that washed detritus to the curb.

He sniffed as he floated over a cigar butt, a discarded gob of Clark's Teaberry gum, a dog turd. He was so close! He drifted up through dilute darkness toward an unhealthy orange glow reflected off the bottom of clouds, and glissaded down murk to search for his reflection in windshields. One car was occupied. As he hovered he made out the man's hands on something, hair, between him and the steering wheel. The man's eyes were closed, lips drawn back from clenched teeth, as his hands moved on the long yellow hair of the woman folded over in his lap. Rivulets of dark air kept the boy afloat as the woman jerked away, her mouth open, lipstick smeared, exposing a monstrous thing of flesh that groped blindly upward from the man's lap. She seized it with one hand and pumped it until the man's mouth opened and his arm that groped for the woman's head relaxed.

A gust of night air buffeted the boy. In a trembling hurry lest by touching the car he lose his flight and his invisibility, he threw his head to the side, strained upward and plunged through the warm, thick flows that rushed above the Avenue traffic. An ochre miasma tumbled him head over heels, but his momentum popped him into the easier air of his own street, where he skimmed level until he turned a reckless somersault upward to alight on his frozen granite windowsill.

TWO

*Ten is relaxed and casual, yet alert. He has himself and his skills
in hand; he takes things in his stride . . . the 10-year-old . . .
has a fairly critical sense of justice. . . . Individual differences,
apparent at nine years, become still more manifest at ten. . . .
The exercise of skills with social approval serves a valuable double
purpose. It serves to strengthen that self-respect and self-confidence
which is so important in meeting the perturbing demands of
adolescence. Simultaneously, society thereby protects itself
against the delinquencies of adolescence. . . . Boys express their
camaraderie with other boys in wrestling, shoving and punching
each other.*

—GESELL AND ILG, *THE CHILD FROM FIVE TO TEN*, 1946

"I have a surprise for you," his father said. "Now that you are ten years
old you can go to overnight camp like your cousin Stevie."

The light caught Albie's mother's dark hair and dark eyes, and the
glass of water she held. He needed more time. He wished she would
help him.

"My little man," said his father, "don't you want to go to camp?"

Albie ran out of the living room, through the carpeted foyer and skidded
on linoleum in the hall. He slammed his door.

His mother tapped. "Please, honey, may I come in?" The latch-snap
sounded from the whole door when it yielded. She sat beside him and
stroked his brow. "My terrible-tempered Mr. Bang."

He squeezed his eyes shut and held his breath until she picked up
her glass and stumbled back to his father.

Three years after the birthday party when Uncle Eli had shown the movie
of the Mighty flying mouse, directors of summer camps for boys visited
to hawk their wares. Each camp director spread brochures and albums on
the coffee table. The pictures showed boys in matching tee shirts in rows
on a grandstand; boys playing baseball; boys at the edge of a lake. His

father and mother sat high up on side chairs at the corners of the coffee table. "Does it look like fun, honey?" "Would you like to go there?"

The colored photos were not as real as the pictures in Albie's mind after he had read a book himself. Crouched beside the coffee table, he bent his head to think his thoughts. The camp director and his parents believed he was still looking at the pictures.

After the third such presentation Albie's father asked, "Which one do you like best?" Albie couldn't think. "You have to like one of them best."

When Bear Brewer came from Bear Lake Camp, Albie's father said, "He's the athletic director of Aiken Academy. You might go there for seventh grade."

Bigger, faster, stronger boys were athletes. Clinton in Albie's class bragged about his football team. But when Albie's father played golf on weekends, all Albie saw was his mother's sadness as she carried a glass of water with ice cubes in it from room to room, her red shoes wide apart. The time he found a bronze medal in his mother's bureau drawer that celebrated her third place in a Junior Girls' race in New Jersey, she took it away from him with an odd smile. Uncle El could hardly walk. His mother's brother had danced in a ballet, with makeup. What would a boy from such a family do with an athletic director?

"His name is Brewer," his father said.

"Brewer!" His mother shook her head. His father stared at her back with his hands on his hips.

The dark stubble on Bear Brewer's jaw resembled Black Pete's. His hair was thinner than Albie's father's. He carried two black cases and a screen on legs which he set up at the end of the living room, right where the screen had stood for the birthday party.

He unpacked the same brochures and forms as all the other camp directors. The second case was the projector. Albie crawled under the drop-leaf dining room table to plug it in. Stretchy metal cords twanged as Bear Brewer looped them over wheels on the arms where the reels went. Albie loved how the square hub accepted the reel, the way the lens clicked into place after the film had been threaded, the authority of the shiny toggle switches that controlled the light and motor. He was ready for a movie.

In the dark room Bear Lake Camp blazed back at them in silent color. Hordes of smiling boys, all larger than Albie, erupted through a screen door onto the verandah of a big house in the country. They waved at the camera in obvious buffoonery before they swarmed down steps out of sight. The gears of the projector clicked and rattled; the blue loop of film sticking upward shuddered in the darkness. Boys ran across a green field toward the camera. Boys stood in a row on a dock under a blue sky with green trees behind them on the opposite shore; at a silent signal they all jumped into the blue lake.

". . . learn to swim," Bear Brewer said, "in water as pure as Bear Lake."

Smoke from Albie's mother's cigarette floated through the bluish light above the projector. "Would you like to learn to swim?" she asked.

The idea gave Albie a deep uneasiness. Cool water under a hot sky, yes, but water too thick to breathe stung his eyes when Mother washed his face. He leaned his head one way and another, but he could not decide about learning to swim. "I guess so," he said.

Bear Brewer grunted and slapped Albie's back before he carried his baggage out through the foyer. Had a decision been made? Albie sensed momentum. And disturbance—not one of the boys in the film had been reading—but he quelled the feeling. Bear Brewer went as the others had gone, and he wanted to get to his bed, where he could dream.

How much time did he have? How many miles away would camp be? The pulp science fiction magazines his allowance bought said that time was no more than another dimension of space.

The first time his parents permitted him to cross the avenue that separated the block where he lived from the park, he dutifully looked both ways before he scurried to safety on the far sidewalk. But one day he dared to pause in the middle to follow the white line from his feet to where it disappeared in the distance. That night he imagined a bare plane, as white and featureless as a sheet of paper, with a single line extending before him like the line in the middle of the avenue: downtown. The line appeared black in his mind's eye when the paper was white, or he could say 'red' and make the line red. The line extended behind him, too.

So there was uptown and downtown. On his right lay west, and on his left hand, east. He stood at his imaginary intersection on a plane with the matte finish of a page lit by his Bakelite lamp. The city was a grid, but camp was off his map.

What about up and down? Despite his flights of fancy, his expeditions from his fifth floor apartment to the street occurred in the new self-service elevator in which a solid door with a tiny window had replaced the old sliding gate. The elevator clucked when it started, but Albie felt so little that the motion didn't seem real.

In his father's office building, the weight of his blood rushed down to his legs and tried to topple him as the elevator ascended. That was an elevator!

When his mother took him to visit there, he drifted away from adult conversation to admire and covet the stores of pencils, ink, erasers, paper clips, envelopes, message pads, and paper in the supply room. Yellow legal pads stacked in piles! Reams of white typing paper! He extended a small hand to touch these riches.

"Excuse me, son." His father's law clerk rested a heavy hand on his head. Albie stepped back as a man in khaki wheeled in a hand truck bearing two cases of stationery on their ends so they would fit through the doorway. The law clerk had black hair down to his fingers, a gold ring, gold cufflinks through holes in his white shirt. He took the top box off the hand truck and set it flat on the floor with a loud slap. He set the second case on the first, opened it, tore the wrapper off a ream of paper, and riffled through the printed sheets. "Okay," he nodded to the man with the hand truck, "over there."

After the men left, the boy who could not fly, the boy who loved books and stationery supplies, imagined that the sheets of paper were maps, one above the other, each for a different day. Perhaps the future was up and the past was down!

His mother found him in the corner stroking the hard edge of a wrapped ream of paper. "He was playing by himself," she told his father.

Albie turned his face away from adults he did not know and his father's disapproval. Time was up, up was up. Even if he could not fly or remember, he would imagine. Later, when the falling elevator stole the floor from under him, he rose up toward the future, and did not turn away.

The night after Bear Brewer's visit, Albie awakened from a dream of movement and crowds, and cried out. That was his mother's footstep in the hall, but when the door opened he did not recognize his room in the trapezoid of yellow light that followed her in. He pressed his face against her warmth. "Mommy?"

She stroked his damp forehead. "What is it, my honey darling?"

"Where did we go?"

"I couldn't understand you. Can you say it again?"

He shook his head, his face tight against her. "I'm too disappointed," he sobbed.

Years before, she had shaken him awake in the night and dressed him in bathrobe and slippers. The family left the apartment. Father, in a raincoat and a flat steel helmet, wore his binoculars on a strap around his neck. Mother, in a bathrobe, carried something wrapped in a blanket. The stuccoed hall was dark and the lights on the stairway went out as father led them by flashlight down flight after flight to a strange apartment in the front of the building.

Inside, blankets hung over the windows. There was no furniture. Many adults sat on the floor under dim yellow lights, while Albie's father walked up and down in the raincoat and helmet and gestured at people with his flashlight.

Albie sat on a rolled-up rug between his mother and the mother of a girl he played with. The other woman's chalky face was sweaty, the brown hair outside her kerchief pasted down in ringlets over her frightened eye, a girl's eye, not a mother's. Her silent husband cradled Albie's playmate in his arms; he wore a vest but no tie. They both wore white sleeves down to their wrists.

"Thank goodness Eliezer isn't here," his mother said.

His playmate's grandmother wailed opposite them on another rolled-up carpet. "Oy!" she wailed, "not on the camps . . ." Her mouth was wide open, her pale ochre face the color of the light. She lifted her arms in sleeves to Albie's father until he blew a whistle and told her to be quiet. She cringed away from his flashlight. In the morning Albie awakened from the blackout in his own bed.

Albie's grandfather came for dinner on his way home after he had stopped to pray. Praying was asking God for things, but Albie had never seen anyone do it. People in books prayed in churches. Boys in books knelt by their beds and clasped their hands as they prayed aloud while their mothers listened behind them.

Barrel-chested Grandfather unbuttoned his vest at the table and took off his rimless glasses to peer at Albie with a concern his parents did not show. He never addressed Albie directly. He was bald. He sang little songs after dinner even if no one listened, even if Albie's mother asked him to stop.

Sometimes grandfather introduced the songs like a disk jockey: "This was one my mother knew. It's about two old mares . . ." And sometimes he didn't, so they were altogether incomprehensible. He sang with his blue suit jacket off, vest unbuttoned, trousers unbuckled, shirt collar open but his tie still clasped by a little chain.

Albie's father wasn't there. His mother interrupted her own father's singing. "Albie's going to camp this summer, Papa."

Grandfather opened his eyes. "A camp? A camp?"

His mother shook her head and looked at him hard. "A summer camp, in New Hampshire, with other boys. They will walk in the woods, and swim. Albie will learn to swim in a beautiful lake."

His grandfather hummed and waved a finger in the air. He said. "The Talmud tells us, 'You shall teach your boy to swim.'" He nodded and hummed and tapped the table. Albie's mother made a sour face. Grandfather beckoned Albie closer and stroked his hair. Albie saw thick blue veins among sparse hairs and pink scars on the back of the hand that smelled like a cigar. "You should be a fighter, a fighter," said Grandfather.

Albie doubted that such a thing was possible.

"He should fight for the land." Grandfather muttered words that sounded like static, or coughing. Mother stood against the wall and twisted a dish towel in her hands. After Albie retreated to his bedroom, the adults talked and argued and the door opened and closed. Later, Albie's mother came to check on him.

If the surface of time gets folded, now can be close to then, or right beside a decade from now. That is when Albie will visit his aunt in Zurich. His aunt? She is the wife of his father's father's double first cousin. When he first hears of this woman's existence, he will ask, "What's a double first cousin?" He has in mind a relative twice as large as life, like a double scoop of cherry vanilla.

His mother will avoid his eyes and strain to sound offhanded. "It's when two brothers marry two sisters." As Albie tries to frame a question about the relationship and the nexus of unarticulated feeling surrounding it, his mother will take him by both shoulders and kiss him. He will wipe lipstick from the front of his cheek. He will not ask again.

His aunt, or whoever she was, and the family there in Zurich had escaped, but at ten Albie did not know what they had escaped from. Later he learned from scraps of conversation that when these double first cousins of his father's escaped to Switzerland they assumed the name of a noble Swiss family that had died out hundreds of years before. When they got some money they wore rings that bore the crest of the now-reborn family.

They became what they were not. Albie found this fakery magnificent: if you are going to escape you should make a good job of it.

Albie sensed that the Europe his father's parents had come from was a darkness like the back of the corset shop his grandmother ran, or the hospital room where her bald, remote husband died. When that happened no one explained to Albie what was wrong. He had been the shortest of the four grandparents.

Albie's grandmother sold women's underwear, bras, and stockings from boxes marked with size, model, color, ready to wear. In the back she fitted and made custom foundation garments. That was private: Albie was not welcome in back.

From the store's front window Albie watched workmen across the street pour concrete pillars around metal reinforcing rods like the whale-bones in his grandmother's corsets. A boy needed facts to strengthen his memory. The tissue of Albie's imaginings fell away from the thin parts of his history he was sure of. He yearned to add the distant truths he would see with binoculars to what he already knew and remembered. If he could only observe he was sure he would remember.

Among the grown-up books in the living room shelves Albie found *A Treasury of Jewish Folklore*. Even without pictures, the places and characters in the tales it told were as vivid and strange as his day in Chinatown. But the family never talked about them.

At dinner he asked his father, "What's a treasury?"

His father beamed. "The Treasury is part of the government," he said. "It's the second cabinet post in line for the presidency, ST. WAPNIACL." He told Albie's mother, "He's taking an interest. He's very advanced."

The saint part didn't sound right. The *Treasury* said that Jewish people revered the stones of the Wailing Wall beyond any other reality on earth. "What's the Wailing Wall?" he said.

His father scowled. "Who's he been talking to?" His mother drank water from her glass. "I don't want your father filling his head with that stuff," Albie's father said. "It's hard enough without it."

"I read it myself," Albie said.

"He should know because of Eliezer," his mother said.

"He won't get anywhere if they think he's an immigrant. He has to fit in." He pointed a fork at Albie. "Keep up with your school work. Never mind that Bible stuff."

The next day after school, Albie opened the Bible on the living room floor to look for the Wall, and imagined the awe he would feel if he were to stand before it. Why didn't his family discuss the Bible? In fairy tales, shoemakers taught their sons their trade. Indian chiefs taught young braves to track beasts and enemies. Albie turned page after page in search of the Wall, or awe, or anything that invited him.

Albie knew that there had been a war, and that it was over. 'D.P.' meant displaced person. In some news photograph Albie had seen a man his father's age with gleaming eyes in a drawn face, his arm around a woman with a shawl over her head. Behind them stood a ragged column of men and women in threadbare clothes, on a dirt road in a place without buildings, people without context or destination.

Albie dared not ask who they were. Perhaps his mother's voice had changed. Perhaps his father had moved a hand to shush some adult guest. The meaning was clear: the world's survival rested on Albie's not asking when he shouldn't. Albie's father led the conspiracy to thwart his son's desire to know how the world worked and force him into an unnatural posture in regard to it. When in effect he said, "Stand like this, wear this, speak this way — "Albie understood, " — so that you will be safe from the monstrous harm in the world."

But the worlds of adventure and victory Albie read about in library books weren't like that. Could it be that his father was wrong?

A decade after what happened that summer at camp, twenty-year-old Albert Greenberg flew alone to Zurich where his great aunt, the widow of one of the double first cousins, ran her deceased husband's optical shop in the Theaterstrasse. He wanted to see a part of his family with whom he ought to have a double connection for himself.

The telephone was a challenge, but on the third try he got through.

" — ?" said a woman's voice.

"*Ist Clarice zum Geschaeft?*" he asked. "*Ich bin Albie Greenberg, ihr, ah, Grossneffe.*"

"*Moment,*" said the voice, with a French accent.

Great double aunt Clarice came on the line to invite him to dinner. She gave him directions to the optical shop in French-accented English. He could not tell whether she could not understand his German or preferred not to speak it.

On his way a street vendor sold him a bunch of flowers as bright as a mountain meadow. He stood on the shop's thick carpet. The gleaming wood and glass of the counter reflected the ceiling lights like the fake lenses in the frames on display. Those frames were thick plastic, and the lenses the staff wore were thick, too. Great Double Aunt Clarice was a heavy woman in a black dress. A black rope connected her thick glasses to a gold pin on her dress. She had huge, heavy breasts, so the pin sat on a nearly horizontal surface.

"Hello," Albie said, over the suspension spans of serious corset engineering. "I'm Albie."

Clarice answered in rapid Swiss German he could not understand. She said something about "*Brille*," and touched Albie's face. "*Walther wird*," she said, and more German before she hurried into a back office.

"Albert, *ja?*" said a tall man in a starched white lab coat. His hair was an odd orange color, brushed straight back from a receding hairline. His tanned face was lean but square; he wore glasses with thick, honey-colored tortoise shell frames and perfectly rectangular lenses.

"Albert," Albert said, and extended his hand.

"So. I am Walther. Your *Tante* wishes give you a pair *Brille, gratis.*"

"I don't wear glasses," Albie said, "but thank you, thank her." Despite his awkwardness in the foreign language and his discomfort before this relative he had written to only once, he saw his chance to have binoculars of his own. "I was planning to buy a pair of,"—he did not know the word for 'binoculars'—"*Fernsehern*." He held up his hands to mime and pointed to a display behind the counter.

"Ah, *Fernstecher*." Walther stood straighter, bowed a little to Albie, and chattered to Clarice through the door to the back office. She muffled the mouthpiece against the top of her huge breast and answered as rapidly. Walther straightened again and took a step backward toward Albie. Clarice spoke again. "*Ja, ja,*" Walther said, and pulled the door to the back office shut.

Another employee, a short woman in a lab coat with a black pony tail and black harlequin frames, greeted a customer as fat as Clarice, who leaned over the counter to point at something under the glass.

"So!" said Walther. "Your *Tante* say, perhaps you have one pair *Sonnenbrille*, dark, with no prescription, that is *gratis*, but the *Fernstecher, Binokel*, she gives only ten *Prozent Rabaat.*"

Albie coveted the gleaming black metal, the perfect iridescence of the coatings, the supple black leather of the straps. "How much are they?"

The price was high. "*Karl Zeiss*," Walther said, and lowered his chin.

Albie knew the precise extent of his traveler's checks. He prepared to decline as he examined his inner sense of loss. He would survive without the binoculars.

Walther, impassive in his rectangular glasses, brightened. "Please," he said, "we have here one old pair of these glass. You will wait, please." He spoke with Clarice through the door and hastened to another part of the shop.

He returned with a black leather case even more battered than Albie's father's brown one, and extracted the glasses. Fingers had worn the crinkles on the barrels smooth and rubbed through the black finish to expose dull brass.

"They are long ago made," Walther said, "but they are very precise."

Albie picked up the binoculars. They had two knurled knobs in the center, one larger than the other, next to each was a ring marked with lines and numbers. The white filling was rubbed away, so even the grooves seemed shallow. Albie made out what had been either an E or an L on the larger ring, and part of an M or perhaps an R on the smaller one. The smaller wheel moved the right barrel with the smoothness of his father's field glasses. The larger wheel was stuck.

Walther turned his hand palm up and gestured toward the shop window. Through the heavy binoculars the scene was out of focus; Albie could not make it right with the small wheel. "Please, I will clean," Walther said, and took the binoculars to a corner of the shop.

The fat woman and the clerk with the pony tail concluded their business and leaned across the gleaming counter to touch their cheeks together. The clerk smiled and waved until the woman was out the door. She glanced at Albie without interest and polished the counter.

Walther returned with the binoculars in one hand and a dark green rag in the other. "*So!*" He crossed his arms as Albie raised the glasses to the street window.

The blur of color and light didn't change until Albie's finger found the larger knurled ring. It glided a tenth of a silent turn. The scene came into focus; Albie caught his breath.

"They have seen very much," Walther said. "Very much."

Beyond the glass and the corner of the K in 'Optiker' Albie saw the face of an old man on the far side of a tiny grassy park with perfect, preternatural clarity: blue eyes, frown lines, a mustard yellow shirt collar under the threadbare tweed jacket. Albie felt the man's fear as he waited to cross.

Would drivers respect his gray hairs? "Oh!" Albie said, as he remembered the road he had not crossed beyond the camp.

"*Ja?*" Walther opened his eyes wide, "Yes?"

Albie looked backward to that summer half his life before and forward to a future still concealed. Now he would explore that future with these old binoculars, and understand the past. His heart beat faster, raprapraprap, with a tap at each beat.

"Here is, for the hand," Walther said, and picked up the short strap on the case. He touched his extended index finger to the side of his nose, and to his lips. From the pocket of his white lab coat he produced a brand new leather strap with a buckle on one end. The polished black surface shone through its crinkled cellophane envelope in which it was rolled up like an anchovy bound with a rubber band. "Here is, for the head, yes?"

"How much?"

Walther glanced over his shoulder at the still-closed door. He wrote a price on a foolscap pad.

"Yes," Albie said, "yes."

Walther nodded with vigor as he made change, but when Aunt Clarice opened the door with a boa over her shoulders he backed away into the corner. Her eyes took in the parcel under Albie's arm, the flowers, and the two shop assistants. She walked around the end of the counter to take his elbow. He held out the posies to her.

"*Alors,*" she said without accepting them, "you have come to see Clarice, *n'est-ce pas?*" Double Great Aunt Clarice and Albie walked out the door, as summer heat wilted the flowers, memory and imagination faded, and past and future collapsed back to the present.

Albie's mother sewed name tapes after dinner, in the living room arm chair, in her eyeglasses, under the brightest lamp in the room. She held shirts up to his chest again and again with a strange light on her face. "So handsome," she said. It seemed to Albie that she might cry. Piece by piece the never-washed, never-worn new clothing marked ALBERT GREENBERG disappeared into the new camp trunk with its shiny brass studs. Brand new blue blankets went into the duffel bag of unforgiving canvas. Until Albie left he would sleep under his familiar tan ones, with the torn satin binding he used to rub against his lip.

One night when the trunk was still open his father came home from work and sat in the wing chair. "Come here, Babble-boy," he called into the shadows behind him, "I want to see you in the hat."

Albie carried the crimson baseball cap with a gray 'B' like the ones the boys had worn in the film by the button at its top. He stood before his father.

"Put it on."

Hollowness deep in Albie's chest spread upward into the corners of his jaw. His father held him at arm's length by the shoulders. "What do you think, honey, Joe DiMaggio!" He pulled the brim of the cap down over Albie's eyes and drew him close to hug him.

"Uh," Albie said.

"What is it, Babble-boy?"

"Can I take your pocket knife to camp?"

A look passed between his father and his mother. His father rubbed the baseball cap back and forth on his head. "A boy should whittle, and play mumblety-peg," he said. He lifted Albie's chin. "Do you know how to play mumblety-peg?"

Albie shook his head.

"I played mumblety-peg when I was his age," his father said to his mother's back. She stayed in the kitchen. His father said, "Yes, okay," and opened the newspaper.

The baggage in the foyer intruded on the normal life of the apartment. Nowhere in that hill of property was any object over which Albie had sovereignty. Even though the gray camp shirts bore Albie's name tape, they were not his because he had never worn them. The baseball cap made his ears stick out.

One hot June morning the doorbell rang after Father left for work. A man with a red face and a brown uniform wrote on the clipboard he carried, tore the paper and gave Mother a piece before he took the duffel bag and the trunk away. Where they had sat the crushed carpet appeared dirty in the horizontal light from the living room window.

Once again Albie could breathe. He stuffed the zippered gray and crimson bag into the bottom of the hall closet. Lazy June days passed in dreamy fantasy. Albie read a library book every day, sometimes two; he would return from a pirate ship or the Sahara desert only to accompany his mother as she shopped for groceries or visited neighbors.

Early Sunday morning before he was to leave he woke early and tip-toed down the hall stuffy with summer heat. He had not joined his parents in bed for years. Their door stood open a few inches; behind it, a lamp gleamed brighter than the dawn outside the blinds.

"Invasion," his father said, and "Communists." A little later he said, ". . . going to war."

Albie could not make out his mother's soft words.

"Of course not," his father said. "I didn't go the other time . . ."

Albie was too old for this. He shuffled away in his cloth slippers with squirrel faces, but when his mother sobbed, he edged back and pushed the door open. "Mommy?"

The bedside lamp silhouetted his father, who was hugging his mother and patting her back. Newspapers were strewn all over his side of the bed. His mother cried, "Oh!" His father relaxed his embrace and his mother turned over. She held up the covers on her side. "It's okay," she said.

The air felt strange. It was not okay. A ten year old boy going away to camp should not get into bed with his mother. Albie hesitated. His father grumped and pulled on a brown bathrobe that hung from the bedpost to walk around Albie to the bathroom. Yellow light clicked on; the door closed; water ran.

Albie remembered how high the bed had seemed once. His mother embraced him. Something wet, a tear on her cheek?

"My Albie. I don't want you to be a soldier."

The toilet flushed. His father opened the bathroom door. "MacArthur," he said. "Ground troops. Maybe it's on the radio." Leather slippers scraped linoleum until he reached the carpet. A man's excited voice echoed from the big radio.

Albie's mother got out of bed and left him alone.

The family breakfasted in pajamas and bathrobes as they did every Sunday. His mother drank orange juice and coffee, but she did not eat. His father ate scrambled eggs and bacon, drank tea and read the newspaper. Albie peered over his father's shoulder. "Where's Korea?"

"On the other side of the world, like China."

Like Chinatown? "Do they drink tea?"

"I guess so," his father said.

"Do they have fireworks?"

Both parents stared. He had said something wrong.

"More than fireworks," his father said. "They're having a war. We have fireworks on the Fourth of July because we won the war."

"The Revolutionary War." Albie knew that from school.

"That's right." His father returned to the paper.

"So is the war in Korea about tea?"

His father pushed his eyeglasses up onto his forehead. "The bad Koreans in the north, the Communists, attacked the good Koreans in the south. We might have to send American soldiers to help them fight back."

"Why?"

"Because they invaded. They came in where they didn't belong."

"Could they invade here?"

"Of course not," his father said. "We're safe here."

"How would the soldiers get to Korea?"

"By train," his father said. "They would get on a train —"

"Like when I go to camp?"

"No," his mother said, "not you." She touched her face with a napkin.

". . . to the west coast," his father said. "They would sail on a troop ship . . ."

His mother held her head with both hands. "Those boys going off alone!"

"They're not alone," his father said. "They have their buddies. Like you." He rubbed Albie's head. "You'll have lots of buddies at camp." He rattled the paper.

"I hope he never has to go," his mother said, and reached for the front section his father put down. "Albie, honey, may I see that, please?"

He passed it to her. She studied the headlines through her glasses and held the page up so she could see the bottom. "Oh!" she gasped.

"What is it, Mommy?"

"Listen to this. Morris?"

His father took off his glasses.

"They attacked the queen, listen." She adjusted the paper to see it better. "'Queen Mary sleeps through hunt for burglar assailant in palace,'" she read. "'An armed man broke into Marlborough House, Queen Mary's residence, early today, stabbed an elderly housekeeper several times, beat her female assistant and then hid in a basement until he was caught by the police two hours later.'"

"The queen?" Albie said.

"The Queen of England," his father said.

His mother lifted the paper up to turn pages. "'It appears that shortly after midnight the intruder scaled a five foot wall, climbed to the second floor in the rear of the servant's quarters and entered Mrs. Knight's room through a partly opened window. Awaking, Mrs. Knight screamed, where-upon the intruder stabbed her repeatedly with a small knife until Mrs. Ralph, hearing the commotion, ran into the room and was herself beaten.'"

Albie's mother said, "If even the queen isn't safe—"

"Let me see that." His father slapped the front page and folded the inside page back. "It's not political," he said. "It's only a crazy man." He put the paper down. "It's not important."

It was important to a boy who dreamed of climbing out windows, and who had witnessed a stabbing. Albie passed the paper back to his mother while his father drank tea.

"I'm afraid," his mother said.

"We're safe here," his father said.

"No, listen to this. 'Mayor pacifies prowler in home,'" she read. "'A youth who had drunk too freely at a friend's graduation party entered Mayor O'Dwyer's bedroom at Gracie Mansion at an early hour yesterday. He walked right over to the Mayor's bed, his right hand in his coat pocket, and asked, "are you O'Dwyer?" The Mayor, putting to use the presence of mind that comes naturally to an old-time member of the police force in an emergency, answered as casually as he could in the circumstances: "No, he's downstairs." She smoothed the paper. "It's on page 32, you have it."

His father rummaged through the sections at his end of the table. The hand his mother rested on Albie's trembled. Maybe someone would invade the house while he was gone at camp. He sipped milk from his glass to feel the rim of liquid on his upper lip, and peeked under his eyebrows from one parent to the other.

His father read. "'The youth, identified later as Michael McDermott, 18 years old, had climbed the six-foot ornamental iron fence surrounding the Mayor's official home.'" He chuckled; "He's a climber like our little man, here." He scanned the article further. "'He entered the mansion by a rear door and made his way to the Mayor's bedroom on the second floor.' It's like the other one, he was disturbed, listen. 'The Mayor, once downstairs, asked the youth about his background. "He told me about his mother, and that his father was dead," the Mayor said.'" Albie's father raised a finger. "You see, he's from a broken home, it's not important." He pointed at Albie. "Finish your eggs."

Albie moved the congealed mass from side to side with his fork.

"The real danger is the Communists," his father said.

Albie's mother wept. Albie stared down at his egg. His home was not broken, yet he already dreamed of climbing fences and buildings. Perhaps these intruders wanted to find out how queens live, or mayors, so they could change themselves. Perhaps the bad Koreans wanted no more than to find out how to be good.

The night before the trip to the railroad station Albie's mother made him salami and mustard sandwiches on rye bread, two of them, his favorite. She packed them in a brown paper bag with an apple, a peach and a hard boiled egg. What about salt for the egg, half a teaspoon, folded into a little pocket of wax paper and wrapped in with it? Yes, here. What about Fruitana biscuits containing raisins trodden flat, with the unique doughy taste that concealed the sharp sweetness of the raisins until three bites released it? Yes, we'll put them in, too. What about SenSen, a red cardboard box of tiny black licorice squares, sold for the breath? His parents deplored his taste for them, but yes, yes, for the boy who is going away, anything, everything. Everything into the paper bag and fold it shut.

His mother wrote his name on it with a red crayon. When he awakened during the night he padded into the kitchen in seersucker pajamas. The light in the refrigerator dazzled him, but the cool air that rolled out felt delicious. Even though the bag stood sideways, he could read ALBE GREE in red letters. He touched the bag so it rustled before he returned to bed.

The summer morning oppressed even before it got hot. His father dressed the way he always did in a suit with a hat, and his mother put on a dress. They watched Albie shake white tooth powder into his hand and brush his teeth. They watched him dress in gray shorts and a crimson camp shirt.

"Where's the bag?" his father asked.

Albie knotted his shoelaces.

"I'll get it for you, son." His father returned with his briefcase in one hand and the zippered gray and crimson canvas camp bag in the other. "One for me, one for you." His father buffed the toe of his shiny shoe with his handkerchief while Albie put books into his bag and stood at the bookshelf to memorize the light, the reflection of the windows in the mirror, and the spines of his books he could not take along.

He did not want to eat. His father would not let him take the scrambled eggs and toast his mother made him to his room. His mother put her hand on his father's arm and took his plate away. "Don't forget your lunch," she said.

The brown paper bag with his name, ALBERT GREENBERG, stood unwrinkled next to the milk bottle. He enjoyed the cold weight of the peach and the apple, but the bag was too big to fit into his camp bag with his books and sweater and toys. He picked up the lunch in one small hand and the canvas bag in the other.

"Okay?" His mother settled the baseball cap on his head. "They said you'd get milk on the train."

"I have a surprise for you," his father said, in the tone that meant a gift. From the top shelf of the hall closet he produced a long object wrapped in gift paper. ". . . in good health," he said. "It's a real Wilson."

Albie tore wrapping paper from the odd shape and saw his name, Albert Greenberg, in black paint on a wooden handle. He did not recognize the tennis racquet because a red canvas cover with a zipper concealed the strings, and a heavy wooden trapezoid distorted its oval head. With the weight of the press, his thin wrist could hardly hold it up. His heart beat raprapraprap as he met his father's eyes.

"Do you like it?"

"Oh, yes, thank you."

"Let's look at it." His father loosened shiny silver wing nuts, removed the cover, and pointed at a thin red string wrapped around the other strings near the handle. "This is rough and this is smooth." He spun the racquet. "That's how you decide who serves." He checked at his watch. "We'd better get going."

His mother took her pocketbook from the hall table. Albie picked up his lunch and the canvas bag. His father zipped the cover back on the racquet and replaced the press. "Always keep the press tight," he said as he held it out, "so it won't warp."

Albie put the paper bag under his left arm and reached for the racquet.

"Like this." His father wrapped the top of the paper bag around the racquet's neck and Albie's small fingers around the bag. As his father rang for the elevator, his mother caught the racquet press before its shiny screws could scratch the hall table.

When they got out of the taxi Albie clutched his bag of books to his chest with both hands and left his lunch and the tennis racquet on the seat. His father paid and directed Albie and his mother under a great dusty arch. "That way." He led them to an arcade out of sight of the sun, through a heavy door and down a brown marble staircase to the huge space of the concourse around the clock.

Grand Central Station looked like a *Life* photo about the war. Throngs of children clustered around standards which bore the names of camps, as parents bid them good-bye with embraces and tears. Separation and immensity and unremitting noise reverberated in the dim air to render announcements incomprehensible. From time time a whistle blast or a child's cry rose above the din until the weight of so many people subdued it.

A sign on a pole said CAMP BEAR LAKE in crimson letters on gray. Under it Bear Brewer wore white shoes and a dark blue jacket with gold buttons like one Albie's father had, over a gray and crimson camp tee shirt like the ones in Albie's trunk. He fawned at Albie's mother and flipped his clipboard under his arm to shake hands with Albie's father.

He winked at Albie. "Ready to go, son? Ready to win?"

Albie examined the white shoes.

Bear Brewer jiggled the new racquet and tousled Albie's hair. "You must be Pancho Gonzales."

Raprapraprap. "I'm Albie Greenberg." He looked at his mother for reassurance.

Bear Brewer laughed. "You're not going to turn pro on me, are you?"

"He's pro material, all right," Albie's father said. He and Bear Brewer grinned at each other. Bear Brewer beckoned to a man in a faded red sweatshirt and tan pants, who nodded and approached them. His pink chiseled nose and cleft chin reminded Albie of a picture in a magazine. "This is Uncle Jesse," Bear Brewer said. "He's the counselor in Panthers. Jesse, this boy says he's Albert Greenberg but we're going to make him into a Pancho Gonzales."

"You bet," Uncle Jesse said. When he reached out to tousle Albie's hair, Albie didn't duck in time, so Jesse's ring hit his scalp and caused a little pain. The ring was a heavy brown metal with a piece of red glass set in it.

Uncle Jesse looked Albie's father right in his eye and called him 'sir.' They shook hands. Cryptic announcements echoed through the dark air overhead. A cluster of boys and counselors around a nearby sign moved toward one of the track gates. A mother waved even after the group had disappeared.

"Better get ready," someone said.

"All right!" Uncle Jesse cried. "Hup, two, three, four!"

"Visiting day's in three weeks," Albie's mother called. His father pulled her by the arm. A thick-limbed, meaty boy behind Albie pressed against him.

"Mommy!" Albie cried in panic, but he was curious, too.

Uncle Jesse blew a whistle. "Let's go! Hup, two, three, four!" The group of men and boys detached itself from mothers and fathers to edge toward the tracks. Albie started away without a good grip on any of his three burdens. One step, two, and he dropped his lunch. He bent to get it; when he stood up he couldn't find his parents in the crowd. 'Wait!' he cried, but the crowd pressed him on through dark noise, away from home.

He could not see his parents. Larger boys surrounded him, so he could not see Uncle Jesse or Bear Brewer. He scrambled to catch up. "Track twenty-six," boomed a loudspeaker, "track twenty-four." Up ahead the gray and crimson sign disappeared into an archway.

"You need help," said a much larger boy with a dark crewcut and pimples. "I'll carry that for you." Albie tried to proffer the tennis racket, but the boy reached into the circle of his arms to take the lunch. Even that help was welcome. "Thank you," Albie said. "My name is Albie Greenberg and I'm in Panthers."

The larger boy jogged toward the archway. Albie stumbled after him. Down on the platform camps lined up as conductors directed them to the cars that would carry them to the correct part of New England for the summer. Camp Rinoma, said a sign above green and white tee shirts. Sail-A-Way, in blue, had girls as well as boys. As much as Albie wanted to run back against the flow, he knew what was expected of him. With the tennis racquet as the point of his phalanx, he forced his way through campers, counselors, and conductors until he found the gray Bear Lake sign, and Uncle Jesse's red sweatshirt.

Uncle Jesse shouted, "Twenty-one, twenty-two, twenty-three." At 'twenty-three' he pushed Albie through the train door by the back of his head.

"Check!" a man's voice replied. "Twenty-three!"

"Twenty-three!" Uncle Jesse shooed Albie into the car from the vestibule. Most seats were taken. Boys who knew each other talked, shouted, pushed, read comics.

"Cubs and Panthers at that end," the man on the train said in a gravelly voice. He bent down to Albie. "You?" His face was gray with whiskers, but as smooth as Albie's father's after he shaved.

"I'm in Panthers."

"Call me Uncle Charlie. I'm the boss." He rested a large hand on Albie's thin shoulder. "Sit over there." He pointed at a pile of board games, baseball mitts and baggage at the aisle end of a backward-facing seat designed for two adults. Black hair curled from the backs of his knuckles.

Two boys beside the pile faced backward across from three others facing forward. Albie hesitated.

"Whatsa matter?" Uncle Charlie pushed Albie toward the boys, who appeared hostile and united. "Get that crap outa there," Uncle Charlie said. The boys glared at Albie, and whined. "Don't gimme that." Uncle Charlie pointed at a boy near the window. "You, what's your name?"

"Raddy Tarrant." He had a freckled pug nose and blue eyes.

"Get outa there."

Raddy pressed his lips together. Uncle Charlie grabbed his shirt. "You hear me?" He dragged Raddy into the aisle and shoved Albie toward the seat near the window. "That's your seat." Albie opened his mouth to protest. "Sit down."

The other four boys didn't make room. Albie clutched his bag and tennis racquet as he sidled past knees. As he sat, the train jolted him into the lap of the boy opposite. "Moron," the boy said between his teeth. Albie pushed himself back into the vacant seat. The boy opposite was the heavy, meaty boy who had pressed him forward in the station, but he had an open, smiling face and curly brown hair, and he winked.

In the aisle, beside the pile of toys and baggage, Uncle Charlie held Raddy by his shirt. "What about me?" Raddy said.

"You men work it out." Uncle Charlie released him and strode toward the front of the car. "Jesse!" he called, "Come back here and keep—"

Once the train was under way Albie peered out the window as houses, trees, a town, a train station slipped by. If he was quick he could pick out the name on the blue sign before a colored blur of advertising posters covered it and the station disappeared. His reflection floated through the scenery beyond the glass without effort, as fast as the train. The clangor of steel machinery rose through his seat, but he could not feel this head-long passage through the world. If he could wish himself into the image beyond the window, he would fly through a cool, sharp wind, past fields and stations and towns and fields and trees, in tandem with the train. Out there, not in here, disembodied and invisible, they could not touch him.

The other boys ignored him. Three of the five had been together in Lion Cubs, the youngest bunk, the summer before. Raddy Tarrant had accepted the seat on the aisle, but in the first hour had arm wrestled with the small dark boy in the middle opposite for his seat, so the two smallest boys — Albie's size — who were destined for Lion Cubs sat on the aisle, separate, like Albie, from the group.

The meaty boy across from Albie joined the boasting and scuffling, but he was less strident than they, and less determined to assert his superiority in everything. Raddy perceived a slight or a challenge in every comment; he bumped his knees into the others and took offense at the contact; he asserted rules and enforced them with blows.

"Anybody who can't name four American League teams in ten seconds," he said.

"Yankees, Red Sox, Orioles," the boy next to Albie said.

"Except Mullaly," Raddy said.

"Yankees, Red Sox," said the meaty boy. His gray camp shorts were tight around his thigh muscles.

"Gets a noogie." Raddy hit the larger boy in the shoulder.

"What about me?" Mullaly said. He had pointed ears and thick, black eyebrows over worried green eyes. "Yankees, Senators, Red Sox—"

"Too late, time's up." Raddy hit him, too.

"No fair!" Mullaly stood up, but the train jerked and threw him back into his seat. Albie and the small boy on the aisle moved away from the impact.

"What about them?" Mullaly said.

"I'm not playing," the small boy said.

Raddy shook his fist in the air. "Everybody who didn't name four teams!"

"Hey Raddy," the meaty boy said, "I don't want to play."

"Hey Raddy," Raddy said in a falsetto, "I don't want to play."

"Jerry!" Mullaly said, "Let's get him."

The meaty boy pinioned Raddy's arms while Mullaly tickled his ribs. Raddy kicked Albie's leg. Albie withdrew toward the window. Raddy uttered a long, piercing scream. Astonished, Albie whirled around to a tableau of Jerry pinioning a grinning Raddy and Uncle Jesse looming in the aisle behind Mullaly and the two small boys.

"He's fighting," Raddy said.

"Mullaly, Roth, you want a noogie?" Uncle Jesse said.

"He started it." Jerry Roth let Raddy go.

"Hold it down here." Uncle Jesse withdrew.

As soon as he was out of sight Raddy hit Jerry again. "That's for snitching."

"Hey," Jerry said.

"You're a sissy," Raddy said.

Jerry turned in his seat and hit Raddy's shoulder with his fist hard enough to make Raddy flush, and fall silent.

"Pow!" Mullaly said.

Quiet followed. The ride went on and on. Albie's empty stomach complained, but he did not have his lunch and had no idea how to find the boy who had carried it. Albie faced backward as the train rattled forward and Albie's sunlit other self flew through towns and stations and fields. At one point he thought, this eternal riding on a train was not all bad. Camp might be no worse.

Uncle Jesse appeared with a tray of cardboard milk containers. "Time for lunch," he said. "Regular or chocolate?" The boys opened paper bags and metal lunch boxes.

"Uh," Albie said under the gaze of the boys and Uncle Jesse. "Uhhh." To call a stranger 'Uncle' would dishonor his real uncle.

"It can talk!" Raddy said.

"You okay," — Uncle Jesse unfolded a piece of paper from his tee shirt pocket — "Greenberg?"

"I don't have any lunch."

"Didn't your mother make you lunch?"

Albie quailed: the question dishonored his family again. He remembered the deli smell of his two salami sandwiches and his pickle.

"Somebody took it."

They all stared.

"I mean, somebody helped me carry it, but he didn't give it back."

"Who was that?" Uncle Jesse said.

"A big boy, in the station."

The other boys relaxed.

"What big boy?"

"I don't know."

Uncle Jesse examined Albie's face. Noise from the wheels and the conversation of others in the car filled the train, along with unwelcome pressure from so many people so close to Albie for so long. The moment of Uncle Jesse deciding whether to believe him drew out as the train whistled in a curve. Uncle Jesse steadied himself on a seat. The other boys ate sandwiches. One small boy had a hard boiled egg, but he didn't have salt folded in wax paper.

"You guys," Uncle Jesse said. "You got any extra?"

They avoided his eyes.

"Mullaly, Roth, Tarrant, your new bunkmate Greenberg is a regular Pancho Gonzales. Who's going to give him half a sandwich?"

No one moved. The train entered a dark tunnel, but no sooner had the lights come on than they were out in daylight again with the engine whistling. The smaller boy on the aisle offered Albie half of a sandwich.

"Thank you." It was two square slices of orange cheese and lots of mayonnaise on white bread. The mayonnaise smell told Albie how hungry he was.

The boy with the thick thighs extended a Graham cracker. "My name's Jerry."

"Thank you. I'm Albie Greenberg." He should shake hands but his hands were full. Jerry smiled at him.

"Regular or chocolate?" Uncle Jesse said.

"Chocolate." The decision his mother would not have permitted him made Albie feel wicked and grown-up. He had lost his lunch, but he had found something better. These real boys had fed him. Might he now reach out to them? His life-long hesitance before others at his school on the other side of town might mean no more than that he didn't know them well. Neighborhood boys were strangers to him, but at Bear Lake he would eat and sleep beside these boys. Yes, in time he might dare to befriend them. Albie ate, and eyed the boys around him as much as he watched the scenery outside.

After lunch the boys went to the bathroom at the end of the car one by one. When Albie returned, Raddy had taken his seat near the window, Mullaly sat next to Jerry facing forward, and the small boy who had given Albie the sandwich had moved to Mullaly's seat. The aisle seat was all baggage again.

"Hey," Albie said, astonished. "That's my seat."

"Oh yeah?" Raddy said. "Who are you?"

"I'm . . . Albert Greenberg."

"No, you're not," Raddy said. "He said you're Pancho somebody. I'm Albert Greenberg, and this is my seat."

"I'm Albert Greenberg, and I don't have any lunch," Mullaly said.

"I'm Albert Greenberg, and I don't have any seat," Jerry said.

Raddy pointed at Albie. "Who's that guy?"

"It's Uncle Jesse," Mullaly said.

"It's Uncle Charlie," Jerry said.

"It's Raddy Tarrant, and he's a troublemaker," Raddy cried. "Get him!" He seized Albie's wrist to pull him over the knees of the five boys. Jerry and Mullaly tickled him so that he wriggled and struggled between tears and laughter. Raddy hit Albie's skinny shoulder with his fist again and again. "Troublemaker!" he shouted. He leaned close to Albie and said, "This is my seat," before he let him go and folded his hands in his lap to grin at Uncle Jesse, who had returned to stand in the aisle.

THREE

Azazel was originally a divinity symbolized and embodied in the goat, that lively, swift, high-climbing yet earthy, sexually potent animal with a strong odor. It is an animal both combative and nurturant, able to live in inhospitable terrain and willing to be domesticated . . . . these aspects of the goat god have been lost to Judaeo-Christian culture.

—SYLVIA BRINTON PERERA, *THE SCAPEGOAT COMPLEX*

Fine gray gravel surrounded the station house where the Bear Lakers got off the train in New Hampshire: no curb, no pavement, no traffic. Younger boys stood in rows with bags and sports equipment while milling boys bigger than Albie, many much bigger, responded to the counselors' commands sluggishly or not at all. Albie grew angry when he saw the boy who had stolen his lunch, but another boy looked so similar he could not be sure. He lost his anger when he wasn't sure. Anger felt better than fear, but Albie felt afraid again. His arm hurt where Raddy had hit him.

At a signal from Uncle Charlie, a yellow school bus drove onto the gravel. The thin driver wore a tan baseball cap with a very long brim over a hawk's nose and pink cheeks.

"All right, listen up!" Uncle Charlie's unshaven jaw appeared blue in the sunlight. "Answer your name when it's called. Baird!"

"Here!" a blonde boy a little taller than Albie replied.

"Get on the bus."

One by one large and small boys climbed aboard. When Albie got on, the window seats were all taken. He chose a seat near the back next to a thin boy who stared out the window and ignored him. Albie became invisible again. He watched rural life over the shoulder of the boy beside him the way he had watched the stabbing across his street, the way he had watched Tom Sawyer whitewash the fence, the way he watched the world of his dreams. He did not participate.

The paved street crossed a highway with a broken white line down the middle to become a blacktopped road that wound through fields and woods.

Small trucks stood outside white houses with green shutters. Trees; an empty meadow under a bright blue sky behind a ragged hedge of plants as tall as Albie; more trees. Barns, silos, cows with big black spots. A heavy woman in a yellow dress with a baby on her hip watched them pass.

The boy beside Albie had a head like a light bulb and hair shaven to a stubble the color of Uncle Charlie's chin. As long as the boy pressed his head against the window, Albie could see past him, but after a while the boy covered his eyes with his hands and rocked back and forth. Albie tried to watch the scenery behind him, in front of him, behind him again, but it was no use.

The others on the bus laughed and called to each other as Uncle Jesse shouted something from the well next to the driver. The boy beside Albie hummed just loud enough to hear above the bus engine and the other boys. He held his fingers over his eyes so his thumbs pointed backward below his huge ears, which stuck out, and had long, pendulous lobes like Grandma Greenberg's. Perhaps he was sick.

The boy's wrist bones bulged like marbles under the sallow skin that stretched over his flat forearms. The button at his collar was closed even though the bus was very hot. Albie touched his shoulder. "Are you okay?"

The boy stopped humming. He stopped rocking and slid his hands away from his eyes to peek at Albie before he rested against the window again.

"Are you sick?" Albie said. "My cousin gets sick on buses."

One of the boy's large hazel eyes turned in toward his nose; one looked at Albie. "Destination Moon," he said. "I'm accustoming myself to lower gravity."

"This isn't the moon. It's New Hampshire."

"It doesn't matter. It's higher up."

The bus turned onto a dirt road and the bus driver blew the horn. "What's your name?" Albie asked the strange boy beside him.

"Joe," he said to the window. "This is my second year."

"I'm Albert Greenberg."

All the other boys sang, "We're here because we're here, because we're here, because we're here," and stamped on the metal floor of the bus. Uncle Jesse shouted through cupped hands.

"It's my first year," Albie said.

The bus bounced under wooden signs that said 'Bear Lake – Camp for Boys' and 'Mistlewood – Camp for Girls.' It rolled past a barn, between a lake and baseball fields, and up a hill through tall trees to stop in a parking area at the end of a row of rough wooden cabins. The engine, and the boys, fell silent.

Across the parking area from the smaller buildings, but further uphill, stood the huge white house from the Bear Lake movie, with many green-shuttered windows above its two porches. The boys filed off the bus. The man who watched from the porch above the steps the boys in the movie had descended was Bear Brewer. The woman with him waved. Dust hung over the road. The row of cabins stretched into the distance toward a forest. Uphill from them stood more pines, wooden tables, stone fireplaces spread across a band of hillside. Further uphill stood a handful of windowless buildings smaller than the cabins.

"Wave to Uncle Bear, boys!" cried a counselor in baggy dungarees and a cowboy hat. He led boys who were Albie's size to the first cabin in the row. "Come on, Lion Cubs," he called. The little boys scrambled up the wooden steps. The youngest bunk's counselor might be more likable than Uncle Jesse. The small boy who had given Albie the cheese sandwich waved before he went in, and Albie waved back.

The identical dark brown cabins stood side by side on the hill in a straight row. At their uphill end two wooden steps, or three, led down to the ground, while at the downhill end the screen doors opened onto eight or ten wooden steps. The windows had screens instead of glass. Albie's cabin was Panthers, the second one. The third cabin was Woodsmen.

"Panthers!" Uncle Jesse stood on a tree stump and waved a clipboard. "Follow me!" Raddy pushed forward. Jerry, Mullaly and two others crossed the pine needles and gravel in the flat area where the bus had stopped. Albie followed at a distance, and Joe followed him. The group of boys stopped. "One, two, three!" cried Raddy. All the boys made small circles with their fingers at their temples, turned, and pointed at Albie.

Before Albie could consider whether he dared protest, the pointing fingers swung past to follow Joe, who ran in a broad circle through the picnic tables and into the third cabin, Woodsmen. The laughing boys who had mocked him shambled together toward the wooden steps of the second cabin. "Panthers!" Uncle Jesse repeated from the steps. Raddy pushed past him into the cabin. The screen door's slam rang in the air.

Inside Panthers metal cots stood on the unpainted floor with their ends against the side walls. A camp trunk sat at the foot of each bed; a duffel lay on each camp trunk. The shade of the trees and the small screened windows dimmed the interior even though it was still midafternoon. In one far corner a large boy had already made his bed and stacked clothes on two wooden shelves.

"Find your trunk, that's your bed," Uncle Jesse said as he walked down the row of trunks. Albie clutched his tennis racquet and camp bag against his chest. "Philip Mullaly, here." Uncle Jesse pointed to a bed on the left. "Jerry Roth, here." He pointed to the bed next to the large boy at the end. "Roth, this is Cooper Brown, he's from Boston. Brown, this is Jerry Roth."

The two large boys examined each other. Cooper Brown looked even stronger than Jerry Roth. His face was oval sideways; he had combed his straight, light brown hair all the way across the top of his head from one side to the other. Jerry Roth said, "Hi."

"How do you do."

At the bed next to Jerry Roth Uncle Jesse said, "William Hobeck." A tall boy stepped forward.

"That's my bed," Raddy said. "We're together."

"Take the bed where your trunk is and come get your keys. You can trade later." Uncle Jesse sat on his own bed with the clipboard and a manila envelope full of small keys. His khaki blanket was folded at the corner like the back of an envelope.

"No!" Raddy cried. "I'm the pitcher and Jerry's the catcher, same as last year, we're supposed to be together."

Albie found his trunk at the foot of the fourth bed on the right, opposite Jerry Roth. "This is mine," he called out. The thin mattress smelled damp, but a fresh pine needle scent floated in through the screens. Above the wooden shelves he found a nail in the wall: he hung his tennis racket on it by the corner of the press.

"Where's your trunk?" Uncle Jesse asked Raddy.

"I don't know."

"Look for it."

Raddy scowled. He peered at Cooper Brown's trunk, at Jerry Roth's, and for a long time at William Hobeck's.

Albie saw that the trunk beside him said Tarrant. "Is this yours?" he asked.

"Who's speaking?" Raddy looked all around the bunk and up at the ceiling.

Outside, from the direction of Woodsmen, boys' voices burst into a cheer. "Yayy!" they cried. Hands clapped. "Two, four, six, eight, Who do we appreciate, Uncle Dan!" They clapped again.

Uncle Jesse examined the tag Albie had found. "Randolph Tarrant, you're over here."

Raddy stuffed his hands into the pockets of his shorts, shuffled across the wooden floor and kicked his trunk. "No! It's in the wrong place." He wheeled and stuck his hand out at Albie. "Trade?" He pressed his thin lips together and pushed his jaw forward as if he were going to spit.

"This is mine," Albie said.

"Yeah, but you're a tennis player and we're the battery." He looked over Albie's shoulder to Jerry. "Right?" No one answered. "Right, Uncle Jesse? We're the battery, right?"

Uncle Jesse rested his hand on Albie's shoulder. "Do you mind?" Albie's head shook itself no even before he was sure. "Thanks a lot," Uncle Jesse said. "I'll move the trunk for you." The sound of Albie's metal trunk sliding over grit on the wooden floor echoed in the empty space under the cabin.

When the transfer was complete Raddy jumped on the mattress that was to have been Albie's and cried "Yayy!" He kicked Albie's new racquet to the floor between the beds.

Albie's face grew hot. His eyes wouldn't focus on the metal leg of the cot that had been his.

"Foot lockers!" Uncle Jesse cried. "Hup!" Each boy who had been at the camp the previous summer sprang to attention at the foot of his bed. Albie did the same. Uncle Jesse passed out keys; the boys threw their trunks open. "Any boy who needs help making his bed, ask me or Brown," Uncle Jesse said. He examined the list again. "Brown! Where are the twins?"

"They went to the nurse," Cooper Brown said, "to give her the medicine. They'll come to dinner."

Uncle Jesse grunted. He lay down on his own cot and opened a magazine with a blonde woman on the cover.

Albie unzipped his duffel bag. Sheets, fuzzy blue blankets, new towels, and a pillow: everything bore a name tape that said ALBERT GREENBERG in black characters on white. He piled his clothes on his shelves and hung his canvas toilet kit on a new nail with his racquet. Cooper Brown and Jerry Roth kept their toilet kits in their trunks: Albie returned his to his trunk.

A bugle sounded outside. "Ten minutes," Uncle Jesse said with his face in his magazine.

"What's that?" the tall boy across from Albie asked. His short black hair stood straight up over a pale face, but one of his cheeks was purple blue. When his dark eyes met Albie's, Albie realized the color wasn't a mask, and averted his eyes.

Jerry Roth said, "It's the warning. In ten minutes they ring the first bell for dinner and we have to leave the cabin. After ten more minutes they ring the second bell and we have to be at the table. You can leave now to wash your hands if you want."

"Get the beds later," Uncle Jesse said over his magazine.

"Are you going to wash your hands?" the boy with the mark on his face asked Jerry.

"Yeah, Jerry Roth," said Jerry, extending a meaty arm to shake hands. "I'm Will Hobeck," said the boy, with the normal side of his face toward Albie.

"What's *that*?" Raddy said.

"It's called a birthmark. It's how I was born. So don't say anything."

Raddy seemed to contract. "I just want to know what you do," he said. "Are you a shortstop or what?"

"I'm a jumper," Will said. "I won a gold medal in the Junior Olympics."

"Broad or long?" Raddy stared at Will's face.

"Both." He jumped into the air to touch the cord that hung from the bulb in the middle of the cabin.

"Let's see who can jump further out of the bunk," Raddy said. "somebody hold the door." Albie pushed the door they had entered through open. "Get out of the way, moron," Raddy said. Albie stepped outside and down the three wooden steps to the ground. He held the door open against its spring.

"I'm first!" Raddy's footsteps rattled. When he landed two feet from the steps, he fell backwards onto his hands. He dragged his toe through the pine needles to make a line. "Now you."

A bell rang. "Let's go," Uncle Jesse called. Footsteps bumped, and Will Hobeck flew from the doorstep to land much farther from the cabin than Raddy. He swung his arms forward and stood with grace as other boys followed him out the door.

"He won!" Albie cried.

"You dope!" Raddy hit Albie in his arm with his fist.

"Hey!" Uncle Jesse said, "break it up, that's a noogie." He grabbed Raddy by his elbow and struck Raddy at the top of his arm with his other fist. Raddy's face flashed as dark as Will's birthmark, and he bared his teeth at Albie. "Get out of here," Uncle Jesse said, still holding Raddy.

Albie trembled as he followed Cooper uphill to the bottom of the big white house. In a dim room with urinals on one side and sinks on the other they washed their hands in cold water and dried them on a damp roller towel. On the narrow stairway Albie hunched his shoulders together to avoid jostling other boys, and smelled water, and soap, and dirt on his hands. He pressed forward because he was afraid that Raddy would pursue him. Larger boys parted to let him through.

At the top of the stairway open double doors revealed long tables in rows with benches on their sides and chairs at the ends. Bear Brewer and Uncle Charlie stood near a round table in front of a huge fieldstone fireplace. Cooper led the way across the dining room to join other Panthers at a table near a window. Uncle Jesse arrived and stood at the end of the table near the aisle to the kitchen.

Counselors closed the double screen doors to the great porch. The doors to the kitchen on either side of the fieldstone fireplace were jammed by boys and counselors carrying dishes, trays, metal pitchers; steam rose in the dark, noisy space beyond. On the side of the mess hall a hook and eye fastened a swinging gate of unpainted wood across a stairway up only wide enough for one adult. A crude black sign on yellowing cardboard proclaimed 'PRIVATE.'

"What's up there?" Albie said.

"Nobody uses that," Jerry said. "It leads to The Bear's family, and nobody goes up there unless they're in big trouble."

From here on there could be no escape. Albie did not know the names of the boys at the next table. He closed his eyes. The chatter of boys and the rattle of metal utensils swelled and dimmed.

When the sound softened, Albie opened his eyes. A huge man in a Bear Lake sweatshirt had paused to shake Cooper's hand. "Who was that?" Albie said.

Cooper took a seat. "Uncle Bart, the waterfront counselor. He swam all the way across the lake last summer. It's two miles."

Two miles was forty city blocks, as far as from Albie's house to the far side of the museum and back along the park, twice: it was a long way, even to walk.

"I'm going to do that some day," Cooper said.

"Swim across — ?" Albie swallowed 'the lake,' afraid that Cooper would ask him to swim with him so he would have to confess that he didn't know how.

Increasing noise in the mess hall drowned conversation as the other Panthers pushed their way to the table. Prayers preceded food. A microphone squealed. The mess hall fell quiet. Philip Mullaly clasped his hands and bowed his head, and Raddy did, too.

Albie's family ate without praying. Besides, if you asked God for too much you might be branded selfish or rude. Albie sat on his hands and bent his head like the others, but peeked under his brows to see how normal boys behaved.

Uncle Charlie pointed into a book. "Give us this day," read a large boy on the platform near the huge fieldstone fireplace.

Philip's eyes were closed. Raddy and Jerry were giving each other horse bites on their thigh muscles, daring each other to make a noise Uncle Jesse would notice. A tall, thin boy at the Woodsmen's table prayed like an angel with his palms together in front of him, his blond hair tumbling over his forehead. At the same table Joe stared into the middle distance and picked his nose until his counselor, Uncle Dan, hit him on the back of his head and whispered at him.

". . . something something something Jesus Christ," finished the boy on the platform, and the campers responded, "Amen."

"On Saturday night the Dodgers got so many runs they had to stop playing at midnight," Will Hobeck bawled.

All the boys talked at once.

"Nineteen," Will said.

"Why'd they stop?" Jerry said.

"You can't play baseball on Sunday morning," Philip said. "They have to go to Mass."

"The Pirates won," Will said. "Kiner hit everything, two homers, a triple, a double and a single. They beat the Dodgers sixteen eleven."

"Says who?" Raddy said.

"I heard it on the radio, with my father," Will said.

"Pirates make you walk the plank," Philip said. "It's like a diving board."

"Yeah," Raddy said, "they make sharks swim around. They stab you with swords so you walk the plank."

"They have cannons," Will said.

"That doesn't have anything to do with walking the plank," Albie said.

"They do have cannons," Will said. "Don't they, Jerry?"

"If there's no sharks," Philip said.

"You have to swim," Cooper said. "The plank's the same as a diving board."

"Across the ocean?" Will said. "They'd shoot you with the cannons."

"The cannons are for shooting other ships," Albie said.

"I'd swim back to the ship," Raddy said. "I'd get a sword and I'd kill all the pirates."

"You couldn't," Jerry said. "You've gotta be in advanced before you can dive off the board."

"I *could*!" Raddy said. "I'm going to be advanced." He glared around the table. "How many can swim?"

Cooper raised his hand. "I can! I can!" others called, even boys at the next table who hadn't been part of the discussion.

Raddy poked Albie. "Can you swim?"

Albie glanced from his plate to Cooper. "I'm going to swim two miles—" He saw admiration begin in some faces and mockery in others. "—after I learn how."

Cooper regarded Albie with curiosity. Albie blushed. Most of the time he told the truth, but other boys lied to gain status, and sometimes Albie found it hard to remember what was real and what he had imagined. Yet Albie had a deep regard for the truth, for the whole truth, for nothing but the truth, which arose near his yearning for the absolute, for what was most intense, what was most itself. For instance, New York where he lived was the largest city in the nation, and therefore the best. New York was real, its preeminence was true, but the worlds that burst into color and life in Albie's head when he read a book, or when he dreamed, felt just as real, just as true. Some days he noticed the puzzle that his imaginings could feel more real, more true, than the world itself, and resolved to figure it out. Reading, going to school, was how you found answers. Easy problems, like long division, had yielded, so maybe hard ones, like how to be a normal boy or how to swim would, too. However slight his progress, Albie would never stop trying. What was certain, what was true, was that Albie loved to learn. "I'm taking lessons," he said, and hoped it would come true.

"I can swim *under water*," Raddy said. "Can you swim *under water*?"

Albie spooned red Jell-O into his mouth. Would Uncle Bart teach him? If he put his face in the water and breathed in through his nose, the water would shut off his breath like a flap of red Jell-O over his nostril. The harder he tried to breathe the more surely the cold red plug would drown him. He coughed, and a bite of Jell-O fell out of his mouth onto the table. Cooper was still staring at him, but Raddy had turned away.

Cooper raised his eyebrow. His silence squeezed Albie shut. Albie blushed, and surrounded the blob of Jell-O with a napkin. He peeked at Cooper again. "Did you, were you, ah, afraid to put your face in the water?" Even as he spoke the words he couldn't imagine doing it.

Cooper said, "My father showed me how when I was little."

The conversation moved on and Will shouted and all the boys at the Panthers' table sang a song Albie didn't know.

On the way back from dinner, Albie stayed behind Raddy, who walked toward the cabin with a bigger boy from Woodsmen. "We have an Olympic jumper," Albie heard him say. "Really."

The sky had dimmed to a soothing blue a shade darker than Albie's blankets. "Regular camp articles on the shelves, special personal articles in the foot lockers, duffel bags folded up in the bottom of the foot lockers," Uncle Jesse said. He patrolled the cabin to help the boys unpack. "Pull those beds *tight*, so you can bounce a quarter."

Albie envied Cooper's impassive competence. He copied the way Cooper had arranged his shorts, shirts, socks, and books on the shelves. After his third or fourth look Cooper walked over to him. "First summer at camp?"

"Yes."

"I mean at any camp."

Albie wanted to say, "Yes, it frightens me, I want to be your friend. If I were big, strong and normal like you, I could manage."

Cooper stood still for as long as it would have taken Albie to say all that, and a little longer. He held out his hand. "Call me Coop."

"Coop." Albie shook a hand as cool and big as a grown-up's. "I'm Albie."

"Pleased to meet you, Albie."

"I go to Hunter College Elementary School," Albie said.

"I go to Noble's."

"I never made a bed before."

"I'll show you." Cooper centered Albie's bottom sheet and tucked the ends under the mattress at the bottom and at the top. "You take it like this," he folded the edge over the top of the bed so a triangle hung down, "then this, and this." Now the sheet had the same tight fold as Uncle Jesse's blanket.

"Wow," Albie said.

"You do this end."

Albie tucked the bottom in tight, for Cooper's approval.

"Now the blanket."

Albie's blue blankets came out of his duffel wrinkled; they were fuzzier and thicker than the gray ones on Cooper's bed. When they were finished, the hospital corners on Albie's bed weren't as sharp as Uncle Jesse's, or Cooper's. Albie fretted at the round contour. "It's not as neat as yours."

"Your blanket's thicker, it's new."

Until then Albie had thought that new things were to be preferred.

"My father used my blanket at camp," said Cooper. "He got it from Grandfather, who got it in the Navy."

Albie's father had worn the metal hat, but Albie didn't know whether he had been in the Navy or not. "Thank you for helping me," he said.

"If you're all set you can knock off," Uncle Jesse said. "Anybody doesn't know where the latrine is, it's across the road, downhill from the Main House. Any of you know Michael Wooley?"

"Who is he?" Raddy said. "Some kind of new kid?"

"He's a new kid," Uncle Jesse said, "like the Gardners." He squinted around the cabin. The bed between Albie's and his had been made with a red blanket with a black stripe at its end, as had the one across the aisle in the corner. "I guess they're here," he said.

"They went to the nurse," Cooper said. He walked out the door next to the foot of his bed, at the downhill end of the cabin.

Albie ducked around the foot of Raddy's bed and followed him out. "Where are you going?"

"Wash my hands."

They crossed the thick bed of pine needles downhill from the bunk, over roots and pine cones, under trees so tall their lowest branches were far out of reach. The wind that pressed through the trees absorbed the chatter of boys' voices from the cabins. Far down the hill they heard an engine and the crunch of tires on gravel; headlights led a car up the road behind black trees. When the beams swung from the far side of the road toward where they were standing, Cooper said, "Look!"

In the light and shadow Albie caught a glimpse of something brown that bounced and rustled down the hill.

"Did you see it?" Cooper asked.

"What was it?"

"A rabbit."

"It was invisible," Albie said. "If it hadn't moved I wouldn't have seen it."

"That's how they hide, so hunters won't see them," Cooper said. "When you don't move you're the same as the background."

"Camouflage."

"It's not just how you look, it's what you do."

"How'd you learn that?" Albie said.

"At camp," Cooper said, "last summer."

Albie felt hopeful as he accompanied the larger boy across the gravel parking lot where the black convertible had stopped. Further on, a narrow path led down over damp earth to a doorway at the far end of a building made of grooved boards. The latrine had no door. Along the back wall were three urinals and a row of open booths. Sinks with only a single faucet were attached to the wall next to the door. Long windows no more than six inches high along the top admitted little light; the interior was darker than the evening outside.

Albie peered around the first partition into the stall to see a board with a hole in it, and no cover.

"If you have to do number two," Cooper said.

The pine needle scent had changed to a smell of dampness, and a city stench that was far worse. Albie swallowed, and breathed through his mouth.

"The switch is here," — Cooper pointed to a box next to the first sink with a twisted metal tube leading to it— "but it's better not to use it."

"Why not?"

"Moths." On the deepening blue screen over the narrow window the color of one of Albie's mother's dresses were two small dark triangles and a larger one. "Watch," Cooper said. The switch made a hollow snap. Two bare bulbs hanging by wires from a twisted metal tube along the ceiling came on and changed the blue rectangle to flat black. The triangles became dull brown creatures that waddled across the screen, while the larger whitish one flew off the screen past Albie with a dull buzz to circle one of the bulbs. Within seconds three, ten, twenty moths of different sizes and shapes flew around the lights; from time to time one rested on a wall or one of the sinks. Dozens of new moths fluttered in through the door.

"They leave the lights on," Cooper said. "You have to brush the moths off before you sit down."

Albie shuddered. Cooper shut off the light. They felt their way out the door and swung their arms to dry their hands on the way back.

Panthers was now lit by a single bulb hanging from the middle of the ceiling. Uncle Jesse stood across from Cooper Brown's bed with his hand on the shoulder of a thin boy with light brown hair. The boy, who wore dungarees instead of camp shorts, slumped forward. A thin, blonde woman with pink glasses that swooped up at the corners and a pink ribbon in her hair set down one end of a camp trunk; a man in a wrinkled suit of narrow gray and white stripes and a dark blue tie set down the other.

"You'll try out, okay?" the woman said.

"He always wanted to play shortstop," the man said, "like Phil Rizzuto. I always played shortstop."

Uncle Jesse said, "This is Michael Wooley."

"Mike," Michael Wooley said to the floor.

"Pleased to meet you, Mike." Cooper offered his hand.

"Pleased to meet you, Mike." Albie did the same.

Mike touched the two hands and edged toward his mother.

The man arranged a duffel on top of the trunk. "Okay?"

Mike met his father's eyes. His mother stepped away and touched her mouth. Mike's father patted him on the back. His mother kissed his forehead. His father put his arm around her shoulders to walk her out of the cabin.

Mike was as thin as Albie and not much taller. Albie extended his hand again. "My name is Albert, but my nickname is Albie," he said. When they shook hands, Albie looked right at Mike the way Cooper had looked at him. "Pleased to meet you."

Mike glowed. Albie returned to his bed. Uncle Jesse and Uncle Charlie talked outside. Will Hobeck poked at the bed with the red blanket. "Somebody came," he said. "Who is it?"

"It's the kids who aren't here yet," Philip said, standing in the aisle between his bed and the one in the corner with its matching red blanket.

"Okay," Uncle Jesse said from the doorway, "finish changing, bedtime."

"No story?" Raddy said. "We never go to bed without a story."

"A story, tell us a story!" Will jumped into the air, but missed the light bulb. "If I touch the light bulb can we have a story?"

"Please," Albie cried in the voice that would wheedle a treat from his mother, "please read us a story."

Raddy stamped his feet. "We want a *story*," he chanted. "We want a *story*, we want a *story*."

Mike joined in. "We want a *story*!" All the boys stamped. "We want a *story*, we want a *story*."

"Hold it down." Uncle Jesse burst into the cabin, but Uncle Charlie in the doorway said something and hit him in the shoulder with his fist. "All right," Uncle Jesse said, "I'll read you one, only,"—he threw up his hands toward his shelves and stepped backward—"I don't have any books to read from!" He hit Uncle Charlie back, and Uncle Charlie left.

"You could read one of mine," Albie said, "I have six books." To contribute thrilled Albie. The cabin was silent. "I like books, I could read . . ."

"Big deal," Raddy said. "My father has a hundred books."

Uncle Jesse pointed at him. "Pajamas."

"Two hundred books," Raddy said.

"Hey!" Uncle Jesse came over to Albie's bed. "What stories do you have?" He peered at the shelf. "I don't know, *Penrod and Sam*, what's that about?"

Albie reached for his favorite novel about two boys who fly planes and capture criminals. "This one," he said.

"Don't read one of his," Raddy said. "Tell us a story."

"Tell us a sports story," Jerry said.

"All right," Uncle Jesse said. "I'll tell you a short one. Once upon a time . . ."

Before he could continue the screen door opened again. "They're here," Uncle Charlie said to Uncle Jesse. "The parents took them to the Inn for dinner." He rolled his eyes. "Meet the Gardner boys," he announced. "This is Walter and that's Wayne." He rested his hand on the shoulders of a boy with a face like a fox and waved at a boy with round pink cheeks, who peered into the cabin around him. "These are, hell you tell 'em, Jess." He clapped Uncle Jesse on the shoulder and left.

In the light of the single bulb, the thinner boy pursed blue-tinged lips under prominent cheek bones. His eyes studied everyone in the cabin. From behind him the other boy said, "Waynie, he thought I'm *you!*" and pushed his way past to jump up on the camp trunk at the foot of the bed between Uncle Jesse's and Albie's.

Both newcomers had straight ash blonde hair long enough to fall over their faces and dark eyes, but the resemblance ended there. The ruddy second boy was much taller and heavier than Waynie, but he didn't open his eyes all the way. "Hey!" the plump boy bellowed, "This is my brother Wayne!"

The thin boy shuffled to the bed in the corner without speaking.

"Waynie!" The plump boy jumped up and down on the trunk. "I *told* you they were here."

Uncle Jesse guided the boy to the floor by the elbow. The boy kept jumping. "You!" Uncle Jesse said, "what's your name?"

"Walter T. Gardner," the boy said. "That's my brother Wayne T. Gardner." The skinny boy's narrow face scanned the bunk.

"I'm Uncle Jesse. I'm your counselor. You been to camp before?"

"Not this camp," Wayne T. Gardner said. Raddy eyed him from across the aisle with his hands on his hips.

"Get changed," Uncle Jesse said. "I'm telling a story, welcome to the bunk."

The larger boy bounced up and down on the bed next to Albie's. "I'm Walter!" He tugged off his shoes without untying them and dropped them on the floor. "That's my brother Wayne, but I call him Waynie. What's your name?"

"Albie."

Walter took off his socks and bounced on the bed again.

Raddy scuffed toward Walter in leather slippers. "I'm Raddy Tarrant. I'm the pitcher for Panthers. What do you do?"

Walter beamed at Raddy. He pulled on his pajamas over his jockey shorts and a ribbed undershirt. "I'm getting in bed, Waynie," he called.

"I'm Raddy Tarrant." Raddy extended his hand to Wayne. "I'm the pitcher."

Wayne took his hand. "I can pitch, too."

"No, I'm the pitcher," Raddy said. The boys eyed each other. Raddy squeezed Wayne's hand. Wayne squeezed back. Their faces reddened. Raddy pressed his lips together; the way Wayne's eyes moved from side to side, Albie thought Raddy was winning.

"Walter!" Wayne shrieked.

"Here I come, Waynie." Walter scattered his bedding as he sprang across the aisle and seized Raddy in a bear hug from behind. "Leave my brother alone!" As Raddy struggled, Wayne did something to his hand that made him cry out.

"You stink!" Raddy cried.

Uncle Jesse pulled Raddy and Walter apart and sent Wayne to the bed in the corner. Raddy leaned so far backward away from Walter that he almost fell. They glared at each other across Albie's bed while Albie counted the books on his shelf until Raddy turned his back on the rest of the cabin.

Walter, rearranging his bedding, caught sight of Albie. "Hi," he said.

"Hi," Albie said. "I'm Albie Greenberg."

Walter's sweet pink face glowed.

From the other side of the cabin Will called out, "What about the story?"

"Only if I get some cooperation," Uncle Jesse said.

But when the boys were undressed and in bed, Uncle Jesse called, "Lights out," pulled the string and walked to the door. The door slammed. Uncle Jesse walked away on gravel.

"*Pleeease* read my story," Albie called in the dark.

"It stinks," Raddy cried, "and you stink too!" He jumped out of bed, hit Albie in the shoulder, and retreated to pull his covers over his head. The noise from under Raddy's covers must have been laughing, because Albie couldn't imagine Raddy crying, or feeling as small and vulnerable as himself. With his own eyes shut tight Albie saw the brothers in his book as they flew their plane over a great lake far in the north, out of sight of human habitation.

When Albie awakened to his first full day at camp, the weight of still-tucked-in blue blankets pressed his thin shoulders to the mattress. It was hard to make sense of the sloping roof and wooden rafters above him, but the smell of dew and pine needles reminded him where he was before he could call, "Mommy!"

To his right Raddy slept on his side, mouth wide open, one arm under the covers and one above the pillow, a Raggedy Andy doll tossed onto a pile of rags. Beyond Walter Gardner, Uncle Jesse snored with covers over his head.

Outside the screen door, a breeze swayed the branches of a great tree so its shadows moved in silence through daylight on the wooden floor. No traffic rattled on pavement; no one shouted in the street.

Albie sat up. Across the way Cooper Brown read a book. When he saw Albie watching him he closed it. Albie waved; Cooper lifted his hand.

A bugle sounded. One by one, the Panthers got up.

On the way up the hill to breakfast Raddy said to the bigger twin, "I'll show you where to sit, okay?"

"What do you mean?" he said. "I sit next to Waynie." He turned his palms upward. "Right, Waynie, we sit together?"

Behind them Albie marveled at how clear and sweet the air was. Perhaps that was because houses here were made of wood instead of stone like the sidewalks and buildings at home. He listened to the tiny sound of breeze in the trees instead of the conversation.

The orange juice tasted sour. Uncle Jesse spooned hot cereal, glutinous and gray, into a heavy white bowl. Albie passed it down with alarm. His family never ate hot cereal, so he wondered whether the rules required that he eat it. The energy with which the big twin mashed milk and butter and sugar into it revolted him.

Albie passed a second bowl down to Cooper. "No, thanks." Cooper gave it back to the boy with the stain on his face, who poured milk into it.

The next bowl felt fuller than the others "No, thanks," Albie said. Uncle Jesse seemed to discover him for the first time. "Eat some oatmeal," he said, "put meat on your bones."

So this was oatmeal. If normal boys ate oatmeal perhaps it would make him bigger.

"Go on," Uncle Jesse said.

Pressure to eat when he didn't want to was familiar. Albie added milk and sugar like the other Panthers. The sweet liquid tasted okay, but the moment his tongue penetrated a slippery wad of oatmeal something closed his throat. He couldn't swallow. He tried not to taste as kicks, jostles and bumps passed around the table to end in a pinch on his arm. Startled, he cried out, so the mouthful of oatmeal flew onto the center of the table.

"Upchuck!" Raddy shouted. "Hey, upchuck!"

"Jesus Christ," Uncle Jesse said. "What's the matter with you? You gotta clean that up."

Albie flushed and dabbed at the mess with a paper napkin with little effect.

"No, get a rag," Uncle Jesse said. "What are you, stupid?"

An aide wiped the table with a damp gray rag from a bucket. The puddle he left smelled sweet but unpleasant as it dripped off the table onto Albie's lap. Albie dammed the dripping with a forearm and rested a hand over his shorts; he ate neither the oatmeal nor the scrambled eggs that followed it. Not one of the other Panthers paid attention to him for the rest of breakfast.

Cleanup followed breakfast. At the foot of his bed, Wayne Gardner received an imaginary throw from an imaginary outfielder. Mitt on his left hand, he swiveled with violence to tag an imaginary runner in the corridor between the footlockers. At first he smacked the pocket with his fist to simulate the slap of the ball into his glove, but later he shifted to one-handed catches and slapped an open hand on his right thigh.

Slap! He caught the invisible ball, wheeled, and tagged the foot of the invisible runner sliding toward him. "Yer out!" he cried for the invisible umpire.

"Yeah, he's out," Walter Gardner said next to Albie.

Slap! "Yer out!"

Silence.

"I got him again, Walter," Wayne called.

"Oh, yeah." Walter raised his head and his voice. "He's out!"

From his foot locker Philip Mullaly extracted a new brown glove tied up with string. He set it on his pillow with care, and frowned as he held a small pocket knife away from his body with a straight elbow.

"New mitt?" Raddy was making throwing motions at the far end of the corridor.

"Yeah." Philip cut the string and unwound it turn by turn.

"How many fingers?"

"Four."

"You gotta break it in," Raddy said.

"I guess." Philip removed a baseball from the mitt and tucked it under his pillow. He raised the mitt to Albie. "Over here," he said.

Had Albie somehow missed a ball that had been thrown to him?

"Hey, catch!" Raddy shouted and mimed a throw. Albie saw Raddy's arm fly, and ducked to examine his new baseball mitt, as virginal as his tennis racquet. A chilly hopelessness took him as he slid his hand in. The cold, stiff flesh, sensual and a little scary, didn't let him open his hand or close it. He hefted the leather. It didn't matter that he didn't know how to take part, or that the space the mitt claimed on his shelf would accommodate four, perhaps five, more books; his duty here was to endure. In silence he tried to adjust his camp hat at a slant the way the boy with the stain on his face wore his.

"We swim second period," Uncle Jesse said as he patrolled the aisle. "Take your bathing suits." He stopped at the skinny twin's bed which looked worse than Albie's, even though the blanket was thin. "What's this, hey?"

At the cabin door, Wayne sneaked a look at Uncle Jesse, then ignored him.

"Hey! Gardner, Wayne!"

"Yes?" Wayne said, with artificial sweetness. His forelock fell over his eye.

"Pull this bed tight, it's a disgrace."

Wayne pursed his blue lips. "I can't."

"There's no can't, not on this team."

His brother pulled at Uncle Jesse's shirt. "He can't," he said. "He has to be very careful."

Uncle Jesse pointed a finger at Wayne. "You, be careful to make your bed right. Now!"

Wayne shuffled back to his bed with his mitt on. His puny one-handed pull hardly moved the blanket. Uncle Jesse gave the wrinkled blanket a second perfunctory tug and shooed the twins ahead of him toward the door.

Albie hung back. He would not have gotten away with what Wayne had done. As he trotted over the thick carpet of pine needles to baseball he resolved to be perfect for the rest of the summer.

Shouting boys ran ahead to the second of three baseball diamonds. Ordinarily the youngest boys were relegated to Fenway Park, off beside the stables and riding ring, where shaggy grass overgrew the base paths and the pitcher's mound was little more than a chalk circle. Today the Panthers were allowed to use Ebbetts Field, which afforded each team a single unshaded bench. Left field was the archery range. Only the oldest campers played at Yankee Stadium, where all of Bear Lake could watch contests against other camps from stands made of wood and metal painted Bear Lake colors above rudimentary dugouts along the base paths.

The game was Three Old Cat, which permitted one team to use three bases and the whole infield. Raddy pitched; Jerry Roth caught. Cooper swung three bats. When Albie's turn to hit came, the light tan one looked the smallest and easiest to manage.

He swung at the first pitch well before it hit the ground in front of the plate.

"No batter, no batter," Jerry called.

"Take it easy," Uncle Jesse told Albie over Jerry's head, "keep your eye on the ball."

Albie watched the ball with perfect concentration as it flew from Raddy's hand to the center of Jerry's catcher's mitt.

"Strike two," Uncle Jesse said. "Look 'em over."

Albie's mouth hung open. The bat rested on his shoulder. The wild third pitch flew over his head as he remembered past humiliation in gym.

"Ball one," Uncle Jesse extended an index finger. "One and two. Way to look 'em over."

Jerry retrieved the ball from the backstop. "Hey, Raddy, let's bear down." Raddy scowled and started his windup, but interrupted it halfway to make chewing motions with his mouth, and to spit saliva, which landed on his shirt.

"Play ball," Uncle Jesse said.

Somewhere up the hill a bell rang.

"That's it," Uncle Jesse dropped his hands to his sides. "Swimming!"

"C'mon," Raddy said. "I was going to get him."

"Sure," Uncle Jesse said. "Roth, Greenberg, take the equipment back."

"Same game tomorrow," Raddy said. "Same score."

"There isn't any score," Cooper said. "we aren't playing a real game."

"I was ahead of him," Raddy said. "I want to see if he's Joe DiMaggio."

"He's not Joe DiMaggio," Cooper said, "he's Billy Goodman."

"I'm Albie Greenberg," Albie said.

"I don't care, I was going to get him." Raddy bumped Cooper as Cooper walked past. Cooper stopped to face him; he was a foot taller than Raddy. When he walked away, Raddy glared at Albie.

Jerry tucked his big catcher's mitt under his arm and took the extra ball out of his pocket. "Get the bats," he said. Albie secured his fielder's mitt and new crimson swimming trunks under his arm; he knelt to retrieve the three bats, which he supported on his flexed forearms with the respect due important instruments. Yes, he could carry them, and to do so made him proud.

Across the road from the backstop Jerry raised the top of a wooden box four feet square attached to the side of a small building. Albie deposited the bats among the jumble of balls, masks, chest protectors, baseball mitts, square canvas cushions he recognized as bases, Indian clubs, and a medicine ball. "How come they don't have tennis racquets?" he said.

"Girls play tennis," Jerry said. "Over at Mistlewood they play tennis and softball. Boys play hardball."

"I thought boys played tennis, too." Albie's racquet hung publicly from the nail near his bed. He thought back to the railroad station. "What about Pancho Gonzales?"

"Who?"

Did he have the name right? "Franco Gonzales?" He was about to say that his father had given him a tennis racquet when Jerry said, "Sissies, maybe."

Albie didn't feel like a sissy. He followed Jerry to the waterfront. A wooden dock in the shape of an L extended out into the water. One row of white floats divided the water inside the L into shallow and deep; another long row of floats enclosed water beyond the L. A huge red canoe bobbed next to the unenclosed side of the dock.

The sky was hazy blue, the water gray. The Lion Cubs' counselor squatted to untie a small boy's shoelaces. Uncle Jesse studied a piece of paper on the dock. Behind him Uncle Bart, who was much bigger, wore a tiny black bathing suit and held a bamboo pole twice as tall as he was. He blew a shiny steel whistle on a red and gray lanyard around his neck. ". . . when I blow the whistle," he said in a loud voice. "Put your clothes on a hook and your shoes and mitts on the bench." He blew the whistle again.

A few boys started toward a wooden building under a large tree a few yards back from the edge of the lake. Uncle Bart blew the whistle. "What did I say?" he shouted. He stalked over to one of the Lion Cubs. "What did I say?"

The little boy who had given Albie the sandwich on the train put his hands in his pockets and looked at his shoes. The Lion Cubs' counselor went to stand behind him and rubbed his head. "What's your name?" Uncle Bart asked.

"Stuart," the little boy said to his own feet.

"I'm Uncle Bart, the head waterfront counselor," the man said in a voice more than loud enough to reach all the boys. "When I blow the whistle, everybody stops. He blew the whistle again. "Is that clear? Everybody stops." Stuart remained frozen. Uncle Bart passed a severe glance over the crowd of motionless boys. "Okay, change!"

"Yay!" The Panthers ran into the wooden building ahead of the Lion Cubs. The Lion Cub counselor held Stuart's hand as they followed.

The building, half the size of the cabin Albie slept in, smelled of mildew. Low wooden benches lined the single room except for one corner where a stall without a door contained a wooden seat with a hole in it. Wooden pegs covered the walls; painted lines divided them into regions corresponding to the bunks. Bathing suits hung from the Big Bears' and Ranchers' pegs. "We leave our bathing suits here," Uncle Jesse said. "Everybody remember which hook is yours."

Albie held his breath to escape the smell of the bodies and faced the wall to conceal his own nakedness. He ducked his head as he changed lest he indulge forbidden curiosity about how others were made; he succeeded in not touching any other boy as he sidled out the door with his elbows close to his sides.

He found a place to sit on sparse grass as far from the lake and the changing cabin as possible. As other boys filed out, something tickled the hand he leaned on. A daddy long legs with a pale brown body smaller than a baked bean and legs like hairs stood half on his hand and half on the sparse grass. He would have shaken the creature off, but surprise stopped him dead.

Though the spider had no eyes Albie could see, he felt it was studying him with cautious optimism. It wanted to understand. To reassure it, Albie held his fingers still. The daddy long legs took a step across his hand. Amazing! For one moment of communion, the living spider rested on Albie's living hand fixed on living grass, before it ran away and the shouts of boys brought Bear Lake back.

Uncle Bart made all the Panthers and Lion Cubs sit in rows, and called each boy by name. "Cooper Brown!"

"Here!" Cooper raised his hand.

"I don't have to ask if you can swim," Uncle Bart said. "You start intermediate and you can take the advanced test today."

"What's intermediate?" Albie asked Jerry.

"Beginners is only up to here." Jerry pointed to his navel. "Intermediate is past the floats and around to the end of the dock where it's over your head. And advanced is past the dock, so you can swim out to the raft."

Halfway from the dock to the far line of white floats, a square wooden raft floated on oil drums. A small diving board on the raft pointed back toward the diving board at the end of the dock.

"Walter Gardner," Uncle Bart called.

Walter raised his hand.

"Can you swim?"

"I can swim, and so can Waynie."

"Good." Uncle Bart scanned his clipboard. "But you weren't here last year."

"We can swim," Wayne said.

"Beginners," Uncle Bart said. "Take the test." He examined his clipboard. "Greenberg."

Albie blushed. "Here," he whispered, and raised his hand.

"Can you swim?"

Before he could answer Raddy said, "Can't hit, can't swim."

"What did you say?" Uncle Jesse said from behind the boys.

"Greenberg?" Uncle Bart said.

"No."

"*Greenberg?*" Uncle Bart sounded irritated.

"*No.*"

"Beginner." Uncle Bart put Albie and Mike Wooley in with the Lion Cubs, and sent the other Panthers off to take the intermediate test. He explained safety and buddies and how the water is your friend so it holds you up, even if you hit it or kick it. The little boys paid close attention.

Though Albie heard everything Uncle Bart said, what was going on couldn't affect him any more than a picture on a movie screen could become real. Yet that detachment did not bring a sense of security. Rather, Albie experienced an uneasy lack of smoothness in the flow of time. Each sentence out of Uncle Bart's mouth and each moment was not correctly attached to the next one. The morning had become a string with knots in it being pulled through a narrow place, sticking and rushing ahead only to stick again. It didn't seem possible that before lunch Albie would put his face in the water of the lake.

"Count off!"

A boy at the far end of the group said, "One."

"Two."

"One!"

"Two!"

"One."

A pause. Albie shook his head to clear it. The others were waiting for him. "Two," he said.

Stuart sat in front of Albie with admiration in his eyes. "We're buddies," he said. "I bet I'm the only Lion Cub with a Panther for a buddy. That's great!"

Albie breathed in.

Uncle Bart blew his whistle twice and banged his long pole. Most of the Panthers walked out onto the dock. Uncle Bernie, the Lion Cubs' counselor, conferred with Uncle Bart before he came back to squat with the beginners. He still wore his cowboy hat with his bathing suit.

"We're going to go in the water," he said, "is that okay?" When no one spoke he said, "Everybody hold your buddy's hand and walk into the water until it's up to your knees."

Stuart clutched Albie's index and middle fingers. The last few feet of land were darker and colder underfoot than the rest of the beach. The sun felt less warm once Albie touched the water. Step by step he followed Stuart across a dim sandy bottom until the lake licked Stuart's kneecaps.

"How's that?" Uncle Bernie said.

Stuart tugged Albie's hand.

"What?"

Stuart pointed to Albie's knees. "They're not wet yet."

Albie let Stuart pull him further out into cool water that rose to the top of his kneecap and then above it. Delicious, better than the bathtub.

Uncle Bernie blew a whistle; he was pointing at Albie and Stuart. "That's deep enough for now."

Stuart's face glowed with admiration. Albie was by no means the tallest of the beginners, but he had gone the furthest from shore. Extraordinary! He hadn't thought he was doing anything special.

Uncle Bernie cupped water in his palm and splashed it on his arm. "Now we get used to the water. Wet your arms, wet your bellies, you can even wet your heads."

The beginners splashed themselves.

"See how nice the water is?" Uncle Bernie said. "Now bend your knees and get wet." He squatted to submerge his bathing suit. "Is that okay?"

"Okay!" some of the beginners called.

"Now buddies hold hands and we'll walk out further."

Stuart seized Albie's fingers again. They moved farther from the shore; Albie shivered when the cool lake licked his belly button. Water reached Stuart's armpits, and well up Albie's chest. "It's really deep," Stuart said. "Let's jump!"

Stuart held tight and Albie jumped. Weightlessness delighted him: he jumped again and Stuart kept pace. "Yay!" Albie cried. He jumped higher, higher again, until he missed the timing and went down with his knees bent and Stuart came with him. Albie saw Stuart through green-brown water instead of sunshiny air. Surprise became fright: Albie thrust his knees straight so he and Stuart emerged from the water, spluttering.

In the familiar air other boys were still jumping. Uncle Bernie had his back to them. Stuart inspected Albie before he shouted. "Uncle Bernie, Uncle Bernie! We went under water!"

"Better come in a little," Uncle Bernie said. "We have a lot to learn." Albie let Stuart tug him in, but the intermediates swimming short laps in the deeper part of the enclosure behind him inspired his excitement, and fear, and longing to challenge and best those dangerous waters.

A bugle announced the end of swimming period. On the way back to the changing building Uncle Bernie rubbed Albie's wet hair. "This one's okay," he told Uncle Jesse. "He'll be swimming before you know it."

Uncle Jesse grunted.

When Uncle Bernie winked, Albie wished he were younger than he was, so he could be a Lion Cub.

Cooper and Jerry were standing next to a small canoe pulled up on the beach. Jerry gestured at the canoe. Cooper leaned forward to take it by the thwarts and for a moment lifted it into the air by himself. Jerry clapped; Cooper let the canoe tumble to the ground; Uncle Bart blew his whistle.

Albie changed his mind: he wanted to be bigger and stronger.

At rest period after lunch on the third day of camp Uncle Jesse announced mail night. To be admitted to dinner on Wednesdays and Sundays every camper had to present a letter home; no exceptions. Letters might discuss the sports each boy was playing and might state what a good summer the writer was having. Uncle Jesse offered help but he didn't have to read every letter.

A few boys started writing. Uncle Jesse reclined and closed his eyes. Albie reached for his stationery box. Wayne Gardner crossed the cabin to his brother's bed, and tied Walter's thumbs and ankles together with string. Walter shrieked for help; Wayne opened a pocket knife; he feinted, stabbed, parried with imaginary assailants, and when he had vanquished them, cut Walter free. "Let's go! Giddyap!" He pranced away on tiptoes lifting his knees and waving his shoulders.

With his eyes closed, Uncle Jesse barked, "Put that knife away, Gardner."

Albie rested his pencil point on a blank piece of stationery. The line he drew became the line down the avenue; the paper on his knees became a map. He was facing downtown. A line to the side was his street; it stopped in front of the apartment building his mother was in at this very moment. Now a tiny line at right angles, into the lobby, and another, into the self-service elevator. With another piece of paper he could represent 'up,' to the fifth floor better, but that wasn't necessary. He led the line out of the elevator, right, left, right, left, right, left—and brought himself to his bed.

He extended the first line down the avenue, half an inch, an inch, bent it for the way the avenue angled below the park and swung it left to Grand Central Station. As best he could, he drew the train's course up the East Coast. The scale change didn't matter. There, he was on the gravel station platform, and on the bus—the line wavered, because he couldn't remember the whole ride—but he got the detail of the road in past the stables, the right turn at Yankee Stadium, the curve up through the great trees, the left at the row of cabins, left in the door and right to the cot where he sat.

When Albie folded his map just so, the place he was now came together with the place he wanted to be in a silent, secret kiss. He had bent space and time, and he was home. With great care he creased his map so it would stay.

On a blank sheet he wrote *Dear Mom and Dad*. He didn't want to reveal that he called his mother 'Mommy.' And he never addressed his father by any name, so *Dad* was a bold but false grab for the brass ring of normalcy. Albie avoided his father's eye. On the rare occasions when he needed to initiate a conversation he increased the volume of a wordless, open-mouthed hum until his father looked his way to find out why he was making the sound. At such times Albie felt imprisoned by his father the way Wayne's bonds of string imprisoned Walter, but Albie had no brother to rescue him, and his father never cut him free.

Back to the letter. *Dear Mom and Dad*. He wrote, *Camp is*, and a flash of rage turned his consciousness bright, bloody red. When that faded into despair, it left him unable to think of a word. His bare arm rubbed the post that supported the cabin.

Camp is nice, he wrote. That was a lie. He crossed out *nice* and replaced it with *fine*. He moved his lips to recite what he had written so far, "Dear Mom and Dad, Camp is fine." He thought he might vomit, and cringed from the hot vibration of food lumps in sour flux that would ride over his tongue. His mother wasn't there to support his head as he knelt on cool tile before a porcelain toilet bowl. He held his breath so he would not smell his own vomit.

Uncle Jesse said, "Ten more minutes."

Albie crossed out everything he had written. In a bolder hand he wrote, *I hate it here, take me home*, and signed it *Albert Greenberg*. Shaking, he thrust the folded paper into the envelope his mother had addressed and stamped for him, but he tore it. Tears blurred his vision as he crumpled the envelope and his mother's handwriting; he was careful with the next one. He positioned his seditious message between two of his books before he buried his face in his pillow to savor the taste of the gummed flap and await the end of rest period.

In the afternoon Uncle Jesse led the Panthers down the hill and away from the lake into a region of trees and low shrubbery for riflery. Larger boys on the trail ahead of Albie scuffled and pushed. He ducked backward as big Jerry Roth with his good-natured face checked Raddy into a patch of thorns. Jerry grinned at Albie; perhaps he was an ally. From the head of the column Uncle Jesse called, "All right, men, let's straighten up and fly right there, hey!" Albie held his arms at his sides in the middle of the path.

Around a corner the group approached a shed roof over a wooden platform on which four thin, stained mattresses lay side by side. Sun beat down on a corridor twenty feet wide and fifty feet long beyond the shade of the roof. At the far end tacks held paper targets to a pockmarked wooden frame set in the earth. Tin cans on the ground beneath it were full of holes. Six feet behind the frame, grass and shrubbery grew from the top and sides of a pile of earth and gravel higher than a man's head. Behind the frame and backstop was a cleared space, a wooden fence, and behind that, deep woods.

Albie smelled the bone-dry dirt in front of the platform and imagined the cool earth aroma in the lovely shade beyond the range. "Listen up, listen up!" said a man wearing a long-sleeved tan shirt with epaulets, shorts, and a squared off greenish brown cap. "Listen up to Uncle Lou," Uncle Jesse cried.

Uncle Lou lined them up in order of size. Albie was the smallest, but Raddy was only two places away. Uncle Lou shouted about soldiers, and about safety, and about obeying. That would be easy: Albie always obeyed.

Uncle Lou held up a rifle. "The front sight," he said. "The ramp sight, the barrel, the stock." Albie paid close attention. "The sling," Uncle Lou said. A metal clip with two little claws hooked into a double row of holes in the leather strap. Uncle Lou raised the rifle to his shoulder and wrapped the strap around his elbow with deftness like when Albie's grandfather wrapped leather straps around his arm to pray. Albie would have to learn and practice.

"Hey c'mon, we want to shoot," Jerry said.

"Hold it down out there," Uncle Jesse called from the shade at the end of the platform. The cover of the magazine he was reading was a picture of a woman wearing gloves that came up over her elbows.

Uncle Lou's transparent eyes were as bright as the summer sky behind him. "The bolt. The chamber." He opened and closed the bolt. Albie smelled oil and saw smooth motion. The bolt clicked as it closed and made a dull thunk when Uncle Lou pressed the handle down toward the stock.

Albie fell in love with the shiny silver ball on the bolt handle, its smooth, positive closure, the oil smell. He hungered to touch the rifle. Uncle Lou demonstrated first. "You will take a position on one of the mats," he said, "and shoulder your weapon. I will distribute live ammunition. When there is live ammunition on the range the rifles will point down range at all times. Is that clear?"

"Yes," a few boys said.

"Is . . . that . . . clear?"

Most of the boys cried, "Yes!" Albie's 'yes' caught in his throat because he felt so moved. For him to hold the rifle himself would be to help fight the war, for his parents and sister, for his Uncle Eli, for his neighbors at home, for all of America . . .

"I can't hear you!"

"*Yes!*"

Walter Gardner squinted and pointed his forefinger at a crow on a leafless branch at the far end of the range. "Can we shoot the bird? Bang!" He bent his elbow to pull an imaginary trigger.

"You missed," Wayne Gardner cried. "Pchhh, Pchhh!" He directed imaginary small arms fire at the crow.

Philip Mullaly swung his imaginary machine gun. "Da-da-da-da-da!"

Uncle Lou blew a whistle. "That's enough, men! Order on the range or nobody's going to shoot." The boys fell quiet. "Discipline," Uncle Lou said. "Our forces defeated the Krauts and the Nips with discipline. And that's the way we're going to whip the Koreans, with discipline."

The crow cocked its head at Albie. Let me fly with you, Albie thought. The crow spread its wings, hopped on the branch, and folded its wings again. Fly, crow, Albie thought. The crow spread its wings and fell through the air into the woods behind the backstop.

Uncle Lou lay prone on a mat and thumbed a bullet from his shirt pocket into the chamber of his rifle. Albie held his breath. "Wait until you hear the command to fire at will." Uncle Lou closed the bolt. "When you are ready you will squee-ee-eeze the trigger." The way he drew the sound out, the word approached unintelligibility. After a moment the rifle cracked — the sound disappointed Albie — and a little dust moved from the pile of earth behind the target.

Albie peered at the target. In the white part, below and to the right of the black bull's eye, was a small dark hole. Uncle Lou snapped the bolt open, so the brass casing flew over his shoulder to bounce and jingle on wood beside his mattress. He demonstrated two more rounds: one went in the black, the other outside it, also low and to the right.

"Take in a breath," he said, "let it out, squeeze the trigger slowly. You should never know when you're going to shoot."

"When are we going to shoot?" Jerry said.

"After I teach you the safety rules. These are real weapons, and you soldiers have to handle them right." Uncle Lou looked from face to face. "Is that clear?"

One by one the first group of boys opened the bolts of their rifles, freed their arms from the slings, pulled themselves up and rested their rifles in the rack with the muzzles pointing up toward the roof of the shed. They ran to the backstop. Jerry raced back waving his target. "A nine, look, I got a nine!"

Albie pushed forward. Thin white lines divided the black circle into zones: white numbers indicated that the very center was a ten; each zone the width of a pencil eraser counted nine, eight, seven, and six. Next came a narrow white ring, five, and the rest of the paper was broader white rings of lesser value.

Jerry had a nine and a hole in the six ring, on the top; tiny tears of paper at its edge barely touched the white ring that separated six from seven. Uncle Lou held the target up. "Close," he said, "I'm afraid it's a six, soldier."

Jerry counted, "Nine, six is fifteen, four, and three, twenty two."

Twenty-two was almost enough to count for the Junior Marksman Award, which required ten targets over 25. Uncle Lou kept records in a notebook.

"Nine, six, four, three, it's only four shots," Albie said.

"Yeah," Raddy said, "the moron *missed* one."

"And what did you do?" Jerry grabbed at Raddy's target. They both pulled and the paper tore. Raddy hit Jerry; Jerry pushed him back against Uncle Jesse. Raddy charged, but Uncle Jesse caught his shirt, and Uncle Lou seized Jerry in a bear hug. Raddy's bright red face and blue eyes wavered between malevolence and tears. When Uncle Jesse let him go, he grabbed the half of the target Jerry had taken.

"Ten shun!" Uncle Lou plucked the two halves of the target out of Raddy's hands and smoothed them out on top of Uncle Jesse's magazine. "Four, four, three," he counted.

"He missed twice." Philip Mullaly frowned with his thick, black eyebrows.

"No, I didn't," Raddy said. "He tore it, the tear went through the bull's eye."

The boys craned at the target. The tear did go through the black, but there was no hole. "Eleven," Uncle Lou said. "Next platoon!"

Albie ran to pick up a rifle. The sling swivel tinkled. Had he broken something? No one had noticed; he marveled at the weapon's weight as he carried it to the mat and knelt between Philip and the twins.

Uncle Lou showed him how to lie at an angle. Damp mattress ticking cooled his bare knees; he smelled oil in the rifle mechanism, and an ashy residue of gunpowder. He imagined he cradled his weapon in the trench in *Sands of Iwo Jima* as he checked his buddies left and right. When he faced the enemy again, his aim would be true. But the front sight in its little tunnel wandered above the target and dived below it. Albie feared he would miss this target as shamefully as he had misthrown the baseball.

"Like this." Uncle Lou peeled Albie's fingers off the stock, wound the sling around his forearm another way, and replaced his hand. "Keep both eyes open."

The sling resisted when Albie pushed the rifle; the sight swayed less. Albie breathed in and out, and stopped pushing. His cheek, the comb of the stock, the sights and the target were all at rest. In the next moment his heart beat, he breathed in, and everything moved. He pushed harder against the rifle.

Uncle Lou repeated instructions as he distributed five rounds to each boy from a small cardboard box in his shirt pocket. The weight of a round in its shiny brass case which said 'W' at the bottom surprised Albie; the greasy gray metal dome of the bullet itself felt unclean and scary.

"Ready on the right," Uncle Lou cried. "Ready on the left, ready on the firing line! You may fire at will."

With fingers he did not quite trust Albie conveyed a round to the dark hole in the chamber by its brass casing. The heavy part of the bullet wobbled; the bolt made that hollow noise when he closed it; the shiny ball on the handle lay next to the stock. Time to aim. Albie peered over the ramp sight toward the target. As he breathed out the front sight lay over the white part of the paper to the right of the black. He pulled the stock to his left and tried to push against the sling to hold everything still at the same time. He heard a crack! as Walter Gardner, behind him, fired, and a second later Wayne fired, too.

When Albie let himself relax, the muzzle wandered right again. He pulled it left and yanked the trigger. I shot a gun! he thought. When he could focus on the target he saw no hole in the white part of the paper. Had he gotten a bull's eye?

Uncle Lou knelt beside him. "Can't close your eyes, soldier," he said. "When your comfortable aim is off you got to change position."

Albie let go of the rifle as Uncle Lou slid his belly and his legs to the right. Now the muzzle wobbled over the black. Other boys fired again. Albie breathed in, breathed out. The front sight came to rest below the target's center. He forgot to squeeze the trigger as he admired how still the sight remained. He was going to tell Uncle Lou when his weapon cracked: he had fired a second time.

"Good one," Uncle Lou said to someone.

Philip fired. Albie reloaded and relaxed. The front sight rested below the black. He was beginning to wonder when he would have to breathe in when the gun surprised him again.

"Take your time, take your time," Uncle Lou said.

'It gets blurry if I don't shoot fast," Wayne said.

"Maybe you need glasses," Uncle Lou said.

"He has glasses," Walter said. "He's supposed to wear them."

"Am not, it's up to me," Wayne said.

On his fourth shot Albie ran out of breath and hurried to pull the trigger, which moved the muzzle right. On his fifth shot he succeeded in watching the moment of stillness again, even after the rifle went off. Shooting gratified him, but was nothing like what he had expected. Shooting was adult, and important, and necessary if a war came, but it wasn't magic. Albie could learn to shoot, and if he were to learn well, perhaps they would all recognize him as a patriot, a hero, as a normal boy.

But as he shambled toward the backstop, joy disappeared. Up ahead, at the very edge of his paper target, outside the scoring area, Albie saw a dark semicircle and felt sick; now he would suffer his usual athletic humiliation. The Gardners seemed reluctant to touch the paper. Albie leaned closer: there was a hole half in the bull's eye, the ten, and half in the nine.

"You got a bull's eye!" Wayne said.

"He got a bull's eye!" Walter shouted.

Albie eased his target off the nail. The twins ran back to the shed ahead of him. He had a bull's eye, but he also had two other shots in the black so close together the holes made a figure eight. One was in the seven ring; the other extended over the white line into the eight. The hole in the edge of the paper lay outside the scoring area: the first shot must have missed altogether.

Uncle Lou accepted Albie's target. "Everybody over here!" he cried. "What's your name, soldier?"

"Albert Greenberg."

"Albert Greenberg is the first man to qualify," Uncle Lou said. "Ten, eight, seven, that's twenty-five." He flipped another target over and put Albie's target on top of it so white showed through the holes. "You shot a tight group."

The other boys clustered around. Cooper traced the four holes in the target with a fingertip. "That's good," he said, "but where's the fifth one?"

"I missed," Albie said.

"You fired a rifle before, Greenberg?" Uncle Lou said.

"No, sir."

"Men, what we have here is a riflery *genius*," Uncle Lou said.

"Oh, yeah?" Raddy said. "He can't throw, he can't swim."

Uncle Jesse swatted Raddy with his magazine. "Let's see some sportsmanship, Tarrant."

The distant bell rang for the end of the first afternoon activity.

"He can't fight," Raddy said, his face red.

"He can shoot," Cooper said.

Raddy grabbed Albie's shirt. "I'm gonna get you," he said.

Albie's consciousness focused down to one point: to end the contact between Raddy and himself—but as strongly as Albie wanted to end the contact, Raddy wanted to increase it. Raddy wanted to touch and Albie wanted to flee. Raddy was right: Albie couldn't fight.

Uncle Jesse dragged Raddy away. Uncle Lou rested a hand on Albie's shaking shoulder. "You shoulda busted him one, soldier, so he'd leave you alone." But Albie squirmed to avoid his touch, too.

The Panthers had to pause behind the platform as an older cabin, the Warriors, arrived for their riflery period. In the crowd on the path, where the sun over the cleared region gave way to dappled shade, Raddy ran at Albie, knocked him down and made circles in the air over him with his fists. Albie saw aggression personified, a human fighting machine, a boy who was death instead of discourse. Raddy was invasion, like a Korean Communist. Albie wanted to escape.

He could not fly up to a perch above the tumult of boys and hostility like the crow. He lingered as Uncle Jesse pushed Raddy down the path back toward the waterfront. Walter bulldozed through the larger boys who crowded into the clearing. Albie did not see Cooper or Jerry. So many strangers, so close. By the time the older boys had gathered under the shed, the woods were silent, and the sun in the clearing was hot on the back of his neck.

Albie stepped into the shade of the woods. He hastened around the first bend in the path, but he stopped when Raddy's voice in his head threatened to get him.

Something moved. Ten feet away the markings of a chipmunk in the path blended with shadows a ray of sunlight cast from tall grass. Albie froze as still as the chipmunk. The chipmunk watched Albie. Albie thought forward in time to the teasing he would receive for being late, to confrontation with Raddy, to the humiliation of wading in shallow water because he did not know how to swim. The chipmunk stayed put. Albie thought backward in space to the riflery shed that now belonged to older boys. He never considered that Uncle Lou might welcome a riflery *genius* as a protégé for an extra session. Trapped. When a quiet breeze moved the tops of the trees, Albie followed the chipmunk off the trail.

In ten steps the well-trodden dirt path behind him disappeared, but these woods were no trackless wilderness: in every direction some way between trees or around a rock would be easier to follow than another. Albie was not lost. As still as a tree, he breathed in, breathed out. Somewhere to his right was the cleared riflery range and its backstop. The dense woods ahead must lead to the dark trees downhill from the main house. To the left the woods ended at the archery range. If he were to walk ahead and a little to the left, he would reach either the latrine or the clearing below the main house. Too far to the right would lead through deep forest to undiscovered territory. The Albie who had found his way to the library and back would map the New Hampshire woods.

The chipmunk was gone. Cheers sounded from the distant baseball field. Someone blew a whistle. Albie started forward over a forest floor of leaves and pine needles. Breeze rushed in the treetops; silence echoed when it stopped. At a place where sun fell between the trees and warmed one side of Albie's face he wished for his bedroom mirror, to see how still he was.

Something rustled ahead of him. He turned toward the sound, but the woods were still. He walked on. The land sloped down and to the left, and the air smelled of damp earth. He squatted to watch a daddy long legs with a tiny orange body walk from leaves onto a root. From far away Uncle Lou's thin voice called, "Ready on the left, ready on the right." Rifles snapped. Excited boys shouted.

Albie pulled himself up into a pine tree. One branch, two, three: he perched at the height of a man's head. He sought the crow. He let go of the tree with one sticky hand to study the milky pitch on his palm and inhale the acrid sting behind the pine's sweetness; he took pleasure from his sticky palm against his lip.

Something moved in the woods behind him. Albie counted in his mind to ten, to fifty; one branch at a time he eased himself down the tree. On the ground he listened with his cheek against the sticky trunk. A plane flew overhead; rifle fire crackled from the range. The trees remained silent.

Reassured, he followed paths that were not paths. The slope steepened so that he slid on dry pine needles. Had he passed the archery range to where the road ascended the hill? The woods grew thicker and darker. Albie heard shuffling, but saw only trees. This was better than baseball. He veered right, lest he come out into the open and meet the Panthers on the road to the waterfront.

Wings whirred: small brown birds flew from branch to branch. The gurgle of city pigeons would be as out of place in these green and brown woods as their iridescent violet collars. Albie stood stock still as another chipmunk near the root of a tree examined him and ran off. The chipmunk is afraid of me, he thought with surprise. Didn't the tiny creature recognize kinship in Albie's stillness?

He stepped from roots to stones, for silence. Riflery crackle fell away behind him. If that faint burr was an automobile engine, he was far from the road. It paused; gears changed, ground and stopped. Albie rested his hand on the white paper trunk of a birch.

A pebble struck the tree above his hand and fell to the ground. Albie saw nothing. Leaves rustled. Joe stepped out from behind a large tree only a cabin's length away holding a slingshot. "I tracked you," he said. "Let's be friends." He offered his hand.

His light bulb head was too big. Dirt smudged his cheeks and forehead, and his right eye pointed in against his nose. Joe's slingshot was a forked branch and strips of rubber tied to a leather pouch with dirty string. As they shook hands, sticky pine resin glued Albie's hand to Joe's cool palm.

"Where did you come from?" Albie said.

Joe pointed toward the riflery range.

"But it's Warriors, not Woodsmen."

"I wasn't shooting," Joe said. "I hide behind the backstop."

That was against the rules. Albie frowned.

"Bap! Bap! Whizz! Whizz!" Joe said. "I can hear the bullets hitting, and flying overhead, it's great, I'll show you. They never see me. I'm invisible."

The larger boy's left eye seemed normal. "How old are you?" Albie said.

"Twelve years, and one twelfth of a year."

"I'm ten and a half."

"Ten years and six twelfths?"

Albie computed. "Ten years and six twelfths and one fifty-second." Joe smiled.

"What's your bunk doing?" Albie said.

"Baseball, but I don't like it and they don't want me there, anyhow."

"Don't you get in trouble?"

"I did last year, but they don't care as long as I come back at night."

The breeze whispered. Joe could share stillness. "What's your last name?" Albie asked.

"Moscow."

"Joe Moscow," Albie said, to see what it sounded like. "I'm Albie Greenberg."

"I know." They exchanged another sticky grip.

A branch moved so that sun lit Joe's face. His left eye studied Albie; his right eye wanted to look, but couldn't. The breeze brought the crackle of rifle fire again.

Bullets spun on their axes to cut clean circles through Fearless Fosdick. Albie remembered the stabbing. "What if you got shot?" he said. "Aren't you afraid?"

"Not me," Joe said. "I'm an Indian scout, and scouts don't know fear."

Albie resolved to become a scout.

"Where were you going?" Joe asked.

"To the bunk. Panthers." But the truth was that Albie had started scouting already. "I was going to find my own way."

What Albie had just said was true, and the truth of it made him weak. No, he felt weak, but truth was that to find one's own way was strong, and important. Albie squinted at Joe.

"Okay," Joe said. "I won't track you anymore." He put the slingshot into his back pocket. "One thing," he said.

"What?"

"I have to swear you to secrecy. Swear you won't tell about the backstop?"

Albie had never broken so legitimate and important a rule himself. He hesitated. But in taking a new way through the woods, had, he, Albie, not become an outlaw, too?

"Swear," Joe said.

"I won't tell," the new Albie said.

"How," Joe said. He took Albie's hand, palm to palm, so their thumbs hooked around. Albie had never shaken hands that way before. "Say 'How,'" Joe said.

"How."

Joe bounded over a ridge to the right and disappeared. In a moment Albie missed him and followed, but when he reached the top he saw nothing but trees, and all he heard was the breeze, and baseball in the distance.

"Sailors!" William Hobeck called during cleanup. He climbed up on a bed to peer out the window.

"Let me see." Walter Gardner pushed him aside and beckoned to the bunk. "Hey, Waynie, sailors, sailors!"

Boys stopped making beds to rush out the front door. Albie followed. Off to the left Joe Moscow and another boy from Woodsmen trudged uphill through the picnic tables with white sheets and pillowcases in their arms. From a doorway, an aide handed folded sheets to a little boy from Lion Cubs. The little boy carried them toward his cabin past Joe and the other Woodsman.

Philip Mullaly cupped his hands around his mouth to shout, "Hey! Joe the Sailor!"

"How do you know his name?" Albie said.

"He pissed his bed every day last summer." Philip shouted again. "Hey, Joe the sailor, how's the yellow river?"

"*The Yellow River*, by I. P. Daily!" Mike Wooley screeched.

Older campers yelled from the steps of cabins. Uncle Jesse neither objected to the uproar nor participated in it. Joe and the other boy bore new bedding back to Woodsmen through the cloud of abuse. Albie flushed and went back in. "I bet he didn't mean to wet his bed."

William Hobeck's stained face registered amazement. "Only babies wet their beds."

"But Woodsmen is an older cabin," Albie said.

"That's what I mean." William adjusted his glasses. "Sailor! Sailor!"

Albie hurried to change for swimming first. Uncle Bart lined all the Panthers up along the dock and explained how to jump into the water.

Walter Gardner looked twice Wayne's size where they stood on the short arm of the L. Perhaps they were just brothers instead of twins. Philip knitted black eyebrows; how could one be older if they were in the same cabin? "Yes, but I'm ten and some of the other guys are eleven," Albie said. To say 'guys' felt grownup. "One could be a year older." Even Raddy was listening.

Philip's blue eyes frowned at Albie. "My cousins are twins and they're exactly the same."

"Let's ask him," Albie said.

When Uncle Bart bent over Wayne Gardner, Walter jumped into the water. Uncle Bart blew his whistle. Walter emerged with an idiotic smile and disappeared under water again. Uncle Bart blew his whistle twice, three times. "Everybody stops when I blow the whistle," he said to the rest of the Panthers, "everybody stay there." He motioned to Uncle Jesse on the shore.

"Ask him," Raddy said. Philip strode over to tap Wayne on the shoulder. A grin spread over Wayne's face as Philip whispered in his ear. He puffed up his skinny chest. "I am," he shouted.

"How much older?" Raddy said.

Wayne beckoned them close. Albie, Philip and Raddy squatted with him. "*Eleven minutes,*" he said in a stage whisper.

Albie and Philip exchanged glances. "So are you twins or not?" Raddy said.

Uncle Bart made Walter sit by himself on the damp part of the beach and sent the others back to their positions. Albie examined the lake surface a foot below the wooden dock edge. Here was a border between what was safe for human beings and what was not, like a subway platform. The swirl of crowds might thrust you over the edge into darkness and filth when the train was coming; unpredictable eruptions of hostility between Panthers could catapult him into the lake where dark cold water could rob him of breath. He could no longer discern a link between this forced exercise and his joyful introduction to the world beneath the surface with Stuart the day before.

"When I blow the whistle," Uncle Bart said.

Philip, hands forward and spread, stood ready to grapple with an opponent in the air above the water. Mike Wooley crouched with hands on knees. But Albie wasn't ready; he stepped back.

Uncle Bart blew his whistle.

Albie stopped; that was the rule. All the other boys jumped into the lake, splashed and shouted. Uncle Bart blew his whistle again. Everyone stopped.

"You!" Uncle Bart called in a deep voice, "you, what's the matter?"

"Jump!" Philip, below Albie, sounded friendly.

"C'mon," Mike Wooley said, "it's great."

"Wait," Albie said. "I'm not ready." Uncle Bart eyeballed him from the end of the dock; Uncle Jesse regarded him from the shore. It was the subway platform with no train coming, but all the Panthers were watching. Under the gaze of all those eyes, Albie felt like prey.

"I have to go," he said. He meant he had to pee. He ran along the dock onto land, and into the changing cabin.

At the end of lunch an aide handed Uncle Jesse a bundle of letters wrapped in a rubber band. From the far end of the table Albie sought his mother's pale blue stationery with the dark blue border. In his mind's eye he saw her blue-black handwriting. Uncle Jesse raised the mail above the boys' heads on the way down the stairs and through the picnic tables to rest period. The Panthers followed in a knot; they jumped and reached like dogs expecting a treat; they ran the last yards to the cabin.

"Everybody on his bunk!" Uncle Jesse pulled off the rubber band and put it around his wrist. "Wooley." Mike took the first white envelope back to his bed. "Hobeck." William pushed his glasses up on his forehead to peer at the address inches from his nose.

The next envelope was blue. "Greenberg," Uncle Jesse said. Walter passed it to Albie. It was here, addressed to Master Albert Greenberg, in his mother's printing. On the back he read the return address he had memorized when he was four years old.

"Hobeck."

"Gardner, I guess it's for both of you."

"Tarrant."

Albie clutched his envelope. Walter nudged him and passed him a postcard for Raddy bearing a message two lines long.

"Greenberg."

A second letter from his mother, thick enough to be three sheets of paper!

"Brown," Uncle Jesse said, "Roth." Then he said, "This one's for me," with a broad grin, and stuffed a letter into his sweatshirt pocket.

"Did I get any?" Philip Mullaly's voice quavered. He stood at the foot of his bed and touched his cheek.

"Mullaly," Uncle Jesse said. "It's a fat one." He handed Philip a big, white office-sized envelope with a printed return address and two stamps.

One of Albie's two envelopes was postmarked June 24, two days before he had left. He tried to remember whether he had seen his mother writing that Saturday, but the time and the place were too far away.

"Greenberg? One more for you." Uncle Jesse proffered a third blue envelope.

"You got three letters?" Raddy said.

Albie clutched them to his chest. His treasures might last for all of rest period.

"He got three letters," Raddy proclaimed, but the Panthers were busy with their own letters from home.

Albie's mother's thick letter described how hot the city was. 'Today when I went to buy vegetables, sweat was pouring off Mr. Mazella's face,' she wrote, 'and when he asked where my big boy was, I told him you were at summer camp.'

The cool shade in the cabin and the green trees lit by sun outside the screened window faded. Albie remembered how sun glinted off mica in pavement, how rivulets of street cleaning water surrounded crumpled cigarette packages in the gutter and floated them to an iron drain. He saw the perfect silence of the lake under the blue sky in Bear Brewer's movie, yet heard the rattle and clash of delivery carts and the groan of a bus changing gears. He smelled exhaust. He missed his home, and his mother.

Tears made it hard to read the next part. 'Your father went to play golf with . . ."

He closed his eyes, but the letter called him.

'How I wish I could see you run and play with the other boys,' his mother wrote. 'You are my darling dumpling.' Below 'Mommy' she had written, XXXXX, which meant kisses.

The third letter was shorter. 'The apartment seems so big and lonely without you . . .' Toward the end it said, 'Anna and Gertrude and Bibsy all send their love.'

On the way down to the playing field, Wayne Gardner jumped across a ditch at the side of the road and jumped back. Albie did the same. "Maybe

I can pitch today," Wayne said, and smacked his bony fist into his mitt. "You can pitch with a heart murmur."

"What's a heart murmur?"

"The doctor said I have a hole in my heart. I have to be very careful because if it was any bigger all my blood would run out of it." He stuck his chin out at Albie and ran ahead to Ebbetts Field.

Albie shuffled after him. Either Wayne didn't understand, or he lacked proper concern about his blood running out of the hole in his heart. If Albie knew him better he would ask more about it.

At Ebbetts Field the Gardners leaned against the wire backstop around home plate. "What do they do over there?" Walter pointed past Yankee Stadium where bodies in white shirts moved behind the trees that concealed the girls' camp.

"They play tennis," Albie said. "They swim."

"I bet they swim naked," Wayne said, and giggled.

"No they don't," Walter said. "I saw them with rubber hats on, like Mom."

"They pee sitting down." Wayne smirked.

Uncle Jesse dusted off home plate with his cap and blew his whistle.

"Uncle Jesse?" Walter said. "What do girls do at camp?"

"Who knows? They pick flowers." Uncle Jesse blew his whistle again. Albie and the Gardners started out to the field.

"That's dopey," Wayne said, "picking flowers." He contemplated Albie.

"Yeah," Albie said, "dopey." Wayne still watched him. "Girls are dopes." Wayne ran off to his position.

Albie pulled on his mitt and tried to smack his fist into the pocket with conviction. The leather smelled luxurious, but a breeze replaced it with a scent of flowers like his mother's perfume. On his way to right field Albie smacked his mitt again and again and again. When he reached his position, home plate was out of focus. He dried his eyes on leather.

Raddy's pitching became erratic. After a walk, he tucked the ball under his arm, spat into his hands and wiped them on his pants. His next throw bounced in front of the plate.

"Pitcher's blowing up," Wayne called from second base.

Raddy whirled and threatened a throw at Wayne. His next pitch went behind the batter.

"Take your base," Uncle Jesse said.

"Jerk," Wayne Gardner called. Uncle Jesse didn't hear him. Raddy ripped off his mitt and charged. At the last moment Wayne stepped aside and tripped Raddy, who sprawled in the dirt of the base path. "Help!" Wayne shrieked. "You can't hit me, I have a heart murmur!"

Uncle Jesse caught Raddy as he scrambled to his feet. "What's the matter? Let's see some sportsmanship." Raddy escaped restraint and hit Wayne in the face. Wayne ran toward the outfield screaming, "Walter, help, Walter, help!"

"Waynie, I'm coming!" Walter Gardner lumbered toward the conflict from center field, waving his arms. Albie edged deeper into right field to watch, as from his window. He felt too small to risk the touch of violence.

"You stop it!" Uncle Jesse shouted before the collision.

"I'm the pitcher," Raddy said.

"You're out of control," Uncle Jesse said. "I'm taking you out." Raddy kicked his mitt and stalked off toward the backstop. No one else moved. "Duke Gardner, on the mound. Scooter Greenberg, second base," Uncle Jesse said.

At the plate Will Hobeck wrinkled his nose and pushed his glasses up on his face. The color of his cheek matched his crimson shorts: artificial and misplaced among the green grass, azure sky, and dark blue of the lake beyond the base line.

"Play ball," Uncle Jesse said.

Wayne pitched. Will hit a line drive over Albie's shoulder to center field, where Walter Gardner stood with his back to the action. Will surged around third like a rocket plane before Walter, unconcerned by his brother's vituperation, discovered where the ball had gone. With a final long stride Will landed on home plate, thrust his fist up into the air, and shouted, "Home run!"

Raddy shoved Wayne off the pitcher's mound with both hands. "I'm taking you out." His momentum carried them out of Uncle Jesse's reach; they struggled and fell and the next moment the bugle ended the Panthers' session at Ebbetts field.

The Panthers gathered around the water tap at the corner of Yankee Stadium. The drinking fountain part didn't work, so one by one they cupped their hands under the faucet. Raddy pressed the heel of his hand against the opening to squirt the others, but the cool water was a pleasure under the hot sun. Will flicked water in his palm at Raddy. Raddy charged but Will jumped aside. "It's holy water," he said, "I'm blessing you."

"Don't make jokes about that," Philip Mullaly said.

"Why not?" Will reached over Philip's head to flick a few last drops at Raddy.

"Because I'm a Catholic." Philip touched a small silver cross on a chain around his neck.

"Can I get one of those?" Jerry Roth asked.

Philip grimaced. "It depends on what you are," he said. He squinted at Jerry. "You believe the Messiah hasn't come yet, right?"

"What's the Messiah?"

"Jesus Christ."

"Well, has he come yet?"

"You're a kike, right?" Philip said.

"What does that mean?"

"You're a Jew. My father says you don't believe the Messiah came yet, right?"

"My father never said anything about it."

"Well, that's what it means."

Will flicked more water at Philip and ran toward the road up the hill. Philip chased him, and one by one the other boys followed. Albie could spell messiah even if he didn't know what one was; he resolved to look it up in the dictionary when he got home. Mike Wooley's mother was in the choir at the Congregational Church. Wayne, right behind him, said the Gardners went to a big stone church on Pell Avenue at Christmas and Easter. Philip assured them that there was no church at Bear Lake. "The bath takes all morning," he said.

That was a relief. Because Albie had never been to church he had no idea how to behave there. Magazines, books, and even movies showed that normal people went to church on Sunday morning in suits like his father wore to work. They sang songs they all knew and shook hands with the minister on the way home.

When Albie accepted the heady responsibility of washing his own hands and face at camp, he had done it his own way. He washed his hands with soap and rinsed them, and washed and rinsed them again. At the end he hurled a double handful of cold tap water at his face, eyes closed, while he held his breath. He enjoyed the shock because he didn't have to fear the sting of soap in his eyes from a washcloth manipulated by a parent.

But a bath with other boys? He had seen no tubs. Perhaps they were in one of the small buildings uphill from the cabin. He quickened his pace. "Hey, Philip? Where are the bathtubs?"

"Bathtubs!" Philip pointed beyond the Indian Circle. "We do it in the lake," he said. "After breakfast everybody takes a towel and soap and clean underpants to Leech Beach. You go in the water naked and get soapy, and when the counselor says you're clean enough you come out and get dressed."

Mike said, "Baths are for babies. My mother said I can take a shower instead of a bath after the summer."

In Albie's house a shower was part of the adult world, unimaginable for a boy. He had glimpsed his father in the shower with darkness at the bottom of his belly, or had that been his mother turning away, before steam obscured his vision? He grabbed at a butterfly on the ground so he wouldn't have to look at Mike right away. "I take baths." He had an idea. "I hate showers," he said.

"Why?" Mike asked with interest.

"They get in my eyes," Albie said with all the authority he could manage. "The lake is a good idea."

Mike asked Philip, "Are there . . . leeches?"

Philip called back to Cooper, "Hey, Coop, they want to know if there are Leeches at Leech Beach!"

Jerry whooped. "They're *that* big, bigger than your dickie. If they get on your dickie they'll suck all the blood out of it!"

Mike paled. Albie swallowed. Cooper said, "I only got a tiny leech," and held his finger and thumb up, almost touching.

"Did it hurt?" Mike asked. Albie was profoundly grateful that Mike had asked what he was thinking. Cooper shook his head. "Don't worry."

Jerry grinned and pushed Cooper. "A big one'll get you this year," he said. Cooper lunged at Jerry but Jerry jumped out of the way; Cooper chased him up toward the cabin. Albie, who had no brothers, put his hands in his pockets. He wondered how much bigger Jerry's dickie was than his own, and whether the other Panthers would make fun of his dickie.

FOUR

Due to their moderate or low level of self-differentiation, scape-goated individuals may have difficulty distinguishing between various emotional states within themselves, such as anger, hurt, sadness, and joy. . . . they do not know how to assert themselves helpfully and harmlessly in a situation.

– VIMALA PILLARI, *SCAPEGOATING IN FAMILIES*

At lunch Saturday Bear Brewer announced that visitors were coming that afternoon. Could deliverance have arrived? Uncle Jesse shushed everyone before Albie could ask. The varsity baseball team from Pastor Ridge, a rival camp, would bring five buses of campers to watch the game from the new stands.

Boys booed. The way Bear Brewer held out his hand, palm down, to suppress the bad sportsmanship, told Albie that anti-Pastor Ridge feeling was not unwelcome. Bear Brewer said, "The cheers of all of us will drive the mighty Bear Lake Bears to victory."

Uncle Charlie stood on his chair to lead the camp in a cheer. "Two, four, six, eight, Who do we appreciate? Bear Lake, Bear Lake, Yayyy!" the boys screamed.

Another counselor stood on his chair. "Two, four, six, eight," he cried. Cheers erupted from other tables to drown him out. Boys joined one cheer or another with shouts; they banged their silverware or their heavy drinking glasses on the tables. Bear Brewer surveyed the tumult as boys stood on the benches one by one to shout a word Albie couldn't understand. "Huddlebug," they seemed to say. Albie rose too, and banged his spoon on the table.

"We need our good luck mascot," Bear Brewer's amplified voice intoned above the din.

"Huddlebug!" the whole camp shouted. "Hucklebuck!" The noise became rhythmic. "*Do* the huckle*buck*! *Do* the huckle*buck*!"

Albie climbed onto the bench to see better. Bear Brewer had flung out an arm toward the kitchen. In the open space in front of the door a stout black man in a chef's cap and apron held a huge pot in his arms as if it were a dancing partner. "*Do* the huckle*buck!*" all of Bear Lake shouted. "*Do* the huckle*buck!*" The man danced in circles to the rhythm until Bear Brewer raised his arm in dismissal, the noise lost all shape, and the chef retreated to the kitchen.

Bear Brewer growled into the microphone. "With a hucklebuck like that we can't lose!"

"Yay!" the boys responded. Benches scraped the wooden floor. Everyone broke and ran for their cabins, as if rest period would end sooner if they pursued it.

While the game itself held little interest for Albie, he might not mind being there if he could watch from the stands with binoculars. Even if the action were too fast and too broad to follow that way, binoculars would reveal the faces of the players without their knowing they were observed. Albie might learn to feel what they felt.

But without binoculars he would be alone in the crowd, too ignorant to respond to either the game or the other Panthers. He dawdled as the others left with Uncle Jesse. He was not the last out the downhill door, but as they broke into a run through the grove of pines, he stopped and made himself small with his back against a tree between himself and the ball fields.

The sound of the whole camp moving down the hill faded behind him. In the distance bus motors raced and horns beeped. The row of cabins was deserted. No one shouted at him to hurry. He rolled around the tree and sniffed sticky pine sap on his forearm. Most of the campers and counselors were out of sight. Hands in his pockets, master of danger, outlaw Albie ambled toward the corner of the lake in no more hurry than a boy who was following rules.

Two aides behind a knoll near the last cabin concealed their cigarettes when they saw him. Albie stepped over boulders onto the path. A bugle sounded amid shouting from the baseball field. Albie hurried. The noise he was making would scare chipmunks, but perhaps he could scout out Leech Beach to learn what was in store the next day. In the forest darkness his breath caught in his chest and he kept track of the places he passed so he could find his way back, like Hansel and Gretel.

Where the path curved close to the water he climbed through thorns and over roots to scramble down to the lake. He wet his hand. Was this holy water? In his Golden Bible, the hand of God divided the waters so the Israelites could cross to safety. He wasn't sure whether he was an Israelite. He held his hand out over the lake, flat, with the little finger down, but nothing happened.

Branches of the great tree over his head dipped into the water. Through the cascades of tiny leaves he could see the end of the lake and beyond it the docks and waterfront of the girls' camp. The woman who hovered nearby in a rowboat wore a bathing cap and a black bathing suit. Albie climbed up on a bulge in the bole of the tree to see better. A few heads in white caps bobbed near the boat.

Back on the path, feet had trodden the pine needles to dark earth littered with gray rocks the size of baseballs. Around a curve to the right Albie found a sneaker-shaped footprint. He measured his foot like Robinson Crusoe: an inch shorter. Someone else was here. A boy or a counselor? Albie stepped on stones to make no sound.

Ahead through the trees a figure knelt at the side of the lake. Albie approached on tiptoe. A boy. Heart beating, he inched closer until the suspense became too much and he said, "Hi."

The figure straightened, turned. It was Joe! Joe waved. "Come here." He was sharpening a stick with a pocket knife on a treeless margin of dirt and pebbles at the edge of a cove. A big tree on a point of land blocked his view of the girls' camp.

"What are you doing?" Albie said.

"Making a spear."

The Panthers' scuffles were violent enough. Woodsmen were larger and more dangerous. "Really?"

Joe spoke with seriousness. "If I'm lost in the woods I have to trap game and cook it over a fire. That's what Indians do."

The white point Joe was making could pierce Albie's chipmunk. "What could you trap?"

"Maybe a rabbit."

"Or a goat," Albie said, "like Robinson Crusoe."

"Yeah, a wild goat." Joe whittled a while longer. He touched the tip of his spear with a fingertip. "It's ready." He folded the knife, then cocked one of his eyes at Albie. "Do you want to make one? Here's another stick."

"I don't have my knife with me," Albie said.

Joe gave Albie his knife. Albie got the blade Joe had been using part way open, but it slipped from his fingers and closed with a click. Joe didn't say anything. Albie got the blade to stay halfway open. With great care he moved the pads of his fingers and opened it the rest of the way.

When he wrapped his hand around where the blade went, the backs of his fingers felt scared. "Is it sharp?" Albie said.

"A hunter has a sharp knife."

Albie touched the knife to the end of his stick and pushed. A curl of gray bark, white underneath, stood away and fell to the ground. "Great," he said, "thanks." When he finished, he tested the point of his stick on the pad of his thumb. It felt as sharp as a pencil. "I could spear a fish," he said, a little frightened.

Joe followed him to the edge of the water. "A hunter never goes without his knife."

Shouting erupted in the distance behind them. Albie caught his breath: a normal boy would be cheering at the game. "Aren't you supposed to be at the game?"

Joe grimaced. "They like it better if I'm not."

Albie tiptoed after Joe and held his tongue until Joe thrust his spear into the shallow water and a fish no longer than Albie's finger swam away.

Like they had slipped away from camp. "Won't you get in trouble?" Albie said, and feared he had offended, but what he had interpreted as a putoff expression was the eye that didn't see. "Won't we get in trouble?"

"We have to stay here for the summer anyhow."

Albie remembered home, his bed, his pajamas, baths before bedtime. "Joe?"

"What?"

"Where is Leech Beach?"

"This is it."

The orange water over the dark lake bottom looked shallow. "Where we take baths?"

Joe nodded.

"Are there . . . leeches?"

Joe nodded again.

Albie took a deep breath. "What's a leech?"

Joe rubbed the dome of his head. His face became serious. "You know what a tadpole is?"

Albie remembered something dark green and dead in a neglected tank in a classroom corner. "Yes."

"Well it's between that and a worm, only smaller."

In a tiny voice Albie said, "What's it like when they bite you?"

"You don't even feel it." Joe marched around the cove.

Albie hurried to catch up and touched his shoulder. "Do they suck your blood?"

"If they bite you." Joe peered into the water. "Look!" He pulled off his sneakers and socks to wade five yards out to thrust his spear in front of him, once, twice, and bent to pick something up.

"What did you get?" Albie jumped with impatience.

"A fish." Joe held a five inch gray and orange sunfish; its eye was milky and part of its tail was missing.

"Did you spear it?"

"Nah, it was floating upside down."

The dead fish smelled like the pails behind the fish market with the metal beaded curtain on the Avenue. Joe put the fish on the ground. With his whole arm he stabbed at it with his spear and caught what was left of the fish's tail.

"My turn," Albie said. More carefully than Joe, he guided the tip of the stick he had sharpened toward the fish. He wanted to spear the thickest part of its body, but he doubted he would be strong enough to drive the point all the way through, so he stuck the fish's eye.

"Good one," Joe said. Albie raised the spear in the air and war whooped with his hand over his mouth. The fish fell off the stick. Joe stabbed it through the body and raised it aloft again. Both boys screamed with excitement as they paraded along the water's edge.

"The hunters!" Joe cried.

"We are hunters!" Albie responded.

They got bored. Joe flipped the fish out into the lake with the stick. His gesture's resemblance to the swing of a baseball bat threw his deviance and Albie's into cruel relief. Albie wished he had gone to the game, but it was too late for that. "Let's track around the lake," he said.

"We'd get to the girls' camp," Joe said. "We're not allowed over there."

Albie imagined following the path all the way around the lake alone. It would be new, all new, but there was a limit on it. Like the branch public library: what was in the books was new, but the known path down neighborhood streets and up the steps made it safe.

The boys explored the woods behind Leech Beach for the rest of the afternoon. They found the foundation of an abandoned shack, and near an overgrown road that was no more than two ruts, the rusting remains of a very old truck. When they couldn't hear baseball sounds anymore they made their way back to the shore near the big tree.

They talked about school and neighborhoods and what was in their rooms at home and radio programs.

"I listened to Dick Tracy and Terry and the Pirates," Albie said.

"And Tennessee Jed and Sky King," Joe said.

His Dumbo ears with their pendulous lobes must have heard the same broadcasts as Albie, from the same five o'clock to the same six o'clock. Albie wanted to ask something else. No parent stood by to shush him or exchange looks with another adult, and yet he could not speak. Across the lake the girl swimmers had gone in. The sun, low over the trees at the far end, made him squint, but he thought Joe's face encouraged him.

"Do the other Woodsmen pick on you?" Albie said.

Joe pressed his lips together. The light at the edge of the lake was changing. Albie felt bad inside. "We'd better get back." They carried their spears until they saw a cabin. In silent agreement they rested the two sticks against a tree.

"Enemy action." Joe nodded over his shoulder and adjusted the spears so they leaned against the tree tip to tip. "Evasive maneuvers." He ran off through the woods to approach Woodsmen from the uphill side. Albie went the other way to join the Panthers on their way to dinner. If Joe's counselor condoned Joe's absence from baseball, maybe Uncle Jesse would turn a blind eye on Albie's dereliction, as well.

A long amplified prayer and cold cocoa left the boys irritable after Sunday breakfast. Raddy glowered around the cabin. "Pee-yoo!" he said. "Somebody needs a bath." Uncle Jesse tapped his watch as Philip Mullaly sang out, "We're goin' to Leech Beach -oh! We're goin' to Leech Beach -oh!" to the tune of a popular song.

Albie heard doubt in Uncle Jesse's instructions to bring clean underpants, soap dishes and towels. Might this be his first summer at Bear Lake, too?

Walter Gardner pulled at Uncle Jesse's sleeve and whispered into his ear.

"In the woods," Uncle Jesse said.

Wayne threw a hand to his forehead. "That brother of mine. He's worried about where to pee before we go in the lake because—"

"DON'T TELL!" Walter lurched across the cabin to clamp both hands over Wayne's mouth.

Wayne slid away and jerked a thumb over his shoulder. "He pees in the tub." Walter colored; Uncle Jesse grabbed him. "That's enough! Anybody has to go, go now." He pointed at Wayne. "It's okay to pee in the woods. We leave in ten minutes, now get!"

Walter stomped out the uphill door.

"What if he pees in the lake?" Will Hobeck said.

"Indian scouts pee in the woods," Albie said. No one responded. "Fish pee in the lake."

"Oh, yeah?" Raddy said. "How do you know?"

Logic made Albie sure of himself. "Fish would die if they got out."

Raddy shook a fist at Albie. "Anybody pees near me, *they'll* die."

Albie was sure of his knowledge, but not of his bladder, which always relaxed after immersion in a warm tub, even when he had just peed. What if that happened as he stood knee deep in the lake covered with soap? Clothed, he could not handle Raddy on land. In the water, naked, constrained by uncertain footing and the danger of attack by leeches, how could he stop a stream of urine that had started? He anticipated humiliation and blushed.

"He's going to do it in the lake," Raddy said.

"You better not," Will said.

Albie decided he would maintain control, no matter what Walter did, and marched out the door Uncle Jesse opened with his head as high as an Indian scout.

The journey to Leech Beach seemed shorter and the woods more friendly than the day before. A campful of boys larger than Albie had obliterated Joe's footprint and shuffled the path wider and darker. Voices shouted and hooted ahead of them. At the cove naked boys and counselors swarmed in the shallows; rinsed-off soap made the lake too turbid to see fish in.

Uncle Charlie directed the Panthers past piles of towels and clothing to where the water was shallowest and most orange. A clump of little Lion Cubs pointed at an aide with pubic hair who was urinating on a tree with a penis as big as a baseball bat. That embarrassed Albie. A small plane flew across the sky high overhead.

Jerry Roth, naked, called Cooper Brown, who took off his shorts and ran into the lake after him.

Albie carried his metal soap dish into the cool water. The bottom started out sand, but by the time the water passed his ankles, muck squished up between his toes. Water he cupped in his palm gave off the dark smell of parsley his mother had forgotten in the ice box. He opened his soap dish but he had no place to put it when he took out the soap. He started back to the shore.

"Greenberg!" Uncle Jesse called. "You're not done yet!" Albie held the soap dish down in front of him. The other Panthers shouted further out in the cove.

A minute later Cooper and Jerry swam out of the cove, away from the rest of the camp. "Okay, Coop!" Raddy shouted. "Jerry! Jerry! Jerry!" the twins shouted together.

Albie forgot to be ashamed. The rest of the camp watched the two big Panthers race further and further from shore. "They're gonna drown," said a boy with a huge bar of Ivory soap. Uncle Jesse and another naked counselor waded out to water up to their armpits and waved their arms. Absorbed, Albie wet his bar of soap, and washed himself as absently as he would have done in the tub at home.

The two counselors swam after the boys. Uncle Charlie shouted and pointed beside the big tree on the point.

Cooper was well ahead of Jerry. "Two, four six, eight," cheered the Gardner twins. "Go, Coop!" Albie cried. To explain his outburst to the boy with the Ivory soap he said, "He's the strongest one in my cabin."

"What's his name?"

"Coop," Albie said. "His real name's Cooper."

"Yay, Cooper!" the boy cried.

The counselors gained. Jerry paused, turned, and dog paddled toward them. When he reached Uncle Jesse they both rested before they headed in toward Leech Beach with slow strokes.

Uncle Charlie cupped his hands like a megaphone. "Stay with him, Woody!" he shouted. "Where the hell is Bart?" His deep voice didn't sound nearly as loud as the treble cries of the boys. The other counselor gained on Cooper. Albie looked left and right for something to climb up on so he could see better, but the shore was fifty feet behind him. Out on the lake, everyone could see that Cooper's strokes remained strong as he made a smooth turn ten feet out of the counselor's reach.

At last Cooper stood up in waist deep water among the Panthers, Uncle Jesse, and a dozen other naked boys. "Yayyy!" the Panthers cheered.

"You shouldn't do that," Uncle Jesse said. "It isn't safe."

"I was okay," Cooper said, and Jerry nodded.

"Two, four, six, eight," Raddy said.

"Who do we appreciate," the Panthers, and Albie, chimed in.

"Cooper, Cooper, Yayyy!" half of Bear Lake responded. Cooper's transgression had been positive: he had done more than the other boys could, and so he deserved praise. When Albie had cut baseball, he had gotten away with doing less and enjoyed it—but his resistance had not been admirable. He felt better in the world he had started to make for himself with Joe, but he hankered for the higher good of fitting in with the normal boys.

Uncle Jesse shooed the Panthers toward shore. Within a yard of the beach, in three inches of water, he tapped Albie's shoulder. "What's the matter with you, Greenberg? You're all soapy."

"The moron doesn't know how to bathe," Raddy said. "I'll get him!" He pushed Albie backward so he sat down hard on a pebble in shallow water. "Wanna fight?" Raddy balled his fists.

Soapy and muddy, Albie stumbled away to rinse off in deeper water that smelled of vegetables. Out across the lake lay distance, solitude, and freedom. He would trade anything to swim as well as Cooper. The lake cooled his hot eyes before he noticed he had put his face in it.

Half an hour standing in shallow water with the other beginners under Monday's gray sky left Albie chilly until a pickup truck put an end to swim when it drove right up to the waterfront so two workmen could work on the diving board. In the changing cabin he dried his legs and hurried to pull up his shorts as Raddy and Philip ran in. "Ta-raa! Ta-raa!" They mimed hunting horns between him and the door.

Albie ducked behind the partition. Philip dressed and left. On his way out, Raddy took Will Hobeck's glasses from the hook where they hung by the shoelace that went around his neck.

Albie joined the others outside and drew patterns in the gravel with a stick until Uncle Jesse led Will out of the cabin with a hand on his shoulder. "Listen up," he said, "anybody see Will's glasses?"

Discomfort surged through Albie. What was Will's favor worth, or Raddy's enmity? Was honesty worth a reputation as a snitch?

Without his glasses Will looked unsure of himself; the stain on his cheek became a stark and pathetic blemish again. He tugged Uncle Jesse's arm. "I need my glasses."

"You don't have another pair?"

"They don't work right anymore." He wrinkled his nose and peered at the small boys around Albie one by one. "Anybody see my glasses?"

Raddy shook his head through an exaggerated arc. His tee shirt concealed the glasses in the back of his shorts, but the shoelace hung down like a tail.

Albie pitied Will. He sidled over to stand behind Raddy. "Hey, Will," he called, "I didn't see them." Will didn't see the shoelace. "I'll help you look," Albie shouted.

"Everybody help Will look." Uncle Jesse walked down to the water's edge. One of the workmen shook his head no.

Panthers stooped to examine the shrubbery behind the changing cabin. Raddy ducked between two bushes and reemerged without his tail. Albie darted into where he had been. Will's glasses hung in the branches of the bush. Once Albie pocketed them, he became afraid Raddy would accuse him of having taken them in the first place. He entered the cabin, and after a moment alone, jumped out the door.

"Will! Will!" he shouted, "Are these yours?"

The taller boy hurried over. "Yes, thanks, Albie. Where were they?" He put them on and adjusted the shoelace.

"Good work, Greenberg," Uncle Jesse said. "Let's hit the road so we're not late for lunch."

"Yeah, where were they?" Raddy stared at Albie.

"Hey, Will," Albie said, "race you to the bunk!" He broke for the road with Will close behind him. They were neck and neck entering the grove of trees, but the taller boy pulled away as they ran up the hill. Albie caught up among the picnic tables, where Will breathed hard in the sun. When Will got red from exertion his birthmark was beautiful.

During lunch a boy carrying an oval bowl heaped high with mashed potatoes slipped on a cooked string bean and fell right next to the Panthers' table. "Yay!" Panthers cheered when the bowl broke. Boys and counselors applauded. The cheers became rhythmic, "Yay! Yay! Yay!"

"Eat it up!" someone shouted.

An outrage! But the rhythmic cheer became "Eat! It! Up! Eat! It! Up!"

The boy who had dropped the dish rose red-faced to his hands and knees. He wasn't hurt. "Eat it up!" Raddy shrieked. To Albie's inquiring face he said, "Anybody who wastes food has to eat it."

A fat boy handed the boy on the floor a spoon. "Yayyy!" all the campers shouted. The kneeling boy spooned up mashed potatoes. "Eat it up!" screeched the boy who had given him the spoon. "Eat! It! Up!" all the boys at his table roared. The boy ate three spoonfuls before he ran out of the mess hall crying and aides picked up the broken crockery and mopped the floor.

Raddy got one postcard. Albie got two blue letters and a small package. 'I hope you are getting used to camp,' his mother had written in the first letter. 'Your father is very proud . . .'

"What's in the package?" Will said.

Albie had hoped to open it in private. "I don't know."

"Open it," Wayne said. "Yeah, open it," Walter said.

Albie tried not to tear the paper. He unwrapped a quarter pound of his favorite sour balls from the candy store on the Avenue.

"I want a red one," Raddy said.

"Would you like to share them around?" Uncle Jesse was one more pair of eyes behind the circle of faces. Albie had no more choice than about undressing at Leech Beach. He extended the box. Panthers pounced; sour balls rolled on the floor. Uncle Jesse took a green one. "Thanks, Greenberg." He surveyed the cabin. "Let's get some rest."

Boys murmured thanks and returned to their beds. Albie chose a pale yellow fallen sour ball, pineapple or grapefruit, to suck while he read his mail. He saved the one remaining red one for another time.

In the morning Albie hurried up the outside stairs to the mess hall in a stream of bigger boys to reach the Panthers' table first. The second seat was close enough to Uncle Jesse's protection without the first seat's obligation to fetch dishes from the kitchen. He chose the side of the table that would let him see the kitchen door, the Woodsmen and Joe.

Even though the other Panthers weren't there yet, the dining room seemed more crowded than usual. Woodsmen scuffled and made faces. Uncle Dan made them stop; Albie couldn't see Joe because everyone was standing up. Someone seized Albie around the waist. "Stand him up!" a voice shouted. Wiry arms tugged. The back of Albie's knees scraped on the bench. Will's eyeglasses and shocking purple cheek all but touched Albie's face when Raddy, across the table, shouted, "Ten-shun!"

The public address system shrieked. Everyone in the mess hall except Albie was standing. "C'mon, Greenberg." Uncle Jesse raised his palm.

Bear Brewer spoke. "In honor of the founding of our free country, in honor of Independence Day, 1950 . . ." The campers cheers drowned Bear Brewer's words. Albie stood up. "Mrs. Brewer will lead us in singing the national anthem."

Mrs. Brewer took off her apron on the low platform beside the head table. Someone played two loud chords on an upright piano in a corner. Albie stood rigid, his hand over his heart, the way he had learned in school. He couldn't see a flag to face because everyone around him was taller than he was.

"Oh, say, can you see," Mrs. Brewer sang through the microphone. Her shrill voice blended with the shriek from the loudspeakers. ". . . Gave proof through the night, That our flag was still there," the camp and Mrs. Brewer sang.

Patriotic music could make Albie cry. He knew all the words and treasured his normal American feelings as one of his few scraps of authenticity, even though tears shamed him. ". . . home of the braaave!" he sang.

Benches scraped. Everyone sat. With relief Albie saw an American flag in a stand beside the stone fireplace: he had been facing the right way.

Will was laughing. Jerry said, "I thought he said 'national antlers,'" and giggled. The sacrilege shocked Albie: the flag and the nation ought to be above jokes. "It's not funny," he said.

Will pointed at a huge mounted deer head over the fireplace. Jerry poked Albie in the ribs. More Panthers giggled. Albie spluttered. Uncle Jesse raised a warning finger.

"But even before that great battle this country was filled with brave warriors," Bear Brewer proclaimed. "During the last two weeks of the summer Bear Lakers divide up into the Red Tribe and the Gray Tribe, for the final Color War of the summer. Every boy here will be a warrior . . ."

Albie doubted that he could be a warrior.

". . . and fight to the last of his strength, for the victory of his team!" Cheers exploded.

Half of the camp would be on the team that lost. When an older camper read a prayer, Albie prayed that if his team were to lose, it would not be his fault.

And then it was the evening before Color War. Counselors talked together on the blackened earth in the center of the Indian Circle as Lion Cubs and Woodsmen filtered through benches around a circle of stones a foot in diameter with numbers painted on them. At the last campfire of the summer, everybody would get marshmallows and sing songs; the best camper on the winning team in color war would paint the year in his team's color and everybody would shake hands and the next day everybody would go home.

A thick white 48 and 49 lay smooth on adjacent stones; the gray team had won the last two years. The red number 46 Cooper's brother had painted after he won the swimming medal four years before had faded to a pale rose on the granular surface of its boulder.

Uncle Jesse and Uncle Bernie sat on logs as Uncle Dan took off his shirt and tied a leather band with a feather in it around his forehead. He raised one hand. "Braves!" he said in a deep voice. "Take your places for pow wow!"

He was taller than Uncle Jesse, very thin, and dark like an Indian. Albie thought him magnificent. He explained that a hundred years before, the Red Tribe and the Gray Tribe warned their enemies they were coming with a war cry that struck fear into their hearts.

"He's not really an Indian," Raddy whispered.

Uncle Dan chose Baird to demonstrate the war cry. The unkempt boy shambled to the circle of stones with his Bear Lake tee shirt inside out. Uncle Dan whispered to him, stepped back, raised his hand, and let it fall. Baird trotted around the circle with awkward, short steps, whooping, and shuffled back to his seat.

"That was the cry of the gray tribe," Uncle Dan said. "Now we will hear the cry of the red tribe." He pointed at Joe, who sat apart from the other boys in the back row. "Moscow! Front and center!"

Joe shook his head.

"I'm warning you."

Joe picked his nose. Uncle Dan ran across the blackened circle and ran on the tops of the logs to the last row to drag Joe to the center. "Do the red war cry," Uncle Dan said.

Joe scratched under his arm.

Raddy, Jerry, and some of the Woodsmen pointed their fingers at their temples and made small circles.

Uncle Dan shook Joe. "Red tribe!"

Joe uttered a shriek that frightened Albie. Raddy and Jerry dropped their hands in alarm. Joe thrust his way past Uncle Dan to dance around the circle once making a far fiercer ululation than Baird. He folded his arms at his seat with his back to the center.

"He sounded like a real Indian," Mike Wooley said.

"He's not," Jerry said. "He's a moron."

Uncle Dan held his hand up and asked who would like to do a war cry. Uncle Bernie whispered to a Lion Cub with two Band-Aids on his knee. The small boy scurried out to Uncle Dan.

"What's your name?" Uncle Dan asked.

"Tommy."

"The brave Tommy is on the war path!" Uncle Dan proclaimed, and leaned down. "Go ahead."

Tommy stumbled around the circle and warbled a thin falsetto. When he finished, he looked up at Uncle Dan, who patted his back and shooed him toward his seat. "Did you hear that? How many heard the battle cry of the red tribe?"

Tommy raised his hand. So did Uncle Bernie, with his other arm around Tommy's shoulder.

Uncle Dan put his hands on his hips. "Who can tell us the difference between the gray battle cry and the red battle cry?" No one spoke. "Anyone!" Uncle Dan said.

A daddy long legs walked out from under Albie's log. He rested his hand on the ground in front of the spider.

"Last chance," Uncle Dan said.

The spider stepped up onto Albie's palm.

Uncle Dan crossed his arms on his chest. "Braves! The battle cry of the red tribe is 'Red! Red! Red!' and the gray tribe's is 'Gray! Gray! Gray!'"

Albie softened his cupped hand to feel the spider's delicate step.

"Everybody up," Uncle Dan said. "We're all going to practice." The counselors guided, coaxed, tugged boys into the clear space between the front row and the stones. "First the gray tribe," Uncle Dan said, "On the war path, now!"

The campers circulated, ululating and tapping their mouths. Albie protected his spider, but he cried, "Gray! Gray!" with the others and spotted the moment when Joe slipped into the woods. Uncle Dan made them practice again. Back at his seat Albie released his spider onto his thigh. It hurried towards a knee and fell to the ground, where it seemed unhurt. Albie picked it up again.

"What's that?" Walter asked.

"My spider."

"Where did you get him?"

Albie touched the log they sat on.

"Hey!" Walter said. "He's got a spider!"

Raddy and Will whooped and approached. Albie deposited the spider between his legs under the shelter of the log.

"Let me see," Will said.

Albie leaned forward to shelter his spider, and willed it to retreat under the log. With suicidal stateliness it marched out into the open toward the ring of stones.

"Red! Red! Red!" Raddy cried, and jumped from the log. His sneaker landed inches from the spider.

"No!" As Albie stood up in alarm, he jostled Raddy, who fell, got up swinging and pummeled Albie. The other campers gathered to watch the fight. Albie threw his arms up to protect his head, then curled himself up to protect the spider. Wayne stepped out of the crowd to kick Albie in the side and disappeared.

"Hey!" Uncle Jesse pulled Raddy away and dispersed the others. "What was that about?"

Raddy jutted his lower lip forward, his face red. He pulled away and ran out to the road and up the hill.

"That's it," Uncle Jesse said. "Clean up for lunch." Uncle Dan took off his feather. Campers straggled out of the Indian Circle in groups of three and four. Albie found no trace of his spider on the hard brown dirt.

That evening the Lion Cubs and Panthers thronged back down the hill in warm sweaters and jackets along with the rest of Bear Lake. They sat on the front two rows of logs. Someone had laid a bonfire in the center ring of stones, but nothing happened for a long time after the boys were seated and Albie grew chilly and bored.

In time a bugle sounded from the dimness under the trees and grownups walked out in a group. "We call upon the bear spirits to give us fire," Bear Brewer said. One counselor splashed liquid onto the piled wood and tossed the can in. Another struck a match. Yellow flames flared up.

"Ohh!" gasped the campers. "Yayyy!"

Uncle Charlie and Mrs. Brewer read from folded papers in their pockets about the Indians and the English and the French, but Albie couldn't follow it over the noise the fire made. The reading went on and on. Boys talked. In the next section, the Warriors arm wrestled with each other. The sky darkened; a few stars appeared.

"At night, from his prison cell," Mrs. Brewer read.

"The Star Spangled Banner," Uncle Charlie read.

"Behold," Bear Brewer read. He flung a hand toward the lake. Shots, or firecrackers, sounded. A rocket sizzled into the evening sky leaving a trail of red, then exploded with a bang! into a sphere of yellow lights.

"Ohh!" the Panthers gasped, and stood on the logs to see better. Something whistled in the night. With a second bang!, green stars exploded, and a third bang! produced an umbrella of red stars above the green ones. "Ahh!" the boys said.

". . . our battle to be free," Uncle Charlie read.

More rockets punctuated the crackle of firecrackers at the edge of the lake.

". . . an end to tyranny, and the birth of a new nation," Bear Brewer read.

Three rockets flew up together and exploded. Their grains of light mingled and floated down toward the lake, twinkling and dimming, until the water extinguished them.

Silent boys shuffled out of the Indian Circle and up the hill to bed. Albie mused about the fireworks, and Korea and the war against the Queen of England when a man had tried to stab her. It all saddened him. He was only a boy, but when he became a man he would fight tyrants and invaders, and his eyes would not fill with tears.

Next morning Uncle Jesse lined all the Panthers and Lion Cubs up in two rows to throw baseballs back and forth. The same meaningless shouted chatter encouraged good performance and chastised errors.

"Eye on the ball," Uncle Jesse cried.

"Talk it up," a teenage aide called.

"See some spirit!"

"Infield chatter, infield chatter."

"Hurl it in there," another aide said. "Go for the strike."

Little Stuart, whose sandwich Albie had shared, stood across from Albie in a baseball cap so much larger than his head that only a bony little chin protruded below the brim. Yet Stuart could throw a baseball straight into Philip Mullaly's mitt.

The thin aide called, "Looka the arm on that one!"

"See the ball," the fat one said.

Stuart tilted his cap and threw. The ball struck the aide's glove with a solid slap. Albie saw no steps, no process to imitate, so he could not analyze throwing. That some little boys had better-developed baseball skills than his own depressed him, which undercut his efforts even further.

The aide returned the ball to Stuart, who threw it to Albie, but Albie missed it. He ran to get the ball and carried it back to the line to throw it to Jerry, but it flew sideways and hit the ground well short of the other row of boys. A Lion Cub Albie's size dropped or missed as many balls as Albie, but he ignored Albie's greeting to shout to Philip, "Over here, over here!"

It was all pointless and desperate. When the drill paused so boys could get a drink of water, Albie ducked away downhill through the woods behind the latrine toward the archery range. In a patch of the forest floor dappled by sunlight he came upon an anthill that stuck through the mat of pine needles like a carbuncle. Albie knelt to admire an ant pulling a brown lump larger than himself over pine needles, around twigs, and up the incline to the opening.

When his knees hurt, Albie lay prone on the earth. Even up close the ants did not shout to each other, nor could Albie hear their tiny footfalls. Though he was happy enough alone, how he wanted to be part of some large, serious enterprise like the anthill, from which he would not want to escape!

Albie carried a thick white office envelope addressed in his father's handwriting back to his bed between his fingertips. The smaller blade of the clasp knife was so sharp the top hissed when he slit it. Inside he found a few stingy lines on one page of stationery and newspaper clippings.

'Dear Babble Boy,' — his father's handwriting was harder to read than his mother's — 'By now you must be a real major leaguer. Here are some articles you will find interesting. We are very proud that a Greenberg is playing sports at Bear Lake. Your mother joins me in sending love.'

Albie looked up from the letter to try to imagine what his father really felt, or really thought, but nothing came. He unfolded the clippings.

The first picture showed a plump boy with a worried frown sitting next to a woman less beautiful than Albie's mother and a man younger than Albie's father. The caption read, 'Mr. and Mrs. Ernest Sperlins and their son Rouls, 11, were among the spectators at Ebbetts Field yesterday when the Dodgers met the Giants. They are displaced Latvians who have been hired to take care of the Deacon's farm in Chestertown, Md.'

Walter Gardner looked over at Albie. "Hey," he said, "what's that picture?"

Albie pointed to the headline. "YOUNG D.P. ATTENDS FIRST BALL GAME," he read. The article was by Doris Greenberg. Albie could not remember a relative named Doris. Had his father sent the article because of its content or because of the writer's name?

"Read more," Walter said.

"They went to a game," Albie said. "The Dodgers and the Giants."

"The Bums!" Walter said. "Hey Waynie, the Bums!" Uncle Jesse shushed him. Walter sat on Albie's bed. "Read more."

"Knowledge He Picked Up in German Camp Helps at Giant-Dodger Fray," Albie read.

"He's at camp, too?"

"Not now," Albie said. "I guess he was in a camp in Germany." With a chill he remembered the woman in the apartment when his father wore the helmet. *Not on the camps.*

"Read more."

"'It's all so strange to him,' whispered one of the adults. 'He's never seen a baseball game, you know.' All during batting practice, the boy sat silently staring about. He seemed bewildered and a little bored." Albie recognized bewilderment and boredom as plausible responses to baseball: perhaps the boy was like him. He glanced at the picture again, and continued.

"He sat without saying a word until the game was about three minutes old. Eddie Stanky, leading off for the Giants, was still at bat, when suddenly the boy spoke up.

"'Ein strike, drei balls,' he said reflectively."

"What did he say?" Walter asked.

"Something about strikes and balls," Albie said. "Listen." He continued: "And he was right. The count was three and one on Stanky and somehow an 11-year-old Latvian boy who had spent the last five years in displaced persons camps knew all about it.

"The boy was Rouls Sperlins, who arrived in this country with his parents last Saturday. Because his parents have been hired to work on the Maryland farm of Branch Rickey, president of the Dodgers . . ."

"The Dodgers, the Bums!" Walter cried. "Hey, Waynie . . ."

"Gardner!" Uncle Jesse said.

". . . he was seeing his first baseball game almost right off the boat," Albie continued.

"That's enough, back to your bed, it's rest period." Uncle Jesse stood up. Walter retreated. "Read to yourself, Greenberg," Uncle Jesse said.

Albie read on. 'With him were his parents and two Church World Service officials.

'How was it that he already knew about balls and strikes?

'Rudy Hansen, the jovial interpreter who had been assigned to help the boy learn the game, leaned over and asked him.

'By this time the boy was standing to see if Whitey Lockman's solid smash to center field would be caught. A bit abstractedly he explained that he had learned a little softball in one of the camps in Germany.

'Mr. Hansen, budget director for the Church World Service, which introduced the Sperlinses to Mr. Rickey, translated the answer, then sat back to enjoy the game with Mrs. Marjorie Morris of the service and the Sperlinses. But every few minutes, Rouls would poke him and ask a question.

'And when Pee Wee Reese, the Dodger shortstop, was called out at home on a close play, Rouls watched the bitter protests with quite some interest, then gave his own verdict.

'"I think," he said in German, "it should be a run."'

Next to the article an advertisement showed two men wearing hats with brims like Albie's father's. Albie imagined his father presenting him with the clipping from the wing chair at home. 'Read it,' his father would order, and Albie would suffer under the weight of the implied comparison. He could never satisfy his father, nor could he believe that his father really cared about all the recommendations he made to Albie, recommendations that became obligations Albie could not meet. Rouls Sperlins had learned a little softball and taken delight in it when Albie could not. Perhaps German camps were better for that. And Albie would not have asked what the Church World Service was, either, because churches were not for him.

The other Panthers read their mail or dozed. Uncle Jesse fell asleep. Albie picked up the second clipping.

'GREENBERG CHECKS SCHREIBER AT NET,' read the headline. A tennis player named Seymour Greenberg of Chicago had defeated a player named Schreiber. Except for the name, Albie could find nothing to connect to in the article. At the end he read that Schreiber had played poorly: 'His confidence deserted him, as well as his control, and Greenberg had nothing to fear thereafter.'

Across the cabin Jerry and Will whispered together. Cooper read a book. Albie doubted that large boys ever lost their confidence and control, but for himself he could not imagine having nothing to fear.

Morning. Albie awakened under warm covers when the others were still asleep and Uncle Jesse's clock said 5:40. He didn't want to urinate off the steps when it was light.

He slid his pajama pants down, unbuttoned the shirt and inched an arm through the chilly morning air to retrieve his camp shorts. He eased himself out of bed and tiptoed outside. He pulled on his gray sweatshirt and sat on the lowest step to put on his socks and sneakers.

The alley between Panthers and Lion Cubs was darker than the open space uphill from the cabins. Albie hurried through cold mist toward the artificial yellow glow of the bulbs in the latrine. Gray moths fluttered in the doorway; Albie did not enter. He left the trail and walked up a steep hill through woods to urinate in a clearing. Pine needles muffled his splatter; the foamy bubbles disappeared into the forest floor.

Relieved! In a pleasurable faintness he inhaled the pine forest. Before him a climbable tree beckoned, cool and damp, its lichens pale in the early light. Albie's bare knees stood out against the rough bark. A heavy branch blocked his progress upward. The wood was slippery, but the sight of his white canvas sneaker, his sock, and his ankle reassured him. Small birds flew out of the tree; Albie smelled darkness and morning mist. By the seventh branch he could see over the latrine roof to the road. This was no dream. He was climbing to a high place. Another branch, two. As high as he climbed, still higher trees shaded him from the rising sun.

From a good perch he examined the roof of Lion Cubs, Panthers beyond it, Woodsmen, then Warriors. Cabin after cabin disappeared into dimness under tall trees. If only he had his father's binoculars! A counselor in Jockey underpants emerged from a distant cabin, stepped barefoot around into the space between his cabin and the next, and a minute later returned the way he had come.

Albie eased himself around the trunk. The campers' route to the mess hall traversed less than half of the Main House verandah; the rest, out of sight from the cabins, commanded a small meadow. Sunlight crept down the white face of the house to touch the verandah roof, a sofa hung from chains, a wicker chair, a screen door.

Time lay quiet. Albie had found this peaceful place himself; his parents had not given it to him. He ran his hand through slippery dew to feel the rough bark underneath. With great care he extracted the stag-handled knife from his pocket to cut an A and a square G into the cold surface. In the morning light his initials in the cut wood were the same pale shade as his leg. He admired the letters: A.G., that was Albie.

Mrs. Brewer came out onto the verandah in a white blouse and a blue skirt with ruffles on the bottom. She put an apron over her head, tied the straps behind her and smoothed her hair backward. She lit a cigarette from the apron pocket—was it a Chesterfield like his mother's?—and leaned her head back with her eyes closed to blow dragon smoke out her nostrils.

She did not know Albie was watching. He pressed the knife in his pocket against his thigh. What if he were the man who had attacked the Queen of England? Breeze swayed the tree; dizzy, Albie held on with both hands.

Bear Brewer stepped out behind Mrs. Brewer in paint-stained khaki pants and a sagging white tee shirt. He had combed long dark hairs across his bald spot like Albie's father. He put his hand under Mrs. Brewer's apron and skirt and touched between her legs. Albie could see her white slip. She leaned back, eyes still closed, and held the cigarette over her shoulder for Bear to puff. He blew smoke out of his nostrils too. The Brewers stood as still as Albie sat, until Bear removed his hand and Mrs. Brewer stroked his cheek. She put out her cigarette in a rusty ashtray on the wicker chair arm and they went inside.

A minute later the bugle sounded reveille. Albie traced his initials with his fingertip and climbed down the tree.

Elements of the Panthers and Woodsmen chose sides for afternoon baseball. As usual Raddy, a captain, pitched. As usual, Joe was missing and Uncle Dan wasn't looking for him. As usual, Albie, conscientious, chosen last, played right field. He batted eighth because they had too few boys for teams of nine.

Second inning, one out, skins led shirts two nothing. Raddy on the mound, ready to pitch. His shirt hung out in back like the paper donkey tail at a birthday party. Albie raised his new orange fielder's mitt to sniff the neatsfoot oil his father had applied to it. Jerry Roth squatted behind the plate wearing the sweat-stained face mask and protective pads marked with a blob of crimson paint to signify the camp's ownership. That sour sweat smell on the face mask would never be Albie's.

Uncle Jesse cried, "No batter, no batter!" Raddy looked over his left shoulder at Wayne Gardner, who tagged up at first and jostled Bobby, the Woodsman. Bobby, whose lobster claw mitt was black with age, sweat, and oil, shouldered Wayne off the base. Raddy squinted at Jerry, who signaled with fingers between his heavy thighs.

Albie watched from far right field. In the distance behind him a hedge-row separated the camp property from the dirt road to the station, the dirt road his family would drive up in eleven days to visit him. He had arguments for his rescue in order: he didn't like baseball, the food wasn't good, he had read all the books he had brought. And he had done his best: hadn't he learned to make his bed, tried to swim, excelled at riflery? You need strong eyes to see the small holes in the targets better than the other Panthers, and as well as Uncle Lou. When Albie and the rifle became one in a moment of stillness and clear seeing, his body performed an act difficult for others. But his skill meant less than when Cooper hit a home run, or Raddy hurled the ball into Jerry's mitt.

"Ball two." Uncle Dan stabbed the air with two fingers.

"He broke his wrists," Raddy shouted and faced Uncle Dan with his hands on his hips. Wayne broke from first base with his cap in his hand; by the time Raddy had transferred the ball to his right hand, Wayne was standing up on second.

"It was time out!" Raddy complained. Clouds drifted across the sky. Albie touched his upper lip with the sun-warmed leather of his mitt.

The short Woodsman on second mimed a throw to Bobby, on first; Wayne left second and the Woodsman tagged him. "Now he's out!" the Woodsman cried.

"I am not!"

The Woodsman pushed Wayne. Walter ran in to twist the Woodsman's arm. Uncle Dan blew his whistle and sent Wayne back to first base, Walter back to the outfield, and the count back to 0 and 0.

Albie saw it all in miniature, in a larger scene that took in saddle horses outside the barn, a yellow butterfly sinking toward a clover blossom, boys crowding downhill out of the woods for the second afternoon activity.

The bat cracked. Something bounded up at him; he threw up a hand to protect himself; the ball hit his mitt, thwack! and stuck. Desperate to free himself from this involvement in a game he disliked, he threw the ball, hard, the way he was facing; it landed, thwack!, in the mitt of the Woodsman playing third base for the skins. It was the hardest and truest Albie had ever thrown a ball. Proud, he started toward the infield.

"He's safe!" a shirt shouted from the bench on the left field line. Uncle Dan leaned toward third base, hands out palms down, and Wayne on second base thumbed his nose at Raddy. Philip Mullaly screamed, "What's the matter with you?"

Raddy threw his glove on the ground. "We had a force!" Uncle Dan restrained him. Bobby, on first base, faced his teammates on the bench and made circling motions near his temple with his index finger; he flung the finger at Albie with a flourish. "You moron!" Raddy shouted, "You moron!"

Albie retreated toward his exile in far right field. He could not ask what he had done wrong, because as far as he could tell he had not done anything at all. His will had never been involved.

Raddy walked a Woodsman to load the bases. His wild throw walked Will Hobeck. Wayne sauntered across the plate. Cooper Brown was up next. "No batter, no batter," Bobby called without conviction, and waved Walter further out into left field.

Raddy threw, Cooper swung, the bat cracked. The line drive flew over third base safely beyond Albie's control. The tall Woodsman scored. The ball bounced fair before it hopped into a grassy ditch between the foul line and the road. Walter still hadn't found it when Cooper jogged across the plate to shake hands with the other shirts.

When they stopped the score was fourteen to one. Raddy caught Albie on the road up the hill. His blows did not hurt as much as his red-faced assertion, "You don't know *anything*," and Albie's heartfelt acknowledgment that the indictment was true. Raddy and he were opposite, separate and irreconcilable, and would remain so as long as they lived.

Uncle Jesse blew his whistle when Raddy caught Albie, but by the time he reached them Raddy had forced Albie's face into the dirt. "Leave him alone," Uncle Jesse said, and dragged Raddy uphill. The other Panthers trooped after them, grouchy and despondent that a double play had been missed, even though they had played on both teams. They climbed the cabin stairs in a knot and let the screen door slam.

Albie remained prone among tall pines on the slippery brown needles. On his face his dirty fingers touched roughness, dirt, and the dampness of tears. That he was unfit to play baseball with the others was incontestable. Why did he have to try?

He imagined his father's visiting day descent from the black automobile, wearing an overcoat, a Homburg, shiny shoes, and with a hand extended: "My little man . . ."

But Albie shrank from even imaginary contact. How could he report that he had not played tennis, or ask to come home? In his mind's eye anger contorted his father's face, the scene darkened into confusion and scraps of images as the static of a mistuned radio and the shriek of loudspeakers in the mess hall became nothing.

He tried again. His mother made her clumsy way toward him, carrying her familiar glass of water with ice cubes. The apartment corridor at home became the corridor between the feet of the Panthers' beds. In her flowing white robe, she passed Uncle Jesse's bed and Walter, Philip and William, who whispered together. She ignored them all, and they fell silent. Albie's mother had come to save him! The boys wondered as she made her way toward Albie's cot.

His mother's image sipped from her glass and glided past the foot of Albie's bed to touch Raddy's head. She muttered, 'Tsk, tsk,' before her disjointed gait carried her out the door, where she floated off into the dark woods.

When Albie stopped crying the shadows were longer. No one would seek him out to force him to the waterfront. His breath trembled. In mid-afternoon, second period, the cabins stood empty. Joe might be reading in Woodsmen or wandering in the woods. Albie strained to hear. Did Joe really lie behind the backstop to hear the impacts of bullets? If Albie were now fifty short feet from a firing squad of Panthers, he would stand up and die. A greasy lead bullet would strike his heart to free him in one cataclysmic jolt from the misery that was Camp Bear Lake. That hot impact would expunge all the pain. A bitter happiness flooded him as he imagined his father and mother uncertain how to act, impotent to call back his brave immolation.

He picked himself up to a crouch and scurried through the bottom of the forest to a rock fence that ran toward the corner of the lake. From its end it was twenty yards to the path to Leech Beach. Albie sprinted to the cover of bushes to lie flat in the dirt. An aide painting a wooden shack near the lake didn't see him.

In a moment Albie found a deer path further from the lake than the well-worn trail. Now he rounded the corner, ducked from tree to tree; once he gained thick forest beyond the cabins, he walked more easily. After a quarter mile he stopped to listen to the wind in the trees. Leaves rustled ahead; a twig cracked behind him. He saw nothing. Ahead the hard path skirted a marsh; he crossed it on stones and firm patches to gain the shore.

Out on the water longer and stronger arms than Albie's drove two gleaming red canoes across the blue lake. Eight older boys and a counselor plied paddles and cried out with each stroke. Their cry sounded like "War! War!" although it was more likely "Row! Row!" Sun flashed in the spray at their bows; two wakes intersected in a tweed of ripples as the others slid away to leave Albie by himself.

Acorns littered the ground; Albie recognized an oak tree. An acorn bounced off a tree trunk. Its woody tap against the tree announced his one human friend. "Where are you?" Albie called.

"Come down to the water," Joe called.

The land grew soft and wet. Albie took off his sneakers and socks. "Over here."

A bright flash from fifteen yards away made him blink. When his vision cleared he still could not see his friend. "What was that?"

"A signal mirror." Joe stood up between the boles of two large trees at the water's edge. Albie scrambled along the shore.

"You have to go in the water."

Lily pads grew under shade in the small cove. Albie extended a foot into dark water. Muck oozed up between his toes; he grabbed for the tree and handed his sneakers around it. The water was knee deep, thigh deep, touched the hem of his shorts before the bottom firmed. Albie sat with Joe on dry ground between the two trees.

"What happened to your face?" Joe extended a mirror the size of a large index card. It had small orange printing on its black back and a circle you could see through with cross hairs in the center. The printing was instructions on how to signal.

Joe pushed the mirror down. "Be careful, don't signal them or they'll see us."

The glass side showed Albie his forehead, nose, and chin black with dirt. One grimy cheekbone bore a red scrape the size of the circle on the mirror. The wound had pierced Albie's perimeter; now he could not be sure he would survive. Albie restrained a sob.

"Wash in the lake," Joe said.

In water up to his thighs Albie lifted cool water to his face with cupped hands. Twice, three times it stung his cheek and wet his shirt. "Up here." Joe pointed to his own brow. Albie washed.

Back on the bank, the air smelled sweet and soggy. Dragonflies hung over the lily pads, and the sun combed bright and black ripples between them. Up the lake paddles splashed and voices cried "War! War!"

"I threw it to the wrong base, so it wasn't a double play," Albie said.

Joe picked his nose. "What happened to your face?"

"Raddy Tarrant beat me up."

Albie thought Joe was trying to look at him with both eyes. Joe took his slingshot out of his pocket and fired a pebble at a water lily before he offered it to Albie. Dirty string wound round and round to fasten the rubber to itself through slits in the leather. Albie gripped the wooden handle and wondered whether he would be strong enough to pull the rubber bands.

"Here," Joe said.

Albie squeezed the pebble in the leather pouch and pulled. The tension between his left hand, the rubber, the muscles of his left forearm and right arm, the balance, all were different from riflery. There was no sight. Through the crotch of the slingshot he saw that his left elbow was straight, and lost his grip on the pouch. The stone flew away and tore through the leaf of a lily pad with a zip! before it sank with a gurgle. Something white fluttered in the air, then landed on a blossom near where the pebble had hit.

"Thanks," Albie said.

"You could kill him," Joe said.

Joe's matter-of-fact tone shocked Albie until he decided it was an imaginary game. "I could shoot him with a rifle, but I'd get caught."

"You could shoot him with a slingshot."

"Could you kill somebody with a slingshot?"

"If you hit him in the eye," Joe said, "if it went in the brain."

"He doesn't have a brain," Albie said. "He's a moron."

Water lapped the shore. The breeze that whispered above the boys carried faint cries from the ball field; distant reports of rifle fire could have come from a radio in another apartment. Albie's lip felt thick. His tongue sliding over his teeth found staleness instead of salty blood.

Albie studied his face again. Sunlight that brightened his tan cheek lit the oozing scrape a vivid red. When he lifted his swollen lip away from his teeth with dirty fingertips he saw a black and blue mark inside, and a scarlet cut. A pulse of rage, a wish to inflict such a wound, rose and faded.

The far side of the lake lay in shadow. The returning war canoes were no color at all. "What's over there?" Albie asked.

"They do secret Indian stuff during Color War," Joe said. "The only way to get there is in the war canoes, so you have to pass the swimming test, and I didn't last year." He faced away from Albie. "In the Color War I was gray, and we were behind, but it was close. They give points for everything you do, I could have gotten twenty points for passing the swimming test during Color War, but I didn't. They took off five points if you don't go in the war canoe, so we lost those points. Bobby was the crimson captain in the junior camp. He wanted to beat me up, so I ran away."

"Can you swim?"

"Yes."

"Why didn't you pass the swimming test?"

"I don't feel like it." He broke a stick and traced a pattern on his forearm with the sharp end.

Albie could imagine no greater gift than to be able to throw with precision, to swing the bat cleanly to bring forth the decisive crack!, to run with grace, to drop to the ground and slide without fear: to have a normal body. "Why not?"

Joe worked on his forearm with the stick. Albie raised himself up: the pattern was an 'L' with an extra line going the other way at the top. The white pattern on Joe's golden skin reddened and oozed blood. Joe added a long line that crossed the upright of the 'L' and short lines at its ends. A cross, with short lines all going the same way: a swastika.

"What's that?" Albie said. "Isn't that a Nazi thing?"

Joe scraped until all four limbs of the swastika were bleeding. "It means I don't feel pain."

Albie hadn't known that his cheek was hurt until he saw himself in Joe's mirror. He examined his red wound again, and peered through the half-silvered circle in the mirror's center at the dark image of the far side of the lake. The shadowed trees and returning war canoes framed a face older than the one he remembered from his bedroom at home.

He comforted his swollen lip with the cool mirror. He tilted it so he could see the scrape on his cheek at the same time as the mutilation Joe still inflicted on his forearm. "I don't feel pain, either," Albie said. It was true when he said it, but how far would he dare to follow Joe into that unknown?

After dinner, after free time, after pajamas and the latrine, after the horseplay that preceded taps, after a story if Uncle Jesse were to read one, came the silence of the night. But not right away.

"All right, that's it, shut up," Uncle Jesse called from outside the cabin. He read his magazine with the woman with long gloves on the cover in the light from a bare bulb until the night patrol counselor came to murmur with him. After they looked in and moved away the boys were alone.

"Hey, let's french Uncle Jesse's bed!" Raddy whispered.

"Hey, two pop flies, Coop's no batter," Will Hobeck whispered.

"No batter! No batter!"

"Hey Coop, why didn't you hit a home run?"

"Hey Jerry, why didn't you hit the ball?"

"Do we have swimming first period tomorrow?" Mike Wooley said.

"Second period," Philip Mullaly said.

"Hey, Yogi!"

"He's asleep." Raddy got out of bed and jumped on Jerry. "We gotta warm up, hey, Jerry!"

A fist hit flesh. Raddy's feet bumped the wooden floor. Sheets and blankets rustled. Raddy again: "Hey, Greenberg! When are you gonna pass the swimming test?"

Albie played possum.

"We can't go in the war canoe until everybody passes and you're the last one."

"Can't throw, can't swim!" Will chanted.

"Can't throw, can't swim! Can't throw, can't swim! Can't throw, can't swim!"

Albie buried his face in his pillow to wait for the silent part of the night to bring him dreams as rich and colorful as his dreams in his red enamel bed at home. He missed his creamy linoleum with its pattern of red ships surrounded by black flourishes. But in those in-between moments after the silence of the other Panthers told him he was safe from attack and before real sleep, he visited his real home.

Prone, right cheek on his pillow, his sheet and heavy blue blankets protecting the back of his neck and his bony shoulder blades, Albie breathed air his own breath had warmed, and breathed it again. The damp pillowcase reminded him of when he used to suck his thumb with a corner of the sheet clamped in his fist. His arms, his thighs, even his hands relaxed; his breathing became less careful, more rhythmic as his small chest rose and fell on a current of life and his simple cot floated on rusty iron legs out on the lake beyond the waterfront. He bobbed on soft dark water out of sight of the dock and the boys in their crimson bathing suits and the counselors with their whistles and tests he must pass.

His bed became a war canoe made of the white bark of birches, ribbed inside with wood like his own ribs that pressed through thin flesh to sustain his rising and falling. Strong, dimly seen lodge brothers knelt behind him in the great canoe. Silent, graceful, as powerful as Cooper Brown, they drove him forward with strokes of broad paddles. He breathed in, and the canoe rushed forward with a frightening acceleration; he exhaled, and the craft glided through glassy water and the whirlpools the paddles cut disappeared astern.

The sunlit waterfront fell behind as the great canoe carried him to the far side of the lake. In the dimness of early morning the fleet glided to a stop in sandy shallows. Under overhanging trees, canoes and paddlers melted away to leave him alone, barefoot and naked, but as warm as he was in bed, to walk ashore among woodland creatures who did not fear him. He knelt to stroke their soft fur. He lifted a chipmunk to feel its heart beat raprapraprap through tiny ribs, and held it against his cheek and lip so it could feel that he would not hurt it.

Alone, he pressed further into misty woods to meet Joe Moscow. Joe's hair was a stubble as always, but a single beam of daylight from above the lake lit his straight and shining hazel eyes, as he strode toward Albie, tanned and glowing, his palms turned forward. Joe knew what Albie did not. Joe would teach him secrets of the dark wood and what lay beyond. Albie, in peace, moved forward to embrace that knowledge as the mists thickened into a bulwark that shielded them from the camp on the far side of the lake.

Boys crowded up the stairs to breakfast. Albie and Joe would cut baseball together. Joe put his finger to his lips. "Where we were before."

"Where we were before," Albie murmured to the friend he had made, and savored the elliptic reference to matters of importance. Things would be different now.

They made their way west along the water. A man Albie did not recognize, in a tan shirt and a cap with a long brim like a bird's beak, fished from a green rowboat anchored off Leech Beach. The boys scuttled through bushes until they had passed him, through woods so deep even their Indian eyes could not discern a path. A point of land concealed them from the far side of the lake. Trees here hung out over the water. The sun near its zenith cast hard shadows on the water and clumps of grass in the warm place where they took off their shoes and socks and shirts. Albie extended the two sour balls from his pocket to Joe.

"Which one do you want?" Joe asked.

Albie hoped Joe would take the yellow one. "I don't care."

Joe closed his eyes and groped for Albie's hand. He touched the red sour ball, released it, took the yellow one, unwrapped it and put it in his mouth.

Albie's red sour ball was so sour it could as well have been lemon.

"Which one did I get?" Joe said.

"Can't you tell?"

"You taste it."

The startling idea violated a rule. Albie closed his eyes, extracted the sour ball from his mouth, and held it out; in a moment Joe tapped the other sour ball against his teeth. Joe's lips were wet on his finger. Joe's teeth opened. The new sour ball, definitely lemon, drew from Albie a welling up of saliva. He was ready to bite down to crush it when Joe said around his sour ball, "Switch?"

Albie opened his eyes. Joe held out the red sour ball. They exchanged again. Albie bit down as soon as he had the red one in his mouth and delighted in the vivid cherryness; when it faded, his teeth stuck together.

"They say you shouldn't share stuff," Albie said after the sugar dissolved.

"Indian scouts share what they have." Joe tilted his light bulb head and smudged cheek to one side. The bulletin board of his flat left forearm bore three scratched-in swastikas. The oldest had faded; the second gleamed bright pink on the golden skin, and the newest and smallest, up near the elbow, hid in purple crusts and ooze. Joe followed Albie's glance and picked scab off his newest mutilation.

So carefully had Albie's parents protected him from the forbidden symbol that all it meant to him was rebellion, and the world outside his room. "I want one of those." Albie offered his arm. "You do it."

"I can't." Joe gazed across the lake to the dark, tall trees that concealed the place where Bear Lake did Indian stuff during color war.

Albie touched his shoulder. "I want you to."

"I'm not allowed." Joe hung his head between his thighs and crossed his arms over the back of his neck.

Albie stretched to see Joe's face, but when he saw it was suffused a dark red, he withdrew and blushed himself. "What?" Albie said.

Joe pointed a finger at Albie's face. "Swear to secrecy, pain of death?"

"Swear to secrecy, pain of death."

Out on the lake, the fisherman rowed past the point. Joe waited until he was out of sight. "My friend's mother was taking us to the zoo," he said. "I forgot my magnifying glass, so I scouted to my house from the back and climbed the tree to my window. I was scared, but I got outside of my room, in the tree, and I saw my mother . . ." Joe fell silent.

"I promise I won't tell."

"She took the covers off my bed. Then she took her clothes off, and—"

"Everything?"

"Everything. Then my father came in, and, and she did things with his body and he did things with her body, and I fell out of the tree and they heard me crying, so they told me not to tell the doctor, and that only grownups can do things with other people's bodies."

Albie was on the trail of something important. He remembered the rich darkness of his own parents' bedroom with a strange excitement. He ought not intrude and yet he might ask this friend—but Joe slid away. Albie leaned toward his back. "Were they . . . scratching things on their arms?"

Joe's face was a mask of misery. "She took his pee-pee thing in her mouth, and he did other stuff, and my mother was yelling, I could hear them both yelling before I fell."

"Are you sure?"

"I think so."

Albie wanted to hug Joe to comfort him. He picked at a lichen on the rock he was sitting on. "Then what happened?"

"My mother came out in a bathrobe and told me all that stuff while my father got dressed, then my father stayed with me while my mother got dressed. On the way to the doctor in the car they told me that grownups and doctors could do things to other peoples' bodies, but kids weren't allowed, and nobody could talk about it. The doctor gave me stitches, see?" Joe pointed above his brow where irregular skin underneath his close-cropped hair was lighter than the skin around it.

"I'll tell you how." Joe broke a stick, examined the ends and gave one to Albie. "Start with the up and down part. You don't have to do it hard, as long as you keep doing it."

Albie marked his skin with the stick so his suntan turned white. "It doesn't hurt," he said.

"It'll feel hot after a while."

A breeze rippled the lake as Albie scratched a swastika the size of his thumbnail into the back of his forearm. He moved the twig at Joe's direction until a little blood welled up from each of the four limbs, and each of the cross bars. The wound felt hot, and heavy, but it was not a pain he had to withdraw from. His blood welled up, his blood ran out, but he was alive. The pain didn't frighten him as much as the anger of the other Panthers, or his father's insistence that he play tennis.

"There," Joe said. "Wash it in the lake."

"It might attract leeches." At home Albie's mother cleaned his cuts at the sink and painted them with iodine from a square brown bottle. He remembered the medicinal smell; the glass applicator attached to the cap felt cool before the hot bite of the liquid. But he was in bright sunlight now, and iodine was a dark city thing.

Joe said, "The doctor told me, if you get a cut you should wash it."

Albie waded into shallow water. Sunlight fell between the leaves of trees on the red swastika. Blood darkened and gelled. When it had become a purple crust with substance Albie waded back to Joe, who extended his marked left forearm. They shook left-handed: this tradition they had created required ceremony.

As the boys and counselors shambled back to the cabins from lunch, a white truck with a red light over the cab drove up the hill from the ball field, siren keening. Boys hurried across the road to clear a path as it stopped in front of the Main House. Men in dark blue pants and white shirts with red crosses sewn on the sleeves got out of both sides of the cab and opened the back doors, which had a small oval window near the top.

Uncle Jesse shooed Walter Gardner ahead of him and tried to press Philip Mullaly toward Panthers, but Philip wriggled around him to stare at the word AMBULANCE painted in an arc over a red cross outlined in black.

"Is it polio?" Philip said.

The driver, who wore a white policeman's hat with a red cross above the shiny black brim, slid out a rolled-up canvas stretcher. The men disappeared around the side of the main house.

"Show's over, let's go." Uncle Jesse put a hand on each of Philip and William's shoulders. Philip swatted the hand away.

"Hey," Uncle Jesse said, "you want a noogie?"

Philip's blue eyes were frightened. "My sister had it," he said. "You can't breathe, and you have to be in an iron lung, and your leg doesn't grow and you can't walk. My sister has a big shoe with a metal—" He frowned even harder than before and ran toward the cabin.

Uncle Jesse nudged Albie and Will toward Panthers. When Albie reached the steps of the cabin Uncle Jesse still stared at the open back doors of the ambulance from the edge of the road.

Will held the screen door open. "Did you ever hear of polio?"

"My mother said you shouldn't have your tonsils out in the summer because of polio." Albie said. He was as glad to have something to contribute as he was aware that he didn't know what he was talking about. Inside the bunk he unlaced his shoes for rest period. Philip lay prone on his bed with his face in his pillow. Will asked Wayne whether they took kids' tonsils out in the infirmary.

When Uncle Dan, from Woodsmen, scratched at the screen door, Uncle Jesse shot a warning glance around the cabin before he stepped outside. Walter stood on his bed. "They're whispering!" he announced in a stage whisper. When Uncle Jesse glared in at everyone, the boys pretended to sleep. Right before the end of rest period, Uncle Jesse stood up next to his bed and said, "Listen up, men, I have an announcement. Everybody knows that today is Wednesday, right?"

"Right," Jerry said, "it's the All Star game."

"That was Monday," Raddy said.

"It's Tuesday," Wayne said.

"It's Christmas Day!" Raddy shouted.

"It's the last day of camp!" Mike Wooley shouted.

Uncle Jesse held up his hand. "This is serious, men. It's Wednesday, so everybody has to hand in a letter home before dinner." He surveyed the cabin. "How many have already written the letter?"

Cooper sat impassive. Mike shook his head no.

"Well," Uncle Jesse said, "since Saturday is visiting day—"

The boys clapped and stamped on the wooden floor. "Yay!" Raddy shouted. Albie joined in. "Yay! Yayyy!"

"—and there isn't time for the letters to get home, nobody has to write a letter and we won't have to mail them." Philip, prone on his bed, hugged his pillow and gazed at him with bright blue eyes. Uncle Jesse rubbed his nose. "So if anybody wrote letters today, give them to me."

No one moved or spoke.

"Okay, let's go swimming!" Uncle Jesse cried with a heartiness false than usual. The boys were subdued on their way down the hill. Albie tried to walk with Philip, but Philip hunched his shoulders with his hands in his pockets and kept to himself.

The microphone shrieked. Bear Brewer held it away from him until Mrs. Brewer had adjusted the box at the back of the platform. "Listen up, listen up," Uncle Bear said. "Some of you know that one of the campers"—boys whispered a name—"had to go to the hospital because of ah, an illness."

A boy at the next table whispered, "Polio!" The counselor swatted him. "What's polio?" someone asked.

"We have to be careful you all don't get the infantile, ah, illness," Bear Brewer said, "because last year was the worst—" Mrs. Brewer stopped twisting a white handkerchief and signaled to him. "—the third worst —" She signaled again. He put his hand on the microphone with an amplified 'thump.'

Mrs. Brewer whispered to him and stepped back. Bear Brewer stepped to the front of the elevated platform. "—so the doctor said everybody has to take a pill two times every day."

Mutters and whispers filled the hall until someone shouted "Quiet!" and someone else called out, "What kind of pill?"

Bear leaned over to his wife. When he stood up, he said, "It's a sulfur pill."

"Uncle Jesse?" Mike said.

"What is it?" The counselor's face was pink above the faded red of his sweatshirt.

"I can't take pills."

". . . after dinner and after breakfast," Uncle Bear said, and put down the microphone.

"Don't worry, Wooley," Uncle Jesse said. "We'll figure it out. Take Greenberg here and get the food."

Albie climbed backward over the bench, careful not to jostle either Raddy on his left or Philip on his right. He followed Mike into the kitchen.

"Can you take pills?" Mike asked as they waited in line.

"I just learned," Albie said. "It's not too bad."

"I don't think I can."

"My mother used to mush up aspirins in apple sauce," Albie said.

"You tasted it?" Mike stared at Albie with respect. "What was it like?"

"Kind of sour." At the high counter, an assistant counselor lifted down the heavy bowls the cooks put out. Mike and Albie carried them back to Uncle Jesse, who served out the boiled carrots and mashed potatoes with meat loaf and a thin red sauce he ladled from a soup bowl.

"That ain't ketchup," Jerry Roth said from the far end of the table.

"Oh yeah, what is it?" Mike said.

"Blood."

Four

"No it isn't," Mike said.

"It is," Raddy said. "When I went to the nurse with a bloody nose she put it in a big glass jar. I saw her."

"No you didn't." Mike lacked conviction.

"Yeah," Jerry said, "they get girls' blood from across the lake."

Raddy made a face and rolled his eyes. "They get blood instead of ketchup from nosebleeds, and from girls, and," —he made the face again —"they get blood from kids with polio." Mike paled. Philip clutched his cross and made a little sound. Raddy stood up and pointed a table knife at Mike. "That's how you find out you got polio. They call you down to the nurse and she takes out all your blood, to put in the ketchup."

Uncle Jesse pointed a finger at Raddy. Raddy dipped bread into the ketchup, and made growling sounds as he ate it. Uncle Jesse slammed the table. "You want a noogie, Tarrant?"

Raddy rolled his eyes.

When the boys passed their empty plates, Albie put the silverware in the mashed potato bowl while Mike scraped leftovers into the carrot bowl with a rubber spatula. "It's not true," Albie murmured when he caught Mike's eye. Philip touched Albie's shoulder with a hopeful smile.

"Yes – it – is!" Raddy shouted from the other end of the table.

"It's not!"

"I said, hold it down!" Uncle Jesse grabbed Albie's thin upper arm. "You're cruising for a bruising." Albie recoiled. Uncle Jesse shook him and let go.

It was Mike's job to carry the bowls and dishes back to the kitchen in two trips, and Albie's to wipe the table clean with a damp rag from a pail in the kitchen before an adult carried a tray of individual desserts to each table. The sweet, corrupt smell of the dishrag was perfectly distinctive, like its gray color and stringy texture. The public address system squealed while Albie was still wiping. Bear Brewer and his wife both leaned over the box behind the platform. The boys fell quiet as more electronic bleats sounded.

". . . each table," Bear Brewer said. "There's chocolate ice cream for dessert!"

Many boys cheered. But instead of dessert, the waiters brought each table a full pitcher of water and an envelope. Mike pushed away from the table, but the weight of four other boys held the bench still. "Uncle Jesse?" Mike said.

"There's one pill here for everybody," Uncle Jesse said. "Fill up your

glasses. Take one from the envelope, don't drop it, hold it up where I can see it. When I say, you take the pill, like this." He rested a shiny white tablet larger than an aspirin on his tongue, and looked from face to face around the table before he swallowed it with water. "Any questions?"

Mike held on to the edge of the table with one hand and raised the other as if he were in school.

"Wooley?"

"I can't—"

Albie, beside Mike, could hardly hear his voice. "They're gonna suck all your blood out," Raddy said.

Uncle Jesse passed the envelope. Albie wondered whether the pill would crumble on his tongue. "Ready," Uncle Jesse said.

Mike sobbed and set his pill on the table in front of him.

"Now!" Uncle Jesse said. Albie opened his mouth. His tongue stretched near his back teeth. Willing himself not to taste, he closed his eyes tight, placed the sulfur pill on the back of his tongue, and didn't gag even though he wanted to. The first swallow of cold water scratched the pill against the back of his mouth, but the second washed it down. Albie opened his eyes.

Uncle Jesse studied the boys, one by one. Philip frowned, his lips pressed tight. Raddy's pill was gone. Jerry grinned. Will was pale; he was cleaning his glasses on his shirt. Mike hunched on the bench squinting at his big white pill, which rested on the table like a full moon in the night sky.

"I can't take it, Uncle Jesse," he said.

"Let's go, Wooley, straighten up and fly right."

Boys at the other tables had taken their pills. Trays of chocolate ice cream were coming from the kitchen. "Hurry up," Jerry said.

At the pace of a man approaching the gallows Mike picked his water glass. He inched the pill toward the air between his open jaws, tongue extended, but he did not put it down. Albie thought he was holding his breath.

"Now!" Uncle Jesse said.

Mike gagged and dropped the pill. He tried to drink from the tumbler but he had not filled it. He gagged again and vomited on the table.

"Pee-yoo!" Jerry leaned away. Albie swallowed hard and tried not to breathe. Mike was crying.

"Jesus Christ! Clean that up!" Uncle Jesse's cheeks flared even redder than usual.

The pill lay in the vomit. Albie could not move his rag toward the mess. Uncle Jesse gestured to one of the kitchen help, a tall black man with a mustache, who brought Mike a handful of paper towels. The man wrinkled his nose as he cleaned the table with a separate rag and bucket.

"Thanks, Eddie," Uncle Jesse said. "We need another sulfur pill."

The other boys watched in silence as Eddie brought back the pill with a tray of desserts. Uncle Jesse stood behind Mike for his next try. The pill fell from Mike's fingers onto the table before he got it to his mouth.

"Go ahead and eat the ice cream," Uncle Jesse said, "except you." Other tables were excusing boys who had finished their ice cream. Uncle Jesse brought a slice of buttered white bread from the kitchen. "Put it in here," he said.

Mike laid the pill on the butter.

Uncle Jesse folded the bread over. "Jesus Christ, even Greenberg can take pills," he said. "Eat it."

Mike nibbled the corner of the bread furthest from the pill.

"More."

Mike retched.

Uncle Jesse shook Mike, who took a big bite. Albie heard the pill crack as Mike bit through it. His jaws closed, but he didn't chew and he had fear in his eyes.

"Okay!" Albie said. "Drink some water."

Mike filled his mouth. There was a pause during which Raddy sniggered. Mike gurgled and swallowed the bite of sandwich, the piece of pill, and the water. He coughed, but that was all.

"Good work." Uncle Jesse pushed the last dish of chocolate ice cream down the table, but Mike shook his head. The boys at the other end of the table scuffled for it. Albie had seen Mike drop the rest of the sandwich on the floor, but he didn't say anything.

"Excused," Uncle Jesse said.

Albie carried the dustpan and William wielded the broom as they moved the morning dust toward sunlight that slanted through the blue column of Uncle Charlie's pipe smoke. The boys strained to hear what he muttered to Uncle Jesse.

"Upstate New York is worse than last year," the head counselor said, and noticed them. "Get out of here, will you?" The two men ambled outside. William pushed his glasses farther up on his face, and peered through the screen door, and Albie listened too. Uncle Charlie pointed a finger. "Get out of here," he repeated.

Mike Wooley scuffed two paths through the dirt on the way to dinner. Albie ran back to walk beside him. "What's the matter?"

"Uncle Jesse said if I throw up he'll give me a noogie." His eyes were sad. "I can't help it."

The dust Mike kicked up smelled dry, even in the late afternoon air. In his imagination Albie reviewed the gallery of mess hall odors: faint disinfectant at the beginning of the meal; the soapy smell of oval crockery bowls newly filled with mashed potatoes; damp rags, Mike's vomit. He winced. "Why don't you practice?"

"It wouldn't work."

"You could roll up a little piece of bread. If it didn't work you could eat it."

Mike kept one hand in his back pocket and rubbed the other round and round through his light brown hair. "It wouldn't be a real pill."

The bell rang while they dried their hands on gray roller towels. Albie tugged Mike's shirt sleeve. "Sit next to me," he said. "You pretend and I'll take your pill."

Mike brightened on their way up the stairs, but slumped again as they approached the table. "What if we get caught?"

Albie pushed him ahead to two seats together at the far end and shushed him as an older camper on the platform asked God's blessing on the food.

Bear Brewer switched the microphone back on while the tables were being cleared. "It has come to our attention," he managed to say before the loudspeaker shrieked. "It has come to our attention that some campers have not taken the sulfur pills."

Albie and Mike glanced at each other.

"The pills are very important." Bear Brewer touched his brow with a red bandanna. "As you know, one of the campers had to go to the hospital in an ambulance." He paused. "That's why we take pills. So if any boy has trouble, raise your hand, and the nurse will help those boys take their pills in the infirmary."

Only two hands went up in the whole mess hall. "It isn't a real nurse," an older boy nearby said. "It's Mrs. Brewer." Everyone pretended they hadn't heard. Mike nudged Albie with his knee and mouthed 'okay.' One aide wiped the Panthers' table as another handed Uncle Jesse the envelope and nodded at Mike. "Him?"

"Wooley! You want to go to the nurse?" Uncle Jesse said. That sounded like a threat to Albie.

Mike shook his head.

"You ain't gonna york again?"

Mike avoided Uncle Jesse's eye. Raddy got up. "I don't want him yorking on me."

"Sit down." Uncle Jesse tore the envelope open.

"I want to go first," Philip said.

"Show us how it's done," Uncle Jesse said. "I want to see that sulfur pill on your tongue."

Philip pressed his narrow lips together as he accepted the pill. He picked up his water tumbler, stuck out his tongue, placed the pill and turned left and right so all the Panthers could see it before he swallowed water. "Down the hatch," he said.

"Who's next?" Uncle Jesse said.

"Please," Philip said. "Just swallow it fast."

Raddy pointed past Albie's face at Mike. "Uncle Jesse, he didn't take one."

"I'm going to," Mike said.

"I want to be next," Albie said.

Uncle Jesse passed a pill down the table. Raddy rubbed it with his thumb before he gave it to Albie. Albie rested it on his tongue, closed his eyes tight and made a face as he swallowed. "I did it!" he said.

Raddy clapped. "He's a sulfur pill genius! Too bad he can't throw." He stood up and mimed a hard throw at Albie, who flinched.

"Sit down," Uncle Jesse said. "You ready, Wooley?" He passed a pill.

"You better take it." Philip said.

Mike took a deep breath, put his left hand to his mouth and pressed his lips together. He seized his water tumbler with his right hand and drank while he passed the pill to Albie under the table. He drank until the tumbler was empty, and still held it up against his mouth.

"You okay?" Uncle Jesse squinted.

"He didn't swallow it," Wayne said. "I saw."

"I saw too," Walter said.

Uncle Jesse put both his palms on the table, half stood, and leaned forward. "Okay, Wooley, open your mouth. Stick out your tongue."

Mike stuck out his empty tongue and turned left and right, the way Philip had.

"It's in the glass," Wayne said.

Walter grabbed Mike's glass.

"It's empty," Philip said. "He took it. Good work!" He clapped, and all the boys applauded. Uncle Jesse tousled Mike's hair before he passed the next pill.

Dessert was a biscuit with blueberries and whipped cream. Albie clasped Mike's pill in his left hand and passed dishes with his right. That he had broken a rule for his friend was no problem, noble even. But he had told Mike that he would take the pill, so to put it in his pocket and dispose of it later would be dishonest. He must redeem his pledge with a feat of strength, like when Cooper lifted the canoe.

The other Panthers finished their desserts, licked the dishes and spoons, jostled and joked. Uncle Jesse's unfocused eyes drifted toward the screened window behind the next table.

The pill softened in Albie's sweaty palm. He reached for his water glass, still a third full, and glanced right and left as the boys stacked their empty dishes together. No one watched him. He sipped, and brought his left hand to his mouth.

The pill landed close to the tip of his tongue. He would have to taste it to swallow it.

Raddy's dish knocked the stack over.

Albie gagged. The huge white pill landed amidst the crockery with an audible click. Albie slapped his hand over it. Uncle Jesse hadn't seen.

"He didn't take his pill!" Wayne cried.

"Yes he did," Philip said.

"He got another pill!" Raddy shouted. Albie flushed as red as Uncle Jesse. "In his hand!" Raddy twisted Albie's wrist in an Indian burn. "Let it go!"

Albie dropped the pill. One by one, the Panthers turned from the pill to Mike. "I get it," Walter said with delight. "It wasn't his pill, it was *his* pill!" He tugged his brother's shoulder. "Right, Waynie, it's *his* pill, right?"

"Right," Uncle Jesse said. "Wooley, that's a noogie. Greenberg, that's a noogie. Wooley, take that pill now!" Uncle Jesse pushed his way behind the bench to make a fist and hit the side of Mike's arm hard enough to shake his trunk. Mike flushed but he didn't cry. "You gonna do it?" Uncle Jesse said.

Mike shook his head.

"Hey, Eddie! We need a rag and a bread and butter." Uncle Jesse held Mike by the collar of his tee shirt and glowered at Albie. "You're next," he said.

Eddie brought rags, a pail and a buttered slice of white bread. "Don't let him mess again, okay?"

Uncle Jesse plucked the pill off the damp table and folded it into the bread. The rags Eddie spread in front of Mike smelled sour, like some harsh kind of soap.

"I ain't sitting here," Raddy said, and climbed back over his seat and around the other side of the table.

Uncle Jesse slapped the bread into Mike's hand. "Go," he said.

Mike rolled sad eyes upward before he ate it, bite by bite. Albie saw him pause, so he knew which bite contained the pill. Mike got it down. Eddie collected his rags and the dessert dishes, and was gone.

"Now for you." Uncle Jesse moved toward Albie. Albie could not control his trembling. Where was his credit for loyalty to Mike, for being normal? He couldn't speak. The other tables had been dismissed; the Panthers were restless. "Dismissed," Uncle Jesse said, and in the confusion of the boys getting up he made a fist and hit Albie's skinny arm.

Even in the pain of the blow and the humiliation of getting caught, Albie understood that he had not been hit as hard as Mike. "It's only fair," he thought Uncle Jesse said. It had not been fair. Albie ran from the mess hall to hide his tears.

But in getting hit he had become more like the other boys, and therefore more nearly normal. Two short days remained before visiting day, when he would see his parents. He would not tell them Uncle Jesse had hit him: that would be snitching, and Uncle Jesse and the Panthers would hold him in even greater contempt.

Perhaps he could spread this seed of normalcy to his parents! If by suffering one blow Albie could sweep away the dark sense of strangeness that pervaded his apartment, that hung over his grandparents and his memories, that menaced the safety of his room, well, it would have been worth it.

On visiting day his father would drive the car and his mother would ride beside him. Or would she stay in the back to save the front seat for him? As Albie crossed the road outside the main house he imagined the crunch of gravel as the black car rolled to a stop before him. The doors swung open, one then the other, like the wings of a lazy crow. His mother and father stood before him.

Only two days, only two days. What about Joe's mother and father? Dare he look at them, knowing what they had done? When Albie lifted his hand to Panthers' screen door, his shoulder ached where Uncle Jesse had hit him, so he had to work not to cry at the unfairness as he walked the ten steps to his bed.

In his dream Albie lay safe with his mother on a faded red rubber raft. Warmed by sunshine, they floated together in a soft motion a few yards off the sandy beach of the Nassau Point guest house.

Back when he was too small to go to camp, his mother led him, hand in her hand, down a path that emerged from dark woods into sunlight. Sand edged a blue cove. A rowboat bobbed and gleamed in shallow water. His mother took off blue Chinese pajamas to uncover her bathing suit as he removed his shirt, shorts, and sandals. He smelled her perfume as she retied the drawstring of his bathing suit and poked his belly button.

Together Albie and his mother blew up the raft and carried it over a sand crust that squeaked and cracked under their feet. Nearer the water violet fiddler crabs scrabbled into their holes in the harder wet sand. Ripples tickled his ankles. His mother murmured to him, and bright sun lit his closed eyelids redder than the raft.

He would have slept, but the sun faded, wind howled and the water beneath the raft grew cold. Gray clouds scudded across the sky. Dark shadows slid over the causeway, chilly rain fell and Albie awoke on visiting day morning in bedclothes soaked with urine.

Walter was asleep. Beyond him Uncle Jesse lay on his back, eyes closed, mouth open, hands crossed under his pillow behind his head. Across the aisle Philip whispered to Will, who sat up in bed without his glasses. In morning light the stain on his cheek looked black.

Feigning sleep, Albie flopped over. Raddy was out cold. Beyond him Mike sat up in bed. He opened his mouth, stuck out his tongue, touched it with his finger, put the finger back down on the bed, and closed his mouth: practice for the morning pill. Cooper was out of sight.

Albie rolled back. "Uncle Jesse?"

Neither Walter nor Uncle Jesse moved. Someone walked past outside: almost reveille.

"*Uncle Jesse!*"

Uncle Jesse rubbed an eye with his fist.

Albie wanted to whisper into Uncle Jesse's ear, but he was wet so he stayed in bed. "I wet my bed," he muttered.

Walter sat bolt upright between them. "Sailor!" he brayed, "Sailor! Sailor!"

"Yay, sailor!" Philip cried. Raddy leapt out of bed. "Pee-yoo! I can smell it from here!" He ripped Albie's blankets away to leave him exposed in wet pajamas under a wet sheet.

"Sailor!" Panthers cried. An impassive Cooper Brown watched from his bed over the top of a comic book. Albie closed his eyes and tried not to hear.

"Greenberg!" Uncle Jesse called. "Strip your bed and put the sheets outside, we'll get you new stuff after breakfast."

Reveille sounded. "I can't get dressed because it smells in here," Raddy whined.

Uncle Jesse moved his hand as if to threaten a backhand slap, but that was a joke, too. The fullness behind Albie's eyes threatened more flow, more humiliation as he peeled off his sodden pajamas. Small beads of urine glowed beside blue veins on his smooth abdomen and thighs. He dared not meet anyone's eyes as he dried himself with a towel beside his bed.

Albie lowered the cold pajamas into his laundry bag with his fingertips. His blanket lay on the floor, still secured to the foot of his bed by its hospital corners. When he piled his sheets outside, a tiny boy in Lion Cubs was doing the same thing.

The prayer at breakfast was about honoring your father and your mother. They served pancakes with syrup, and bacon. If Albie held his head right he could see a rainbow in the milk film on the side of his glass in the sunlight that slanted through it. Mike got his pill down on the first try. He touched Albie's shoulder and smiled, but Albie bent his head again.

Bear Brewer spoke over the pubic address system. "As you know, today is visiting day."

"Yayyy!" the campers cried. "Yayyy!" Even Albie managed a "Yay," like an obligatory response to a prayer.

"We had Dr. Meredith, who gave us the sulfur pills, come out here last night." Mutterings of 'polio' arose. "Today he said we have to have a quarantine."

A boy's voice cried, "I don't want a needle." At the sound of a slap, the mess hall fell silent.

"What's a quarantine?" Mike said.

"When you can't go to school with mumps," Will puffed his cheeks out so the purple stain dominated the table. Mike stuck his tongue out at Will.

"Listen up, listen up!" the loudspeakers shrieked. "Your fathers and mothers can see your cabins next visiting day."

For Albie that day would never come. The car would carry him home to the bed he never wet. He would escape the boys who hated him and the counselor who struck him. He would sit in the front seat and hand the coins to the toll collectors. He would roll the window down himself and roll it back up, and watch the red speedometer needle as his father drove them back to the city.

". . . across the road," Bear Brewer said. "Are there any questions?"

The Panthers talked, shouted, raised hands for Uncle Jesse's attention. "Does that mean," Wayne Gardner said.

"Dismissed!" Uncle Jesse stood up. "Let's make the beds, pronto."

If Albie were to run ahead he could exchange his soiled sheets before the crowd of campers gathered to humiliate him. He stepped around Cooper and jostled Raddy on his way down the same stairway boys had smiled and waved from in Bear Brewer's movie. On wings of excitement and anticipation he flew across the road, around trees and small buildings, to grab his damp sheets from the steps of Panthers.

Cold urine drowned summer smells of pine needles and morning sunshine. Albie ignored a Woodsman who cried "Sailor!" at him, but Panthers blocked the path to the laundry cabin. "Ready?" Raddy called. "One, two, *three*!"

"SAILOR!" Panthers shouted in unison.

"Again," Raddy called, "one, two, *three*!" Cooper was with them. Had he shouted 'Sailor,' too? Albie ran off the path and around a picnic table as boys laughed and pointed. Uncle Jesse shooed them toward the cabin, so when Albie, dry-eyed, returned with his clean sheets, the other beds were made and Cooper was sweeping.

"We will visit along the second part of the road, along Yankee Stadium up to the waterfront," Uncle Jesse said. "Uncle Bear will tell the parents to park on the far side and we will remain on the ball field."

Baffled, Albie raised his hand.

"Greenberg?"

Across the cabin Philip's frown twisted so tight that Albie felt he had intruded. His fluttering heart, rapraprap, would not let him ask how he could embrace his mother from across the road. He shook his head.

"No touching," Uncle Jesse said. "It's a quarantine, so you can't give anything to your parents."

Albie missed what Will asked in a rushing which could have been the wind, or could have been within him. He stopped breathing to listen very carefully.

"Yes, if they brought you something I'll bring it across to you, or one of the aides."

Albie imagined himself a movie Indian who stood tall on his own side of the road. A leather strap around his forehead bound his long hair in a slow breeze, as with hard eyes he pointed to his heart with a rigid index finger. 'I,' he signed. He made a fist and held it up, palm forward, because that would mean 'have,' or 'hold.'

'I want to have.' He slid his open palm forward at chest level toward the other side, and up, in a gesture of flying; he brought the hand down and pointed toward his father, who held the keys to the car. 'I want to go with you.' At the end of his utterance he crossed his arms over the fringed leather shirt he wore. Its short sleeves showed the emblem he had scratched on his arm. 'I am a man who feels no pain,' it proclaimed, as the wind swayed his black hair.

Albie picked scab off his forearm to expose a Chinese red line of blood with new pink scar on either side as Uncle Jesse shouted and boys scrambled down the steps. They hastened through the grove of tall pines to the road, where they ran despite Uncle Jesse calling them back. Amazing! The other boys were as anxious to see their families as Albie. Far ahead, past red and yellow archery targets casting shadows across the athletic field at the Indian Campfire circle, adults who were not counselors or aides stood next to unfamiliar automobiles on the grass beyond the ball fields.

The boys hurried forward. Aides stood at intervals along the road, on the near side; a dark green pickup truck with a yellow rotating light on top of the cab rolled up and down between the ball field and the visitors.

"C'mon," Will shouted. Mike ran. The Panthers reached the batting cage of Ebbetts field in a rabble, half running and half walking, when Uncle Jesse stopped them. "Hey, listen up."

"That's mine!" Will pointed across Yankee Stadium, "That one, the blue one, it's a Buick! Mommy!"

"Hey, Hobeck," Uncle Jesse seized his arm and shook him. "I'm warning you."

Will's face reddened around the birthmark. The pickup truck reached the end of the road near the waterfront and drove back the other way, no faster than a man would walk.

Uncle Jesse said, "I don't want anybody crossing the road, because I'll just have to bring you back. I want the Panthers to follow the quarantine." He slapped Mike's back. "Wooley here learned to take his pills, right?" No one answered. "I know you can do it. Any questions?" In the awkward silence Uncle Jesse said, "Okay, let's go."

The Panthers broke for the road. Albie ran through Lion Cubs who waved and called to adults across from them. Ahead were aides, the road, cars. There, there across the road was his mother in front of the black convertible, in a white blouse and red skirt. There was his father in a brown jacket and a brown cap, and a tie with stripes. They were not reaching out for him.

Albie forgot Bear Lake. The flying boy whose sneakered toes barely touched tufts of infield grass was no brave who could feel no pain, but all trembling feeling, all unconsummated union with his mother, until, ready to jump the shallow ditch, he was body checked, and arms around his chest lifted him into the air.

"Good one, Dougie," Uncle Jesse called.

"Mommy!" Albie cried.

"Remember the quarantine," Dougie, the aide, said. "You can't go on the road. I'll put you down."

Not quite able to discern his mother's expression through his tears, Albie howled his message across the no-man's land of the dirt road: "I hate it here! Take me home!"

The green pickup truck rolled up between them and stopped. Uncle Jesse held Albie by his shoulder. Dougie was there. The driver of the truck leaned out the window; his pressed khaki shirt bore a policeman's badge. "Better watch that," he said to Uncle Jesse, "Doc says, any contact, they go in quarantine, too." He beeped the horn and drove off.

Behind the cloud of pickup exhaust—a city smell—his father pushed his mother back to the car with one hand. He swung his other arm. "How's the tennis going?" he called.

Nonplused, Albie watched his father point through the trees toward the girls' tennis court. "I want to go home," he screamed.

His mother touched his father's shoulder and they whispered together. His father reached into the front seat for a paper bag which he waved at Dougie, who had moved down the road.

"*Please*," Albie cried.

"Next time we can see where you live," his mother called across the road in a strange, thin voice. Her eyes glistened. "We can meet your friends."

Dougie investigated the paper bag he carried to Albie. "Lucky you. Hope you'll give me one."

Albie felt lollipops through the bag. He flung it down so hard it tore before it left his grip. "Take me home!" His voice rasped and failed. "I want to go home!"

His mother and father whispered together again. The green pickup truck blocked his view; when it had passed his father stood at the back of the car. They must not have heard him, that was it. He would try the Indian signals. He had two feet of grass before the edge of the road. He moved forward.

"You!" Dougie called from a distance.

Albie glanced toward the voice before he made contact with his mother's eyes. 'I,' he signed, and held up his fist.

His father opened his mouth. The signing didn't work. Albie broke across the road, skidded in the gravel and fell, his hand on his mother's ankle. Uncle Jesse grabbed his leg. Albie gripped and kicked. His mother's stocking tore in his hand as she stepped away. "Please!" he stretched his neck up.

Uncle Jesse lifted him away into a bear hug three feet from his mother. She was crying, too.

"Babble Boy," his father said. "If you stay I'll let you use the binoculars." He dangled the leather case from his hand. "You can watch sports. You can look at the moon."

"I want to come home," Albie sobbed.

"You don't want to quit, son. It will go on your permanent record," Albie's father said. His mother touched his father on the shoulder. "If you want to go to law school," his father said.

Albie struggled harder. Uncle Jesse squeezed him tighter. Albie's father reached the binoculars over the edge of the road to Uncle Jesse. The case swung against Albie's thrashing ankles. Albie's mother sat in the back of the car with her face in her hands. His father got into the driver's seat.

"Take me home," Albie moaned one last time.

Along the part of the road near the stables, the littlest boys in Lion Cubs wailed across the road to their parents. Pinioned by Uncle Jesse, Albie watched the convertible slow behind the pickup truck and beep.

His family rolled out of sight.

A summer breeze chilled his perspiration as he hung limp in Uncle

Jesse's muscular arms. His quiet tears left dark spots on the sleeve of Uncle Jesse's gray sweatshirt and fell with small impacts on his hands and knees. Uncle Jesse frowned after the black convertible as he loosened his grip. Albie's feet touched grass. When Uncle Jesse let go, Albie slumped to the ground.

At the edge of the road a frantic Will pointed to the waterfront and gestured. Near a blue car across the road a man with Will's straight dark hair waved back. He clapped his hands together and moved them up and down over his head in a victory gesture. Further down the road Raddy and Jerry threw a baseball back and forth to the applause of parents across the road from them.

"Show me a screwball," one of the fathers called.

Raddy wound up. His wild throw over Jerry's head bounced and rolled to where Albie slumped in the grass. It bumped against his leg and stopped.

"Let's see the ball," Raddy cried.

Albie turned his back.

"You all right?" Uncle Jesse said.

"Come on, son, throw the ball," a father called.

Albie's hand shook as he threw it with his elbow close to his side. It landed on the road well to Jerry's right and half way to the bigger boy.

Jerry, Raddy, and the father all shouted. The father stepped onto the road to field the ball, when Uncle Jesse shouted, "Don't touch it!" He bounded over Albie's legs, scooped up the ball, and flipped it to Raddy. His face was red when he came back to Albie. "Here." He dangled the battered brown binocular case by its strap. "You gotta work on that pitching arm."

Albie could not bear Uncle Jesse's gray eyes. With the case beneath him, he lay prone with his face in the grass and didn't listen to anything.

On the evening of the first visiting day of the summer, Albert Greenberg lay prone on the third cot on the right side of Panthers. The bare bulb on its wire cast the black shadow of his head on the small territory he must defend where his arms encircled the battered brown leather case that contained his father's precious binoculars.

Somewhere in the cabin William's voice asked, "What did you get?"

A pause. Mike said, "Checkers."

"Can I see?"

After the hollow bump of the cardboard box cover on the floor, the thin clicks of the checkers sounded like plastic, not wood. Albie imagined the feel of the sharp edges of their molded crowns. He wished for Mike to ask him, Albie, to play—but to stand up and leave the binoculars exposed would risk their loss.

And bring him ridicule. The others would see that his father had entrusted him with a magnificent adult possession that made him different the way his rich blue blankets separated him from Cooper. Raddy would snatch the leather case and hold it out of Albie's reach. He would cry, "Saloojee!" and lob it over Albie's head to Jerry. Jerry would hold it beyond Albie's skinny arms and grin at Albie's helplessness without malice, but he would toss to Wayne. Wayne would purse his bluish lips at Albie, slide the beautiful instrument out of the case and flip it to Raddy, who would turn aside at the last second to let the binoculars crash to the floor. Raddy, innocent as an angel, because Uncle Jesse would have come in the door.

What pain Albie would feel when his father's binoculars shattered! He would suffer the shame of explanation, and his father's turbulent wrath at betrayal! The Panthers would rage at Albie because he had accepted something better than what they had. Uncle Jesse would rage because of the disturbance. Albie would never get to inspect life from a high place above the noisy conflict of the Panthers, above Bear Lake and the Color War. They would smash his father's binoculars, and Albie would never understand.

Inch by inch he bent the elbow that supported his weight until his finger reached the catch on the leather case. You pushed a spring-loaded brass button shaped like a shield so the flat edge slipped under a brass barrier to allow the flap to open. The catch made a thin, high-pitched sound as it released. Albie inhaled the subtle aroma of the old leather case, so unlike the brilliant reek of his new mitt.

Pressure of the binoculars had flattened the nap of the red velvet lining into a gray triangle that matched the edge of the lens. A piece of chamois darkened by time to the brown of his father's meerschaum pipe was wadded into a ball that concealed the way its edges had been cut in a zig-zag. Afraid that one of the other boys would see, he pulled the case closer under him.

With his face buried in his pillow he tried to remember the exact white numbers around the eyepieces, and the gliding resistance of the focusing knob. Was it stiffer than he remembered, or easier to turn? He wanted to touch the wrinkled black body of the binoculars with his fingertip.

The hard case became uncomfortable. Albie propped himself up, opened the case and slid the binoculars out onto his blue blanket. With awe he turned the knurled ring with his index finger. It was easy! Joyful, the cold barrel in his hand, he sat up. Cooper was drawing on a pad with colored pencils. Albie focused. Cooper's hand, and the pad, and Cooper's knee filled the circle with the searing clarity he loved.

He guided the circle of his attention to Jerry's bed to watch the checker game. Jerry's hand was a pink blob that rushed into the circle to move a man, and vanished. Mike's hand appeared and withdrew. Albie traced the hand, the forearm, the shoulder, the face. Mike gaped back at him.

"Look what he's got!" Mike bawled as he ran to the foot of Albie's bed.

Will leaned over Mike's shoulder. Albie wanted to examine Will's birthmark with the binoculars, but the light behind him shadowed it. Cooper stood there too, and Jerry.

"They're binoculars," Albie said.

"Wow." Philip stood on the end of Mike's bed to see better. "Where did you get them?"

"My father gave them to me," Albie said. "They're really his."

"My father calls them glasses," Cooper said. "He takes them when he goes birding in the cemetery."

"Birding?" Raddy leaned against the wall on the far side of his bed and extended his hand. "Let me see."

Surely Albie's father would forbid Albie to surrender control of the binoculars, but their very value might earn him a chance to live at Bear Lake. "Tomorrow," he said. "I'll show everyone how they work when the light is better."

"Can everyone look through them tomorrow?" Jerry asked.

"Yes," Albie said.

FIVE

*If there is a story . . . it will take something of a storyteller at this
date to find it, and it is not easy to imagine what impulses
would lead him to search for it. He probably should be an old
storyteller, at least old enough to know that the problem of
identity is always a problem, not just a problem of youth, and
even old enough to know that the nearest anyone can come to
finding himself at any given age is to find a story that somehow
tells him about himself.*

– NORMAN MACLEAN, *YOUNG MEN AND FIRE*

The blue cast of early morning light meant a clear day at Bear Lake Camp.
Dust motes floated in a ray of sunshine; the summer air was cool and
fresh. The bulk of the binocular case reminded Albie in his cot that Visiting
Day had come and gone; he drew in a convulsive breath and controlled
himself so he wouldn't cry. He was the first one awake.

His father had driven the car away toward the city and left Albie here.
Albie could not escape. As long as he didn't get polio he would survive to
go home; it was only a question of time. Under the covers his thighs and
knees felt no skinnier than normal, so he didn't have polio yet. He eased
into clothes and touched the binocular case under his pillow before he
tiptoed out of the cabin barefoot to put on his shoes at a picnic table.

Bear Brewer announced that because the disease in the camp had sent
parents home, the day would be an ordinary Sunday, so the boys would
bathe as usual. Someone asked a question from the other side of the
mess hall.

"No," Bear Brewer said. "Definitely not." He pulled the microphone
cord to free a tangle and walked to the front of the small platform. "A boy
has asked whether anyone with the disease is still in the camp. The answer
is no. One boy had the disease, but he went to the hospital, so he isn't in
the camp."

Another question came from the same table. Bear Brewer assured everyone that no germs remained in camp.

"Ask why we still have to take the pills," Albie said.

"Uncle Jesse?" Philip said. "If the germs are gone, why are we still taking the sulfur pills?"

Uncle Jesse shook his head with an irritated expression. Philip raised his hand. Albie could tell the only reason Bear Brewer faced the Panthers was that he didn't want to attend to the table the other questions had come from.

Philip waved his hand in the air. "Ooh!"

"A question over there."

Philip stood up. An aide put the envelope of pills on the table in front of Uncle Jesse. "Uncle Bear?" Philip said.

The hall fell quiet.

"If the germs are gone, why do we still have to take the sulfur pills?"

Uncle Bear leaned over the railing at the side of the platform to hand the microphone to Mrs. Brewer. The loudspeakers transmitted a harsh scraping before her voice came over the system. "Just in case," she said.

Bear took back the microphone. "Just in case. We're taking the pills just in case, because that's what Dr. Meredith said."

Philip touched his cross. One by one the Panthers swallowed the sulfur pills. Mike got his down even though Raddy tickled him.

On the way back from Leech Beach the undergrowth grew thick between the trail and Albie's great trees at the edge of the water. The bushes and thorns were too dense to see through, but he could find his way to his hidden place on the shore from a faint side trail.

He slowed to let the other Panthers go ahead, so he was walking among bigger boys who paid him no attention. A glance over his shoulder revealed no counselors: he jumped into the bushes.

In hiding, he took inventory: dirty underwear, a towel, and a soap dish in hand; his clasp knife in the pocket of his shorts. He had six books on his shelf and a pair of real binoculars under his pillow. He had shelves of books and a library card at home.

He fingered the contour of the knife through his shorts. The other articles he carried weren't important. He could not see the books, or the binoculars, but he remembered them in as much beloved detail as he could see the towel and soap dish he carried. In his mind he stroked the copy of Tanglewood Tales that had been his mother's, delighted in the old-fashioned type and smelled the musty greenish buckram.

In his head he rehearsed the story about a young hero in a forest. When the woods quieted, he tucked the towel bundle under his arm and retraced his steps on the main trail toward Leech Beach. If Joe were here they could work along the shore from two directions, and call to each other when they found a way.

He knelt. A tunnel between two patches of thorns led to something less than a path toward the water. Short of the bank the thorns and bushes yielded to a grassy oval the size of his bed at home. To his right the two huge willows stood with their roots in the lake; showers of their tiny green leaves concealed the grassy spot from the lake and the camp.

The grass stopped where the bank of dark earth and pebbles tumbled over to fall two feet to water dense with lily pads. Albie smoothed folds from his towel to lie prone on it in his clean tee shirt. The water in this shaded place was cooler on his hand than the bath he had just taken. The bottom was slimy stones, not dirt. Across the lake at Mistlewood he made out individual figures in three small canoes and a rowboat.

One insect buzzed and another scritched, but he heard no human sound. The vegetable smell of the lake oppressed him until he accepted it as an object of interest to be examined. He remembered his mother's mythology book again. Bright green lily pads moved on the dark water. Here and there a white flower glowed, a plume on the helmet of a soldier of the dragon's teeth. Large insects flew around the lilies: he would come back with the binoculars to examine them in detail, and he would show them to Joe.

Straight overhead the branches of the willow covered him; the sun that lit the patch of grass entered between the foliage on two major branches of the tree. The two trunks to his right were as fixed as the wall between his room and his parents'. The opening to the lake, like his window, let him see without being seen. This is my place, Albert Greenberg thought. This is my place.

At rest period, light from the uphill door silhouetted Uncle Jesse with his hands on his hips. "Close your eyes," he said. "You're gonna need your rest."

"Why?" Mike Wooley said. "What are we doing this afternoon?"

"We're playing ball. Even though your folks can't watch we have an exhibition game with the Lion Cubs and Woodsmen."

"All of us?" Cooper Brown said. "Isn't that too many?"

"You'll choose up teams and take turns. Quiet down now." He left the cabin.

"I'll be the captain," Raddy said.

"They'll pick captains from Woodsmen because they're older," Philip said.

"Let's pick teams for now," Raddy said. "Who wants to be the other captain?"

"I do," Philip and Wayne Gardner said simultaneously.

"Choose you," Wayne said. "I got odds, one, two three, shoot!"

They extended fingers.

"Two out of three," Philip said. "one, two, three, shoot!"

"I win!" Wayne cried. "I want—"

"Three out of five."

"No fair, you didn't call it."

"Wayne's the captain," Raddy said. "Now we choose who picks first."

Albie wrapped his thin arms around his pillow and the binocular case as he lay on his side. He would be chosen last and he would embarrass whichever team had him. The other Panthers squabbled over the teams. ". . .on my team," Raddy shouted.

Uncle Jesse stepped into the cabin and let the screen door slam shut. "Hey!" I want it silent for the rest of rest period."

"Aah," Raddy said.

Uncle Jesse glared at him. Albie looked from Uncle Jesse to Raddy. "What do you want?" Raddy said. Before Albie could protest his innocence of bad intent, Raddy said, "I don't want you on my team anyhow."

That afternoon Albie slipped away to return to the side of the lake with his binoculars. From his place under the tree he examined the far shore, leaves, birds, a chipmunk, butterflies on the lily pads, and even the dragon-flies, in peace. He would have shared the binoculars with Joe, but was not moved to look for him. In fact, he was not lonely.

When he returned, all the other Panthers were sitting on the down-hill steps and the pine needles nearby. Every boy had a knife. Walter Gardner bit on his tongue which stuck out of the corner of his mouth as he scraped the bark off a forked stick. Mike cut string into pieces a foot long. Will used the bottom step as a table to cut an inner tube into narrow strips. Slingshots.

Albie stepped out from behind a tree.

Raddy cut a piece of red cord. When he saw Albie, he tapped Will's shoulder and pointed toward Will's left hand. Will extended it. Raddy tied the red cord around his wrist.

"Hey, Raddy, are you making slingshots?" Albie said.

Raddy stuck his lower lip at Albie and started to carve a forked stick. He had a piece of the red cord tied around his own left wrist also.

Cooper and Jerry stood foot to foot. Cooper balanced the tip of a knife on the pad of his index finger and flipped the handle toward the ground. The knife whirled, fell, and stuck into a rectangle of bare earth cleared of pine needles between them. He scratched the ground with the tip of the knife and handed it to Jerry as Albie approached.

"It's on the line, I win," Cooper said.

"What are you playing?" Albie said.

"Mumblety-peg," Jerry said. "want to play?"

Albie did, but the bugle sounded and Uncle Jesse opened the door to call them in.

At the sink on the way to dinner Albie saw that Jerry wore a red cord, too. It was thicker than string, braided; it had been tied with a triple knot.

"Can I get one of those?" Albie said.

"You have to ask Raddy. He's giving them to the red team, for color war."

"Can I be on the red team too?"

"They tell you," Jerry said. "It's not up to me." Someone splashed him from the other side; he threw water back and chased the other boy up the stairs. Albie dried his hands on his shirt and followed.

The next morning would be riflery, which was good, then swimming. The afternoon would be baseball, which was bad. On the other hand it was all bad: if Albie were to excel too much at riflery on the same day as he was too useless at baseball he would become even more of a freak among the Panthers. What if Albie were to aim off on purpose so Raddy could defeat him in riflery? But Raddy's malevolence was fixed. He could not be propitiated.

The universe ordained that Raddy had to excel over Albie and that Albie must remain an outsider to the life of the Panthers, because Albie was different. He could not remove his difference, but the past two days had changed it. He had been the worst athlete in the bunk, even if he had been recognized as a riflery genius; now he was still the worst athlete, but he had his father's binoculars — and even so he would remain different, and less, forever.

The Panthers were ready to leave. Albie dawdled. As the screen door swung shut he reached into the hiding place under his pillow. On the way down to the riflery range he held the case high in his armpit and pressed it to his body with his thin arm as much to conceal it from the other boys as to keep it from falling. As an added assurance he put the case strap around his neck.

"What's that?" Jerry pointed at the strap.

"My binoculars."

"You're a lucky duck."

Albie chewed his lip. He had made a promise which he must redeem; yet he feared the inevitable request.

Jerry pointed to the strap. "I thought it was tefillin."

"What's that?"

"The things my grandfather wraps around his arm." Jerry bent toward the case. "What can you see with them?"

"Anything. You can see the targets better." As he spoke he realized that he would be able to tell everyone's score before they knew it themselves. His binoculars would see their future, and at the same time he could also find out for certain whether Joe exposed himself to the danger of flying bullets.

"Can I?" Jerry asked.

"Sure."

The other Panthers pushed around them and past them. Albie freed the case from under his arm and held his breath as he always did when he eased the binoculars out. He untangled the strap. "You'd better put this around your neck."

Jerry put the strap around his neck and scrutinized the part in his hand with respect. He ran his thumb tip over it. "My grandfather says you have to check the straps to be sure they're black enough."

Albie regarded the cracks on the strap and the rough brown of its underside with discomfort as Jerry inspected the woods. Over his shoulder Albie saw trees, leaves, light and shade, an orange and black Monarch butterfly, the trunk of a tree blotched with lichens in front of a stand of white paper birches. A dust-colored bird flew through the forest to land on a branch. Jerry swiveled from side to side so the barrels of the binoculars swept the forest like the cannon of a tank.

"Turn that knob until it gets clear," Albie said.

Jerry stopped pivoting and focused. "That's good," he said, "great." He leaned back to look up at the sky before he handed the binoculars back to Albie. "Thanks." He ran off toward the riflery range on his meaty thighs.

Albie rolled the strap and unfolded the binoculars so they would fit into the case. In order to catch up he stretched his gait into Groucho Marx strides, but he strode at a slow motion cadence lest he trip, fall and damage the binoculars. He hoped Jerry would be a closer friend now that he had shared the binoculars. Did his own grandfather know the rules about keeping straps black? Perhaps Albie should tell him.

At the range Uncle Lou chose Albie to be one of the first to shoot. Albie lay the case beside him as he stretched out on the mat closest to Uncle Lou's table.

"Whatcha got there, soldier?" Uncle Lou said as he counted out bullets.

"They're my father's binoculars."

Uncle Lou pursed his lips but didn't quite whistle. He knelt but didn't reach for the binoculars. "They're in the case," Albie said.

"Thanks, Greenberg."

They were ready on the right, ready on the left, ready on the firing line. "You may fire at will," Uncle Lou said.

"Hey, Will, get down there and we'll fire at you," Raddy called from the far right mattress.

"Shut up," Will said.

Albie fired first.

"Not bad," Uncle Lou said." That's a seven, high and left."

"Where did you get the field glasses?" Raddy asked.

"Eyes front, soldier. They're Greenberg's."

Small arms fire crackled. The binoculars were safe with Uncle Lou, so Albie concentrated on finding the target above his sights and then on not concentrating, relaxing, letting go, so the rifle would surprise him every time. At the end the boys carried their targets back to the shed, where Uncle Lou's face was only the gleaming objective lenses of the binoculars. "And the winnah!" Uncle Lou said as they stepped up onto the platform.

"Wait a minute," Raddy said. "I got a thirty something."

"No you didn't," Uncle Lou said.

The boys clustered together to examine the targets. Albie had a 34, Will a 32, and Raddy a 24. Raddy folded his target to the size of a playing card and put it in his pocket.

"Next platoon," Uncle Lou said, and handed the binoculars to Uncle

Jesse, who eyeballed them, returned them and unrolled his magazine even before Uncle Lou had completed the formalities for the next set of targets.

In Albie's hands, the binoculars wobbled more than the rifle without the sling. Uncle Lou had rested his elbows on the table. Albie sat back against the rough post that supported the shed roof and rested his elbows on his knees. Now he could see the white rings in the black and the small white numbers like page numbers in a printed book. A gun went off, a black hole appeared in the white to the right of the bull's-eye and dust flew from the backstop. He opened his mouth to speak, but he didn't know whose target he had been watching.

He lowered the binoculars. Wayne was firing from the mattress he had used, Mike was to his right, and Cooper was at the end; all three of them were reloading. Albie raised the binoculars again and found himself looking at the pattern of the grain on the weathered wooden frame that held the targets, rusted nails, staples holding yellowed corners of old targets. Someone fired. The target Albie found was not the one he had been watching before. That confused him: he felt lost until he realized that he was free to look anywhere, or everywhere to find it again, or he could let it go and examine whatever he wanted with his own binoculars.

He eased the magnified circle across the backstop, up to its top, off to the dark green woods beyond it. The shade was black. The accelerated motion of the leaves dizzied him. Leaves played in front of something white that didn't move, a birch tree, not a tee shirt. Guns cracked. Albie scanned both sides of the range, but he didn't see Joe.

Uncle Lou cried, "Weapon safe positions!"

The boys retrieved their targets. A huge, out of focus tee shirt obscured Albie's view of the forest. The crazy motion became Cooper's hair swinging, as large as if he were near enough to embrace, and he was gone. Albie panned and caught him again, moving too fast to see clearly. Weeds further left on top of the backstop moved, not in the slow rhythm of branches swayed by the wind, but fast, and only once.

Joe! Albie stood up. There was the side of the wooden rack for the targets, the mound, the cleared region before the woods . . . "Greenberg!" Uncle Lou said, "you hear me?" Albie flushed. "Stand behind the mattresses if you're not firing!"

At Albie's feet, Walter lay on the right, and Philip was wrapping the sling of the rifle Albie had fired around his forearm. Jerry knelt beside the empty middle mattress. "Tell me how I'm doing, okay?"

Albie stepped back. Uncle Lou distributed ammunition. Albie found

Walter's target, the end of the wooden frame, and the edge of the
mound. Uncle Lou called the readies. Albie moved the circle up to the
dark branches of trees behind the backstop. The place where the weeds
had moved was out of focus.

". . . fire at will!"

Albie focused. The weeds, bright in summer sunlight, leapt into
unreal clarity, like a lantern slide of a flower projected in Miss Chandler's
class. Sunlight flashed above shadow, and lit something blacker than the
shadows and whiter than the sunlight.

Crack! Philip fired and worked the bolt. Walter and Jerry fired
together, crackack! The black and white moved, it was a high sneaker,
and it was gone. It was true! Joe! he almost called, but he was sworn to
secrecy.

His friend could get shot! Albie felt cold and frightened. Crack!
Crackack! He smelled burnt gunpowder, and oil from the rifle actions. If
he were to speak to save his friend he would betray him. Uncle Lou
would stop the firing and tell the boys to unload the weapons. He would
collect the unused bullets before he let anyone go behind the backstop,
so Joe would disappear into the trackless woods. Crack! Albie bit his lip
and tasted salty blood. Crack! Now a breeze moved, and Albie smelled
the woods, but still he saw no movement.

"Is that in the black?" Jerry said. "Hey, Albie, wake up!"

Albie didn't want to move the binoculars. "I can't see."

"That's not even the right direction," Raddy said. "Moron!"

"Over here," Jerry said. "The second target."

"Don't interrupt the shooters," Uncle Lou said.

Crack! Crack! Crack!

Albie sought the sneaker in the light and shade beneath the shiny
green weeds above the backstop. Crack! Crackack! A cloud passed over
the sun and changed the light. Breeze swayed trees in the background
with a chord of sibilants. Things blew and rubbed, and moved on the
forest floor. Crack!

When it was over, Jerry had two shots in the black, one at the edge
and one bull's-eye. Albie put the binoculars under his arm, the strap still
around his neck, and ran up behind Jerry. "You got a bull's-eye," he said,
"I think."

"Really." Jerry went to get his target. Albie ran past him, around Walter, into the corridor between the backstop and the edge of the clearing.
This rough ground wouldn't take a footprint. Close up the place looked

different and unfamiliar; he could not find the weeds he had seen through the binoculars. The woods beside the riflery range grew tall and thick. The road lay beyond them. Straight behind the backstop the land fell down into even darker woods, but it had to rise again somewhere beyond his sight to join the hill the cabins and main house sat on. Near his foot was a crumpled Pall Mall package faded to a salmon yellow.

Albie studied the ground.

"Where's Greenberg?" a boy's voice called from the range.

"Joe!" Albie whispered.

Perhaps he had not been here, perhaps it wasn't true. If it were true and Joe were shot, he would lie on weeds and dirt, the black hole he bled from no larger than the holes in the targets, but his bright fresh blood would gleam in the sun. Albie imagined disorder and consternation. The white ambulance would crush the bushes on either side of the footpath. The attendants would bandage Joe's wound as one eye shone up at Albie with gratitude out of his odd electric light bulb head. Joe and Albie would squeeze hands palm to palm, because they, together, could feel no pain. The attendants would lift the stretcher into the ambulance . . .

"Greenberg!" Uncle Jesse shouted.

The breeze rose again. Albie scanned one more time before he ran around the backstop and back to the shed, where it was once again his turn to shoot.

At the end of the period Albie had three new targets that counted toward a medal. Uncle Lou had written his scores down in the book. Cooper and Will had arm wrestled during the last round of shooting. When their grunts disturbed Mike, Uncle Lou ordered them to do pushups outside the back of the shed. On the way to the baseball field Cooper stopped to do more pushups and blocked the trail. William leapfrogged over him.

"My turn!" Cooper leapfrogged over William.

"Here I come!" Jerry leapfrogged over William and crashed into Cooper.

"Hey!" Cooper pushed Roth, who fell backward over William, who was still doing pushups on the trail.

Albie wrapped his binocular case in his arms. The others were bigger and stronger than he: if he were to scuffle with them Cooper would respect that difference, and so would Jerry, who always seemed easygoing, even when he wrestled with Cooper or Will Hobeck. But Raddy was vicious, and Wayne, too. Walter, who didn't know his own strength, would defend Wayne at any cost, so Albie was wise to stay out with his precious burden.

But what was the worst that could happen to him? If he were to participate and get hurt he would cry. He had seen the others red-faced and out of control after a fight, but he doubted they ever cried the way he did. He wished that someone would tell him the secrets of strength and courage, so he could take part in the give and take of life in the Panthers—but that was impossible. He ducked off the path, cut through the woods, and reached the edge of Fenway Park before the rest of the Panthers emerged near the archery range.

He was not strong, but he was fast. He ran with ease to the edge of the field near the road where his parents had abandoned him. He glanced toward the camp entrance and freedom only once before he raced behind the first base stands of Yankee Stadium and across the intersection to the waterfront, where he was the first Panther to arrive.

At swimming Uncle Bart taught the beginners the backstroke. It scared Albie at first, but once he put his head far enough back to put his ears under water, the shouting of boys and counselors subsided to a swish and a click at the edge of awareness. He could survey the same sky as at home without catching sight of anything that proved he was at Bear Lake. A deep breath let him arch his back to tilt his head further and further until the rim of water moved from his hairline toward his eyebrows, like the ring of water on his knee at home.

Uncle Bart made the beginners race. Albie reached the dock ahead of all the Lion Cubs, and bumped his head. When he found his footing Uncle Jesse called to him, "Way to go, Greenberg!" and banged a bamboo pole on the dock.

But the last part of the morning was free polo, which meant a fight in the water. Even Cooper and the best swimmers in Woodsmen participated in the horseplay instead of swimming more laps. Uncle Bart, Uncle Jesse, and Uncle Dan officiated from the dock as Panthers and Woodsmen splashed, pushed, and tackled each other in the shallow water. A large white rubber ball was part of the confusion, but Albie could discern no structure or purpose to the game. Being near the ball increased one's chances of getting ducked; Uncle Bart seemed to have forgotten his whistle. Albie was afraid again. Joe wasn't there. When the counselors looked the other way Albie left the water, changed, and hurried back to the cabin with his binoculars under his arm.

He could not keep them under his pillow forever. The whole cabin knew where they were. Albie considered his cabin mates no less honest than he, but they were more aggressive. And nothing was locked. At home his mother used two keys to open the two locks on their apartment door, and a third for the wood and glass door that separated the outer lobby from the inner. His parents must have taken those precautions for a reason. His father had patrolled the empty apartment in a steel helmet to protect them all. Because Bear Lake Camp did less, it was Albie's responsibility to defend the gleaming evidence of his father's regard.

He hurried up the hill. He would conceal the binoculars in a new place before any of the others could see where he had put them. The brass catch rubbed his ribs as he breathed hard. His trunk was the first place anyone would look. If he put the case under his mattress the bulge in his blanket would betray him. In Albie's mind's eye, a boy crept under his bed on hands and knees to discover the precious leather case caught between the thin mattress and the wire spring, framed by the blue blanket tucked in on three sides. That was too easy.

With the binoculars in the bottom of his laundry bag, dirty clothes would keep curious hands away, but Albie, too, would be reluctant to rummage through the dampness and urine smell. Besides, knowledgeable eyes would discern the peculiar oval contour of the case through the muslin bag. Even dullard Walter was quick to pick out hiding places when they played Kick the Can. The week before Albie had hidden in leaves and dirt at the bottom of a gully, one eye exposed to track the progress of the game. The others rushed by, but Walter stopped, scratched his crotch, and looked right at Albie. Albie held his breath. Once Walter stepped away, Albie thought he was safe, but Walter cried over his shoulder, "Tap, tap, Albie, one, two three," and sprinted for the can before Albie could stand up.

Albie needed a place as big as binoculars, out of sight but easy to hand, where neither the shape nor the texture of the case would yield to casual inspection. He had reached the steps with no other Panthers in sight. Once in the doorway, he knew: the bookshelf. No other boy wanted to read his books. The wooden shelf was deep enough to accommodate the binocular case between the books and the wall, and he already kept his yellow rain slicker in the space behind the books. He tugged the strap over his head, stuffed the case under the slicker and tucked it back. Except for the bulge of yellow there was nothing to see. The slicker stuck out of Raddy's end of the shelf as before. No one would see. Albie would make no written record.

Done! Albie hurried out the uphill door to the latrine as someone came up the downhill steps.

"No baseball this afternoon," Uncle Jesse said. "We're going on a nature walk."

"What's a nature walk?" Walter asked.

"We can look at things," Albie said. "Like trees and animals and different kinds of birds. With my binoculars."

"What kinds?"

Albie didn't know the names of the purplish-black birds that staggered outside the cabin, or the dusty gray ones that whirred through the shadows under trees. "All kinds," he said. "Like eagles, or cardinals." He glanced at Cooper for support.

"Cardinals?" Philip said.

"My father saw a blue heron," Cooper said.

"No such thing as a blue herring," Jerry said.

"Yes there is. My father saw it."

"Well what does it look like?"

"I'm not sure." Cooper smoothed his hair. "He saw three different grebes, too."

"What's grebes?"

"Birds," Cooper said, "that my father saw in the cemetery. You tell them by how they fly." The boys moved toward the downhill door. "Bring your glasses," Cooper said.

Will touched his glasses and the shoelace around the back of his neck. Albie started for his shelf, but remembered that he wanted to keep the hiding place a secret. He pretended to examine his trunk.

"Let's go," Uncle Jesse said.

Raddy dawdled. Albie watched him out of the corner of his eye. He might not be able to wait until Raddy had left. Raddy was on the doorstep. Albie reached for his pillow; he heard the door open. He took a deep breath, touched the pillow, lifted the slicker behind his books and picked up the binocular case by its strap.

"Tarrant!" Uncle Jesse called from outside the door, "Greenberg! Let's go!"

Albie put the strap over his head and one arm and clutched the case to his side. Raddy, outside on the steps, stared at him. Albie saw murder and envy and love in Raddy's eyes before he followed the other small boy through the door. In silence, because Albie did not know how to speak at such a moment, he and Raddy followed parallel lines, ten feet apart, as they descended the hill through the grove of pines together.

The Panthers had to wait in the Indian Circle because Uncle Richard wasn't there yet. Raddy put his hand on the binocular case.

"No," Albie said.

"Why not?"

"There's nothing to look at yet."

"Yes there is." Raddy cupped his hand to his ear. "I hear a car coming."

"I don't. Anyhow we're going to look at birds."

"I'm not," Raddy said. "I don't care." He walked around the circle once, and sat back down next to Uncle Jesse. "What time is it?" he said.

Uncle Jesse extended his elbow and made the fist that had hit Albie in the mess hall. His watch was silver metal on a black leather strap stained white with sweat. Raddy rested two thin hands on Uncle Jesse's arm and studied the watch. "What time is it?"

"Can't you tell time?"

"Sure I can. I just don't want to." Raddy thrust his little hands into his pockets and stalked back around the fireplace.

"What day is it?" Philip asked.

"Thursday," Uncle Jesse said, with his eye on Raddy's back.

"How long till visiting day?" Mike said.

"We just *had* visiting day," Will said.

"Not a real visiting day."

Heads nodded in agreement.

"You know what it was like?" Will said. "On Armistice Day, my mother and father and my brother and me went to visit my uncle in the cemetery. He got killed in the war, so we visited his grave, where he was buried in Washington." The other Panthers listened in silence, except Raddy, who kicked at pebbles across the circle. "We couldn't touch him, like when my mom and dad visited here. His name was William too. He killed a lot of Germans."

"Wow," Mike said, "What was he like?"

Will shook his head. "I didn't know him."

"I bet he was brave," Mike said. Raddy had taken a seat on a log all the way across the circle. "Hey, Raddy," Mike called. "Will's uncle was a hero in the war, he killed a lot of Germans!"

"So?"

"My father said he was a good jumper, like me," Will said. "We went to visit where he was . . ." The mark on his face flared a deeper purple and he fell silent.

"Nobody was dead on visiting day," Mike said. "Were they, Uncle Jesse?"

"Nobody," Uncle Jesse said.

"Not even," Philip said.

"Not even." Uncle Jesse chuckled and reached out to tousle Philip's hair, but Philip ducked away.

Raddy shuffled back and looked Will up and down. "How did the Germans kill your uncle?"

Will shook his head. "I don't know."

"It's lucky we won the war," Raddy said. "Otherwise they'd kill *you*."

Albie, sitting on a log behind Will, caught the full force of Raddy's assertion. "Why?" he gasped. "Why would they kill me?"

"Cause the Germans killed the kikes," Philip said. "My father said it was on the radio. Isn't it true, Uncle Jesse?"

"I don't know." Uncle Jesse consulted his watch again. "I wish Uncle Richard would—"

"My uncle stopped them," Will said.

Albie remembered the empty apartment. Here was a chance to connect. "My father was in charge," he said "He had a steel helmet."

"Really?" Philip said. "Where was he? In Germany or Europe or what?"

Albie felt lost. "In an apartment on three."

"On three?" Philip said. "On three?"

Raddy tugged at the binocular case.

"No," Albie said.

"Are you going to let me look or not?"

"No."

Uncle Jesse stepped between them. From the corner of the woods, Uncle Richard whooped and held up a poster with pictures of trees on it. "Panthers," he called. "Paa-anthers!"

"Single file, into the woods." Uncle Jesse pushed Raddy toward the nature counselor; he stood on a log with one hand in his hip pocket and the other on Albie's shoulder until the rest of the Panthers were up and walking toward the corner of the lake.

Uncle Richard led them down the Leech Beach trail. Albie tiptoed with the binoculars against his side past the copse that marked his secret place. He suppressed an impulse to seek Joe on the bank with the binoculars lest he betray the place and get Joe in trouble. The others would hoot, and the binoculars, which should be an instrument of freedom, would become chains.

The world was so dangerous, with so many connections between things and people. Raddy, ahead of him, ogled the binocular case. What made people better or worse? Sometimes better possessions, like fuzzy blue blankets or binoculars, made them worse. Sometimes something you knew made you better: for example, the hiding place secret made Albie feel better, even though none of the Panthers knew he had a secret.

"A sycamore." Uncle Richard pointed into the woods. "A white oak." He squatted to pick up an acorn. "This is how the oak has babies."

Panthers leaned to peer into Uncle Richard's palm, but Raddy shuffled off the trail, kicking at leaves and pebbles.

"I know it's not white," Uncle Richard said. "It's the color of the wood."

Raddy kicked a pile of leaves near the bottom of a small bush; a small brown rabbit broke from cover to bound into the forest.

"What was that?" Mike Wooley said.

"A bear!" Raddy charged Albie and tore the instrument from the case to aim it into the already silent woods. He swung the binoculars toward the group of Panthers and the two counselors. "Da-da-da-da-da!" he shouted, becoming an antiaircraft gun. He trained the binoculars on the top of a tree. "Here they come, shoot 'em down! Da-da-da-da-da!"

"Raddy! Those are mine!" Albie reached out his hand.

"Err-oom!" Raddy, now an enemy plane, ran away into the woods. He tripped on a root and fell hard with the binoculars against his face. Uncle Jesse hurried to him. When Raddy stood up, crying, his face was dirty but not bleeding. The binoculars lay on the ground. Uncle Jesse seized Raddy by his shoulders. "This is a nature walk. If you can't behave I'm going to—"

"I only wanted to see the animal," Raddy sniffled. He kicked the binoculars and stalked toward Jerry, who watched him come with disdain on his face.

"It *was* a bear," Raddy said.

"Yeah," Jerry hit Raddy's shoulder with his fist, but not hard, as if it wasn't worth the trouble.

"Yeah!" Raddy hit him back.

Uncle Richard called them further up the trail and held up his tree poster. Albie picked up the binoculars. The unscratched objective lenses gleamed their strange iridescence. The knurled knob turned smoothly. Albie scanned toward the lake, but he saw neither the rabbit nor Joe. He put the binoculars away.

By dinner Raddy had a black eye. Uncle Jesse told him to put paper towels wet in cold water on it. Mrs. Brewer saw him holding the poultice on his eye in the mess hall and came over to take him away before the meal was over. The Panthers met him in the cabin afterwards.

"What did the nurse do?" Philip asked.

"She was going to give me a needle this big," — Raddy gestured with his free hand — "but instead she gave me an ice pack. She said I have to hold it on my eye until all the ice is melted, or I might get blind."

"You won't go blind," Jerry said. "And if you do, you can get glasses."

Will stared at Raddy and fingered the shoelace around his neck.

Raddy met Albie's eyes. "I can get *field* glasses. You'd loan me your *field* glasses, wouldn't you?"

"If you were blind you couldn't see through glasses."

"Oh yeah?"

"He's right," Will said. "Blind people don't need glasses."

"I don't need glasses and I'm not blind." Raddy rotated his head from side to side to swing his good eye from Will to Albie and back again.

"Quiet down," Uncle Jesse had returned to the bunk. "Let's get changed."

Nightfall meant a day closer to liberation, but Albie had to turn away from the pressure of Raddy's resentment before he could fall asleep.

Albie did not accompany the Panthers to baseball. Beyond the picnic tables, away from the lake, he lost track of time. Warmed by the sun, he rested in unexplored territory to listen to the song of birds. From that clearing he worked his way up a rise, back toward the camp buildings. How free he felt in the woods! In the park he had always been alert for predatory bigger boys in gangs, boys with dark skin, boys who carried sticks and knives. Here he roamed at will, guided only by his curiosity, safe. He stopped to listen to the forest and his pulse, and heard a city sound, a radio, ahead of him. With great care he advanced up the hill; near the brow he dropped to a crouch.

The sound seemed to come from the main house, but as Albie edged closer he saw it was a separate, shabby structure off to one side of the other Bear Lake buildings. Its dirty white paint was peeling; the windows lacked shutters. The tinny, distinctive sound of radio baseball came from where a shed blocked his view.

Albie approached. The upper end of the road above the parking lot became two indistinct ruts into the woods he had emerged from. The announcer's excited voice rose into an unintelligible frenzy and descended into the thin radio rendition of a crowd's wild cheers. The noise masked Albie's footsteps on gravel as he stepped around the corner of the shed.

A radio in a square red leatherette case sat on a sill under an open window in the corner. The head cook who had danced the hucklebuck with the great pot reclined in a wooden lawn chair with his stockinged feet on an overturned bucket. His eyes were closed, his round glasses rested in his hand on a crescent of mahogany belly between his olive drab undershirt and his pants. Curly white hair chest hair above the undershirt matched the hair on his head.

"The Redbirds," the announcer said. "Here's the windup, the pitch, strike one."

The cook sat in shade, but his legs and feet were in the sun. He held a beer bottle by its neck in a hand that hung down so the bottle rested on the ground. His other hand reached up to adjust an ivory knob below the radio dial. The mutter of the crowd behind the announcer blended with a breeze that brushed Albie.

What kind of a man would dance with a pot?

Albie stepped forward.

The cook opened his eyes. He put on glasses. "You ain't suppose to be here," he said.

"Ball two, two and two," the announcer said.

Boy and man examined each other. Albie stood silent. The man swallowed beer.

"Paid attendance thirty thousand, nine hundred and sixty-six," the announcer said.

"You suppose to be playing ball, not listening to it," the cook said.

Albie leaned against the corner of the shed. He was a stranger here, but not the way he was among the Panthers, nor even the way he felt at home among his family. The cook closed his eyes again.

"Three and two, full count," the announcer said. "Robinson steps back out of the box."

In the summer stillness the cook was at peace, listening to the game in some far off city. He was not part of it, nor did he demand anything of Albie. The announcer recited statistics.

"My name is Albie."

The cook opened his eyes, then lowered them.

"What's yours?" Albie said.

"The pitch, it's a line drive to left, Marion doesn't have it," the announcer shouted. "Robinson is rounding second, the throw," and with excitement mounting even higher and the crowd howling in the background, ". . . it's over Schoendienst's head, Campanella's home, Robinson at third, he stops, tags up, it's a run, the score is tied at two and two, one out and Robinson is in position to score . . ."

"Yay," Albie cried, caught up by the excitement.

"You like the Dodgers?" the cook said.

"I'm learning baseball. Most of the kids in my bunk like the Yankees."

"You do better to stick with the Dodgers." The cook studied Albie through narrowed eyes. "My name is Hughston."

"Pleased to meet you." Albie stepped forward to look Hughston full in the face and extend his hand. Hughston drew back into his chair, but he transferred the beer bottle to his left hand and shook Albie's hand.

". . . looks over his shoulder at third and Robinson tags up," the announcer said. "The pitch . . ."

Albie sat down on the ground.

"He bunts!" the announcer shouted, "Sacrifice, he lays one down, Robinson on his way, Tommy Glaviano has it, the throw is home . . ."

Hughston opened his eyes. Albie leaped to his feet.

"Safe!" the announcer cried. "It's a three two ball game, the Dodgers take the lead!"

"Yayyy!" Albie cried.

"Okay," Hughston said.

A woman's voice called out from inside the house; Hughston glanced toward the window and leaned toward Albie. "You ain't suppose to be here. You better get back and play ball."

"Thanks a *lot*," Albie said.

"Okay." The cook swallowed beer again.

Albie withdrew and scouted back up the hill into the woods. He had delighted in baseball like a normal person. But once the radio was out of earshot, he remembered that the cook had said that he wasn't supposed to be there, and felt embarrassed. At the end of the afternoon he was careful to return to Panthers by a different route.

A faded dark green station wagon rolled up the hill to the parking area. One by one the boys turned their attention from their before-dinner games and squabbles to the car as its engine coughed and stopped. A tall, stout man in gray pants and a gray vest over a white shirt without a tie got out.

He leaned back into the car for a brown briefcase, like Albie's father's. This must be something important.

The man carried his briefcase up the steps of the main house. Bear Brewer shook his hand on the verandah. Mrs. Brewer wiped her hands on her apron, and the man shook her hand also. He gave Bear Brewer a piece of paper from his briefcase and all three adults shook hands again. When the bell rang for dinner, the man had to wait for the throng of boys and counselors to get out of his way before he could drive down the hill.

The aides who collected the mandatory letters home had an expectant air. Something had happened.

"I have good news," Bear Brewer said over the public address system. The mess hall fell silent. "Dr. Meredith has determined that enough time has passed—" His next words were lost in the cheer that went up from the tables where the boys could hear him without the microphone.

Philip pulled at Jesse's sleeve. "Uncle Jesse, what did he say?"

Uncle Jesse shushed him. Uncle Charlie stepped up on the platform and took the microphone from Bear Brewer. "For those of you who didn't hear, the quarantine is over. Next visiting day everything will be normal." A boy at a table near the microphone asked something. "No," said Uncle Charlie, "no more sulfur pills." The rest of his words were lost in screeching from the loudspeakers and the cheers of campers.

"Yayyy! No more pills, no more pills!" Mike jumped up on the bench and screamed, "No more pills! Yay!" Mike and Raddy and Wayne jumped up and down on the bench in unison, and shouted with each jump. "No! More! Pills! No! More! Pills!" As Raddy jumped his shirt pulled out of his shorts to reveal the muscle lines across his thin belly. Walter slapped the table with his hands in time with a goofy grin on his face. "No! More! Pills!" The tumult lasted until Uncle Jesse seized Wayne, who was nearest him, by the thigh and shouted "HEY, YOU WANT A NOOGIE?"

Everyone sat down and quieted. Uncle Charlie pointed into a book for an older camper, who read into the microphone, "A psalm of thanksgiving . . ."

Albie, who had received no acknowledgment of his sacrifice, tried to compose an utterance to Mike that would restore their connection, but Mike was chattering to Raddy with shining eyes. "If you throw a spitball really hard," Albie overheard. He stopped listening.

When Uncle Jesse dismissed the Panthers, the rest of the bunk rushed off to play One Old Cat with a pink rubber ball. Albie followed, vibrating with a kind of energy that wanted to run, to strike the ball, to hurl a fielded ball from the furthest reaches of the outfield to the hollow dark bull's eye in the center of the catcher's glove, to single-handedly stop the run that would defeat the team.

"Yay, Albie, Albie!" the camp would cry from the stands in a single voice. But he was unwelcome and inept; the crowd's roar subsided to silence. The only way to proficiency was participation and practice, the way he had learned to scout in the woods, but because he was incapable of even minimal participation in ball games he would never see how things should be done. He could never learn.

So the Panthers ran faster and faster down the hill to play One Old Cat, and Albie fell further and further behind. As early evening and the great trees darkened the sky he saw that an invisible wall separated him from the life of the Panthers, and always would. The wall was growing higher. He could neither breach it nor hope to scale it, but he could see through it.

And he had binoculars! He would find a place from where he could study the behavior of boys unobserved, and when he had mastered the moves, the patterns, the signs and signals that proclaimed normalcy, he would emerge from his hidden place to amaze them with his fluency, his grace, and his energy. The vitality that filled him made him tremble and threatened to break out into the world if he did not control it.

"Albie!" Joe perched on a tree branch five feet above the side of the road. "I saw you coming," he said, "what were you saying?"

"I wasn't saying anything."

"I saw your mouth moving."

Albie wondered how often his body revealed his secrets when he didn't want it to. He thought before he said, "I have a secret."

Joe's eyes lit up, both the one that looked straight at Albie and the one that didn't. "Tell me."

Albie rolled his eyes right and left like a movie detective. He cupped his hands at Joe's ear. "Not here."

Joe peered down the road as theatrically, then up toward the main house where a few boys walked on the road. He beckoned with his finger. Albie crouched low as they made their way toward the corner of the lake. When they tended toward where the Panthers were playing noisy ball Albie touched Joe's shoulder, and Joe stopped.

Albie pointed to the clearing, shook his head no, and put his finger to his lips. Joe nodded his understanding and crouched lower on the pine needles. They reached the trail to Albie's place at the edge of the lake under a pale sapphire sky, a white moon with visible craters hung over the trees on the far shore. In silence the two boys hurried down the path to the small cove under the trees.

The water was black. "What?" Joe said.

Albie threw a pebble. Its 'plop' was as clear as the smooth surface and the evening air. "Look up at the moon," he said.

Joe moved the foliage. "So?"

"Could you see it pretty well?"

"Pretty well."

"Well, now we can see it better. My father loaned me his binoculars."

"Where are they?"

Albie looked left and right. "Someplace safe."

Joe's eye examined Albie. "Real binoculars?"

Another wall sprouted. Albie reached forward to tear it down. "Yes, we can use them scouting." Joe's silence troubled him. "I'll bring them tomorrow." The invisible wall softened. "We can both use them, you can use them too."

Joe made circles with his thumbs and index fingers and studied the lake through the binoculars that were his hands. "Spies operate in secrecy and silence," he said. "We report only in the woods, no written messages."

"No written messages. Secrecy and silence," Albie responded. The evening air chilled him as something scurried over leaves. "We have to write reports to headquarters." He had written home that day.

"Reports to headquarters?"

"We're cut off, I'm going to call in a rescue team, planes and helicopters."

"Gyros," Joe said.

"Autogyros."

"Submarines."

"One man submarines," Albie said.

"How can they rescue us if the submarines hold only one man?"

"In the torpedo compartment."

"Two man submarines," Joe said.

"Okay, two man submarines." The sky darkened through the range of blue crayons from pale to rich and dark. After they went it would move through violet and purple to black. Pale blue stillness would become a purple hum, a black rumble. Darkness would erupt into noise, and far in the distance above the trees, out there among the points of light that were distant stars, one red light would appear. The rumble would grow louder and more insistent; that tail light under a plane would become two, three, then five. 'Look!' Albie would point up and out through the screened window of the cabin, as the crashing rumble tore the sky, roared louder than the subway. He would run outside, chilly in thin pajamas. Through his binoculars he and Joe would watch the squadron of planes sent by a distant power circle and land, one by one, on the baseball field.

They would roll to a stop, their tails low on tiny wheels. Oval doors would fly open above the wings. Combat pilots dressed in dark coveralls and leather helmets would jump to the earth, each holding his rifle out by an extended arm for balance. They would form into platoons to charge up the hill through the grove of big trees. In darkness they would come, and before anyone knew, the attack would begin!

Soldiers with dark goggles would surround Uncle Jesse and herd him off to a picnic table above the cabins. 'This one?' a soldier would ask, and Albie would nod. One implacable soldier would seize Uncle Jesse's wrist in the faded red sweatshirt to hold the fist that had struck Albie down on the rough wooden table. 'Now,' Albie would say, and nod again; the leader of the soldiers would smash the stock of his rifle on Uncle Jesse's hand to crush his ring and break all the bones. Uncle Jesse would cry out before he and all of Bear Lake faded into the darkness as Albie and Joe ran with the soldiers, down the hill into the waiting planes.

In the first dawn light, engines would cough into life as the planes taxied and turned on their small wheels. They would rattle and bump, until with an awful roar, the screaming engines would press the two boys back into their seats and lift them to a silent exaltation above the trees, above the lake. The rescue planes would rise above the darkness to leave Bear Lake behind, to fly them toward morning, into a brightness that was hard to imagine, toward freedom.

"A rescue mission," Albie breathed. He wasn't sure whether he had thought the words or said them.

"Tomorrow?" Joe said.

"Yes, tomorrow."

The bugle that marked the end of evening games pierced the trees. The boys shook hands and stood up to traverse the darkening path back to Bear Lake Camp.

Some Panthers had their pajamas on when Albie got back to the cabin. Uncle Jesse gave him a severe look. Raddy slammed the door coming back from the latrine. No one watched Albie. Fine: he would give them nothing. Careful not even to peek at his hiding place, he took his toilet kit to the latrine.

The light inside Lion Cubs silhouetted two little boys against the screen door. "Hi, Albie," one of them called. "Hi, Stuart," Albie said.

On Albie's way back Uncle Bernie was reading the Lion Cubs a story with a flashlight. In Panthers, something was in the air. The others read or played games on their beds; not one of them acknowledged Albie's return with even distaste or enmity. Uncle Jesse had left.

Albie looked from bed to bed. "Where's Uncle Jesse?" he said.

No one responded. Walter Gardner on his cot next to Albie's put his pillow over his head and giggled. Wayne hissed, "Shut up!" at him, but when Albie looked at Wayne he was reading a comic book. Puzzled, Albie hung up his toilet kit and changed into his pajamas. Cooper drew on a pad. Jerry smacked his fist into the pocket of his catcher's mitt and held the mitt up in front of his eyes. Even Raddy lay silent on his bed facing Mike.

Albie looked over Raddy's bed at Mike. "Hi, Mike."

Mike swung his gaze from the floor to the far side of the cabin.

Something new excluded Albie. Careful not to pull his blankets out too much he lifted the cool sheet and slid in under his blue blanket, anticipating the peace of night and the adventure of dreams. He slid down until his feet met the obstruction of the sheet tucked in at the bottom of the bed, but the blankets didn't even come up to his waist. Something was wrong. He pulled harder, but the blanket and sheet were tucked in so tight they did not yield. He pushed harder with his feet, but as hard as he pushed he could not feel the metal rail at the foot of the cot.

Walter giggled again.

Albie opened his eyes and sat up. No one in the bunk was looking at him. Uncle Jesse came in zipping up his fly. "Okay, bedtime." He walked past the foot of Albie's bed to his own. "Five minutes, lights out, let's go." Albie closed his eyes again, pulled hard at the blankets, and kicked his feet toward the foot of the bed as hard as he could. His left foot tore through the sheet with an audible rip and found the rough texture of the mattress.

"Yayyy!" all the Panthers shouted. "Moron tore his sheet!" Raddy cried. He jumped out of bed and danced up and down in the narrow aisle between his cot and Albie's. "Yay! First he's a sailor and then he rips his sheets. Moron! Moron!"

"Hey, moron," Will called from across the cabin. "Moron! Moron!" Walter shouted. "That's enough," Uncle Jesse's voice said from near Walter's.

Albie opened his eyes to find every other pair of eyes in Panthers trained on him. The mark on Will's face glowed below the glints on his glasses. Albie didn't understand.

"Your bed got frenched," Uncle Jesse said. "It's all over. Make it again and lights out."

Albie had heard them speak of frenching beds, but he had never asked what it was. Like a wooden boy, a Pinocchio without spirit, he moved over the cold wooden floor. Chill night air flowed through the now-dark screens as he pulled out his blanket. They had folded his bottom sheet back to make a bag half the length of the bed; he had torn it in an L. The flap and the strings that hung from the ragged edge looked terribly sad.

"How do I—"

"Just make it."

The other Panthers sniggered as Albie took his bed apart. They pretended not to watch. Should he use the torn sheet for the top or for the bottom? To rest his bare ankle on the mattress with its faint urine smell seemed a violation, but to be covered by only the blanket risked exposure. Someone whispered. Walter giggled again. Albie memorized where the tear was, so he wouldn't put his foot through it as he remade his bed. It was only a sheet, only a bed, only one more humiliation, yet in the moment it felt like a wall he could not scale. He closed his eyes even before he was all the way in, and tried to close his ears against the whispers. When that proved impossible he listened for the sound of sleep coming, and the roar of the planes of the rescue mission.

Albie did not wet his bed that night, yet in the morning he was ashamed. In the scrap of time Uncle Jesse gave him he advised exchanging the torn sheet for a new one after breakfast, as if what had happened had not been important. Uncle Jesse strode ahead.

The rest of Bear Lake would hoot 'Sailor!' at Albie because his bladder had once reduced him to a baby, and that calumny would be no easier to bear because it was false. Albie would get through breakfast, get through the cleanup, make his bed whatever it cost—and run free with his binoculars to meet Joe. They would look at wildlife and climb trees from which they could examine camp life without being seen. The morning would bring pain before joy; that was the best life offered.

Uncle Jesse served thick pancakes and thin, dry bacon. "No pills," Mike Wooley said with a broad smile. Albie stared out the window. A wing of the main house blocked his view of Panthers. Eyes unfocused, he imagined a line that would pass through the obstruction, through the end wall of Panthers, through the books on his shelf to the oval-ended leather case and its rolled strap under his yellow slicker. After breakfast, after breakfast.

Without drinking, he tilted his milk glass up and down, up and down, to feel the liquid edge move against his lip. The beloved sensation soothed him. If he carried his sheet so as to show that he had taken part in rough horseplay with the other Panthers, all would see that he hadn't suffered humiliating incontinence. Maybe Bear Lake wasn't so bad. Maybe. By the time he left breakfast he had convinced himself that the frenched bed was positive, and wondered how he could participate in frenching someone else's bed.

He bounced up the steps into the cabin. The others were already sweeping. "Hi, Raddy," Albie said. Before he attended to his bed he reached over the books on his shelf to stroke his slicker. The hand he pressed down toward the binocular case found hard shelf rather than yielding leather.

Raprapraprap! The world closed. Albie's bright morning vision contracted to a tunnel. He kept his hand on the slicker while he inched his head around. Cooper tightened a hospital corner. Jerry arranged clothes. When Will saw Albie's eyes he made a face and pretended to dance with the broom. Philip read a comic book. Wayne was making his bed.

Albie groped nothing but wooden shelf and wooden wall. No! He threw the slicker on his bed and took down books and shirts. Nothing. The binoculars were gone.

Shock slackened his face; he feared he would cry with Raddy watching him. He faced Uncle Jesse's corner while he replaced the shirts, the book, the slicker. He walked around the end of Walter's bed. "Uncle Jesse?"

The counselor squinted at Albie's unmade bed. "Let's go with that sheet."

"Uncle Jesse?"

"What is it now?" Uncle Jesse's chin whiskers were light brown.

Albie stood on tiptoes and whispered, "I can't find my binoculars."

"You, ah, leave them in the woods, maybe?"

Albie shook his head.

"You lend 'em to your pal, what's his name, Moscow?"

Albie shook his head at Uncle Jesse's gray eyes.

"Listen up," Uncle Jesse said. "Anybody here see Greenberg's binoculars?"

"Anybody here see Greenberg's binoculars?" Raddy said.

"Hey!"

Raddy pressed his lips together and rolled his eyes.

"Look around some more," Uncle Jesse said. "Let me know if you don't find 'em. And Greenberg? Change that sheet or they're going to close."

If anyone called Albie sailor, he didn't notice.

"You're supposed to bring both," the aide said.

"It isn't wet."

The aide shook out the sheet to display the huge tear. "Be careful, these are Bear Lake property." He handed Albie a folded sheet from the shelf.

On the way back Albie was lost in thought. Could he have changed the hiding place of the binoculars and forgotten that he had done so? Unlikely, but worth checking. His father's precious binoculars enjoyed a status above the toys of children. No one would steal such a valuable article. How could he tell his father he had lost them, when he had not taken the tennis racquet out of its case even once? Compared to this, bedwetting was nothing. No circumstance could excuse this transgression. It would be best for him to disappear into the woods forever, or drown in the lake.

If Albie were threatened in the grownup world—if a real criminal had tried to lure him into a car, say, or leaned out of a doorway and asked him to steal, he would have to ask his father for help, and he would expect to receive it. In this setting, though, he, Albie, would be at fault: even if he were not the thief who had stolen the binoculars, he was the flawed steward who had failed in his duty to protect them.

Yet maybe the binoculars were on the bottom shelf. Or if he had hung them on the nail with the tennis racquet, the strap would have suspended the case out of sight below the bed. That must be it! In his mind's eye he saw the cracked black strap and the flat gray nailhead lit by fading daylight the afternoon before. Yes, he could almost remember putting it there. That he had made a fool of himself before Uncle Jesse and his cabin mates did not matter as long as the binoculars were safe.

He felt relieved when he entered the cabin. "Come on!" Wayne said. "We can't go to swimming until you make your bed."

Albie tucked his hospital corners tight. The bell sent the Panthers out the downhill door. Albie waited in the aisle until the last boy was out; with the slam of the door he sprang to the head of his bed.

The nail and the tennis racquet were as he remembered them. He swung the racquet aside, but he saw no strap. The binoculars must be on the shelf: he had missed them. He took all the books down, and the shirts. The yellow slicker lay flat. Under the left side of the slicker? The right? With a sob he lifted the garment to find only bare wood and dust.

On the next shelf then. In desperation he took all the clothes off all his shelves, and put them back. The cabin was quiet. His heart jarred in his chest. The boys and the counselors had gone to the morning swim. He was free to search, to detect who had stolen his binoculars. He caught his breath: he could steal from the other boys, take back goods in exchange for the pain they had caused him.

He stepped toward Raddy's bed, but another invisible wall would not let his hand touch the property of another boy uninvited. 'Thou shalt not steal,' a voice said in his head. 'I'm not stealing, I'm looking,' he answered it, but his motive was mean-spirited, and what he intended was wrong.

He clenched his teeth, strained in his belly and advanced. Raddy's pillowcase felt slimy and alien; its human odor was not Albie's. Albie had to know. He sidled between the two cots to lift down his tennis racquet. Holding it by the heavy press he raised Raddy's pillow with the handle, but saw only folded pajamas.

Raprapraprap! Someone might catch him! He displaced Raddy's clothing with the racquet handle and knocked a pair of socks to the floor, but found nothing. He crossed over to Wayne's bed and lifted the pillow: nothing. Rushing back to his bed he struck his shin on the metal frame.

Albie cried with guilt and frustration as he replaced his tennis racquet. He raced to the waterfront on a beeline, with his head down, an outcast who had betrayed his father. He deserved whatever was going to happen to him.

On the way to lunch pink-cheeked Walter held the uphill door open as Raddy, Wayne, and Will jumped from the sill and landed outside to cheers. Albie slipped out the other way because he was not sure he could bear the crowded washroom or the hurly-burly of the dark stairway.

Joe was leaning against the latrine door; he followed Albie in. Albie felt intent eyes on him as he urinated, and was embarrassed; he was careful to adjust his clothing. Joe scrutinized him as he washed his hands.

"This afternoon, okay?" Joe said.

"This afternoon what?"

Joe's face clouded; neither eye looked at Albie. "We look through your binoculars, right? To see if they're coming, okay? The rescue mission?"

Even with cold water splashing on his face Albie burst into tears.

Joe touched his shoulder. "What's wrong?"

"They're gone," Albie sobbed. "Somebody took them. I couldn't find them where I hid them." He held his breath to keep from sobbing again.

"It's okay," Joe said. "Sometimes I make stuff up, too."

The expression in Joe's eye was concerned, kind; it was an outrage. Pain in Albie's heart erupted upward into his arms. With an inarticulate cry he shoved Joe against the wall of the latrine with both hands before he rushed out the door and into the woods. Blinded by tears, he skipped lunch.

Albie considered risking death behind the backstop with Joe, but he didn't want to miss a chance to get more targets toward a medal, in case Panthers were scheduled to shoot. He hid in dense brush beside the trail to the range. The Woodsmen approached singing a song about bottles of beer; the red-headed one led them down the trail like a drum major with a stick pointed up in the air. Joe saw Albie and paused. Uncle Dan pushed past Joe and called back from further down the trail, but Joe just picked his nose until his cabin mates disappeared.

After a while Joe said, "I see you."

Albie's heart hammered.

"They talked about your binoculars at lunch."

Albie moved a little.

"I'm sorry I didn't believe you."

Albie wiped his eyes and his nose on the back of his hand. He detached himself from the small tree in front of him.

"You shouldn't have pushed me," Joe said.

Albie stopped ten feet from Joe. "I'm sorry," he said.

Joe extended his hand. Albie's hand was too heavy. Joe came closer and took Albie's. "Let's go that way." Hand in hand the two boys strolled through the New Hampshire woods. Over their shoulders came the crackle of rifle fire and ragged cheers from the playing field. In a little clearing a black bird with a flash of red under its wings flew up and away. "Look." Albie pointed.

"What are you going to do?"

"I don't know, they're my—" He found that he couldn't say, 'father's.' As much as he longed to confess what was wrong to Joe, it was all too complicated, too long, too shameful to recite.

Into Albie's blushing silence, Joe said, "Let's go to the place."

Together, the two boys scouted uphill around all the Bear Lake buildings a new way to a trail that came back to the corner of the lake from a different direction. From their hidden spot they watched boys swim and girls canoe. They didn't talk much.

Saturday morning Albie said, "Let's go early. We can go all the way around the lake."

Joe scratched himself and swayed his head from side to side. "I have to go with Uncle Dan to get a new mattress wrapped in wax paper. I wet my bed again." His blank tone and normal volume said humiliation didn't matter any more.

"Let's go after that."

Joe swayed his head from side to side.

The Panthers' lackluster cries of 'Sailor!' trailed off, but a Lion Cub who had mastered his bladder screeched "Sailor! Sailor! Sailor!" as Joe stood on line with his sheets, and kept it up while Joe and Uncle Dan exchanged the mattress.

Albie sat down to read his mythology book. The other Panthers chattered about the impending game with the Woodsmen; they expected Albie to run away and were glad he would not be there to make errors on whichever team would be stuck with him. Uncle Jesse said, "Hey, Greenberg. Find your field glasses yet?" Albie shook his head. "Too bad, keep looking." Uncle Jesse's eyes went vague again.

They didn't understand and they didn't care. Albie would be a fool to expect any help. He touched his pocket to check his knife once more before he walked past Raddy and Mike and Cooper and out the door. He left his mitt. Cheers and clapping arose from one of the cabins. The Warriors and the Guides streamed down to morning activities; Albie cut through them before he looked back. Someone who moved like Joe bounded down the Woodsmen steps. At that distance Albie could not make out the face. The figure waved to Albie and sprinted the other way to duck between Woodsmen and Panthers.

Uncle Dan appeared on the Woodsmen's porch. "Joe! Joe Moscow!" He went back in. A few seconds later he called from the uphill door. "Joe! Joe Moscow!" Joe broke from the corner of his cabin and ran diagonally through the pines toward Albie in a blue tee shirt that wasn't a Bear Lake shirt. A hoarse shout came from Woodsmen and Uncle Charlie burst out the door in pursuit, his pipe clenched in his teeth upside down. When he caught Joe they were close enough for Albie to see Uncle Charlie's dark whiskers, but Uncle Charlie did not see Albie, and Joe did not look toward him.

"Er!" Uncle Charlie jammed his pipe into his pocket as he restrained Joe by the wrist. "Where's the other one?"

Joe struggled in silence.

"Greenberg," Uncle Charlie said, "where is he?" He scanned the woods before he towed Joe back toward the main house without a glance over his shoulder. They cared more where Joe was than anyone cared about Albie.

Albie owed it to Joe to find a new track to make up for what must be happening to him now. He broke into a run past the place he had made his own, past Leech Beach, past the trail to the abandoned truck. Further on, the shoreline curved away to the left. Albie clambered over boulders to the water's edge: he had come more than halfway around Bear Lake from the camp to where the war canoes went. From a sunlit knoll set back from the water he saw a lone pine on a ridge further from the lake.

It was a straight shot to the tree, but when he thought he was getting close, it got harder to see, and when he could see it again it looked further away than before, even though he had walked in the right direction. When Albie realized he was lost, he peered into darkness and thick woods to retrace his path to the water. Sun twinkled off ripples in the thousand colors of Albie's mother's diamond like a crumpled wrapper from the sour balls he and Joe had shared.

Albie inspected Bear Lake and Mistlewood in miniature with something like nostalgia. There was the Indian Circle. Tall trees concealed courts where Mistlewood girls played tennis. Well to the right stood four widely separated small houses with short wooden docks. Albie could make out a canoe tied to one of them.

The little houses must have driveways, and roads. Albie could scout the rest of the way around the lake to telephone to beg his father for his freedom. Would people let him or would they drive him away? Or capture him for Uncle Charlie? Tomorrow was Sunday. The people in those houses would go to church, so Albie could climb in through a window to telephone without their knowing—if he could get there.

He left the lake to seek the lone pine on the ridge again. When his route uphill was no longer clear, he climbed a tree. Four branches, six, eight, much higher than when he watched Mrs. Brewer smoke. The wind murmured, chilled him, swayed the tree. Down far below his toes the ground moved back and forth. Albie felt hot and cold, and a panicky fear he might fall.

Joe's parents had taken Joe to the doctor, but no one knew Albie was in the wilderness. Beyond Bear Lake and the camp lay the road, the railroad station, miles of track, and somewhere at the end of the line his city and his street. As Albie closed his eyes and clutched the tree, his parents contracted and lost importance. He reached out to his real uncle with the ropy scars on his neck through the railroad station, but the seacoast and home were too far away. Bear Brewer was real, and nearby.

The bark of Albie's tree was out of focus, but not the swastikas on the arm that clasped the trunk. I will not be afraid, he thought. With all his will he forced himself to loosen his grip on the trunk until he could lower one sneaker to the branch below the one he stood on. There he enjoyed the tree's motion the same way he enjoyed subway stations rushing toward him through a dark tunnel. He carved a block A and G into the bark and stroked the white letters before he made his deliberate way down the tree.

On the ground he felt weak. A low, distant sound might have been a truck or the wind. His tracks in the pine needles around the tree were a hodgepodge. Which way had he come from? He wished Joe were with him. He set out down hill and up, and in a while passed from a clearing into a very dark part of the forest. Low branches and thorns threatened his face. He pressed ahead bent over until the undergrowth became too dense for him to continue.

Behind him looked just as bad. The darkness became the gloom of Grand Central Station the day he departed from the city. The echoing speech of a thousand campers and parents became the rumble of the train and the growling of beasts and a black wind that soughed among a thousand trees. The noise grew to tumult, battle. The flow of campers had rushed him away from the world he knew and the room he loved and tumbled him into this gloomy wilderness to hunt his food. In his imagination Bear Brewer loomed before him, unshaven like Uncle Charlie. Curls of black hair erupted from their shirt collars, from their cuffs, and their faces bulged. The hand Bear Brewer reached out to Albie became a paw. He was a bear. Albie, alone in the woods, would meet the bear.

He had tracked alone from the lake's brilliance of blue sky into the unmarked darkness of the wilderness where light failed so even white mushrooms under trees were hard to see. Curiosity would draw him deeper into the closed book of the forest, where the bear would smell him first, but he would hear it gruffle. Albie would sniff damp air to discern the animal reek in the vegetable darkness, and though he would long for the light above the lake, he would not look back. He would hurry because he was pursued. The bear's passage through the dark undergrowth would echo the crackle of twigs Albie's own feet broke and the rub of vines he kicked out of his way.

The bear would gain on him. Its rough breathing would drown his cry. No, he would not cry out, because no one could hear him. He must survive alone. Sweaty with fear he would glimpse the awful black muzzle, the heavy paw that swiped at him the way the aide, Dougie, had seized him on visiting day. The bear would take him in a hug the way Uncle Jesse kept him from his parents and deliverance, and leave him with red, ropy scars like his uncle.

Some day Albie would say to some little boy, Joe's son, 'It was a New Hampshire bear,' but to survive now he would have to overcome it. How could a skinny boy who was afraid of Raddy Tarrant defeat a bear?

The bear's hug bound Albie's arm to his side. With his free hand he scrabbled in his pocket for the clasp knife. There! Gnats wheeled around the bear's cruel eyes, but in the shower of its spittle and meaty breath, with his thumb and a finger Albie gripped the blade and with a convulsive gesture—now he might cry out, to deceive the beast—he threw up his arm so the weight of the handle opened the knife!

How could a small boy stab through the matted filth in a bear's dark coat, the leathery skin beneath its fur, the muscles of its powerful chest, even thicker than Uncle Bart's? No, a boy with a pocket knife could not reach a bear's heart. The monster growled and drew him close, but as the jaws yawned Albie plunged the knife into the bear's eye, yes, the whole length of the large blade, into the vulnerable eye, and as the bear shook its head, Albie's open hand hammered the whole knife, blade and handle, deep into the bear's eye and brain, to kill the bear!

The bear stumbled, wept, coughed and tried to growl. Albie, still caught in the monster's embrace, glanced back over his shoulder to be sure his head would not hit a stone as he fell. The bear crumpled to the ground and released him, but Albie held the flat of his hand over the handle of the knife until he was sure. When it was over he walked to the lake to wash the amber ichor that had run from the bear's eye off his knife, and off his hand.

Fist clenched on pine sap, Albie had to wash, he had to wash. The lake and Bear Lake Camp lay between him and visiting day. He charged downhill through the brush and thorns; he did not protect his face. The scratches on his face burned hotter than his forearm under the stick, but he pushed through, pushed through, and emerged in a clearing with a circle of stones in the center: he had found the other Indian Circle!

Albie came back to himself. Among the burnt pieces of wood in the center were a Coke bottle, a Mars bar wrapper, a red and white Lucky Strike package not faded at all. Down the cleared lane at the water's edge, keels of war canoes had grooved the narrow beach. Albie scrubbed his hands with dirt. From his point of view inches above the water he rinsed in, the lake appeared an ocean. He could never swim that distance. He dried his hands on his shorts as he walked back to the circle.

Ten feet above the ground where he had come out of the woods, two skulls had been nailed to a tree facing each other. They were too big to be dogs, and their top parts were smaller than the picture on the iodine bottle at home. One was broken.

"These bears are dead," he said aloud. "They're dead!" Now he had something to tell Joe. He wanted to tell his real uncle. The pebble he threw missed the tree. Near the water he found an opening toward through which he began his long return around the lake.

As he worked his way back he tried to limp like his uncle, but it was too hard to keep doing. The sun moved through the sky toward the side of the lake he had reached, the way it moved from the park in the morning to the Avenue in the afternoon. He trudged past Leech Beach, where tomorrow the other Panthers would haze him as they bathed. His face felt as stiff as a sunburn. He knelt to make a face at the water but a small breeze disturbed the surface so he couldn't see his reflection.

He threaded his way through shadows to reach Panthers in the quiet time before dinner. Jerry saw him coming. "Look who's here," the larger boy said, but his face changed as Albie slumped up the steps. "Hey, what happened?"

Albie pushed past him. "Hey," Jerry said, "you should go to the nurse." Walter pointed at him from the other end of the aisle. "I know," Walter said. "He went in the woods where it isn't safe and a lion attacked him." Wayne pursed his thin blue lips and fixed piercing eyes on his face, and Jerry and Cooper stared too.

Albie stood in the aisle. His face felt stiff, that was all. Wayne took Uncle Jesse's shaving mirror from its nail. Albie's dirty forehead, nose, and cheeks were torn by a dozen deep scratches. Most of them had dried to purple crusts, but a few were still bleeding, and one, which extended through his eyebrow and onto his eyelid, gaped open to expose a trail of red blood, like a fresh swastika.

"Who'd you fight with?" Raddy said.

"None of your business." Albie stepped to his bed. He wanted to lie down to read, but he would do better to wash his face first. He pushed past Raddy and Jerry, but as he descended the stairs he had just climbed Uncle Jesse said, "What's the matter with Greenberg?" Albie jumped, but Mike ran after him to grab his wrist. Albie let himself be pulled back up to the cabin.

"He was in the woods again," Raddy said.

"Let me see," Uncle Jesse lifted Albie's chin into light from the doorway. He colored. "We better get you cleaned up. Brown! Make sure everybody's at dinner on time!" He propelled Albie out the door and up the hill.

They waited on a bench outside an unfamiliar entrance to the main house, where the ambulance men had gone. Uncle Jesse picked up a small stick between his feet. He broke it in two, and broke each half in two. He rubbed his nose. "You want to tell me what happened?"

Albie shook his head.

"Why don't you play ball with your teammates?"

Albie wanted nothing more than teammates, but he had only enemies. He shook his head again.

"Why don't you come to baseball like everybody else?" Uncle Jesse rubbed his nose with the back of his hand. "You're a good shot, you could use that eye to throw better."

Scratching inside the door became a snap and jingle as someone released the hook and eye. Mrs. Brewer said, "Come in, Jesse." They followed her down a narrow corridor with faded linoleum on the floor and dark brown enamel woodwork. She turned on the light in a small room with two chairs, one painted white, a table with a thin mattress wrapped in a sheet on it, and a white cabinet with glass doors.

The medicine smell frightened Albie. "I'm okay." He tried to duck out, but Uncle Jesse held him by the arm.

"Close the door, Jesse," Mrs. Brewer sat on the white chair and motioned the counselor to the brown one. He rested his hands on Albie's shoulders to keep him between them. Mrs. Brewer smelled of perfume and cigarettes. "Oh, my." She opened a black and white notebook like the ones Albie used in school. "What's his name?" She riffled through pages.

"Greenberg," Uncle Jesse said. "Alan."

"Albert." Albie said.

"Oh, my." Mrs. Brewer wrote in the book with a fountain pen. She touched Albie's eyelid. "Does that hurt, Albert?"

It did, but Albie shook his head.

"Boys shouldn't fight at Bear Lake," Mrs. Brewer said. "In this beautiful country, you can play as hard as you want. We have every sport. We have Color War so you won't have to have a real war. Oh, my, Mr. Brewer and I can't understand why boys fight." She opened a package of cotton balls and cleaned his cuts with a gentle touch. She didn't hurt him. Albie was relieved that she had stopped talking. Cool water ran down to his neck.

"He's the best shot in the bunk," Uncle Jesse said.

Mrs. Brewer worked on Albie's face. "Shooting," she said, "fighting." She stopped daubing. "I thought the world had enough fighting, and now we're going back. I hope you don't go to Korea."

"Me?" Uncle Jesse said.

There was a heavy step in the hall. "Dinner," Bear Brewer said, and leaned into the room. "What happened?"

"Coupla scratches," Uncle Jesse said.

"Which one is it?"

"Greenberg. The one who goes off with the one from Woodsmen."

"Oh, yeah." Bear Brewer tousled Albie's hair from behind. "Your mom and pop sent you here to play sports. You ought to take advantage." His voice changed. "Hurry up, Hildie. It's dinnertime."

He left. Mrs. Brewer poured the remaining water into a sink and opened a smaller bottle.

"Is that iodine?" Albie struggled against Uncle Jesse's restraint.

Mrs. Brewer poured a liquid that was both orange and green into a metal cup. "No, dear. This is mercurochrome." She dipped a Q-tip in the orange liquid and painted a spot on the back of her hand. "It's good for your cuts." Albie watched, fascinated, as the liquid dried from orange to cherry red.

Mrs. Brewer dipped the Q-tip again. Albie cried out as the tincture bit the open scratch; Uncle Jesse held him still until Mrs. Brewer was done. "You shouldn't fight," she said as she put the small bottle back into the cabinet. "I wish boys wouldn't fight."

"Say thank you to Mrs. Brewer," Uncle Jesse said.

Albie muttered at the floor.

"You're welcome, Albert," Mrs. Brewer said. "I'll be watching you."

Halfway down the narrow corridor Uncle Jesse stopped Albie with a hand on his shoulder. "You want to tell me who you were fighting with?" He knelt down. "Was it your pal from Woodsmen?"

Albie shook his head.

"Attaboy," Uncle Jesse said. "At least you're not a snitch." He stood up and smacked Albie on the buttock.

By the time Albie reached the Panthers' table he was no longer the topic of conversation. Conspicuous in red war paint, he chose the corner seat as far from Uncle Jesse as he could get.

On his way to the next table, Joe whistled when he saw Albie's face. "What happened?"

Uncle Jesse poked Jerry Roth. "Tell him to get back to his table." Jerry poked Joe, who ducked away when he saw Uncle Jesse hold up a forefinger with his head tilted in admonition. Albie struggled not to look at Joe. Uncle Jesse aimed his cleft chin at Albie, and winked.

"When we purify ourselves in the waters of Bear Lake today," Bear Brewer read from a typed piece of paper at Sunday breakfast, "we call upon the two great spirits." He lifted his palm. Uncle Jesse reached under his seat, and with half a dozen other counselors scattered through the mess hall, stood up and beat a tom-tom with a wooden ball on the end of a stick.

"The secret of the great spirits belongs to every boy here," Bear Brewer said. "What is the secret of the Bear Lake spirits?"

A few boys called out. Raddy poked Cooper. "I know what the secret is. You do too, don't you, Coop?" Cooper nodded.

"Oh, rubber, rubber," Bear Brewer intoned, and gestured again.

"Oh, rubber, rubber," the counselors responded, and beat their tom-toms.

"Oh, rubber, rubber," a few campers answered. Joe slumped at the Woodsmen's table. He tore pieces from the edge of a paper napkin and rolled them into little balls.

"Oh, rubber, rubber," Bear Brewer chanted.

"Rubber, rebber, Redbear, Yayyy!" responded campers, the red-haired Woodsman among them. Joe kept silent.

Jerry stood up with his hands raised. "Oh, Redbear, Redbear!"

"Yay, Redbear!" Raddy shouted.

"Redbear!" Albie said.

"No!" Raddy pushed Albie, "You're on the gray team."

"Nobody's on any team yet," Albie said. He wanted Uncle Jesse's support, but the counselor wasn't listening.

Raddy poked Wayne. "You know, don't you?" He nodded his head up and down in an exaggerated way.

"Oh, grabber, grabber," Bear Brewer proclaimed, and the counselors drummed their response, "Oh, grabber grabber."

Wayne returned a grotesque wink. "We know, don't we, Walter?"

"Know what?" Walter said.

"About Red Bear and Gray Bear," Wayne said.

"Oh, mighty Red Bear!" Bear Brewer said, "Oh mighty Gray Bear!"

Tom-toms thundered. Uncle Jesse looked over at Woodsmen to be sure when to beat his drum.

"Everybody in the bunk knows except you," — Raddy pointed a fore-finger at Albie — "because you . . . can't . . . swim!"

"I *do* know," Albie said.

"Oh, grabber grabber!" A cacophony of cries and tom-toms filled the air. "Oh, rubber, rubber!" Boys beat on the tables with their fists and stamped on the floor. "Oh Redbear, Redbear!" Raddy drummed the table. Both Gardners joined him, though Walter said "Rubber, rubber," so Albie could not be sure whether Walter understood or not.

Desperate, Albie cried into the din. "*I do know!*"

The noise quieted. Jerry stared at Albie. All the Panthers at that end of the table were waiting for him. Philip said, "You can't know what the great spirits are because you didn't go across the lake with us."

Albie held a deep breath until he made a decision. He would regain normal status in the Panthers in one fell swoop. "They're not spirits," he said. "They're two old bear skulls nailed to a tree."

"Who told?" Raddy balled his little fists and stuck his lower lip out at the other Panthers. "Whoever told the moron can't be on the red team, that's all!" He pushed Albie. "Who told you?"

Having scouted to the other end of the lake alone, without help, without counselors to guide him or others to paddle him there, had earned Albie no respect. Never mind their respect; he would keep his accomplishment for himself. "I just know!" he blurted, and cried, "Oh, Graybear, Graybear!"

Time stopped. Albie and Raddy glared at each other. Another paroxysm of drumming circulated as Bear Brewer said something into the micro-phone. Benches squeaked as boys pushed back to leave. Uncle Jesse's gray eyes were unfocused over his coffee cup. Albie saw no friendship in the Panthers' faces and Raddy was coming toward him. Albie clambered backwards over the bench and couldn't stop himself from running toward the front door.

On his way back to shore from his two-minute bath, Albie encountered the Lion Cubs and Uncle Bernie standing in a circle. "One!" a little boy cried, and tossed a tennis ball to an even littler boy beside him. The tiny boy failed to catch the gray tennis ball, which floated in the water until he pounced on it and tossed it to Stuart, who was next in the circle. "One!" he said. Stuart caught the ball and passed it on, "Two!" and the next boy cried, "Three!"

Uncle Bernie was next but he didn't catch the ball. "Oh-oh," he said, and picked it up to toss it to the next little boy. "One!"

All the Lion Cubs were laughing or smiling. Stuart waved to Albie. Uncle Bernie waved, too. "Want to play?"

Albie felt sudden shame at the yearning that must show on his face. He shook his head no and ran back to his soap dish, his clothes, and his higher status as a Panther.

On the path back to the cabins Albie felt someone behind him. When he peeked at the cowboy hat the second time Uncle Bernie said, "Hi."

Albie nodded.

"Any time you want to join us," Uncle Bernie said, "the Lion Cubs would be proud to have a big boy join them in a game."

Albie flashed a smile over his shoulder, but that embarrassed him so much he ran back to Panthers, arranged the books on his shelf and hurried to hide in the woods behind the latrine for the hour left before lunch.

During rest period Uncle Jesse shushed the Panthers twice to make them start the letters home that would be required at dinner.

'Dear Mom and Dad,' Albie wrote. 'I want to be a red because the reds are going to win. My whole bunk can't be on the same team. We went to the beach today but I hope we have riflery tomorrow. I'm looking forward to coming home.' He studied his work, erased 'coming home' and wrote in 'visiting day.' They announced official team assignments the morning after visiting day; everything after that would be Color War.

Albie's heart accelerated. All the other Panthers wore red cords, even Mike Wooley. They would judge his throwing, his swimming, his batting, of course; but would they judge how well he made his bed and whether he cleaned his plate of food? Would they judge how happy his letters home were?

"Coop?" he called.

"That's enough." Uncle Jesse smashed his magazine to the floor. "I gave you a break, but that's a noogie." He bounded around the end of Walter's bed to seize Albie's elbow and strike his arm. This time he didn't pull the punch. Albie stood silent, his mouth open, as his eyes filled. It was too much: how could any boy stand up to a world so dangerous?

"Go write your letter," Uncle Jesse said.

"I did." Albie displayed his sealed letter.

Uncle Jesse held the envelope up to the light from the window and squinted at Albie sideways. He must believe that Albie had obtained his knowledge about the other side of the lake dishonestly. A warrior keeps his counsel, Albie thought as he lay down. He would say that to Joe.

Ten days had passed since Albie's father had bribed Bear Lake with the gleaming lenses to imprison Albie. Now Albie imagined the visiting day to come. "My little man," his father would say. But the crinkles at the corners of his father's eyes would fade when Albie confessed. A tremor of his father's wrath passed through all of Albie's slender body. Albie held his breath, because if he let the anger have its way his iron cot would shake, its legs would rattle on the floor, and Uncle Jesse would ask him to explain.

If someone had stolen the binoculars Albie was guilty of carelessness, but not all the fault would be his. If no one had taken them. . . . The idea that he might have lost them was intolerable. Doubt buffeted him. Might he have put the binoculars down and forgotten that he had done so? His memory was stronger than that, but his imagination was strong, too, and the threat of his father's rage would not let him sleep.

Near the end of rest period Albie tiptoed around the end of Walter's bed. Wayne was reading a Captain Marvel Junior comic; Albie felt a connection with the crippled newsboy in his familiar purple suit.

"Uncle Jesse?" Albie pitched his voice low so neither Gardner could hear. "Can I talk to you outside?"

The counselor rubbed his hair and followed Albie out. "Jesus Christ, not your binoculars again."

Fright chilled Albie's stomach. "I don't want anybody to get punished."

Albie crossed his fingers in his pocket. "I think someone in the bunk took them." He surveyed Uncle Jesse's face for a sign of understanding.

Uncle Jesse's face registered gloom. He raised one eyebrow. "What do you want me to do?"

"You could have a search when nobody's here. Or Uncle Charlie."

The bright midday sun cast a harsh pattern of light and dark on the ground among the picnic tables. As Uncle Jesse stared off toward the far end of the row of cabins, a whirl of consequences Albie could not control rose from the ground, licked at his feet, wrapped around his knees. If Uncle Jesse were to recover the binoculars in a search, Raddy, or whichever Panther had taken them, would know Albie had snitched, and take revenge. The folklore of Bear Lake reprisals loomed: dead frogs in beds; beatings behind cabins; duckings in the lake.

"I can't hear you," Uncle Jesse said.

Albie was bound to try to recover the binoculars, but the other things he loved left him vulnerable. His books could be torn, or soaked; the clasp knife his father had given him could be dropped down the latrine. As if he himself had fallen into such a place he shrank from darkness and stench that rose all around him until the bright day contracted to a single opening far above his head. He could do nothing. He crouched, arms close to his sides.

"Hey, Greenberg . . ."

"Never mind." Albie fled away from Panthers, past Woodsmen, down the line of cabins, and through the woods to the edge of the lake. He did not stop until, sweaty from running, he stumbled to his refuge beside the lake. On a grassy mattress that sloped down to dark water, beside trees an arm's length out of reach, he rested his head on the pillow of his fingers interlaced. Above him leaves divided the air into shade and sun. Motes and insects twinkled, appeared and disappeared, as they sifted through these quiet bands of light and darkness: so much motion amidst the stillness!

His breath eased. Two dragonflies hovered, one behind the other. Their many wings glinted as they subsided from shade into light; their silhouetted bodies flashed purple pink, like the filament in an electronic tube that has just come on.

With the flash, the crack of a bat echoed across the lake. Shouts of boys and deeper cries of men who drove them: baseball. A sharp sound nearby, a broken stick. Albie caught his breath. He set aside the dragonflies' pursuit and coupling, and tensed to listen.

Silence. Leaves moved. Another stick broke, more leaves, a step. More steps came his way through the forest, along the lakeshore, from beyond the next cove, from where the Indian Circle was, and the baseball field. A slow cadence: adults. Shoes off and in his hand, Albie was up and in the water. He waded over slimy stones his feet knew well, through cattails and lily pads, to the cleft in the trees. He crouched like a stone and rested his shoes on a root above the surface of the water. Behind him the great trunks and a tangle of thorns protected him from the counselors on the path around the lake. White arcs of sunlight overhead carved the deep shade. He was open only to a boat or to someone with binoculars on the wooded shore opposite.

As he hunched down, damp but not cold, every forceful beat of his heart ended in a tap instead of a whoosh as the path he had made through the lily pads trembled and disappeared. The counselors were baseball players: even if they saw the disturbance they would not understand.

Just in time: slow adult steps stopped in the clearing.

"Little fucker ain't here."

". . . where he came last time." That was Uncle Jesse.

"I thought you gave him a noogie." That older, darker voice was Uncle Charlie. It had been a serious pursuit. Albie considered his next move.

"Yeah, sure . . ." Uncle Jesse sounded uncertain.

". . . seriously wrong with him," Uncle Charlie said. "You gotta straighten him out before visiting day."

". . . if we can't find him," Uncle Jesse said. "But I think he was here."

One of them threw a rock out among the lily pads. Albie knew the story of Cadmus: he imagined that the green and white leaves became the ringlets of strange warriors who arose from the slimy shallows to smite them. Afterwards the two counselors would lie one on top of the other, their bright red wounds faded, white bones exposed, their torn, sodden remains strewn with dirt and leaves and twigs. A passerby who found them would not be sure whether they were two corpses or one.

They stood a few feet away.

". . . when he comes back from dinner," said Uncle Charlie, "and I'll straighten him out."

Adult footsteps dwindled away. Dragonflies with two pairs of wings hung in the dark and light over the lily pads, two, three, four of them, now alone and now in pairs. The boy marveled at how fast they moved their many pairs of wings with no sound he could hear. When he was sure he was safe he waded back to his landing to lie in the sun, where his shorts and the bottom of his shirt would dry.

"Dismissed," Uncle Jesse said. The Panthers pushed back both benches at once and moved out toward a planned evening game of Kick the Can with the Woodsmen. Albie scuffed after them.

"C'mere, Albie." Uncle Jesse touched his shoulder. "We're gonna talk to Uncle Charlie."

Albie felt as hollow inside as when the elevator in his father's office building dropped. "Why?"

"Ah, about the binoculars." The adult hand that had struck him held him fast. Uncle Jesse marched Albie around through the same narrow infirmary corridor to a room across from where Mrs. Brewer had treated him. Papers and index cards all but buried a portable typewriter on an old brown desk. Books with faded cloth bindings and piles of magazines Albie didn't recognize filled a scarred bookshelf. A large can with a tan label sat on top of the mess.

Uncle Charlie strode in and sat in the desk chair. Uncle Jesse propped himself on the side of the desk. Uncle Charlie filled his pipe with sweet-smelling tobacco from the can and lit it with a wooden match. He gestured at Albie's face with the pipestem. "You got cut up."

"In the woods," Albie said to Uncle Charlie's black whiskers.

Uncle Charlie puffed, pawed through index cards, made a face at Uncle Jesse. He pointed his pipe at Albie. "Aren't you happy at Bear Lake?"

Darkness swirled under the desk.

"I want you out on the ball field," Uncle Charlie said. "No more of this woods stuff."

"I like to see things," Albie said.

"See things."

"My father gave me binoculars so I could see birds and Uncle Lou said they were good for riflery."

"He's a good shot," Uncle Jesse said.

"I have to give them back to my father on visiting day," —Albie meant, 'because I'm leaving here on visiting day.' — "but somebody took them."

"What?" Uncle Charlie said. "What is this?"

Uncle Jesse said, "Greenberg asked if we could sort of search the cabin,"

Uncle Charlie moved papers and puffed on his pipe. Layers of smoke under the shade of the floor lamp glided in and upward through the opening at the top. "Er," he said around his pipe, and made a gesture of dismissal with his hand.

Uncle Jesse directed Albie toward the door with a nod of his head. "You want me to look around?"

"Er."

Outside air erased the sweet pipe aroma. Uncle Jesse stood with his hands on his hips. "You know where they're playing?" he said.

Albie nodded.

"Get going."

At the end of Kick the Can Albie raced up the road ahead of the Panthers. Uncle Jesse stood alone by Albie's bed. One by one the others left for the latrine with their toothbrushes. Uncle Jesse beckoned. "I looked pretty good," he said. "They're not here."

"Everywhere?"

"What do you want me to do, look on the roof?"

Albie deflated. His head wilted forward. Through open, crying eyes he watched his tears bounce on the dusty boards of the cabin floor.

"Hey," Uncle Jesse said, "they'll turn up."

Albie shook his head.

"Listen, I'm older than you," Uncle Jesse said. "The world isn't so bad a place."

"Bad things happen," Albie said, "invasions like Korea."

"We're all on the same team." Uncle Jesse tousled Albie's hair, and as when they had first met, his ring struck Albie's head and caused a little pain. "We don't have any Communists at Bear Lake. You better go wash your face."

Albie heard amusement and tenderness in the counselor's voice. The thin lips above the cleft chin softened. As Albie left the cabin, Uncle Jesse slid the rolled-up magazine with the woman on the cover out of his back pocket.

Thursday. Nine days of Bear Lake until visiting day. Albie knew the rhyme: Thursday's child has far to go. He had nine days of humiliations at baseball and swimming ahead of him. His friendship with Joe was marred: why hadn't he shared the binoculars the first day? Joe and he were brothers who had survived in a hostile land. Joe was the best friend Albie ever had, but Joe had survived without Albie and without the binoculars, and Joe didn't have to confess a crime to Albie's father.

The last visiting day had taught Albie not to count on anything. What if his parents didn't come? Or what if his father came without his mother and determined that Albie would have to stay to protect his permanent record? Albie saw his father bend over a golf club on the living room carpet in his bathrobe on a rainy Sunday morning.

"I guess you can't play today," his mother murmured as she wiped condensation from the front window.

His father tapped the white ball into a paper bag. "No, but my little man is playing ball near a beautiful lake in New Hampshire."

And whether it was nine days or twenty-four—it was that long until the banquet—Albie had to live with Raddy beside him day and night. Raddy his enemy, Raddy who goaded him, Raddy the menace at his side when he slept. Albie had not meant to usurp Raddy's seat on the train. If he had known what fixed malevolence sitting there would produce he would have asked for another place.

But no one could care about that ridiculous seat conflict for more than a day. Raddy must hate him not for what he had done but for what he was, and Albie could not change that.

'I'm the pitcher,' Raddy always said. Albie was the goat, fated to be driven out and destroyed. He belonged outside the arrangements of others, outside his family, outside Panthers, in the woods outside Bear Lake Camp. Albie must harden himself to bear a life alone that extended into the distance, always, forever.

After Leech Beach the Panthers replaced their soap dishes and towels on shelves and hooks. Dirty underpants went into laundry bags, and the boys to lunch.

"Let me have your attention," Bear Brewer said over the loudspeaker. "Many of you know that this is the last Sunday before the second Visiting Day, so it is the day of the All-Star Aides' Game with Pastor Ridge."

"The aides are the best players in camp," Philip said.

"Dougie hit a grand slam home run last year," Jerry said. "He ran from third base to home backwards."

"That was funny." Cooper barely showed his teeth when he smiled.

"I hope we get good seats," Philip said.

"The top row is best," Mike said.

"First come, first served," Raddy hissed. "Mike, let's go early."

"Can we?"

"Are you chicken?"

". . . after rest period," Bear Brewer said.

"Hucklebuck!" someone shouted. The mess hall took up the cry. "Hucklebuck! Hucklebuck!"

Bear Brewer held up both hands; the shouting trailed off. "No hucklebuck today, because Hughston is off duty. But let's do a cheer for the aides." He stood up on a chair with the microphone. "Two, four, six eight, Who do we appreciate? Aides! Aides! Yayyy!"

During rest period Albie finished his letter home and Uncle Jesse slept with his mouth open. Will whispered. "The third base stands. The sun's behind you."

"Like the real Yankee Stadium," Wayne whispered.

"Get the whole top row," Raddy said. "Will, you're the fastest, you get there first and save seats."

Albie could listen to the Dodgers with Hughston instead, but the idea of observing from a high place appealed to him. "Let's go now," he said.

Raddy whirled around. "I bet you won't."

"Why not? I want to see the game as much as you do."

"You're chicken," Raddy said.

Everyone watched one thin boy face the other thin boy on the next cot. "No I'm not," Albie said.

"Go ahead," Raddy said.

This was what Albie had practiced all summer: to leave the group, to act alone, to find a high place from which to observe. Uncle Jesse's watch said 1:20, only ten minutes left. Albie walked to the downhill door. "I'll save you a seat, Coop." He stepped out and eased the door shut. This normal kind of rule-breaking made him feel brave.

"Why don't you take your binoculars?" Raddy shouted.

Albie kept going off the bottom step.

At the game, two metal stands of campers roared like the radio. "He's walking him," Will explained to Albie as the Pastor Ridge catcher moved off to the side to play catch with the pitcher. "They'll have a force at every base."

A Bear Lake aide slid into third base, right in front of them, but the umpire called him out. "He was safe!" Raddy shrieked. "Ump is blind!" The Bear Lake stands booed. Even Cooper said, "That was a bad call."

"No fair!" Albie shouted.

Joe wasn't in the stands.

Before dinner Albie propped his letter home against the wall of the cabin to print in pencil on the back of the envelope, 'P.S. We won the All-Star game today 5 to 3.'

But Monday morning dawned leaden. Raddy stamped through a rain puddle in the gravel parking lot to splash Will. Will shoved Raddy. It thundered during breakfast. Rain spattered the wood siding and splashed through the screen. Aides moved around the mess hall to close windows.

"The great bear is growling," Bear Brewer announced. "First Uncle David will lead us in song here in the mess hall, and after that Uncle Dan will tell an Indian story." Thunder flickered the lights during the long delay after the clearing of the tables. The Panthers muttered. Will and Jerry shouldered each other along the bench for more room. Philip slid off at the other end so he pushed back against Mike. Cooper asked to be excused and climbed backward off his bench.

"Now I have room," Raddy said, and spread his arms. One hand struck Albie in the face.

"Hey," Albie said.

Uncle David held up his hands for attention. "How many like to sing?" He had freckles and hair that parted in the middle. A few campers raised their hands. Albie raised his, but as he did so Raddy swung and hit him in the nose with his fist. Albie cried out, and pain blinded him. He put his hand to his face.

"What the hell?" Uncle Jesse said.

"He was fighting," Raddy said.

Albie lowered his hand. Blood covered his hand; a drop landed on his yellow slicker. Uncle Jesse pressed napkins from the metal dispenser on the table against Albie's nose. Uncle Dave sounded a pitch pipe.

"Go to the nurse." Uncle Jesse held Albie still, which pushed him closer to Raddy.

The idea of walking across the public space with his nose bleeding was too humiliating to consider. Albie shook his head no.

Raddy pushed Albie away. "He's getting blood on me."

"Oh give me a home," Uncle Dave sang. The microphone squealed.

Albie tried to slide away from Raddy, but that pushed Walter off the end of the bench.

"He's pushing me," Walter cried.

"Home, home on the range," many campers sang.

"Stop pushing!" Walter hit Albie in the shoulder. Uncle Jesse dropped the napkins to seize Walter by both arms. A splatter of blood from Albie's nose landed on the table; Albie reached for the napkins and Raddy pushed him again.

"We're all leaving." Uncle Jesse nodded to Albie. "You go first."

"Where never is heard, a discouraging word," Uncle Dave sang with the campers. A very loud clap of thunder shook the mess hall, and the lights and the microphone failed together.

Mrs. Brewer waved a finger in the air as she bustled around the treatment room. "I wish boys were not so unruly. I'm sure your mother doesn't want you to fight." She cleaned Albie's face with a wet pledget of cotton while he held a gauze pad against the side of his nose. "Let me see," she said.

Albie's nose bled again.

"Oh, dear." Mrs. Brewer dipped cotton into a jar of liquid with tweezers; held up the tip of his nose with the pad of her thumb and poked the cotton into his nostril. It tickled; he sneezed and spluttered, and blood sprayed again.

"Really!" Mrs. Brewer said. "You have to cooperate with Mrs. Brewer."

When she finished stuffing his nose she washed her hands and dried them on her apron. She stood back with her hands on her hips. "Go back to Jesse," she said. "Tell him you are not to run or swim today, you are not to remove the cotton, and you are to come here after breakfast tomorrow."

Albie backed toward the door.

"And tell him that you will not fight any more for the rest of the summer."

Albie hurried through the rain to the cabin instead of going back to the mess hall. The Panthers didn't return until after lunch, by when the rain had stopped.

"Raddy?" Joe asked when he met Albie shuffling toward dinner. Albie nodded. "Did you hit him back?" Albie shook his head.

"Three weeks," Joe said, "then we get to go home."

Albie meant to go home on Visiting Day.

Uncle Jesse put Albie at the far end of the table and kept Raddy near him. Albie couldn't eat with his nose packed. He raised his hand; when Uncle Jesse acknowledged him he raised his chin toward the exit. Uncle Jesse nodded.

In the bathroom under the mess hall he studied himself in the mirror.

Except for the nostril bulged out by the cotton and his healing scratches, his face looked the way it always did. He pulled at the fluff of cotton sticking out and felt a tickle inside that made him want to sneeze. He would never be able to sleep with the cotton there. Little by little he coaxed it out. Things pulled loose inside, but his nose didn't bleed. As he rested his forehead against the cool glass, a wave of sadness made him weep for his room at home, his books, his bed, the brown Bakelite reading lamp and its beaded string.

He left the washroom to hide in the woods near the latrine until bedtime. He kept his head down and was able to keep from seeing either Raddy or Walter as he undressed, crawled under the covers, and pulled the sheet over his head.

Albie slept and dreamed and awoke under the heavy blue blankets from home, his forehead cold in the night air. His full bladder would not let him return to the sleep world that broke into pieces, faded and crumbled into the ordinary darkness of his closed eyes and the danger of the bunk beyond his eyelids.

He gave up. He opened an eye crushed into the pillow to see bedclothes, Raddy on his cot, measured breathing. Raddy's left arm lay outside the blanket: in the darkness the red cord and its knot looked black. Albie matched his breathing to Raddy's: one, in, rest; two, out, rest; one, in, rest. The regular rhythm soothed him, but his bladder insisted.

He took care with the screen door. The cold wooden steps outside felt damp under his bare feet. The air, too, was chill with moisture that obscured the stars, but moonlight filtered through. The dampness made his sense of smell more acute: he sniffed damp wood, tall grass that grew against the side of the bunk, his urine as it splattered off a rock. He fancied he could smell the coldness of the rock as it refused the warmth of his urine. He redirected the noisy stream against thin blades of grass too close to the building to be mowed. In the silence he rested his cheek against the wooden siding in the deeper darkness made by the shadow of the next bunk, Lion Cubs.

A breeze rustled the leaves of the great trees and chilled him. The wood against his cheek and the earth he stood on were cold too. They united him with the place and the world of things and creatures better than the pages of a book or the texture of a daydream because he was in the real world instead of separated from it. He shivered.

Treetops above him moved and muttered. The fog cleared; the black sky between the trees was shot through with stars. The skin of Albie's feet remembered the drops of urine that had splattered on them from the rock: those drops had been both hot and cold, like the stars. Albie's penis hung outside his pajama pants; he did not put it back in.

A rubbing, a scratching, marred the susurrus of the wind in the trees. The screen door on the downhill side of the bunk opened and closed. A foot descended, less careful of noise than Albie had been. Shod feet scraped gravel near the bottom of the stairs; in a moment Albie heard the hollow splatter of urine on a wooden stringer.

Albie listened and waited. The night, the stars, the wind were the web in which he hung like a spider. The manifestations of the other person who had risen to urinate would pass through the web without disturbing it, as the air left a spider web unharmed; these things do not concern a spider. Inch by inch Albie lowered himself to squat deep in the shadows under the edge of the cabin. His knuckles came to rest in tall grass dampened by his urine; his hand felt a rock the size of a baseball, not quite smooth, heavy, also damp. These were his connections to the universe. He felt all his points of contact; he was at peace, and he waited.

The urine stopped. Footsteps walked into the open downhill from the alley between the two cabins. In a pool of moonlight Raddy looked up through the trees in leather slippers. His left wrist with the red cord hung at his side as he scratched his neck with his right hand. He walked toward Albie.

He walked toward Albie but did not see him. Albie was stillness, he was part of the night. The soles of his feet felt gravel; his hands felt nature; his cheek felt the wooden cabin. Raddy walked to within ten feet of him and glanced back over his shoulder. Then he dropped to his knees.

Amazing! An arm's length from Albie, Raddy pushed leaves aside and crawled into the dark space under the bunk. He moved something and backed out into the night again. The wind blew stronger and the half moon came out to light the ground between the cabins and the trees. Albie felt his heart's motion, but the mystery he had found absorbed him.

Raddy carried something out to the bare place and put something down. From the middle of the clearing he looked up at the moon with Albie's father's binoculars.

A great trembling shook Albie's arms and forearms. His calves jittered, and wanted to run or spring. His fingers gripped and released the stone, gripped and released as the raprapraprap of his heart shook the world. Yet something in Albie remained clear and fixed; he was part of the night and part of the world. As still and as knowing as when he had crouched in the lake, he waited.

In a minute Raddy dropped the binoculars so they swung on the leather strap. He trailed them across pine needles; when they stuck on a root he jerked the strap so they jumped over the obstruction to drag further through the dirt. Raddy ducked back under the cabin even closer to Albie than he had been before, so Albie held his breath. He had never taken so large a breath, and yet he did not move, he waited.

The leaves under the bunk moved again. Raddy backed out, pajama bottoms pale in the moonlight. To take the binoculars back after Raddy had left would not be enough. Albie must face Raddy in the real world, fight if he must, suffer a wound if he must. He touched the scabs on his forearm: I am a man who feels no pain. Raddy was starting to stand under the edge of the cabin when Albie said, "You took my father's binoculars."

In straightening Raddy struck his head against the joist of the cabin with a wooden sound, like a branch cracking, more sharp than loud. He collapsed to his knees in the deep shadow that had concealed Albie and toppled to his side with a rustle like the wind. He lay with his chin upward, his head and face in the dark, but the moon lit his wrist with the red band and the leather slippers on his feet.

Albie squatted. He could not be sure whether Raddy was breathing. The rock he held out into the moonlight was as hard and as cold as before. If he had hit Raddy with it its color would have changed, and it would be wet. A hot red cylinder of anger and hatred rose within Albie from near his heart. God had taken vengeance against this enemy who had robbed him of his patrimony, who had worn slippers to examine the night with stolen binoculars.

Raddy lay before him, false and separate from the world. Albie should have struck him with the rock, he should have. As he watched, the tormentor's head rolled to the side, and dark blood ran out of his ear across the side of his face. Near Albie's free hand lay grass, leaves, a sharp stick— one of Raddy's failed attempts at a slingshot. Raprapraprap. As Albie had once lifted Raddy's pillow with his tennis racquet, so he tried to raise Raddy's eyelid with the stick. Raddy did not move.

Albie shook with wrath. Raprapraprap. His hand was wet on the stick. After a single shudder he pushed it through Raddy's eyelid as far into his eye as it would go. Then he leaned on the stick with his knee so that something cracked like an egg and the stick went in further. Raddy lay there. Albie pulled the stick out. More blood ran out of Raddy's eye, across his nose, to puddle on the black earth under the cabin.

Raprapraprap. Albie shivered with release, completion, like the best part of a book. Justice had been done. He was part of the night, and the avenger. He felt a good weakness, like after he had urinated. Fingerprints, he thought, I must be careful. He rubbed the rock over and over before he laid it down. He waited, and listened, but all he heard was the night, and the wind.

In a squat he took the stick with him as he moved backward a step, remembered and crawled back into the darkness to feel for the rock as well. He backed as Raddy had done, out of the shadow of the bunk and up hill, around the front of the Lion Cubs, into the blackness under the tall trees along the road. A porch light glowed at the main house, but the windows were dark. Albie waited a long time before he crossed the road to the latrine.

Moths wiggled and fluttered on every surface. This life at night was part of Albie now; the breath he held escaped with a sigh. Still barefoot, the damp cement more comfortable than the acorns and pebbles of the road, he dropped the rock through the opening in the first stall. He waited for the wet sound of its impact before he dropped the stick in after it. He washed his hands well under the tap and wiped his cold wet hands over his face.

On his way back, he retrieved the case. The strap chafed his neck as he climbed the steps on silent feet. A scrap of warmth remained under his heavy blue blankets for him and for the binoculars, before he fell asleep.

SIX

The progress of the human race in understanding the universe has established a small corner of order in an increasingly disordered universe.

—STEPHEN HAWKING, *A BRIEF HISTORY OF TIME*

The time Albie witnessed the stabbing from the dark anonymity of his window he watched the hubbub across the street safe in the knowledge that the violence could not touch him because the actors under the street-lights did not know that he had seen what had happened. Five stories of night air and a sheet of glass separated him from the action and muted the siren of the ambulance that rolled into the block from the park. The red lights that flashed before and behind in the night repeated the red that welled from the stab wounds in the sallow flesh of the victim Albie did not know.

As the ambulance floated to a stop under the orange streetlight glow, the closed door that kept Albie's family at bay ensured his safety. To seek out his parents in the living room would have risked a turmoil of blaming his whole life had taught him to avoid.

"Ah," his father would say, "you saw a stabbing, did you? Did you see a weapon? What color was the knife? How long? A switchblade? Did you see it open? No? How can you be sure? You say you know someone was stabbed: my little man, our legal system protects people from others who claim they *know* things. It requires them to prove it."

"I saw him run toward the Avenue, like this." Albie would imitate the man's long, loping strides, arms out before him as if he were swimming. His father would laugh from the wing chair, "Our little Sarah Bernhardt here must be reading too many comic books!"

How could Albie prove what he had seen? Were he to bear witness, the humiliation his father would produce in him would be infinitely more painful than the probing, twisting, biting shiny blade in the belly of the man across the night street. In showing Albie how weak his knowledge was, his father would blame him more than he blamed the murderer who had run away. Better to remain silent and safe, set firm against the side of his window, protected by distance and darkness in the room he had known all his life.

Albie imagined that the night of the stabbing he leaned against the window until it yielded like the mirror and he passed through it like a rim of tepid water. He floated through warm spring air to touch down near the ambulance as whitesuited attendants lifted the heavy form and slid the stretcher into doors that yawned to receive it. As the agitated crowd spoke their anger, Albie murmured agreement and outrage. They would tolerate his presence. They would not suspect him. And when their blaming crystallized into a plan for revenge they would not look to him because he was small and weak, even though he was no longer an outsider.

Albie muttered like a sleeping boy and rolled over. Raddy's bedclothes were disordered. Albie lay prone to conceal himself the way he hid from baseball, and waited.

A little later Philip raised his voice in argument. Mike responded, "You have to."

"No you don't, not a queen."

"Do, too."

Plastic checkers clicked on plastic checkers. Plastic checkers tapped cardboard. Click, tap, tap. They were playing on Mike's bed in the corner, beyond Raddy's empty bed.

From up the hill the bugle sounded reveille. Albie touched the cold metal frame of his cot and waited. Walter Gardner threw off his covers, stood on his bed and sang with the bugle, "Ya gotta get up, ya gotta get up!"

"Shut up, you moron," Philip called down the length of the cabin. "Hey, where's Raddy?"

Albie sat up and rubbed his eyes.

"Yeah, where's Raddy?" Mike asked.

"I bet he went to the latrine," Walter said.

Everyone moved. Albie slid the binocular case up into his pillowcase before he pushed down the covers. In his mind he saw himself from the high rafters of the cabin. His red flannel top fell away to expose bony shoulders; he donned a striped tee shirt with long sleeves. As the self he watched pulled on dungarees and socks, his vision, like Superman's, penetrated the dry boards of the bunk floor. Raddy lay supine on dirt and pine needles, his mouth open. Raddy was dead.

Albie held on to the wooden wall for support and pretended to straighten the books on his shelf until his vision became normal again.

"Hurry up, men." Uncle Jesse tied his shoes. "We were late yesterday. Beds after breakfast."

Somebody let the door slam so Albie had to take a hand out of his pocket to open it.

The morning was misty and sweet, between cool and warm. Albie waited in line for a sink in the crowded washroom. The big boy ahead of him handed him a piece of soap. "You want this?"

"Thanks." Albie washed. In the mess hall an aide stood on a bench to call out, "Letters home for dinner tonight! Letters home for dinner tonight!" Albie threaded his way to a place across from William and Jerry. Uncle Jesse sat down, and one by one the others arrived, except for Raddy.

"Anybody see Tarrant?" Uncle Jesse said. Before anyone could answer the loudspeakers squawked and Bear Brewer announced that one of the aides would read the prayer. Uncle Jesse folded his hands but kept peeking around under his eyebrows.

"Give us this day our daily bread," the aide read.

"Roth," Uncle Jesse said. "Go see if Tarrant's okay."

"I'm supposed to get the food."

"Brown'll get the food, go."

"Where?"

"Check the latrine."

"As we forgive those," the aide read.

Uncle Jesse filled small glasses with grapefruit juice from a dented metal pitcher.

Jerry climbed backward over the bench. "He wasn't in the bunk either." He sat down to the cold fried egg on his plate.

"You sure?"

Jerry nodded and chewed. Uncle Jesse whispered to the aide who poured coffee for him. The aide straightened and pointed to the round table in front of the big stone fireplace where Bear Brewer, Mrs. Brewer and Uncle Charlie were eating with some other adults. "Keep it down for a minute," Uncle Jesse said. "I'll be right back."

He leaned over Uncle Charlie, who gestured with his fork. Uncle Jesse left the mess hall. While he was gone the boys scraped the plates.

"One week," Will said.

"Two weeks," Wayne said.

"One week to visiting day, two weeks to color war, three weeks till we go home," Will said.

"Three weeks, yayyy!" Wayne cried.

"Yay!" Albie responded.

"Let's all be red for color war," Walter said. He held up his wrist with the red cord. "Red team! Yay!"

"Everybody except him." Wayne indicated Albie. "He can't hit, and every bunk has to have both teams."

Uncle Jesse jogged back in to the head table and leaned over Uncle Charlie again. Uncle Charlie pushed back his chair, stood, and tilted his head back to empty his mug. He came to the table with Uncle Jesse and looked at each boy in turn. "Are you the Panthers?" he said.

"Panthers, yay!"

"Who saw Randolph Tarrant this morning?"

"I did," Walter said.

Uncle Charlie's smooth chin and cheeks were black with whiskers. "Where did he go? Why didn't he come to breakfast?"

"I don't know, ask Waynie."

Uncle Jesse tugged Wayne's shirt. "Where's Raddy?"

Wayne shrugged. "Ask the genius. He sleeps next to him."

Everyone turned to Albie.

"You, huh?" Uncle Charlie said. "You know where he is?"

Raprapraprap. "I think he left before I did," Albie said.

"You didn't see him?"

Albie shook his head. The adults whispered together. Other tables finished and left the mess hall. Uncle Jesse held up a finger at Uncle Charlie to say "Dismissed!" but he returned to huddle as the boys departed and the aides cleared the table.

The unsupervised Panthers made their beds and swept. Albie straightened his dry sheets, thankful for having saved himself humiliation by getting up to urinate during the night. As he tucked in hospital corners on one side of his bed and the other he listened to his sneakers slap the wooden floor. He felt his cot's contact with that floor and the posts set in the earth that held the cabin fixed. He counted the days before visiting day, and wondered how to convince his father to let him come home before Color War.

Uncle Jesse ran through the uphill door of the bunk, breathing hard. "Panthers!" he shouted. His eyes were so wide open that white went all the way around the gray part, and the corner crinkles were gone. "Panthers, let's go, on the double!"

"I didn't sweep yet," Cooper said.

"Where are we going?" Jerry said.

"I don't know, waterfront, let's go!"

Walter started for the uphill door. Uncle Jesse hauled him around by his arm. "No, this way, double time, top speed, follow me!" he shouted. "Let's go! Let's go!"

"We were supposed to have baseball." Jerry picked up his mitt.

"Leave it, let's go!" The fright on Uncle Jesse's face was as clear as a Technicolor movie. He swatted Jerry's mitt onto a bed; he propelled Jerry toward the screen door. "Let's go!" Puzzled Panthers stumbled down the steps. "Run!" Uncle Jesse commanded.

Lion Cubs to the left and Woodsmen to the right streamed down the hill over pine needles, between trees, toward the playing field and the waterfront. "I've got a Hershey bar for the first and second!" Uncle Dan cried to the Woodsmen. Bobby and the Woodsman with curly red hair trampled a bush as they led the way downhill. Joe was running, too.

"Run!" Uncle Jesse cried. "Run!"

Albie was the last one out. Before he ran he saw Bear Brewer and another adult standing between Panthers and Lion Cubs near the opening to the space beneath the cabin. Rapraprap. Light on his feet, he bounded past Mike and Wayne with ease where the ground leveled out. He knew and they did not. Knowledge made strength out of fear. He passed all the Lion Cubs and pulled even with Jerry before they reached the waterfront. As Uncle Jesse herded them toward the changing cabin Albie glimpsed the ambulance speeding in past the stables, with the single red light on top going round and round and round.

Uncle Dan made the Panthers and Woodsmen stand in a line and count off; he arranged them in two lines, in four, in a single line again. Without Raddy there were eight Panthers; without Joe there were only nine Woodsmen. Uncle Jesse didn't seem to care whether the boys did the exercises he led or not. Uncle Dan whispered to him; they both beckoned to an aide jogging down the road and whispered to him when he came over. The aide ran off.

Uncle Bernie in his broad-brimmed hat was telling the Lion Cubs a story. One of the little boys in the circle scrunched around from a sitting position to lie prone on the grass with his chin resting on his hands.

". . . and five, and six, and seven, and eight," Uncle Jesse said. Boys waved their arms, touched their toes, and waved their arms again.

The aide returned from the direction of the Indian Circle pushing Joe ahead of him. Joe had dirt on his cheeks and a scrap of blue cloth tied around his forehead. "You were right," the aide called. "He was up to Leech Beach."

Uncle Dan shoved Joe toward the other boys so hard he stumbled. Joe fell into line behind Albie.

"Jumping Jacks," Uncle Jesse said, "again!"

"Where were you?" Albie said over his shoulder.

"Like this," Uncle Jesse said, "one." He jumped up in the air and clapped his hands together over his head.

"Tracking," Joe said.

Some boys jumped with Uncle Jesse but others talked or shuffled in the grass. "*I want complete obedience!*" Uncle Jesse shouted. "All together! Jumping Jacks! One, two, one, two!"

"Boys," Uncle Dan said, "we are responsible for you, so you have to do what we say." He adjusted his baseball cap. "Each cabin must stay together, no running off alone." The eyebrows he raised at Joe caught Albie too.

Joe prodded Albie. "What happened?"

Albie gazed past the two counselors and the lake at the blue sky above it. He remembered the woodcut of God in his children's Bible and trembled: he was afraid to lie. He shook his head, pointed to his pink swastika with its few remaining scabs and brought the pointing finger to his lips. Joe's eyes widened, both the right one and the left one. Albie faced front for calisthenics with the sounds of Joe's exertion behind him.

Later Jerry and Cooper started a pushup match; Will counted. "Ten," he said, "eleven." Jerry had bigger arms and the little smile on his face all the time; he bent his neck up to watch Cooper. "Thirteen," Will said. Cooper's blond hair hung past his face. Albie tried to do a pushup. Would he ever be strong? Uncle Jesse walked away from the row of boys to talk to Uncle Dan again. "Take a rest," he said over his shoulder.

"Nineteen," Will said. At twenty Jerry faltered, stopped smiling and fell to the ground on his side. Cooper's hair dipped and rose as Will counted, "Twenty-three, twenty-four, twenty-five."

Uncle Jesse and Uncle Dan came back with Uncle Bart, who blew a whistle. Cooper stopped with his elbows extended and stood up with care. The three counselors whispered together where the dock met the land; the swimming counselor blew his whistle again. "Today we're going to have a special extra long swim. Change into your bathing suits." The changing cabin was too small to accommodate all the Panthers and Woodsmen at once. Joe and Albie, the least eager, waited at the end of the line.

Joe stood on his tiptoes outside the changing cabin and pulled at his earlobe. "Is Raddy sick?"

Albie gazed out across the lake.

"He didn't come to breakfast," Philip said in front of them.

"Who didn't?" a Woodsman asked.

"Raddy Tarrant."

"The pitcher?"

"Yeah."

"Maybe he went to the nurse," the Woodsman said.

"The ambulance came this morning," Joe said.

"Oh, help me." Philip frowned so hard his eyes closed as he crossed himself. "Oh, don't let me get polio." The line moved ahead but he remained crouched, his fist pressed against his mouth.

Uncle Bart blew his whistle and pointed into the changing cabin. "C'mon, Philip," Albie said, "it's okay."

"Polio's incurable," Philip said. "It means you never get better or you die." He took one reluctant step into the changing cabin. "Don't let Raddy die." He held his cross up toward the ceiling, "Don't let me get polio."

Albie followed his gaze to the unpainted boards of the roof. The underside of Panthers' floor would look the same. God, not Albie, had struck Raddy down for his wickedness. Albie had been God's messenger. The shaken, melting feeling of the night before came back a little. Albie's mouth wanted to smile. Swimming through water could be the first step toward flying like an angel.

"Coop!" Albie called through the crowd, and hurried over before the larger boy went out on the dock. "Coop?"

"Hi, Albie."

"Would you show me," —he stopped until he saw that it would be okay— "how to swim better?"

Jerry pulled at Cooper's shoulder with a meaty arm. "Race you to the float?" Cooper shook his head. He gestured with his chin. "C'mon."

Cooper had defined muscles like a counselor. Albie followed him to the water on his own spindly legs.

"Go ahead and swim," Cooper said.

Albie walked out into water up to his chest, where he closed his eyes tight and extended his neck the way he would draw back from a wash-cloth his mother wielded. He held his breath. He flailed at the water with both hands, as if to beat it down before it could threaten his breathing.

When he stopped Cooper shook his head. "You know how you walk?"

"Walk?"

"I mean, you walk with your eyes open, and you breathe in and out, and you take one step at a time."

"I can't breathe water," Albie said.

"You can breathe out in the water. Look." Cooper put his face in the water and blew bubbles. He turned his head to the side, opened his mouth, faced into the water again, and blew more bubbles through his nose. "Try it."

Albie squeezed his eyes shut, bent his knees, and when his face was in the water blew some bubbles out his nose. He spluttered, jumped up in the air, and flailed his arms.

"What's wrong?"

"I couldn't breathe in, even though I was in the air."

"Why not? Do it again."

Albie did it again.

"You didn't blow all the air out," Cooper said. "You have to blow it out before you breathe more in."

Albie studied Cooper for a long time. He saw a boy who had learned things, a boy not so different from himself. In water up to his shoulders Albie clutched the dock and the rope of white floats with the other. He blew bubbles through his nose. Cooper was right: something inside him wouldn't let go of the precious air. He panicked, emerged, and spluttered.

But Cooper had said that it was like putting one foot in front of the other. Albie blew more bubbles out his nose. Now when he lifted his head from the water he took in the air he wanted through his mouth, ducked and emptied his lungs through his nose again.

"I can do it," he cried.

"Practice that." Cooper slipped under the row of floats to swim around to the deep water.

"Listen up," Uncle Jesse said back in the cabin. "You all know by now that

Raddy Tarrant got very sick. I mean,"—he colored—"the ambulance took him to the hospital."

"I bet he had *polio*," Will said, and glanced sideways at Philip, who held his cross in his fist.

"No he didn't," Walter said.

Albie shivered. Walter leaned against the wall at the head of his bed with a stupid smile on his plump face.

Uncle Jesse rubbed his nose.

"How do you know?" Will said.

"He took all his sulfur pills, I saw him."

Uncle Jesse relaxed.

"If he had polio they'd make us take the sulfur pills again," Mike piped up.

When Uncle Jesse addressed the whole bunk he looked straight at Albie. "The hospital called Uncle Bear and said that Raddy isn't going to be able to come back to camp this summer." He flushed again. "His mother and father are going to take him home."

"Who's going to pitch for color war?" Jerry said.

"My brother Waynie," Walter said.

Uncle Jesse walked out of the cabin. "Get ready for bed," he called through the screen door. "Hurry up, and maybe I'll read you a story." He stuck his head in the door. "Maybe I'll read you one of Albie's stories,"—he looked straight at Albie again—"if it's okay with you."

Albie unlaced his sneakers.

Uncle Jesse started the second chapter of the book about the boys who were pilots, but he stumbled over so many words that the boys were listening to him instead of the story. He stopped in the middle of a paragraph. "That's enough." He leaned over Albie to put the book back on his shelf, and left the cabin.

In the evening dimness Albie said, "It's a great book, I've read it seven times."

"What happens in it?" Cooper said.

"It's about kids like us, well, maybe a little older. They fly planes and everything because their father owns a little airport. They catch criminals with the plane, it's great."

"What did the criminals do?" Will asked.

"They robbed a bank," said Albie, and they—" He swallowed. "They murdered a guard at the bank." The cabin was quiet. "When they try to escape they come to the boys' father's airport and kidnap him to take them up in a plane. They make him fly them to a secret landing strip in the woods, and the boys have to find him."

"Do they?" Mike said.

"Yeah," Albie said. "They fly up there and sneak in because they paint one of their father's planes to match the one that was coming to meet the criminals, so they get their father free, and when the criminals come back they capture them and tie them up."

"Who ties who up?" Mike said.

"The boys and their father tie up the criminals, but one of the criminals always has a knife in his belt, so he gets loose and grabs the younger brother, he's going to throw him out of the plane if the father doesn't do what he says, so the father has to untie the other criminal, and after that—"

"Quiet, Greenberg," Uncle Jesse said from outside the cabin.

Albie was quiet.

"What happens next?" Will whispered.

Uncle Jesse's shoes scraped pebbles as he walked away.

"Tell us what happens," Will said.

"The older brother is flying the plane," Albie whispered. "He does a loop and the worse criminal falls out and the younger brother and the father capture the other one, and they take him back to the police."

"You should tell us stories instead of Uncle Jesse," Mike said in a sleepy voice.

"I'm glad the police caught the criminals," Walter whispered.

The leather bulk under Albie's pillow felt no more uncomfortable than the hard pilot's seat of the yellow plane he piloted in his dreams toward a red sunrise high over the northern lake, with Joe in the co-pilot's seat only inches behind him. He awoke to a symphony of whispers free of Raddy's angry comments. Walter slept, his mouth wide open between plump pink cheeks. Uncle Jesse was gone.

"If he had polio they'd know it," Will said. Walter's breath gurgled. Philip whispered, "I can't remember. I bet they make us take the sulfur pills again."

Cooper pushed down his covers and put on his jeans. "I hope not. Anybody know what time it is?"

Wayne Gardner got out of bed to look at Uncle Jesse's watch on the wooden shelf. "Ten minutes before six."

Before Cooper reached the door, footsteps scraped in the gravel outside and bumped on the step. "Panthers," Uncle Jesse said. "I got something to tell you."

"Excuse me," Cooper said, "I have to do number two."

"Hurry up." Hair uncombed, Uncle Jesse looked from one boy to the next. "The rest of you get dressed."

Walter Gardner rubbed his eyes and sat up. "Hey, Waynie," he said in his normal voice, and in a strange voice, "what's wrong, Waynie, what's wrong?" Uncle Jesse made an ineffectual gesture with his hand. When Cooper returned, Uncle Jesse said, "Uncle Charlie and Uncle Bear wanted me to make an announcement."

The bugle sounded reveille. Uncle Jesse looked happy he had been interrupted. When the last notes floated away down the hill, he said, "Raddy Tarrant had to go to the hospital . . ." Philip's blue eyes brimmed. His eyebrows nearly touched each other. ". . . not because he had a disease, he didn't have a disease." He cleared his throat. "Uncle Bear and Uncle Charlie say that everybody has to stay with a counselor all the time."

"Why did he have to go to the hospital?" Will said.

"He hit his head." Uncle Jesse blinked. "It's very sad. He hit his head so bad he . . . won't be coming back to camp this summer." Albie held his breath. "He injured his head, so everybody has to stay with counselors to be extra careful."

"Even to go to the latrine?" Cooper said.

"Careful about what?" Will said.

"Careful about injuries," Uncle Jesse said. "Careful about your head." He rubbed his messy hair with one hand and picked up a small mirror and a comb from his shelf. "Careful about running off alone." His eyes bored into Albie; he shook his head and combed his hair. "Let's go, breakfast."

Jerry's smile wavered. "Why isn't he coming back?"

The bugle sounded again. "Get going," Uncle Jesse said.

At the table Uncle Charlie whispered into Uncle Jesse's ear; he lit his pipe on his way back to the Brewers' round table. Uncle Jesse watched him until he sat down. "Stop that," Uncle Jesse said to Albie and Jerry, who were scraping plates. "Uncle Bear and some other people are going to talk to some of you about Raddy. I'm going to take you up to see them this morning, so everybody else has to stay in the cabin."

"No baseball?" Mike said. "When are we going to practice?"

"In the afternoon." Uncle Jesse glanced over his shoulder at Uncle Charlie again.

During cleanup he said, "Stay here," and left the cabin. The leaderless Panthers idled in the cabin or played mumblety-peg outside. Mike and Albie played with Albie's knife. Jerry watched from the steps. Albie glanced at Jerry, up at the bunk, toward the main house between turns. Just before his fourteenth turn he spied Bear Brewer and Mrs. Brewer descending the stairs together to meet a light blue car that stopped in the parking area. A woman in a dark dress got out. Bear Brewer shook her hand and Mrs. Brewer embraced her.

"That's Raddy's mom," Jerry said, and retreated inside.

The car parked and a thin man in a dark blue suit and shined black shoes got out. Albie stood a yard from the steps and boys watched from the window as Bear and Mrs. Brewer escorted Raddy's parents up the steps. As Uncle Jesse and an aide packed Raddy's duffel, Mrs. Tarrant cried and twisted a white handkerchief. Mrs. Brewer rested a hand on the shorter woman's shoulder. Raddy's father's big Adam's apple moved behind his open white shirt collar.

Mrs. Tarrant wailed something. Mr. Tarrant squeezed one of her hands in both of his. Uncle Jesse ordered the remaining boys out of the bunk and away from the door. Most of them gave the adults a wide berth, but Will peered at Mrs. Tarrant with curiosity. The boys in the uphill half of the cabin tiptoed because Uncle Charlie was lurking in the doorway. They rattled down the steps, but the minute they reached the nearest picnic table, they all rushed back to the cabin to peer in the window over Wayne's bed.

Cooper and Jerry were caught at the other end. "Excuse me," Cooper said and walked around the adults. Jerry remained.

"Which one is the catcher?" Raddy's mother asked.

"I am." Jerry's back was against the wall near his bed.

"Randolph wrote us—" She wiped her eyes with the handkerchief. Raddy's father worked on her hand, but she pulled it away and caught Jerry's hands between hers. "Oh," she said, "oh, oh." When she let go, Jerry hurried around the adults to join the other Panthers outside.

Raddy's mother buried her face against Raddy's father's shirt and beat on his shoulders with her fists. The boys couldn't hear what she was saying.

Uncle Jesse fidgeted. Uncle Charlie pointed his pipe at the peering boys like a pistol. "Get outta here." He jammed it into his mouth unlit and glared at the retreating Panthers before he stalked off to the main house. A little while later the aide carried Raddy's duffel out toward the parking area. Raddy's father followed with both hands around Raddy's mother's shoulders; he had to guide her because she held the handkerchief over her face. Uncle Jesse balanced Raddy's trunk on a shoulder and followed the Tarrants to the car.

"It's a Ford," Will said.

"We have a Ford too," Albie said.

Uncle Jesse put down the trunk to shake Mr. Tarrant's hand. Mrs. Tarrant stepped back when he turned to her. Mr. Tarrant opened the trunk. Uncle Charlie pointed down the hill and left and right in the air.

"He's going to miss Color War," Will said.

"He'll hate that," Jerry said.

"Maybe he'll get better and come back," Walter said.

Philip shook his head. "My sister stayed in the hospital a long time."

"Maybe he could come back and watch." Wayne's fox face squinted past Albie, who turned his back on the car until the engine started.

The Ford rolled down the hill away from Bear Brewer, Uncle Charlie, and Uncle Jesse. Twenty feet from the parking area, before it passed out of sight behind Lion Cubs, it stopped, but no one got out. Bear Brewer and Uncle Charlie took a few steps forward; the car drove away.

The weight of Uncle Jesse's grip hurt Albie as the counselor piloted him past the mess hall porch, over grass forbidden to campers, into a wide hallway and up a flight of stairs to the room where boys were taken when they were in big trouble. The counselor's knock elicited a man's mumble, and the door opened. Uncle Jesse pushed Albie through.

Four different chairs formed a semicircle across a brown and tan oval rug from a ratty sofa. Black and white photographs of campers' heads in rows on the grandstand hung on bits of wall between the many doors and windows. The interchangeable counselors who sat in front and stood arrayed across the back seemed to guard the boys lest one escape before the shutter clicked.

"Come in," Bear Brewer said from a big white wicker armchair. Mrs. Brewer sat on the couch in an apron over a flowered dress. Uncle Charlie held his pipe in his mouth, unlit and upside down, where he sat in a green chair with rusty stains on its green tartan cushion. Bear Lake and the main house were not as grand as Albie once had thought.

Two strange men occupied the other chairs. The younger one wore khaki pants and a silver badge on his pressed khaki shirt: he had driven the pickup truck on visiting day. His gray hat with a band and chin strap of polished brown leather and a brim like Smokey the Bear's hung over the post of his chair. The tanned older man had colorless hair and hollow cheeks. His pale blue eyes looked out from dark places on either side of a hawk's nose. He wore a white shirt and dark tie with the knot pulled down.

Uncle Charlie examined a clipboard on his lap. "Panthers."

"Panthers, yes, sir." Uncle Jesse squeezed Albie's shoulder to make him stop walking.

"This is the one," Uncle Charlie said.

"Thank you, Mr. Fleming." The older man's voice was a whine, pitched high, with a strange, clipped accent. Albie could see that he was smart.

"Why don't you sit down here." Mrs. Brewer smoothed the threadbare green tartan cover beside her. "You too, Jesse."

Uncle Charlie was afraid. Albie couldn't see Uncle Jesse's face as the counselor propelled him forward to sit next to Mrs. Brewer.

"... a glass of water?" she was asking him.

"... very scary," Bear Brewer said, "but these men want to ask you—"

Albie had listened to enough radio to know they were policemen. The younger one's thick brown belt was attached to a smaller strap that went over his shoulder. The chair arm probably concealed his gun. The older policeman was nothing but hollow blue eyes, watching him. Raprapraprap, Albie's heart beat the way it did when he was hiding, but he was not afraid, he was not afraid. This was a radio mystery, a library book.

Albie closed his eyes. He smelled Mrs. Brewer's soapy odor, mildew on the couch, the dirt on his hands and the fresh cold water and soap he had hurried to wash them with before Uncle Jesse called him. The smell of Uncle Jesse's sweat told him that Uncle Jesse was frightened like Uncle Charlie.

Albie opened his eyes to see Mrs. Brewer proffer a waxed Dixie cup with blue leaves on it. He drank a little. It wasn't as cold as the water he had washed his hands in. "Thank you," he said, and looked her in the eye.

"Greenberg." Uncle Charlie consulted his clipboard, "Albert Greenberg."

"What nationality is that?" the older policeman said.

"I'm an American," Albie said.

"Hebrew," Uncle Charlie said. "We get a lot of them these days."

"Albit," the older policeman said. The policeman in uniform had shifted in his chair to offer a glimpse of the gun. "Albit?" the older man said in his high voice, "That your name, Albit?"

Not Albie, not Albert. Albie met his eyes. "Yes, sir."

Uncle Jesse relaxed his grip.

"You know why we're here?"

"Because of Raddy?"

The policeman's face questioned Uncle Charlie.

"Randolph," Uncle Charlie said.

"Ayuh," the older policeman said. He watched Albie and waited.

Albie waited and listened to his heart. The rug was stained, too.

"Are you afraid, Albit?"

Albie nodded.

"What you afraid of, Albit?"

Albie snuck a glance over his shoulder at Uncle Jesse. Mrs. Brewer put down the metal pitcher in her hand and touched his back. She meant to encourage Albie, but when she touched Uncle Jesse's hand, they both let go of Albie. Albie frowned at the rug. "I'm afraid of getting a noogie."

The policeman in uniform smirked. "Gettin' what?" the older one said.

"Getting hit." The next person Albie looked at would be accused. He put his hands under his thighs. Uncle Charlie made a sound around the stem of his pipe; Uncle Jesse replaced his hand on Albie's shoulder.

"Who been hittin' you?" the older policeman said on cue.

Albie shook his head 'no.'

"The boys fight among themselves," Bear Brewer said. "We put a stop to it when we can."

The older policeman gazed at the director. "This one, Albit, a fighter?"

Nobody answered. Uncle Jesse gripped harder.

"If he ain't a fighter, who's been hittin' him?" He waited one, two, three, twenty beats of Albie's heart. Mrs. Brewer rested her hand back on Albie's back. Again she and Uncle Jesse touched each other, again both pulled away. They left Albie alone.

The older policeman leaned toward Albie. "You know this boy, Randolph, Albit?"

Albie nodded. "He's got, he had the bunk next to mine."

"You and he buddies?"

Albie squeezed his hands deeper under his thighs. Uncle Jesse made a sound in his throat. It got louder for a while until he said "Ah," so everyone could hear it. The policeman turned to him.

"Was they buddies?"

"Ah, Jesse Carpenter, the bunk counselor," Uncle Charlie said.

The policeman ignored Uncle Charlie. "Eh?" He studied Uncle Jesse with hollow blue eyes.

"He used to pick on Albert," Uncle Jesse put his arm back on Albert's shoulder. "He used to, he was, well, . . ."

"Eh?"

"I guess Albert isn't the best ball player," Uncle Jesse said. "Raddy, Randolph, he kept trying to get Albert to play better."

"He hit you?" the policeman asked Albie.

Albie moved his mouth at the floor.

"I can't hear you, Albit."

"Sort of."

"You hit him?"

Here it was, just like on the radio. Being scared was normal. Raprapraprap. Albie shook his head no at the policeman's knees. He did not tell a lie.

"Eh?"

Albie took a deep breath. "No, sir." He thought he saw sympathy in the blue eyes, but he wasn't sure.

"Albert's not a scrapper," Uncle Jesse said. The noises Uncle Charlie made around his pipe might have been assent.

"Shouldn't think so." The older policeman broke eye contact with Albie. Somebody knocked at the door.

"They're not really fighters," Bear Brewer said.

"That's all," the older policeman said.

Uncle Jesse maneuvered Albie toward the door. Albie shrugged off his hand and went back to pick up the Dixie cup from where he had put it on the floor. Mrs. Brewer accepted it with a sad smile.

". . . not strong enough," someone said as Albie left the room. Cooper was outside with one of the aides. Albie preceded Uncle Jesse down the stairs and out onto the off-limits side of the porch.

"C'mere." Uncle Jesse tugged at Albie's shirt. Albie quailed. "C'mere!" Uncle Jesse dragged him toward the stand of trees that separated the mess hall porch from the latrine. Albie wriggled. "No noogie, I'm not gonna hit you." Uncle Jesse steered Albie's shaking, bony shoulder into the darkness of the trees. "I want to thank you for not saying anything."

Albie blinked and studied the counselor's pink face. "About noogies." Uncle Jesse tousled Albie's hair and pushed him away. Albie ran along the row of bunks to Panthers and climbed the steps quietly, to hear who might still be inside.

"This has been a trying summer for all of us," Bear Brewer announced. "A summer filled with boys who had to go to the hospital."

Albie moved the heel of his spoon in circles in the remains of the syrup on his plate and licked the spoon.

"I am sure the boys who had to leave us would have wanted Camp Bear Lake to fight on to the end," Bear Brewer said. "But we told your parents that we had, ah, difficulties . . ."

Albie rested his cheek on his hand.

"For some campers," Bear Brewer said, "this Saturday, the day after tomorrow, will be the end of the camp season. Your parents will take you home then, because they were going to come to visit you anyhow. For the rest of you loyal Bear Lakers the summer will continue through Color War the way we always do."

No cheers. Whispers filled the dining hall. When Albie caught Joe's eye, Joe returned an uncertain wave.

Bear Brewer said, "We look to the Redbear spirit . . ." Older boys near the head table managed a ragged cheer. Albie made circles in syrup until Cooper took his plate to stack it with the others.

At baseball Wayne's pitches missed the plate, the batter, and the nearby air four times in a row. "Walter!" he shouted, red in the face. "Don't say anything!"

"I won't say anything, Waynie."

Albie caught Cooper shaking his head after this exchange, and wanted to say that he, too, saw that Wayne was unreasonable in insisting on silence. He was sure they would agree. But when he missed a second fly ball and Cooper called, "C'mon, Albie," across the field, Albie was still an outsider. He walked up the hill to the cabin alone, behind the others.

He swung his legs as he waited for lunch on the foot of his bed. The cold metal cross bar of the cot caused hot discomfort as it dug into the backs of his knees but he did not stop. I do not feel pain, he thought.

The twins whispered together. Now and then Walter peeked over Wayne's shoulder at Albie. "Ask him," Wayne said. Walter strolled across the aisle. "I want to ask you something." He peeked back over his shoulder; Wayne lifted his chin toward Albie. "Because you're a genius," Walter said.

"I'm not a genius."

Walter bent to Albie's ear. "Do you think . . . Raddy got *polio*?" The bigger boy fidgeted. He towered over Albie with brown, liquid, vulnerable eyes.

Albie swung his legs harder until one foot touched Walter's dungarees.

"We didn't have to take pills again," Walter said.

Albie swung his leg more. "Do *you* think so?" he said.

"Yeah!" Walter nodded vigorous agreement at Albie and over his shoulder at Wayne. "I saw the ambulance." He ran to Wayne's bed. "See?" he chortled. He and Wayne whispered together again. Walter returned to Albie's bed. One of his eyes crossed a little. "My brother wants me to ask you something else. What's a vaggrant?" He pronounced it like 'Tarrant.'

"A what?"

Walter looked helplessly back at Wayne. "A vaggrant."

Wayne pursed his lips and crossed the cabin to join them. Philip frowned from his cot. "V-A-G-R-A-N-T," Wayne said.

"Oh," Albie said, "a *vay*grant. A vagrant is a hobo who travels around on freight trains and things."

"Are there any around here?" Wayne said.

"I don't think so."

Wayne unfolded a piece of newspaper from his pocket. 'RUMOR OF VAGRANT IN DEATH,' the headline said.

"Where did you get this?"

"I lifted it off Uncle Jesse's shelf," Wayne said.

Albie scanned the clipping. Suspicious strangers had been seen near the railroad station. A source at the Union Hospital suggested that a vagrant had been responsible for the death of a boy from severe head injuries. The chief of police advised everyone to take extra precautions, especially with boys. No sign of molestation had been found. The camps would remain open.

"Raddy's *dead*," Wayne said.

Raprapraprap. Albie fixed his eyes on the clipping.

"He's *dead*," Wayne said. "Somebody *killed* him."

"This doesn't say it's Raddy," Albie said.

"But it's a boy at a camp. We better be careful."

"It says extra precautions," Albie said. "Precautions is being careful."

"Does it mean a grownup killed Raddy?"

"It says they don't know."

"I'm scared," Wayne said. "He can go underground."

"Underground?" Albie said.

"They're looking for a mole station."

"That's not what that says," Albie said. "It's mo*les*tation."

"What does that mean?"

"It's bothering," Albie said. "Molesting means bothering."

"You mean killing him isn't bothering him?" Wayne said. "Raddy was right, you're a *moron*."

Uncle Jesse got back to the cabin before the bugle sounded for lunch. He straightened his Bear Lake tee shirts on their shelf. He thumbed through letters in a cigar box. He sat up on the side of his bed, faced the rest of the cabin with his mouth open for a minute before he stood and said, "Hey, Panthers."

Wayne rolled his eyes. Will pushed his glasses up his nose.

"In case you hear rumors," Uncle Jesse said, "about Raddy not coming back . . . he injured his head so bad he's dead."

Mike made a little sound, like a cat's mew, but he didn't say any words. When all the boys had been silent for a moment, Uncle Jesse turned back to his shelves and straightened his tee shirts again.

Mike's mew became a sob. "I'm scared," he whispered to Albie across Raddy's empty bed. "I wish my mother was here. Are you scared?"

"No." Albie shook his head. "I'm not scared."

"I wish I was like you," Mike said.

All the Panthers left the mess hall together. "Follow the leader," Wayne said. "I called it."

"Whoever doesn't follow first has to sweep the middle, okay?" Jerry said.

Wayne jumped down the last five steps from the porch of the main house. Jerry jumped the five steps, then Albie did. Will said, "That's easy," and jumped down eight steps.

"You have to sweep," Wayne said.

"Do not."

"Do too." Wayne looked around for support. "He didn't follow the leader."

"It doesn't matter. I did something harder. That counts, doesn't it? If you do something harder?"

"It ought to," Cooper said, "if it's really harder."

"No," Philip said. "it's not what the leader did. The rule is to follow."

Albie pondered whether boys should get credit when they did something different from other people, if it was harder.

Back in their cabin the Panthers made beds and straightened shelves. While Cooper swept, Will sprinkled water with his hand.

"What are you, blessing it?" Philip said.

"Tomorrow is visiting day. I want to get all the dust so the cabin is really nice."

"Let's fix it up really neat," Jerry said. "Everybody straighten shelves."

The empty shelves and the bare, stained mattress next to Albie silenced all the Panthers. Philip poked the broom under his bed and sprayed dust at Walter and Albie. William sprinkled water for him. Walter pretended to hit a tennis ball with the dustpan; he was still wearing the red cord around his wrist.

"You ought to take that off," Cooper said. "Out of respect."

Albie tucked in his hospital corners. Uncle Jesse stood in the doorway; the other Panthers were occupied. Albie pressed his lips together, reached up to his top shelf for his baseball mitt, pulled it on and ran past the end of Walter's bed. "Uncle Jesse?"

The gray eyes seemed to transmit daylight from the morning sky. "Hey, Greenberg." The counselor was on guard.

"Can you show me how to throw better?"

Uncle Jesse scrutinized Albie a little longer. "Yeah, good, you want to develop the arm, hey?" His face relaxed. "Okay, Greenberg, come with me. Brown, keep an eye on cleanup. Greenberg and I are gonna scout out the ball field."

As they stepped out the door, an aide ran up with a piece of paper. Uncle Jesse read it and glanced at Albie. "I'll take care of it," he said, and guided Albie around between Panthers and Lion Cubs, and over the very spot from which Raddy had looked at the heavens through the binoculars.

On the gravel road down to the playing field Albie had to take double steps to keep up with Uncle Jesse. The still morning air was fresh as they emerged from the trees. Dew beaded the grass and the oilcloth covers on the straw-filled archery targets with the sun rising behind them. At Ebbetts Field Uncle Jesse stopped in the bare base path and cocked his head. "How come, Greenberg?"

Albie faced into the sun. "I want to be like the other . . . boys." 'Guys' would presume: he wasn't entitled to that yet. Uncle Jesse's gray eyes faded into a shadowed darkness and then a silhouette. The brightness behind Uncle Jesse filled the whole sky.

"Yeah, good. Go stand on the mound." Uncle Jesse walked towards home plate.

"Me?" In Albie's head, Raddy cried, 'I'm the pitcher.'

"You."

The power the pitcher's mound conferred on Albie astonished him. Those few inches of height gave him a purview, a command of the surround he had never enjoyed in his window, never atop a tree. And he was at the center. Events would cascade from his action. For once he was the prime mover instead of a watcher from the outside, and he felt like God.

"Here you go." Uncle Jesse tossed Albie a baseball, knelt and held up his mitt. "Let's see the ball," he said.

Albie brought his hand up, threw, and missed.

The counselor fetched the ball and flipped it back. "Try again, Greenberg. Throw hard and aim for the man's eyes."

Albie recoiled from the image of aggression, but did as he was told. The ball flew straight and hard to land in the counselor's glove with an all-American 'thwack.'

"All *right!*" Uncle Jesse returned the ball. "Chuck to me, Albie kid!"

Albie threw hard at the counselor's eyes, and true. Thwack!

"Hey, okay!" Uncle Jesse cried. "Pop fly!" He threw the ball high in the air; Albie watched its flight, watched its descent, and watched it strike the ground ten feet in front of his outstretched arms. With sudden dismay he brought his forearms together to protect himself from the criticism that was to come.

"Hey, Greenberg?" Uncle Jesse's tone was mild.

"What?" Albie's voice was little more than a whisper.

"You can't be a spectator. When you threw the ball? You focused on my eyes, right?"

Albie nodded.

"I can't hear you."

"Right!" Albie shouted.

"Don't just stand there, you gotta keep your eye on the ball till you get it. Now, chuck it back here."

The ball flew too high; Uncle Jesse caught it without comment. "Here's another pop fly." The ball descended to Albie's left, but he was there to lock the ball into the pocket of his mitt with his right hand. He hurled it back to Uncle Jesse. Thwack!

Other Panthers arrived. Uncle Jesse and Albie played catch. Will Hobeck called, "Hey, Albie! Are you going to stay with us today?"

Uncle Jesse squatted behind the plate with an open, inquiring face. Albie squinted at Will's birthmark. "Sure," he said.

"Let's see the ball." Will ran across the infield toward first base.

Uncle Jesse took off his mitt. "Go ahead and warm up," he called to

Albie. Will rested his hands on his knees; sun flashed on his glasses. Albie threw hard. Will caught the ball and threw it to Mike at shortstop, and all the Panthers were throwing and catching.

"Three Old Cat," Wayne called. The others cried assent.

"You pitch," Albie said, and descended from the mound.

"That's okay, you pitch first," Wayne said.

"I'll get the bats, okay, Waynie?" Walter ran off toward the box of athletic equipment as Albie, high on the pitcher's mound, smacked his fist into his mitt. "Jerry!" he called. "Let's see the ball!"

Albie missed the catch. He ran to pick it up, returned to the pitcher's mound, and threw it back to Jerry. Thwack!

"Good one," Jerry said.

After an hour Uncle Jesse called time. Albie sat a few feet from Uncle Jesse. "Okay?" Uncle Jesse said.

"Thanks," Albie said.

"You're okay," Uncle Jesse said. "Just focus on what you're doing. And you have to practice every day. You can't be running off in the wilderness with . . ."

Albie didn't want to hear him say something bad about Joe.

". . . and Greenberg? Strip your bed before lunch." He unfolded the slip of paper. "Your folks are taking you home today."

"Today? Before visiting day?"

"I guess." Uncle Jesse shook his head and stood up. "Hey okay," he shouted, "let's play ball."

Giddy with connection Albie ran toward lunch between the two biggest Panthers. "That was great," he said. "I wish my father wasn't coming today to take me home." The three boys entered the grove of trees together.

Cooper brushed his hair back from his forehead with spread fingers. "I'd like it if you stayed. My parents are in England and no one else can come to get me."

Jerry said, "Maybe you could come home with me . . ."

"Thank you very much," Cooper's voice wavered. "I'm . . . not worried."

"I mean, what if it's —" Jerry paused. Albie froze at the silence. "— a grownup?" Jerry peeked over Albie's head at Uncle Jesse.

Cooper brushed his cheek as if a fly were bothering him and disappeared into the cabin.

At lunch Albie carried an oval white plate of grilled cheese sandwiches from the kitchen. As he sat down Will gave him a horse bite on his thigh. "Ah!" Albie shouted with surprise, and shrank from further attack, but Will was smiling, eyes open behind his glasses. This was not danger.

"Hey, look!" Albie pointed out the window.

All the Panthers looked. Albie gave Will a horse bite. "Ah!" Will cried, and stood.

"Both of you," Uncle Jesse said, but in no time he was serving green beans to the other side of the table.

After lunch all the Woodsmen but Joe walked together through the maze of tables to the door. Joe took a longer, more circuitous route, and stopped on the porch to let the rest of the Woodsmen get further ahead of him.

The Panthers left together. "Race you to the bunk," Wayne said, and ran before Albie realized Wayne had been speaking to him. Albie sprinted, jumped, dodged trees, and overtook Wayne. "I win!"

"I have to be careful," Wayne said.

The two boys climbed the steps together.

"I want rest period quiet," Uncle Jesse said. "We have archery first this afternoon."

Mike mimed shooting an arrow at Wayne. Wayne clawed his chest. Albie grasped the imaginary arrow. "I'm coming, Waynie," Walter said. "You hold him," Albie said. "I'll pull the arrow out." Walter's face went blank. "Help me," Albie said, "we have to save Wayne."

Wayne slumped against Walter; Albie pulled out the arrow and held it up. "It's a Sioux arrow," he said, and threw it back to Mike. "Hey, Mike!"

"On your beds," Uncle Jesse said. "Greenberg, get packing."

"But I don't—"

"I'll help you," Uncle Jesse said.

Albie stripped his bed and packed his trunk. Uncle Jesse helped him. The others watched in silence.

Albie's inert duffle bag crowded him on the bare mattress. He closed his eyes. A boy's voice shouted outside, "Panthers is the second one." Albie's father walked in the uphill door and peered around the dim cabin in sunglasses. "Babble-boy!"

Albie met him half way. "Where's Mommy?"

"She isn't feeling well. You'd better pack your things."

Albie tilted his head at the empty wooden shelves and the two bare mattresses between Walter's red blanket and Mike's dark green one.

The tennis racquet in its dusty red cover and press leaned against the shelf. His father picked it up and extended it toward him.. "Maybe you can play in the city."

After a moment, Albie took it and rested the press on the floor. He slipped the strap of the binocular case over his head while his father hoisted the duffel bag. The middle of the urine stain didn't show on the grimy ticking, but a deep yellow band ran along its borders, like the countries in the historical atlas at home. He was going home! The binoculars were safe in their case! Albie tucked the racquet under his arm and forced a smile over his shoulder. His shoes scratched in grit on the wooden floor. He didn't dare look at the other Panthers' faces. He wasn't sure what he would do when he got to the door.

His father beamed. "Are you all ready?"

Boys chattered outside. Albie stepped past Wayne and Walter's stares and gazed out the screened window of the cabin at the roof of Woodsmen.

"Look at me," his father said. "Take your hands out of your pockets."

Uncle Jesse stood in the doorway. "Is this your father?" He shook Albie's father's hand. "How do you do, Mr. Greenberg."

". . . very difficult for you." His father set down the duffel. "Thank you for . . ."

". . . come a long way." Uncle Jesse rested a hand on Albie's thin shoulder. ". . . natural ability . . ."

". . . tragic situation," Albie's father said. "His mother . . ."

Albie's heart leaped up: he was going to see his mother! But in the next second something inside him paused. *They* had sent him away, both of them, so that now the distant world he had come from seemed like a story in a children's book. A babyish story, sweet but false, no longer appropriate for a man who felt no pain. What had happened separated him from the comfort of family forever — but bit by bit, hour by hour, his desperate need for that comfort was falling away.

Albie inspected Uncle Jesse's gray eyes, tanned face, and faded red sweatshirt. He scrutinized his father's checked sport jacket, the pipe in his mouth, and balding forehead. The adult glances dismissed Albie; the weight of Albie's father's attention shifted to the counselor. "*In loco parentis*," Albie's father said, "in the place of a parent. Can you imagine how your father — "

"I don't have a father," Uncle Jesse said.

The adults talked over Albie's head. The hard binocular case dug at his ribs and the inside of his arm.

". . . in Germany, the last month of the war, when I was fourteen," Uncle Jesse said.

". . . if you should be interested in the law." Albie's father returned a leather card case to his vest pocket. The men shook hands. "Thank Mr. Carpenter," his father said. Albie blinked at his father. "For keeping you safe. For protecting you." His father's face reddened as he pushed Albie past Uncle Jesse and out the door.

Uncle Jesse shouldered Albie's camp trunk and duffel; Albie stepped aside to let him pass. His father had left the black Ford's trunk lid up. Back in the Panther windows, pale ovals over Wayne's and Uncle Jesse's beds watched him hesitate and start back to shake their hands, but the trunk lid slammed and his father tooted the horn.

He hurried. "I have the binoculars," he said.

"Don't you want to say good-bye to your friends?" his father said.

"Good-bye!" Albie waved with his elbow at his side so as not to expose the case.

"'Bye, Albie," someone called from the bunk.

Uncle Jesse stepped toward Albie with his hand extended. "No hard feelings," he said. It could have been a statement or a question.

Albie touched the hand. "No hard feelings," he mouthed, and remembered every torment of the summer. He scrambled into the car and his father drove down the hill and out onto the flat between the archery range and the Indian Circle. The landing across the lake and the bear skulls winked and hid behind the trees on the waterfront. The car slowed as they rolled past Yankee Stadium. It stopped.

Had his father changed his mind? Would he take him home or make him stay? The morning had been heaven, but his father's arrival had revived all the dark feelings Albie had ever had. Did he really want to go home? His brain churned: what should he say? What entreaty might ensure that his father would take him away from Bear Lake forever? Would his mother survive if he dared to stay?

"Uhh." Albie said to summon his father's attention, but under the tweed cap his father's eyes stared forward in a sad expression Albie had not seen before. The face was red. The little wrinkles at the corners of his father's eyes that went with teasing were gone. His father leaned over to crush Albie's face against his own. Albie smelled aftershave on his cool cheek, and pipe tobacco. When his father released him, Albie said, "What church do we go to?"

His father frowned. He drove the car past the Yankee Stadium third base, where he stopped again and shut off the engine. He gripped the steering wheel in both hands; he pulled back his lips to reveal the yellow teeth that clenched his pipe. "Uhh," he said. "Uh. Were you close to the boy who went to the hospital?"

"No," Albie said. "I didn't know his name."

"You didn't?" His father's tone made Albie look. Their eyes met. His father faced the windshield again. "You didn't know his name?"

"He was thirteen. I never even saw him."

"Not him. The boy who slept next to you."

Albie's voice shook. "Are you really taking me home?"

"Oh yes," his father said. "Thank God." He started the engine. Albie knelt on the seat so he could watch through the small back window. No one had followed them. The *Addequant Valley Union-Observer* lay on the back seat, folded open to the same article Wayne Gardner had shown him. 'RUMOR OF VAGRANT IN DEATH.' Albie read it again. When he finished, his father was staring at him.

"Wait!" Albie threw himself away from the accusation in his father's eyes, against the door, and snatched at the handle for balance. The door swung open to let him tumble out onto dirt at the entrance to the camp. The binocular case kicked his ribs.

"Babble-boy!" His father's face leaned out the door. Albie glimpsed the stables and the road to freedom before he was on his feet and running. Back toward Bear Lake, past the backstop, past Mistlewood and the edge of the tennis courts; he flew past the building with the athletic equipment and down to the shore. The horn tooted. From the Indian Circle the fastest feet in Panthers made the corner of the grove of trees, where Albie hurled himself flat in pine needles to hide from older boys on their way to lunch. He crawled on his belly to safety behind a tree.

He braced shaking hands against the tree to focus the binoculars on Woodsmen. From the top of the downhill steps Uncle Dan and a tall boy looked straight at Albie through the grove of trees but did not see him. When they went inside, Joe Moscow emerged from under the steps they had been standing on.

"Joe!"

Joe ducked back under the steps. Larger boys at nearer cabins turned toward Albie's cry. His father's car disappeared behind Lion Cubs on its way back up to the parking lot. In two minutes the grove of trees was empty and Joe ran down to where Albie was hiding.

The trees along the trail were his furniture; the gray-brown lake was his window. At the grassy oval Albie put a finger to his mouth and signed Joe to wait. With his clasp knife he cut a branch from a sapling to sweep leaves and debris over the faint path from the main trail and propped it across the access to the grass.

"Secrecy and silence," he mouthed.

"Secrecy and silence," Joe mouthed back.

Albie drew Joe to the water beside the root of the larger tree. He took off his shoes and gestured to Joe to do the same. "They're coming for me."

"Who?"

Albie put his finger to his mouth and led Joe around through the water to the hiding place between the two trees. Their bodies pressed together against the lakeward side of the boles. "My father," Albie said. "My father and counselors."

"Visiting day isn't till tomorrow."

"He came today. He thinks I killed Raddy."

"He thinks *what*?"

Albie drew away from Joe, but the angle of the cleft and the weight of their leaning bodies pressed them together again. "I killed Raddy," he blurted. He enunciated: "He thinks — I — killed — Raddy."

"Why?"

"I don't know. He saw the newspaper."

Joe rubbed Albie's shoulder. "Grownups never believe stuff kids make up." He picked his nose. "Is your father really here?"

"He was taking me home in the car."

Joe stared into the air above the lake. The glare of midday sun sliced through an opening in the shade to light up Joe's right eye. Albie sought a dragonfly in the column of sunshine, but its luminous pink color was gone like a dream. Indistinct dark shapes moved through the air.

Albie churned inside and listened for pursuit, but they were alone. "I played baseball this morning," he said. "Uncle Jesse showed me how to throw."

Joe's eyes stared out at two different places across the lake.

"I liked it."

Joe dug in his nose.

"Want to look through my binoculars?"

Joe squinted across the lake. "Indian scouts have the eyes of eagles." He raised his elbows, touched his thumbs and fingertips, and made goggles with his hands before he scrambled through the water away from Albie.

"Wait!" Albie hurried to follow. Joe crashed through underbrush to the main trail, and away. Albie could not protect the binocular case and keep up. Once it was quiet again he stumbled to his refuge beside the lake, where on a grassy mattress that sloped down to dark water, he rested his head on the pillow of his fingers interlaced. Above him leaves divided the air into shade and sun. Motes and insects twinkled, appeared and disappeared, as they sifted through these quiet bands of light and darkness: so much motion amidst the stillness!

And how still this place was! Two dragonflies hovered, one behind the other. They subsided from shade into light as the crack of a bat echoed across the lake from far to Albie's left. Shouts of boys and deeper cries of men who encouraged them: baseball. A sharp sound nearby, a broken stick. Albie caught his breath. He set aside the dragonflies' pursuit and coupling to listen.

Silence. Leaves moved. Another stick broke, more leaves, a step. More steps came his way through the forest, along the lakeshore, from beyond the next cove, from where the Indian Circle was, and the baseball field. A slow cadence: adults. Shoes off and in his hand, Albie was up and in the water where he waded over slimy stones his feet knew well, through cattails and lily pads, back to the cleft in the trees. He crouched like a stone and rested his shoes on a root above the surface of the water. Behind him the great trunks and a tangle of thorns protected him from the adults who approached. White arcs of sunlight overhead carved the deep shade. He was open only to a boat or to someone with binoculars on the wooded shore opposite.

As he hunched down, damp but not cold, his heart beat a raprapraprap as the path he had made through the lily pads trembled and disappeared. Just in time: slow adult steps stopped in the clearing.

"He likes to come here," Uncle Jesse said.

"I thought you were taking him home." That was Uncle Charlie.

"He had a hard time at first." His father's voice.

"Yeah, sure . . ." Uncle Jesse sounded uncertain.

His father spoke again. "I don't like him going off alone. The other boy—"

". . . independent for his own good," Uncle Charlie said. "We tried to straighten him out."

Albie cringed in anticipation of punishment.

"Albie!" Uncle Jesse called. "Albie Greenberg!"

One of the adults threw a rock out among the lily pads.

"We're looking for you," Albie's father called. "Babble-boy!"

"We don't find him," Uncle Charlie said, "we better notify . . ."

Footsteps dwindled away. From down the path Uncle Jesse's voice sounded: "Hey, Greenberg!"

Dragonflies with two pairs of wings hung in the dark and light over the lily pads, two, three, four of them, now alone and now in pairs. The boy marveled that they could move their many pairs of wings that fast with no sound that he could hear. When he was sure he was safe he waded back to his landing. He tied his shoes before he backed away from the grassy oval, bowing, as if he wanted to delay as long as possible his last glimpse of the lake. He followed the trail toward the camp for a few steps before he broke off into dark woods, in a new direction.

Albie scrambled far uphill in a wide circle around the westernmost parts of the camp, on paths that were no more than suggestions. At first he ran, but later he strolled through the cool vegetable smell of the forest. His footsteps rustled over twigs and leaves and quieted on pine needles or rocks. On the side of a hill he all but stepped on a bird that whirred up from the ground to gain a treetop too quickly for him to see it. The gentlest of summer breezes eased the crown back and forth, but his binoculars magnified the motion so he could not follow a single leaf.

He traveled north, away from the lake. When he stopped to look back no one pursued him; when he listened he heard only the breeze. In an open area sun fell on a fallen gray tree trunk full of ants. He sat down a few feet away. Through the lenses the little ants became huge creatures that popped into his field of vision and out in a disorderly and dangerous motion, when in fact they were only going about their gentle, purposeful ways.

Distance had enlarged and distorted the normal activities of boys, but close up, baseball with the Panthers had delighted him. Perhaps one could see too clearly, imagine too vividly, remember too much for one's own good. That had been Albie's way, and it could be his father's way, too. Perhaps that was why his father owned binoculars.

Daylight blued. The forest cooled. Albie came to a road. No houses, no traffic, no sign of human interference other than the blacktop itself. No sound. Here at the limit of Bear Lake, he stepped out of the shelter of the woods. Step by step he advanced to place one sneakered toe on the center line. To the left the line pointed to where the sun floated a finger's breadth above the trees. To the right it ran toward the railroad track, the ocean, the Poor Children in Europe and the Russian bears. Toward where his uncle had come from.

Across the road lay night in the chilly north. Albie held a deep breath, blew it all out, and turned back.

My darkling route was strange because I had followed no particular trail. As shadows lengthened I veered to my right, toward where the sun was setting. I knew that country the way I knew my way to the library at home.

On the top of a ridge behind the camp, I embraced a tree even larger than the one I had climbed at the far end of the lake. I closed my eyes and rubbed my cheek against rough bark. That darkness behind my closed eyelids was the same everywhere, in New Hampshire and at home, by day and by night. Except for a soft soughing of breeze in the tops of the trees, the woods were quiet, and I felt quiet inside.

I could not hide there forever. Downhill from the ridge I found a defined path that led to two ruts of the old logging road past Hughston's house, to the upper end of the Bear Lake parking lot, to the three men and the black Ford.

"Hey," Uncle Charlie called. "Hey, you!" He scrabbled at his chest for the shiny whistle on his lanyard.

I descended toward my father and Uncle Jesse at a steady pace.

"There he is!" My father ran toward me.

"Hey, Greenberg!" Uncle Jesse ran, too.

I shrugged off their touch.

"My little man, I demand that you explain . . ."

Uncle Jesse squatted to less than my height. "Your father worried. You know, this rule about boys staying with their counselors."

"All right?" Uncle Charlie said.

Uncle Jesse waved him away. Uncle Charlie jammed his unlit pipe into his mouth and took a big step before he wheeled and extended his hand to my father.

I knelt again to position the binocular case on the back seat. The newspaper was gone. As the car edged out onto the road next to the playing field for the second time, I raised the binoculars to scan the far side of the lake, which lay in deep shadow. The eyepieces bumped the bones of my face and the motion kept me from seeing anything clearly. If I held the binoculars a few inches away, I saw in their two bright circles two images of the setting sun, orange flames that danced together over the new world I had discovered.

My father touched my thigh and said, "Albie," in a choked, indistinct voice. At the entrance he steered the car right, away from the railroad station. We wound our way over hills, between meadows and small farms, and descended into a forest. I watched the road so I would remember it.

My father drove with both hands on the wheel. We slowed to pass through darkening small towns of white houses with green shutters. Black and white cows stood in fenced fields. A rusty pickup truck came the other way with headlights on; I knelt on the seat to watch it disappear into the dusk. No one followed us. I sat back down as the car descended a long hill and came out onto a bridge over a river. We stopped once more at an intersection before we drove onto a highway with other cars.

"Seven hours, maybe eight," my father said, "but we'll be home tonight."

The red needle of the speedometer crept past the 40 toward the 50. Yellow headlights rushed past the other way; some red taillights ahead of us contained the same blue spot as cars that passed my window on the way to the Avenue.

My father glanced at me and touched my cheek. "Do you want to go back to Bear Lake?"

I shook my head. "It was *great*, Dad, but some other camp might be even better."

"Well," my father said, as he turned back to the road ahead, "That sounds normal."

ACKNOWLEDGEMENTS

Heartfelt thanks for kindness and support are due to my teachers, especially Margot Livesey, and to my fellow Emerson students;

To the Thursday Nighters, my writers group of decades: Lori Ambacher, Cynthia Anderson, Louie Cronin, Blake Hammond, Judy McAmis, Richard Ravin, Adair Rowland, Jep Streit, and Frankie Wright;

To friends and family who read the manuscript and told me what they thought, and especially to my old roommate Alan Berger, who encouraged me to exhume these pages from the bureau drawer;

To Jane Rosenman, who edited the words, and Jean Wilcox, who made them into a beautiful object;

And last, because she is first, to my wife Lise Motherwell, whose simpatico surgeon became a curmudgeon cloistered in his own head for hours and hours and hours.

ABOUT THE AUTHOR

R. S. Steinberg studied linguistics and Middle English poetry before going on to medicine and the practice of orthopaedic surgery. After an injury ended his career, he turned to writing fiction and personal essays which have been published in *Fiction, Bananafish, Mulberry Fork Review, The Boston Globe* and elsewhere. He lives in Massachusetts with his wife.